Rosie Protects the Coded Disc of Phaistos

Natalie Petraki

The Hovering Pen Publications

First published by Natalie Petraki 2021

Published in Amazon 2021

The moral right of the author has been asserted.

All rights reserved.

Without limiting the rights under copyright reserved above, no part of this publication may be reproduced, stored in or introduced into a retrieval system, or transmitted, in any form or by any means (electronic, mechanical, photocopying, recording or otherwise), without the prior written permission of both the copyright owner and the above publisher of this book.

Formatted by: Waseem Khan

Illustration: Natalie Petraki

Project Editor: Teal Radford

Copyright © Natalie Petraki 2021

All Rights Reserved.

ISBN-13: 979-8549946330

About the author

Author and Illustrator Natalie Petraki was born in Iraklion, Crete, Greece, in 1977. She has always enjoyed playing video games, reading, and writing books since her teenage years. She wrote her first adventure book at the age of thirteen, using a typewriter. Her mother Melanie introduced her to the world of painting and illustration at the same time. That led her to studies at the former Kent Institute of Art and Design (current University College for the Creative Arts) in Canterbury and Maidstone, in England. As soon as she completed the course of HND Illustration and Graphic Design, she proceeded with further studies in HND/BA 3D Computer Animation for video game design at the University of Portsmouth, England. She earned an additional Masters degree in Art, Design, and Media with a Merit, and has been writing novels since her graduation day. She is currently working on the second adventure book of this series along with a crime novel for adults and teenagers. She has written a number of shorter stories as well that she is considering developing into novels. Natalie has found that being a Writer and Illustrator is the profession that truly makes her happy. Her main target is to offer her readers adventures that are fun, with helpful messages and a great sense of humor.

In her free time, she loves reading, playing video games, going for walks, cooking, yoga, watching movies, listening to classical/epic music/Frank Sinatra and jazz, and playing with the family's dogs Titos, Babis, and Asproula. Babis and Asproula happen to be rescued dogs.

She lived in England for approximately ten years and she currently lives in Iraklion, Crete. She has received various awards in painting and karate tournaments, and has decided to combine her writing of mystery-adventures with her own Illustrations. In her work, she offers 100% commitment and uses unorthodox ways of presentation. When she creates, her appreciation of nature and beauty is apparent, along with her sensitivity, respect, and high awareness of her environment. She loves focusing on the positive side of life and sharing it with other people along with useful tools that will guide them in their lives. As a creator, she pays much attention to detail in order to produce a beautiful outcome that emits love, thought, and concern for the reader. Her stories are full of adventure, action, romantic moments, beauty, surprises, interesting discoveries, and great humor. At the same time, she shows her readers how to never give up on life and that there is always a solution.

Devoted to

This book is devoted to Skip Lucas, Mike Tappenden, John Howard, Ken Devine, Mark Way, Mary Stockton Smith, Nikos and Anna Karaiskakis, Mrs. Georgia Fountoulaki, Mrs. Euterpi Bali, Mrs. Kaiti Kikivaraki-Chnaraki, Mr. Astrinos Damianakis, Sister Melanie, my friends Fanny Papadaki, Mel Fang, Cesilia Poon, Eleni Foka, Rena Tsiknaki, Rena Pavlidaki, Aspasia Zacharioudaki, Isabella Lianeri, my parents Melanie and Sotirios Petrakis, and my beloved cousins Nitsa Petraki, Mimis Petrakis and Kalliopi Petraki for their constant support.

Special thanks to Skip Lucas for his constant support and for helping me believe in myself and my abilities, with a huge amount of patience and respect toward me. Also, special credit is given to Gareth Owain for his formal interpretation of the disc of Phaistos code, and to the Hellenic Institute of Holography for their exceptional creations of the 3D holograms, to the Archaeological Museum of Iraklion, Crete and to the Museum of Natural History for their beautiful exhibits.

For YOU Mike!
I do hope you will enjoy this adventure and feel the magic.
Have a wonderful Christmas!

Natalie.

1/12/2021

Table of Contents

1. A Day of Surprises. 1
2. Some Very Good News. 9
3. A Bad Omen... 15
4. Roserin's Key of Life. 23
5. The Hidden Cave. 30
6. The Monster...And His Friend. 38
7. Confrontation with the True Self. 55
8. Sir Hipparchus and the Star-Net Astrolabe. 69
9. The Astrolabe. 80
10. An Upside-Down Situation. 88
11. The Coffee Pot with the Mirror 98
12. The Bottles of Life 109
13. More Than Meets the Eye 121
14. 'Georgiadi' Park. 132
15. Where Did the Mysterious Lady Go? 141
16. Now You Are Here, Now You Are Not. 153
17. A Very Powerful Stamp. 163
18. Three Floating Octopuses. 172
19. The Dragon's Eye. 183
20. The Rescue… 194
21. A Trapped Spirit… 206
22. The Grapple. 219
23. Skeletons, Pirates, and Earthbound Ghosts. 233

24. 'Dancing with Jack Ketch'. 242
25. A Wish is Granted. 247
26. At the Akashic Records. 256
27. Searching for the Hidden Treasure. 272
28. Equilibrium. 283
29. Projection. 299
30. Centering the Souls. 317

Rosie Protects the Coded Disc of Phaistos

1. A Day of Surprises.

- 'Ouch! 'Roserin winced. Something had hit her arm. She rubbed it to ease the pain and looked to her right. A copper pot with a long arm was now hovering, spinning like a top from the strong impact.

'It's a 'briki'!' Stamatis told her, using its Greek name. 'It looks like the one that grandma used to make granddad's coffee!' He grabbed the tiny Turkish coffee maker to examine it up close. It was a funny looking pot that Cretan people used to make their Greek coffee, one that reminded Roserin of Pinnochio's long nose.

- 'It could belong to Pinnochio!' She thought and felt amused by the idea.

- 'It DOES belong to me!' The puppet's voice sounded suddenly within her consciousness. 'Help! I will not lie again!' was the second sentence that she heard right after. And then...silence.

- 'Why is the briki's main body so small? I always wondered why they made them so small.' Alexander said.

Before anyone had the chance to reply, Roserin, whom her friends and family also called 'Rosie', was startled by something that pulled her backward violently. A dark arm was visible right in front of her stomach, as well as the same distorted face that had been seen out of Roserin's and Stamatis' house. Some parts of the face seemed to dissolve in dark energy, before it would connect its particles together again to form evil expressions. This face was one that was NOT afraid of crocodiles or any other threatening animals in its former life. Its eyes, with miniature crescent irises, were popping out all round, a hollow spot appeared in place of its nose, and it grimaced, showing a number of razor-sharp teeth. Its chin was doubled and had a few dark spots. But what kind of entity was this? The dark spots were spread on the rest of its face too, causing it to resemble a mountain of sand with pebbles in it. It was a 'Goliath's Tigerfish, the most terrifying fish of the Congo River in Africa.

On the ship's deck, everyone froze in their positions, apart from a penguin wearing a scarf around his neck, who ran away from the threat, terrified. Alexander ran after Roserin, while the dark entity used its fists to start hitting the girl on her sides continuously. Rosie cried in pain with every blow. She was now floating in space far away from the ship. Astrapi, an African cat, floated after Rosie and the entity, in his effort to save his friend. Everyone was now on the one side of the deck, not having the slightest idea how to help the girl.

- 'He is taking her toward a black hole!' Stamatis shouted desperately. We MUST do something NOW!'

- 'The Astrolabe!' Bernard, a little boy, shouted. We can turn back time! Then Rosie will be pulled back to the ship, and we will stop his attack!'

- 'We cannot do that my boy!' Sir Hipparchus shouted to young Bernard. 'We cannot play with Time. It is the Astrolabe itself that will decide that. We can only freeze time…'

- 'Let's do it then! Quickly Sir! My sister is disappearing!' Stamatis shouted in despair.

- 'I would have already done it if I could, my boy. But you see…this device is more complicated than you think.'

Alexander suddenly took a crystal out of his pocket. It blazed in colors of turquoise and green on its surface. Henrietta turned to tell him that this was not the time to admire his pebbles, when the boy raised his palm and blew the crystal in the direction of Roserin. A rather long turquoise flame surrounded Rosie and formed a big round energy ball, from which emerged a face that blew the dark entity away. Alexander took another pebble, this time a blue one, out of his pocket and placed it onto his palm. Once again, he blew the crystal hard, in the girl's direction. The stone remained in his palm. Nothing seemed to be happening. Everyone stared in agony, unable to utter a word to ask whether something would happen. The words would not come out of the mouths of these souls, who felt their hands tighten in front of grave danger. After a few seconds of unbearable silence and no reaction, Henrietta's voice filled the huge void.

- 'Alexander?'

The sound of breaking branches made everyone turn their heads. And branches they were…they materialized from the trireme's (an ancient Greek warship with many paddles) mainmast. While everybody's attention was drawn to the newborn branches above, some thick roots appeared behind them and hugged the malus mast (one of the ship's main masts) tightly. They seemed to be originating from Roserin's side.

- 'They are growing out of my feet!' The girl shouted from a distance. Everyone looked at these thick roots that resembled a Giant's long beard (if the beard's hair had been magnified a few thousand times). As the roots grew away from Rosie's body and wrapped around the mast, the branches grew toward the girl. They stopped growing right behind Astrapi, who was still hovering in the air. They were knitted to each other and formed a bridge. Roserin was suddenly pulled forward like a comet, almost past Astrapi. The African cat changed his direction and ran across the bridge, back to the ship. The girl was now standing on the deck, still glowing in turquoise-green light. Sir Hipparchus and the children all sighed with relief. The roots started to dissolve from her feet and the remains were now floating away from the mast.

- 'That was close!' Bernard sighed and relaxed. Henrietta's eyes popped out:

- 'Get away from there! Get away from there!' She shouted, panicked, at Roserin, while Bernard jumped as if he had just been electrocuted.

- 'How many are there?' Stamatis asked, terrified, and looked around in all directions.

- 'There seem to be more than there are stars...' Alexander commented, and in his panic, he grabbed something that looked like a mop, to defend both himself and his friends.

- 'Use the Mirror Rosie! Use the Mirror!' Sir Hipparchus urged the girl, in his despair to keep her, himself and the other children safe. Rosie stood still and focused with a decisive look in her eyes.

- 'What do we do now uncle? What do we do?' Henrietta asked in panic.

But wait! Let us pause the story at this point...Who is Alexander? And who is Henrietta? Who are Stamatis and Roserin, and why does she seem to have been somebody's target? Who is Astrapi and who is Bernard? Are there any black holes in the sea? And how about the dimension in which we seem to find these people? They seem to be in space!

You are not afraid...are you? Our hero depends on us and our help! The dark entity is not able to pass through these pages unless you give them power with your fear...So, do not be afraid, and follow me!

Roserin, Stamatis, and Astrapi –Roserin's African cat- were having their breakfast. The siblings were pondering how to spend their holiday. Astrapi was a beautiful big cat with a funny curly tail. Between his eyes, he had a white line of hair, whereas the rest of his body was brown, with a few white patches in front of his chest. He was a very clever African big cat and sometimes he would play hide and seek with the children. The children would ask him to 'stay', and then they would hide somewhere and call him once they were ready. He would always find them by using his nose! This cat even knew how to go down the slide by himself at the park! He would do anything to make Rosie laugh! And beware anyone who would try to hurt his friend or her family. He would bite that person's leg at once, and not let go!

- 'At last!' sighed Stamatis. 'We are on holidays. After such an exhausting semester at school, we do deserve some good holidays. But where would we go? We cannot stay here in such heat.'-The weather was too warm and the children felt unable to do anything.

- 'I did enjoy school a lot though.' Roserin said. 'I loved the breaks and especially the last day when we celebrated.'

At Roserin' and Stamatis' school, several athletic activities had been organized last year, including ice skate racing where students had been divided into groups and tasked to find a lost treasure within a certain time limit. With the use of a map and a pair of ice skates, each student would come across various clues that would lead them to the treasure. It had been a rather complicated route, and therefore a great challenge, inside an enormous labyrinth in the shape of a snow flake. Every student had carried a personal flashlight on their forehead to find their way inside the dark slippery grounds of the maze. Stamatis had somehow managed to lead his team to the treasure: a giant frozen-looking ice skate with embedded diamonds. It had been lent to the school by Mr. Stone –the owner of a cute and welcoming jewelry store in their city of Iraklion. The team that found the treasure was awarded with a very respectable amount of beautiful crystals along with diplomas of excellence and a grade of distinction in the lessons of 'Sixth Sense' and 'Awareness.' And the best part of the final celebration was that all the students were winners in the end. They each received an individual basket with their name on it, a letter of appreciation concerning their efforts and respect of rules in this game, along with several wrapped gifts that served as useful tools in their spirit lives. And had a student offered their total focus in finding the treasure, they had the chance of being awarded wrapped chocolates and sweets, gathered from all over the world. These treats were wrapped in the most beautiful paper that had ever been made, which, when unwrapped, made the most mesmerizing sounds that could ever be heard. No wonder every single school in the city would participate every year in the big treasure hunt.

- 'Ha! Another hilarious memory' laughed Stamatis. I remember when Rosie made that sculpture...you cannot imagine what she went through to make it and then transfer it to school! It was a bust of a girl wearing a hat. And not only did the bust weigh almost more than Roserin, but all of a sudden, the hat was lifted in the air along with the wig, and it flew away to God knows where!' He giggled. 'So poor Rosie had to go to school carrying a bald head! When I imagine it lifting in the air...' He was not able to complete his sentence though, due to his loud laughs that he could hardly control.

- 'You are so insensitive! It was a horrible moment for me and you are laughing! What else can we expect from a boy? Anyway, let's get back to our subject. Does anybody have an idea as to how we could spend the holidays?'

- 'What would you say to asking your friends Henrietta, Barnard and Alexander to stay here with you? I bet you would be having a great time together!'

- 'His name is Bernard...' Stamatis corrected his mother.

- 'But of-course! –Roserin shouted- What a splendid idea mom! I believe that they will love this idea!'

Then, it was their father's turn to speak. He had not said a word since they sat for breakfast; He had only picked up the newspaper and sat listening to his family's conversation.

- 'I find your idea very good. I am sure it will be very good news to them too, since you are always having such a nice time together. Am I right?'

Mr. Leon Elephantinos and his friend and colleague Sir Socrates Marmeladas - the latter one being the father of Stamatis and Roserin- had just been transferred to another department of their scientific job of Astronomy, Lightworking, and Research, and had to travel by train every morning to get there.

- 'I have something else to tell you.'- Mrs. Adele Aurora continued, who came from Finland.

'A few days ago, we received the tickets to Finland. I want to get my books published and attend a crafts presentation. We are leaving soon; Tomorrow noon is our departure.' –said their mother, who happened to be a crafts presenter and a writer of comical stories. She loved imagining and creating situations that would cause a sudden mood lift in her readers. In her last book, she wrote about some young boys who kept diving in the sea with their masks on to peek at the body of a half nude overweight lady underwater.

- 'This is perfect! We will have a great time! You have made me happy with this news, mom!' –Roserin shouted while her mother looked at her, astonished. Was she happy about her friends' possible visit, or was she feeling ecstatic because her parents were leaving? 'Henrietta will be very happy as soon as I tell her! Where is she now? Is she still sleeping?'

- 'However, that does not mean that you will do whatever crazy thought comes into your mind, during the time we will be away.-'Mr. Socrates said, to bring his daughter back to her senses....-'Well, why are we sitting here? We need to call them and their parents as well, to ask them whether they want to and whether they can. We have a lot of preparation to do for the children, in case they accept our invitation.'-At once, Mr. Socrates ran toward the living room to make the phone call, and the children ran behind him glowing with excitement.

- 'Freeze! Police! You have the right to remain silent!' –A shout was heard all of a sudden. This shout disturbed neither the children nor Astrapi.
- 'Malaka...malaka...malaka!' The popular swear word sounded in the Greek language, from the same source.

- 'Shut up you stupid thing!' –Roserin shouted playfully. This voice came from a mynah bird, which Rosie and Stamatis had taught to say a few words and phrases. She looked like a crow, with a yellow stripe around her ears, very black feathers, and a beautiful orange beak. She was the sixth and not least member of the family. She was very clever and funny. She would perch on a thick beam in the inner garden and fly around freely. She always stayed close to the children and liked to land on their shoulders.

- 'Petra feels like talking today! My efforts to teach her have bloomed...it may have taken me three months to teach her: 'You have the right to remain silent' but, I did succeed in the end!' Stamatis said.

- 'Yes. And you have driven me nuts all this time! Both you and her! I should have bought you an owl or a tortoise. At least THEY would let me sleep in the mornings. I wouldn't even consider a hamster who might start running around on their wheel at night, so that nobody can sleep! Yesterday morning I woke up again by this dinosaur's distant cousin...I was dreaming that I was in the middle of an adventure, and as soon as I was about to get inside a crypt, I heard a voice saying: Peeeeeetraaaaaaaa...' 'Petra' being the mynah's name.

- Right at that moment, their dad hung up the phone receiver and walked toward the kitchen with Roserin and Stamatis behind him, asking: 'Did you call them already? What did they say? What did they say?'

2. Some Very Good News.

- 'Well, it seems that the children will be staying here since their parents are traveling too...to the Lost City of Atlantis specifically.' –Mr. Socrates said while frowning and wiping his mouth with a napkin. - He continued: 'They have some relatives there, as well as friends who invited them to spend the holidays together. Your friends will have to stay here along with their little cousin since their holidays do not coincide with their parents' and they still have to attend a few classes. So as soon as they heard about your idea, they felt very happy about it, since they were looking for somebody to look after the children. I assured them that you would not be alone in any case and that Margaret would take care of you.' -Margaret was a lovely lady who worked in the children's house as a cook.

- 'Yes, indeed. They have some uncles and aunts, and I remember one of Henrietta's aunts who visited here two years ago, or was it three years ago? What was her name?'-Stamatis wondered with a pondering look on his face.

- 'Do you mean Mrs. Maya?' –Roserin asked him. - 'The lady who had a cute white-furred llama? Let me think what his name was...Adonis! Of course! That must be the lady. I was impressed by warm-hearted

Adonis!'

- 'Now that you mention it, I am sure that it was her. I liked her llama a lot too, and I also recall that she was very kind herself. I would say that she was perfect...' –Their mother, seeing that they were deeply absorbed into their thoughts, interrupted them, and, face shining with a smile, she addressed them while placing her hands onto the table.

- 'Come Rosa...we have lots to do since they have decided to come. Everything must be ready by this evening. We also need to prepare their beds.'

Everybody agreed and started cleaning and tidying up the house. Even Astrapi wanted to help by eating the leftovers, and Mrs. Adele said to her with a smile:

- 'What a mischievous big cat you are! You would do anything to get inside! You do not have to eat the leftovers inside the house; you can very well do that outside.' She gave her the lunch on the porch. While Rosie's father was busy packing his suitcase, everybody started cleaning the house as quickly as possible. Roserin took the initiative to clean Petra's cage, where the bird had to stay every time they had visitors Petra had the bad habit of flying onto a visitor's shoulder to do her "business"! However, Bernard, Henrietta, and Alexander had never had any problems with her. This was simply because Petra recognized them, loved them, and always respected them! The situation was very different with guests. She had to leave her mark and say: "Hey! I am here too!"

Henrietta was a beautiful girl; she had long straight golden hair that looked especially soft and healthy. The way she brushed her hair to fall over her face suited her very much. She also had kind blue eyes. Rosie, on the other hand, had long curly blond hair that looked a little wild– just like her character- and brown eyes. Stamatis had many of the same characteristics as his sister, with the exception of his chestnut hair, which was a little long behind his neck and brushed to the side of his forehead. Henrietta and Alexander's cousin, Bernard, had dark brown hair, cut very short and covered with a hat in the shape of a paper boat. Alexander did not look much like his cousin; his hair was brown too, but not as straight as Bernard's. He had a slim, athletic figure, and loved to dress in a unique, stylish way. He was the type of person who appreciated the soft feel of silk and velvet on his skin.

As far as their hobbies were concerned, Henrietta and Roserin adored adventures, like hiding a 'treasure' somewhere in a field, and having everyone else search for it with the help of a map they had drawn. The girls also loved ice skating and exploring. Sometimes they would visit Rosie's neighbor, who happened to own a number of iguanas and chameleons. They enjoyed observing the various breeds as the lizards ate, slept, and stared back at the girls. Rosie however, had started showing a greater interest in fish exploration as well. Colored fish mostly, that had been born with the most amazing color combinations, and in the most unique shapes and sizes. She was especially fond of fish with metallic colors.

She felt free in her soul when she was ice skating, so she would often visit her school's rink to practice. She also loved making macrame wristbands, along with potholders that decorated their house so nicely. She enjoyed making wristbands with beads inside, mostly colorful beads. When she happened to create decorative pieces of macrame for her room, she preferred using brown wooden beads. She had made an Easter Bunny with beads all along its outer edges.

The boys were a different story. Stamatis loved making miniature wire trains using beads, stones, shells, or any other materials that would suit as wheels. He and Bernard were also interested in racing old cars from time to time, whereas Alexander loved to be occupied with flying miniature planes in his free time. He also had the habit of collecting colorful crystals.

Henrietta was a different type of character. She loved doing other things, and you will see that she will surprise us more and more as the story evolves. Bernard and Alexander also have a very important part to play in their spirit lives. Just wait and see...

But let us go back to a few minutes earlier. Stamatis had started tidying up his room, and as soon as Roserin had completed cleaning Petra's dome-shaped cage, she began helping her mother pick out the most appropriate bed sheets for her friends' beds.

- 'The floral lavender sheet for Henrietta, the olive green silk sheet with the top hats and old car prints for Alexander, and the sheet with the sugary and chocolaty doughnuts for Bernard!' Rosie said. 'But where will Robert sleep mom?' Robert was a very cute Penguin who belonged to Bernard; He had come all the way to Crete to be adopted by a child who would appreciate his company.

In the meantime, Margaret was preparing some traditional 'myzithra' goat's cheese pies with sugar and cinnamon for the following day. She decided to make some chocolate fudge also, and combine it with vanilla extract. As soon as the cream with walnuts had been prepared, she covered it carefully and put it in the freezer. After two hours, she cut the fudge into cubes and placed it inside two illustrated tea boxes, which depicted some of Santorini island's white houses: their white walls, brown and blue wooden fences and window shutters, and some figures of people behind the windows, occupied in various activities.

All of a sudden, the noise of a breaking object caught everybody's attention. Everyone ran toward the living room where it came from and saw a goblet full of cherries lying on the floor. Or let's just say...what was left of the goblet. Nothing strange, you might say, as anyone can accidentally break something. Well yes, I agree. The peculiar thing, in this case, was that none of the family members had been around. It is usually because of someone's actions that an object breaks. However, this time, everyone was busy in places other than the living room when it happened. Mrs. Adele started collecting the pieces...

- 'I don't understand! What happened?' Stamatis asked, confusion in his eyes.

Petra, along with her cage, flew toward the living room window that looked out toward the house's main entrance and looked outside. The olive trees in the garden were shrinking and drying out at a fast pace. Something had provoked this very sudden draught. Did the sun become stronger? Were the olive trees hungry? Or were they thirsty perhaps? The bird moved her head in all directions. The olive trees took on a shriveled appearance, and the leaves had lost their beautiful green-silver color. They were now yellow-ochre. So was the sky itself. The whole atmosphere outside looked yellow and sandy as if there was sulfur in the air. The shadow of a human figure with long hair floated quickly past the front yard and disappeared past the dry olive trees.

- 'Police! Police! Police!' Petra started shouting as soon as she saw the dark intruder. She flew back to the living room's central table, along with her cage, and hopped around, all upset.

- 'Petra, it is not time for games…' Stamatis said to her. 'Was it YOU perhaps who threw the goblet on the floor?' He asked her. 'You do exercise a lot, don't you?'

- 'Police! Police! Police!' Petra replied to her friend. Then she lost her balance on the beam that she was standing on, and fell onto her cage's floor.

From within the olive trees, somebody was staring at the house's main stairs. Whoever this entity might have been, they saw Astrapi walking down the stairs. As soon as the African cat reached down the ground, he paused and looked around carefully. He sniffed in the air. He kept walking slowly and steadily. After a few steps, he stopped again and looked around. This time he used both his eyes and his ears in his effort to detect the slightest unusual motion or the slightest unusual sound. He kept looking around. Not the tiniest fall of an olive tree's leaf would escape his attention, especially from the spot where he was currently standing. There was absolute silence in the dry garden. Not even the cicadas that sang loudly every summer could be heard. There was hardly a breeze of comforting air either. And then it happened:

The entity's eyes aligned with Astrapi's eyes. Astrapi had found what he was looking for. Without blinking and without taking his eyes off his now discovered target, he started running toward the mysterious entity that had just left its spot. The dark figure with the long hair floated at great speed toward the garden's stone wall which divided the family's premises from the neighbor's olive tree garden. The African cat ran behind, as no other cat had ever run. The strange shadow permeated the stone wall and disappeared. Astrapi climbed onto the wall and remained on top, moving his tail in an agitated way. He looked along the wall, in case the dark figure tried to enter again from another part of the wall…

Within the house, Petra flew into her cage's door and opened it wide. She flapped her wings out of the front door, right into the garden. She landed onto an olive tree and looked around carefully. She did not dare fly past the stone wall, as there was hardly any protection beyond it. Her friends Roserin and Stamatis had used a visualization technique of a huge white bubble that they had placed around their garden to keep them safe from negative energies and entities. A strong gust of warm wind blew suddenly against the bird and almost threw her off the branch with the hot sparkles it carried. She struggled to find her balance on another branch when an olive happened to enter her orange beak by accident. Her beak was forced to open so wide that she finally lost her balance and fell onto the ground, with the olive still inside her…

3. A Bad Omen...

- 'This is what I saw in my dream...' Roserin said after a few seconds of complete silence. Everyone else looked at her in the eyes. 'I saw it! I saw it exactly as it happened...and you were all standing in the very same positions you are standing in now!'

- 'And what else did you see in this dream of yours Rosie? Did you see that we missed our flight because we did not prepare our luggage on time?' Her father teased her while picking up the cherries one by one.

- 'I am not joking! This is a bad omen...' Roserin replied, slightly annoyed with her dad's lack of seriousness at what she had mentioned.

- 'There is a good omen too, though!' her mother added to Rosie's comment, 'We all stood silently for a few seconds, which is a clear sign that a Guide has passed near here...they may still be near us, guarding us!' she said with a smile, 'So don't worry, whatever the danger may be, we have protection.'

Despite her mother's reassurance, Rosie could hardly calm down. There must have been a reason she had had that dream. She suddenly felt a cold stone of deep sadness within her soul. She was the only one left in the living room. Stamatis and their parents had returned their attention to the task of sorting out everything that needed to be done to prepare for their trip. After a while, Henrietta also woke up and was very glad to hear the news. After having eaten the rice with vegetables that Margaret had prepared for her breakfast, she joined Roserin and her mom as they discussed the necessary things the kids would have to sort out during the holidays. The housework was too much for Margaret to handle on her own, so Rosie and Stamatis would be responsible for looking after the animals. Henrietta enjoyed watching Mrs. Adele giving advice to Roserin, telling her things like: 'And watch after Henrietta and her cousin so that they will not lack anything. Also, never let Petra out of her cage should anyone come over. And please don't use the liver pate to feed Astrapi...we bought it to spread on our bread. This is for you. It is NOT for the monster cat!"

Once everything had been accomplished throughout the day and Mrs. Adele had prepared her suitcase, they all went to sit out on the porch. When the old cuckoo clock in the living room struck 10:00 p.m. Rosie and Henrietta made sure to light the candles within the lanterns that Rosie's mom had hung up on a piece of string. They emitted a warm, caring atmosphere. Dinner looked like a great temptation so it was not a surprise when they all started tasting everything early. There was some sweet fresh apple pie that Margaret had prepared, along with a few sandwiches filled with crab, mayonnaise, and vegetables, some marinated 'gauros' –anchovies- fish that Roserin adored, in their lemon sauce, and Stamatis' most favorite ice-chocolates filled with coconut oil that Mrs. Adele had neatly placed within a little wooden trunk. On top of everything, there were a variety of cold fruit smoothies that the children had the chance to enjoy every summer, along with pieces of ice-dinosaurs inside them. There were different smoothie flavors, made with mixtures of various fruits that Margaret put in the blender. There was mango with coconut, as well as tropical and exotic fruits including mango, pineapple and passion fruits, blueberries with strawberries and banana and Margaret's special recipe.

- 'You may only have one or two ice chocolates though after you have eaten your sandwiches,' Mr. Socrates said to the children. 'You can still enjoy your cold juices while eating a sandwich.' He continued.

All of a sudden, as Astrapi returned from the garden, a large piece of apple pie landed on his head. He instantly lifted his ears; Once he made it fall to the ground by pushing it with his paw, he examined it with his nose.

- 'Is that edible?' He seemed to be thinking. 'It smells very good, yes...I am sure I can eat this!' So, without thinking for too long, he grabbed it in his mouth, and swallowed it down his throat. After two seconds, his eyes popped out and he started coughing intensely. 'WHAT is that? Are you trying to poison your beloved cat?' He spat out as much as he could. 'Whatever happened to raw birds?'

- 'The blueberries with strawberries and banana are mine!' Roserin grabbed the drink she loved the most and drank from the pink straw.

- 'I'll have 'Margaret's special recipe'! Henrietta chose her cup, which was a lighter cream color.

- 'And I am choosing my cream Goddess!' Stamatis lifted his favorite smoothie, a blend of mango, pineapple and green lemon. 'What's inside yours, Henrietta?'

- 'It's a mixture of banana, yoghurt, sugar, cinnamon and milk.' Margaret said as she appeared with one more chair in her hands.

- 'Have you added something extra in my smoothie Margaret?' Rosie asked.

- 'I haven't added anything more apart from banana and blueberries in yours, my dear. And some yoghurt!' She replied, and chose mango with coconut to treat herself. Roserin's and Stamatis' mother also chose Margaret's special recipe, and their father accepted the last smoothie, which included mango, pineapple and passion fruits.

As soon as everyone had completed their dinner, they went straight into bed. Everyone, that is, but Roserin and Henrietta. It was not an easy thing for them to just lie down and fall asleep. They were too excited, so they decided to play a game which was called: "The Treasure of the Frozen People." It was one of their favorites. Henrietta selected the white pawn, which consisted of a big glass bell that had a big white polar bear on the top, whereas Roserin chose the blue pawn, which was also a glass bell, with the shape of a frozen goat emerging through it. Within the bell, one could see the goat's legs as she stood up. The children had to find the frozen people's treasure that was hidden somewhere inside a long labyrinth, under the frozen ground of the North Pole. The person who found the treasure would have to return to the start, but always with the danger that their enemy might steal it from them. Rosie started first and rolled a pair of dice that looked like frozen crystals. She could make out, through the frozen glass, a six and a five. She could move six steps to the North, or any other direction she wanted. Another alternative she had, was to add the numbers and move accordingly. This is what she finally decided to do, and she moved 11 steps toward the West. She had to be very careful, though, not to fall inside a frozen lake. In such a case she would be able to use a rescue igloo: The 'Igloo of Life'. She would be able to use it only once though. In the case that she fell into another trap, the igloo would then be useless.

It was Henrietta's turn. She got a three and a five when she rolled the dice, and she decided to walk five steps to the East, where an underground frozen temple was standing invisible beyond her steps. She decided to open its main entrance in case the treasure was inside. She was unlucky though. Instead of the treasure, she found a scroll that would instruct her how to proceed. Although the information on the scroll might help her, these scrolls were very risky to unfurl because there was a possibility that they might bring unfortunate news too. There was also a heap of 'frozen mirrors' -cards that would unveil a special message to her, if she leaned the mirror slightly toward a certain direction. The scroll's message to Henrietta was to pick up one of the mirrors that was placed inside a sleigh, which had been parked in the center of the game board. Additionally, there was another heap of letters that were rolled and secured by a white silky rope, and which contained positive messages only. They had the stamp of a glowing diamond.

Rosie Protects the Coded Disc of Phaistos

The game continued for a long time until Roserin found the treasure, which happened to be a round device that emitted fire. As Roserin tried to return to the start with her treasure, Henrietta chased her and took it away. It was difficult because of the presence of many obstacles which both of them had to overcome. However, this time, Rosie encountered many more traps than Henrietta, like for instance a whole herd of Polar Bears- protectors of the precious cargo- who had been hiding behind certain numbers. There were also various other thieves, mainly pirates, who had laid life-threatening traps.

- 'I will reach you!' Henrietta said. 'I will -cross my heart! And I will take the treasure away from you!' She said with amusement, and rolled the dice. 'And just look at that!' She got two sixes. She moved her pawn twelve steps ahead and she still needed one more step to get Rosie. The latter one, on the other hand, rolled a number one.

- 'It is MY turn to play!' Henrietta said, full of confidence, and rolled the dice happily. 'A two and a four! How lucky for me! So, here I come two steps ahead, and I take the treasure away from you! Thank you very much!'

- 'Oh, God! I cannot believe this!' Roserin said with disappointment. 'I am usually the one who wins at board games...so, what happens now?'

- 'I will lock you inside one of these nice, frozen igloos!' The girl said, and grabbing Rosie's frozen goat pawn, she moved it toward one of the furthest igloos of the North Pole. The front half of the igloo resembled the treasure's shape- a huge crystal ice skating shoe. Rosie would now stay away from her and the treasure. 'It is very easy from now on!' And victory soon came to her, after two or three turns.

- 'So, that was it! You win! Now, I can go to bed because I am starting to get tired; I cannot carry on anymore.' Roserin's eyes would hardly stay open. Henrietta, on the other hand, did not want to sleep yet, and as soon as she put the igloo of life, the mirrors, and the envelopes back in their protective box, she went to bed only to read a book. It was soon midnight, and the cuckoo clock in the living room chimed twelve times. She put on the magenta pajamas that Rosie had lent her, and as soon as she closed the door of her room as silently as she could, she slipped under the fresh, cool sheets. Next to her bedside table was a beautiful antique lamp that offered a nice dim light. She found the page that she had stopped reading on, and picked up the story where she had left off. It was an interesting tale of a girl who discovers a crypt in an old house. The girl's name was Henrietta too...

As she read, she became aware of a bright white light which appeared under Roserin's door. What was going on? Did Rosie turn on any strong lights? She had said that she was very tired and wanted to sleep...so what was that bright light? All of a sudden, the door opened slightly, and Rosie was sitting on her bed, surrounded by a big bubble containing white light. She had taken a position that indicated she was meditating, and traces of what looked like pieces of golden leaf spread around the bubble's surface.

The next morning, Margaret awoke very early and soon went to wake up the children, since their parents wanted to say goodbye and give them some last instructions. It was not very easy for them to wake up though, so Margaret had to walk back to their rooms a few times, ringing a bell that released a sweet sound. Henrietta and Roserin had the greatest difficulty waking up after their late bedtime the night before, and they were the ones who got up last. As they began to blink their eyes open, they overheard Mr. Marmeladas talking on the phone, exchanging muffled words. Then, with a shove on his office door, he opened it wide and came out of his private space.

   - 'Listen up! Your friends are coming here at eleven. So get ready as soon as you can; Make sure you have your breakfast before they arrive. And Rosie, mom wants to give you something.'

   - 'Mom?' Roserin asked with curiosity. 'What is it?'

   - 'Follow me to my bedroom Rosie; There is something that you must have during our absence,' Mrs. Adele said while walking toward her room with Roserin right behind her. After they closed the door, Rosie's mom revealed something she had been hiding inside her closet. The shape of the object looked like a big cookie, with a layer of something delicious in the middle. The only difference was that it was bigger, and it looked more like a flask. It was gold on the surface and had the embossed image of an olive tree. There was also some sort of reflection under the tree that looked like the mirror image of the tree itself. However, the difference was that the reflected image of the tree was hiding something else that could not be seen on the image of the actual tree itself. It was embellished with what seemed to be round lanterns with balls of light. The 'flask' also had a lid on top of a narrow tube that had been embedded on the side. It very much resembled melted golden candle wax that had been pressed down by somebody's seal. There was a symbol on top: The drawing of an open eye.

While the girl was pondering the symbol, a hooded figure outside the garden was observing them both through a looking glass.

In the meantime, in the dimension of the living people, outside the Aquarium of the city of Iraklion in Crete, a young blond girl of about ten years was standing in front of a giant octopus that decorated an entrance. Next to her stood a much older girl who seemed to be her companion. The latter one took something out of her red fabric backpack and offered it to the girl. It looked like another miniature fabric-silk bag, with big red poppies on a green background, tightened by a deep red silk ribbon.

    - 'For you my dear,' she said. 'It's for good luck. I carved it myself.' She added.

    - 'How pretty!' The girl smiled as soon as she opened it and pulled the contents out.

    - 'It's the Phaistos disc! I love these symbols! I wonder what they mean...' Her finger caressed the round wooden disc with symbols carved on its surface.

    - 'You can wear it around your neck.' The girl, who looked to be about twenty-five, said. 'But if you don't like the rope, I could give you a nice ribbon that matches.'

- 'The Phaistos disc!' The girl repeated with excitement. As soon as she uttered the words, a crow landed on her shoulder, and the giant octopus' eyes turned toward the girls, looking as threatening as they could possibly appear…

4. Roserin's Key of Life.

Stamatis, Henrietta, and Mr. Marmeladas were sitting on the porch when they heard a carriage approaching all of a sudden. Everyone was anxious to see whether it was their friends. Unfortunately, it was not them. After about fifteen minutes, one more carriage appeared on the road, and this time, some familiar voices sounded in the air.

- 'Stamatis! Rosie! We are here!'

Lots of excited voices sounded in the front yard, and the children seemed to be happy. They would all spend the entire summer together. Mrs. Jasmine also got off the carriage, which had the shape of a rabbit and was being pulled by six strong goats, and carried a few bags she had prepared for both of her two children, as well as their youngest cousin.

In the meanwhile, Roserin was admiring the golden 'flask'. She passed the leather strap attached to the flask over her head, and attempted to unscrew the lid. She used all of her strength, but the lid would not open.

- 'Not from there!' Her mother said. 'From here!' She showed Roserin a small hidden opening on one side that looked like a small keyhole. Then she gave her a key of a very unusual kind. 'Now, let's place it on the table and try again!'

As soon as Roserin placed it on the wooden table, she took the key from her mother's hand and rushed to unlock the golden 'flask.'

- 'There is a partition!' Roserin shouted, excited. 'Look at that! And it is so beautiful...a surface of stars!' She opened the golden partition from the hinges in the center. A mirror appeared underneath, and the girl tried to feel it with her fingers.

- 'No!' Her mother shouted with anxiety. 'Do not touch it! Never, ever touch the mirror!' She pushed Rosie's fingers away. 'Have a look at this:'

She leaned over the reflective surface and blew a small stream of air out of her mouth. What happened next was beyond Roserin's comprehensive abilities. There were ripples in the mirror. The solid surface was not that solid after all...

- 'Rosie! My brother is here. And our young cousin Bernard!' Henrietta interrupted suddenly with a noisy and unpredictable entrance. Roserin closed the flask instantly and hung the key around her neck. 'Come on!' Henrietta urged her to follow to the entrance. Once the latter one got out of the door, Mrs. Adele held her daughter back for a few seconds.

- 'Be careful with the key Rosie...Never give it to anyone. Never lose it from your sight,' she said seriously. 'This is the key of Life...'

- 'But what is the mirror for? What does it do?' Roserin asked anxiously, eager to know the answer.

- 'You will know,' her mother said. 'When the time comes, you will know.'

Once the parents had greeted each other, they became engrossed in catching up on many serious topics, discussing recent news with tension, as Greek people tend to do. There was much news to be exchanged, by all means. It was a beautiful day for everyone, and Astrapi was happy to see Bernard and Alexander once again. Every time he felt he was not being given proper attention, he would walk toward whoever was the center of attention, then, without making the slightest noise, he would dive his nose into the most sensitive area of that unlucky person's body. Most of the time, it happened to be Mr.Marmeladas who was busy with the talking whenever guests appeared at their home. Astrapi was a very clever African cat. He had finally discovered how to make people pay attention to him, and it would work every single time! The chosen 'victim' would, out of shock, instantly release a loud piercing cry. Then all the surrounding people would laugh their heads off and give the cat a lot of praise, turning him into a hero!

- 'Adele, should we prepare our bags?' Henrietta's mother asked in a friendly way. 'I still have a few things that need to be packed. You see, I did not do that at home because the children wanted us to come to you as soon as possible. Fortunately, Henrietta has her things here already,' she added. 'That makes things a bit easier.'

- 'Yes, Jasmine. I am coming right away. Just give me a minute to feed Petra because she has spread her food all over the floor.' Mrs. Adele filled Petra's plate with pieces of banana and apple, fruits that the bird adored the most. This was a very successful trick to make her enter her cage every time there was alarm for the possibility of her doing her business on the guests' shoulders.

- 'Where is that bird again?' Roserin's mother was afraid that Petra would start her tricks in order to be noticed. She could not trust her! She searched for the bird first inside and then outside the house.

And then, just as soon as Mrs. Adele had reached the inner garden, a young penguin appeared in the hall. He was holding a big stone very tightly in his beak.

- 'Hey! I have an idea!' Stamatis shouted all of a sudden while they were all busy greeting Astrapi. 'Why don't we go to the caves? There are some really nice caves on the mountain right across from the house,' he said, and looked at his sister for confirmation. 'I have heard that they are the most beautiful caves in the dimension, with lots of lagoons inside with the most wonderful colors!" His face was lit with enthusiasm. 'I have never been there, so today is a good chance for all of us to visit,' he added.

- 'Chrrrrrrr,' was Astrapi's reply, as if he wanted to say 'Yes'. He sure was in the mood for a walk. It was boring for him to be in the same place for a long time. Besides, his instincts were telling him that something unusual was on its way. Everybody agreed as soon as they heard Stamatis' idea. Robert the penguin flapped his flippers, a behavior that showed his excitement for anything going on with his friends. He went along with almost every idea as long as he had the chance to participate too.

- 'We will have to ask mom and dad,' Rosie said. 'We also need flashlights. I am sure it will be very dark in there and I am not in the mood to break anything, especially now that we are almost on holidays,' she said, forgetting the fact that since she was now in the other dimension, there was nothing left to break in her body! After her face took on a mischievous look, she added, 'I would not mind if I had an accident during the school semester! Besides, mom always takes good care of me...' She winked at Stamatis with a smile.

- 'I know about the caves!' Bernard interrupted with excitement. 'Mrs. Daphne, our neighbor, mentioned them once. She said that there were many secret passages beneath the lakes, and even more lakes and hidden waterfalls beyond the passages themselves! Yes!' he said with enthusiasm and carried on talking when he saw he had succeeded in drawing everybody's attention. 'There is a whole maze down there that is full of booby traps! Have you heard of the two tourists who went in there and nobody ever heard from them again? I bet they are still inside somewhere, rotting in their liquid graves!' he said with a twinkle in his eye, trying to give his friends goose pimples.

- 'Yuk!' Stamatis said with fright.

- 'Don't tell me things like that!' Alexander said with his hair standing up. 'I would not like to get lost in there in all that darkness and then run into two ghosts that have appeared from nowhere...'

- 'Sounds great!' Roserin commented with an air of adventure that was in her blood.

- 'So that's it then!' Stamatis said with excitement. 'Let's go tell mom and dad. But don't say anything about what we have just said; Otherwise, they will never let us go.' Stamatis said, worried that he might miss this opportunity of a lifetime- to experience a close encounter with two ghosts in a haunted cave.

- 'Why not tell them? Astrapi will be with us,' Bernard said. 'He will keep us safe.'

- 'You know how hysterical parents are...They always think we are too young!' Stamatis said. 'Don't go to that place, don't go to the other, be careful on the street, always be at home before eight o'clock, be careful who your friends are.' He carried on while attempting at the same time to close the door behind him as soon as everybody else had entered the house. 'Don't run on that steep road, a carriage might suddenly appear.' He carried on imitating his mother's voice when all of a sudden, due to his excited mood, he ended up closing the door just before he managed to walk through it, and it hit him on the head. He rubbed his aching forehead, and because of his disappointment that he had hit himself in such a careless way, he closed the door hard this time, only to find the handle left mysteriously hanging in his very own hand! His eyes got as wide as an owl's, and he rushed to put the handle back on the door before anyone noticed.

- 'Mom!' Henrietta shouted. 'We want to visit some caves at the mountain opposite here. Is it fine with you?' She pleaded. 'Astrapi will be with us.' At that time, all of the parents were sitting on the back porch drinking iced coffee and having some pyramid cookie ice creams. These were ice creams that Margaret had managed to hide from the children, since they would eat anything sweet that appeared in front of their eyes.

Especially Rosie...

- 'Yes, you may go,' Mrs. Jasmine said. 'We are leaving in a few minutes too, so please remember everything I have told you, Henrietta. And do NOT be late! Don't be gone more than four hours!' she said to her daughter. As soon as the children hugged their parents goodbye and wished them a safe journey, they set off for the caves. Astrapi looked very excited and ran toward the outside gate, roaring with enthusiasm. Robert followed behind him, still carrying the same stone he had had in his beak when he arrived. Roserin was the last one to leave the house since she had to find a safe place to hide her very special mirror. When she found the spot, she felt proud of herself for finding a place nobody would ever think to look. She went out to meet her friends. As they were about to close the gate, Roserin's mother appeared at what seemed to be a Gothic window.

- 'Please keep in mind everything I have told you Rosie! And do NOT be too late! I don't want you to worry Margaret!' she said. Stamatis turned instantly to Bernard and commented with a mischievous smile:

- 'See? What did I tell you?'

-They set off for the caves as soon as Roserin replied: 'Yes, mom!' Bernard carried on describing even more hair raising details and stories about the creepy caves. Astrapi was running in front, exploring every spot that had captured a smell from either another animal or human being that passed by, leaving something behind them. Most of the time, it was a delicious leftover from the food they had consumed during their short breaks: a rabbit's bone, some chicken or turkey. Other times it was the smell an animal like a fox or even a raccoon had left behind. Weasels were the first creatures of the forest that would run to pick up most of the leftovers, especially during the night. Astrapi always got annoyed when he was not able to prevent them from stealing HIS food. The bushy mountains belonged to HIM! What right did all of the other animals have to take his food? He was the only African cat of the mountains, so everything that was left behind belonged to him! He suddenly found a piece of sausage on a tree branch, and snapped it up instantly and gulped it down. While trying to avoid a weird, unpleasant smell that came from somewhere, and which most likely belonged to a certain plant that was in the area, he looked hungrily for more pieces of meat. He was too busy to notice the presence of a mysterious animal. He could not see the spider-like fingers that pushed a pair of thin olive tree branches aside. Somebody was watching them. Somebody with a pair of big fiery eyes...

- 'It doesn't stink. It stanks!' Astrapi thought, and the children laughed as they covered their nose with their shirts.

- 'If only I could tell what that smell is,' Alexander said. 'Sorry you have to suffer like that Astrapi.'

As for Robert, he might have started out last, behind everyone, but he had soon turned into a racing penguin who was ahead of them all.

- 'Did someone fart?' Bernard asked. 'Did you know that an ancient Greek city with the name Fartmoon existed?' He giggled.

- 'Shut up Bernard,' Alexander said, and strode behind Robert.

5. The Hidden Cave.

After one hour and the discovery of a few new animals that the children had never seen before, they reached a valley with seven waterfalls nestled in its depths.

- 'Are we there yet?' Bernard asked.

- 'Yes. This is the place,' Stamatis answered. 'The cave is down there. All we need to do is walk over the bridge.' He pointed to a wooden bridge that would look rather unusual and more like an illusion to people from another dimension. It looked the same as any bridge that existed in the parallel world of the living people; However, this bridge had something unique in the way that it was made. It looked as if it was suspended in the air, with no suspension cables around to support it. One end of the bridge started a few meters away from the slope, where the children were currently standing. Anyone who came from this other dimension, would assume instantly that they would not be able to jump over such a big gap to the bridge. They would dread that they might fall and disappear into the abyss. Henrietta took the first steps forward, along with Astrapi, and they were both seen by their friends...walking in the air.

- 'Come on! What are you waiting for?' she shouted to the others.

- 'I am just thinking; Should we be doing this?' Roserin hesitated. 'We left Margaret alone at home. I feel bad about this now. Maybe we should do it another time.'

-Henrietta sighed, 'Rosie! Do not worry about Margaret...She is always fine on her own. Besides, Petra is there to keep her company. I am not going all the way back now that we are almost there!' She assured her friend, and continued walking across the air. Once she reached the floating bridge itself, with Astrapi by her side, Stamatis followed, along with Bernard, then Alexander, and finally Rosie. They kept walking forward when Alexander noticed the gigantic forms of various figures that seemed to be either rocks that had been sculpted, or real live beings that had been frozen for some reason. They looked as if they had emerged from within a mass of water and were floating in the air. In fact, this 'water mass' was a tiny piece of Universe, filled with galaxies, nebulas and falling stars. The children approached one side of the bridge to look at the frozen figures. The figures were made of a very special crystal- a blue quartz crystal that seemed to be alive. The crystal reflected every passerby's true hidden self. The surface of the figures worked like a mirror, with the only difference being that they would only depict a person's true nature. This time, they reflected the forms of some very familiar people.

- 'Look! That's us!' Stamatis said. 'I can see us!' he shouted, full of excitement.

- 'Yes! And see there? That is Henrietta!' Roserin said. 'There you are Henrietta! Not there...over here, to the right! You are holding a bow! And you are wearing something that looks like a crown!' Then her eyes moved to another figure close to Henrietta's, recognizing herself. 'Is that me? No, it cannot be!' She doubted.

- 'But it IS you!' Bernard said. 'You look like an interpreter of some sort. You are holding something that looks like a letter! And you look a bit anxious I must say.' The boy noticed and paid attention to Roserin's frozen long curly hair that was in motion as if the stone figure was struggling to run.

- 'Look at Alexander!' Bernard continued. 'There!' The figure with the long gown that looks like a scientist!' he said excitedly. 'And you are doing something...You have a patient! You are treating a patient!'

- 'It looks as if he is about to touch someone's body,' Stamatis said, 'like a healer!'

'And where are YOU?' Alexander asked, feeling slightly uncomfortable as he did whenever people spoke about him. He was a little sensitive and he generally preferred that the subject of discussion revolved around somebody else.

- 'He is behind Rosie!' Henrietta said. 'See? You are a warrior! That is a big surprise.' She looked at him thoughtfully. 'You aren't hiding something are you?'

- 'There is Robert! Do you see him?' Bernard made his friends jump with his sudden observation.

- 'He has a fish in his mouth!' Rosie noticed and smiled.

- 'You look so cute Robbie! Do you see yourself? There?' Alexander pointed with his finger.

- 'Look at that intense light inside his heart!' Stamatis added.

- 'He is beautiful!' Henrietta said. 'Our young cute Robbie!'

- 'Hey! Look at Bernard!' Alexander shouted with amusement, interrupting Henrietta, as a cloud unveiled the depiction of his cousin's true self. Everyone looked at the frozen figure that stood behind the other stone sculptures and they burst out laughing loudly. Bernard's figure had its tongue stuck out from a grimacing mouth, thumbs touching its ears with palms wide open toward the others.

- 'He is right behind us and teases us!' Alexander commented. 'You are very funny, young cousin! I wish I had the same...' He tried to complete his sentence, but the sound of an arrow whizzing past his ears made him freeze, just like his petrified figure. Henrietta's stone-made depiction had turned slowly toward Roserin and released an arrow aimed at her. Rosie was right behind Alexander when she grasped the arrow right before it pierced her throat. The movement of her hand to catch the arrow was spontaneous and performed within a fraction of a second.

- 'What on earth was that?' Stamatis asked with his eyes popping out. 'The stones have never behaved in such a way before.'

- 'Rosie?' Henrietta said with great worry, feeling slightly guilty that her own figure had almost hurt her close friend. With relief, Rosie exhaled the air that she had trapped inside her lungs.

- 'It is a message. I will receive a message...'

- 'What sort of message?' Bernard asked.

- 'I don't know...' Roserin answered. Deep inside her, she felt a cold hand touching her heart, which was not a good sign at all. She thought Henrietta was in danger. 'She is asking for help, even though she does not know it yet,' she thought secretly, not wishing to reveal her interpretation to anyone. 'I think we had better move on,' she said aloud, looking first at the arrow and then back to the stone figure itself. 'We don't want to be late...'

The children gave a last look toward the stones, with shocked expressions, before they kept walking along the bridge. Henrietta's figure had frozen once again, and it looked as if its glance was piercing right through every single one of them. After a while, they started climbing up a lot of stairs that seemed to stretch far beyond the horizon. However, the more stairs they walked up, the lower they found themselves down in the valley. Roserin took a quick look behind and saw thousands of narrow stone stairs leading upward that they had just descended. It looked like an ancient Greek temple of vast proportions, decorated with large strong pillars. It reminded her of a dream of hers that had tormented her a great deal. She had seen herself as a tiny person, trying to run up the stairs and save herself from a huge powerful monster that ran menacingly after her with the speed of an agitated bull! But she was too small and slow to outrun him; Her only alternative to escape him was to use her brain...

As soon as Roserin looked ahead of her again, a few hundred stairs behind the children somewhere on the top of the stairway, the small entity with the big fiery eyes made his appearance once again...

They reached the valley very soon and right away started looking for the cave.

- 'Where is it?' Bernard asked.

- 'It should be under one of the waterfalls,' Stamatis said, 'but I am not sure which one.'

'And there are only six waterfalls. Where is the seventh one?' Henrietta asked, full of curiosity.

- 'We need to follow those trees...' Roserin said, and pointed to a cluster of thousand-year-old olive trees, which all had one common characteristic: They all leaned in the same direction.

- 'They look like ghosts,' Alexander said. 'So huge and old...yet, as strong as a mountain. And look how thick they are! But why do they lean toward that direction?' he asked, feeling overwhelmed by this phenomenon.

- 'They lean to the East,' Rosie answered. 'This part of the woods has become so dark; They yearn for the sun's light.'

- 'So how do you know we need to go this way?' Alexander asked.

- 'I know. I don't know how, I just do. It feels as if somebody has planted this knowledge inside my head,' she murmured, mostly to herself.

- 'Well, you have been correct before,' Alexander said. 'I trust...' he tried to continue, but a loud sudden noise that felt like the coldest hand touching their hearts prevented him from even completing his thought inside his head. A few seconds of the sound and sensation were enough to freeze them and make them unable to even think of running away. Robert dropped the stone he was carrying in his beak and huddled against Rosie's leg. She touched his head unconsciously.

- 'What is that?' Bernard whispered, horrified. Nobody dared to open their mouths. They waited until it stopped. And then, there was a hair-raising silence. It was almost as if Death had spread his wings onto these mountains. They all ran in the hope that they would get out of the olive tree woods as soon as possible. They ran and ran, following a path that had been created alongside some very big thick bushes, until they reached a small piece of land- the only spot that was blessed to be still nourished by the warmth of the life-giving sun. And there it was: The most beautiful waterfall the children had ever seen in their lives. Its crystal-clear water gleamed with the most enchanting turquoise-green colors that anyone could ever imagine. In the sunlight, the greenish-brown stones underneath and beside the waterfall shimmered wonderfully. This small waterfall had been formed by the convergence of hundreds of other water sources that gave this huge mountain life. Henrietta admired the way the sources faded away, the higher on the mountain she looked for them.

- 'Like the water of Life that hides within the mist...' she whispered.

Bernard stepped closer to the waterfall, like a mouse charmed by a Piper. A small, unusual detail drew his attention.

- 'The water is moving upwards!' he said, imitating the movement with his hands, unable to utter another word.

- 'Yes,' Henrietta agreed with admiration. 'This place is sacred,' She could not take her eyes off the waterfall. 'Spirit goes back to its creator...' she whispered to herself.

Henrietta decided to look for the cave, so she moved closer to the waterfall and looked around. However, she could not see a cave anywhere, and neither could her friends. So, where was it?

- 'It was supposed to be here!' Alexander said, and then he noticed something not quite right about what he was staring at. The stones on the waterfall's base were not wet.

'What sort of trick is this? I don't understand...'

- 'It is not a trick!' Henrietta said. 'It is an Illusion...and a very good one.'

- 'Yes, I can see it is an Illusion,' Alexander answered back. 'I have not eaten a proper meal recently, and this is the result! I should have listened to mom and...'

- 'No! I mean a real Illusion!' Henrietta continued. 'It is a reflection from another part of the planet, or it could be from the place with the other waterfalls we saw before. It works in the same way an eye works when it perceives an image upside down and then it rotates it so that we can see the object right side up. In this case, the opposite thing happens. But do NOT ask me how...'

- 'Then how do you explain the fact that I can feel it?' Roserin asked her friend, and took her hand out of the waterfall. 'It is not wet, but I feel a very pleasant energy running over my hand. It feels as if a hundred spirits are caressing me. I am sure that if we went underneath it, the cave would be right there!' She stepped forward and disappeared under the ascending waterfall.

- 'Rosie!' Stamatis shouted anxiously.

- 'Rosie?' Henrietta approached, and put her hand through the water. All of a sudden, Roserin's head appeared again, her hair moving upwards along with the ascending current.

- 'Come on! It's here!' She shouted ecstatically. 'You can breathe without a problem. And it feels so good!' Astrapi had already gone inside with a jump since Roserin was there. As her close African cat and the friend that he was, he would follow her anywhere. Henrietta was the next one to go, along with Bernard, then Stamatis. Alexander followed, with Robert running behind them as quickly as he could, not wishing to be left behind on his own

6. The Monster...And His Friend.

As soon as the children walked under the waterfall, the quiet area outside was not at all quiet anymore. It was disturbed by the shrieking noise of a peculiar animal with a long tail. It was the small monster with the red eyes. He carefully approached the spot where the children were last seen and tried to detect any faint sounds. When he felt that none of them were close enough to discover his presence, he decided to follow them under the ascending water.

- 'Look at that!' Henrietta said, standing still with her mouth open, frozen by surprise. 'I have never seen such a thing!'

- 'Isn't it beautiful?' Roserin said with admiration. 'Look at the nice turquoise color in the lakes, and how luminous it is in here!' she noticed. 'It seems that we will not be needing the flashlights after all.'

Robert ran toward the first lake that lay ahead of them. He climbed an ascending rock and jumped from its peak. He found himself in the lake with a big splash. He swam underwater like a fast torpedo.

- 'This is huge!' Alexander said and hugged a very thick and strong column that had been formed from stalactites. 'Even if the five of us surrounded this, we would not be able to cover it!'

- 'It is full of stalagmites as well!' Stamatis said, still standing in the entrance. 'And look at the size of the cave! It must be kilometers long!' he said in surprise. He had to duck low to avoid bumping his head on the ceiling; He was becoming quite tall recently. He had reached one meter and fifty centimeters already.

Bernard, who was the most curious of all, had already walked a long distance ahead of them when he reached a point where he could no longer see where the walls of the cave went.

- 'Do they exist at all?' He wondered silently.

- 'Yes, they do! You just need to find them!' A voice sounded from behind him and Bernard turned around with astonishment. He realized that somebody was standing right behind him although he had not heard the sound of a single footstep approaching him. A small dirty boy was standing there, slightly shorter than Bernard himself. It appeared that he had recently eaten chocolate, judging by the traces of smudged brown substance around his mouth.

- 'Who on earth are you?' Bernard asked the young boy, 'and what is that creature on your shoulder?' he said as his eyes met a pair of large eyes.

- 'I am 'Sweet Tooth,' the boy replied, 'and this is my friend Bigeyes'. He is a very rare soul given to us by the world of the living people. He is a monkey.

- 'Monkey? He looks more like an owl to me!' Bernard said after watching the small 'monkey' creature with the big red fiery eyes turn its head ninety degrees sideways.

- 'Do you see its hands?' Henrietta asked as she approached her cousin, feeling curious to meet the stranger he had encountered. 'They remind me of this scary creature I once read about that exists in our former world of the living people. They call it a tarantula.' The small monster's hands had a very peculiar shape and a hairy quality.

- 'Have you been to this cave before?' Sweet Tooth asked his new friends. 'It is sacred! If people do not respect it, the cave will eat them!' He was proud for being able to repeat exactly what his grandmother had told him, in the same tone and suspense, especially when pronouncing the word 'eat'.

- 'Right!' Bernard said and could hardly hide a smile on his face. He chuckled.

- 'Bernard!' His cousin said with a warning tone in her voice. 'You never know what can happen in this world,' she said, trying to make young Sweet Tooth feel important, and also in the hope that she might receive some more information. 'Sweet Tooth, we have heard that there is a whole maze inside here, is this true?'

- 'Yes! Whoever follows these lakes gets lost and can never come back. There were these two people who came to see the cave, but the cave ate them!'

- 'Are you talking about the visitors from the world of the living people?' Alexander asked, appearing at Bernard's side and very interested in finding out more about this topic.

- 'Oh, please...' Bernard murmured in a tone of disbelief. He rolled his eyes upward to stare at the stalactites.

- 'Yes,' Sweet Tooth answered, 'and now they are ghosts and they have haunted the cave forever! But they don't want me to say anything more.'

- 'Why are you whispering?' Bernard asked him.

- 'We must not wake up the cave. Shhhhh!' young Sweet Tooth said, and placed his index finger in front of his lips.

- 'We must not wake up the cave?' Bernard said in whispers. 'We must not wake up the cave! Hello? Cave? Are you sleeping? Sweet Tooth does not want us to WAKE YOU UUUUUUUP!!!' He shouted, gradually raising his voice louder as he walked toward the various lakes that had been shaped in the area. He was not paying any attention to his friends who were trying to calm him down. He continued, his voice booming louder and louder until, within a fraction of a second, he slipped and landed in a small hole filled with water, enough to wet his pants and make it look as if he had not made it to the toilet in time. The echo of his last words filled up the vast space that looked like a secret water temple.

- 'I think that's enough for today,' Henrietta said, slightly embarrassed about her cousin's behavior. 'We came to see the cave and we did, so it's time for us to get back home. We cannot stay here any longer now that you have transformed yourself into a frog!' she said funnily. 'You might catch a cold in here with these air currents, and then mom would say it was MY fault! So, say goodbye to our young friend...'

- 'Hey! Stop dragging me...you are my cousin, NOT my mom!' Bernard complained to his cousin and took his hand back by force. He was old enough to walk on his own and most importantly to have his own voice...he was eight already!

- 'Sweet Tooth do tell me. There is something I just do not quite get,' Roserin approached Sweet Tooth. 'Astrapi here, my African cat, usually senses when somebody is close to us. How come she did not smell you, and especially your ah... cute small friend?' she asked the boy. She found this 'monkey' creature or whatever he chose to call it, slightly scary. (The longer souls stayed in the 'In-Between World, the less they recalled the usual animals from their former dimension. They were getting used to seeing animals that were slightly different instead.)

- 'Well, it is simple!' Sweet Tooth replied. 'Bigeyes rubs some very special leaves on us. These leaves keep the mosquitos and all of the other insects away!'

- 'They do?! So that explains it!' Roserin said. 'It seems that Astrapi took you both for plants!' she said with a sense of admiration toward the young boy who knew something as important as this.

- 'Amazing!' Bernard said, impressed. 'What a splendid idea. I could use some of those leaves every now and then!' he said carelessly and tried to hide his secret mischievous idea to use the leaves to pay a visit to the kitchen when his mother made that delicious apple pie! That dough was just too enticing for his tongue's taste buds- even better than the cake itself.

'Just to smell fresh! You know...' he said with the most innocent look that a child would ever choose before they committed the greatest mischief that was ever possible to be accomplished in the Universe.

- 'To smell fresh?' his cousin smiled, as he could read his cousin's every single thought. 'You are lucky you do not have a mother like Timmy's, who brought the authorities home to teach him a lesson when she realized he had snuck the whole chocolate pudding! Remember? The one she had prepared for that dreadful aunt of his,' he paused and pondered for a while. Then, he could not help but chuckle when he imagined young Timothy's ecstatic moments, having gulped the pudding a few minutes before his aunt had arrived!

- 'I feel sorry for him...' Rosie expressed what she felt.

- 'Well, at least he prevented his aunt from eating it!' Bernard laughed and praised the boy. 'It serves her right! That thing is not an aunt, it is a monster!' he said and hugged Bigeyes, as he jumped into his arms. 'Do you agree my cute monkey? Yes! And you are much more attractive than her, aren't you? And you would bite her if we happened to meet her, would you not? That's my cute, clever Bigeyes!' he said and caressed him on the head.

- 'We should be getting back.' Roserin told her friends. 'We cannot leave you wet for too long,' she said to Bernard. 'Fortunately, Stamatis has got a few clean clothes at home; They should fit you. Do call Robert. Is he still swimming?'

- 'Well, bye then!' Sweet Tooth said to them while Bernard gave young Bigeyes back to his owner as if he had been a baby. Then he looked for his Penguin.

- 'Wait a minute! How will we get through that part of the woods?' Rosie asked with a slight tone of fear in her voice. 'You know? That creepy noise that we heard?'

- 'You are right,' Henrietta replied. 'Maybe there is another way to go.' She turned toward Stamatis. 'Do you know another path perhaps? A safer one?'

- 'Don't worry about the woods!' Sweet Tooth shouted to his new friends as he was left behind. 'They are friends of Bigeyes'!' But nobody seemed to be paying attention to him. They were distracted by small discoveries on their way out, which they had not noticed before. Like the way stalagmites were shimmering. A thin cover of silver dust that stuck on the surface made them look as if they had been dipped in some sort of magical broth. It took their breath away...

- 'It feels as if we are walking on the moon!' Henrietta thought.

The children all found themselves outside the cave soon, except for Bernard who did not want to get out of the waterfall.

- 'It feels wonderful! It is so pleasant...and it makes me feel great! Very great!' he said with his face protruding outside the water, his hair moving upwards. Robert appeared right next to him, with his feathers looking wet already. As he stood, the flow of the water caused his feathers to move upwards.

- 'But it will not dry your pants!' Henrietta said and pulled him out of there by force. 'Come on! We have a long way ahead of us. And do not even think about wandering off! Especially with these low clouds,' Henrietta warned her cousin when she saw the thick layer of fog that approached. This phenomenon happened every day, caused by the coming of the second sun. The second sun would give life and energy to their world for another twelve hours. In the meantime, the moon would cover the first sun for the next thirty-six hours, until tomorrow morning. It was a total eclipse that offered a dim golden light. Then, the moon would uncover the first sun for only twelve hours and return for its eclipse once the second sun started to appear.

- 'Maybe we should choose another way and avoid the path through the woods. The fog comes from there,' Roserin said. 'I think we should ask Sweet Tooth. He could have another path in mind. I am going in again,' she said decidedly and disappeared again through the waterfall.

- 'Maybe we should call it waterflow!' Stamatis mused, watching his sister, then he looked toward the sky. 'I can hardly make out the second sun approaching.'

Roserin started looking for the boy inside the cave and walked a bit further inside since she could not see him close at the entrance. She went past the hole that Bernard had fallen into, but she could not see any sign of Glykodontis, -as the name Sweet Tooth is called in Greek- or Bigeyes. She stood there for a few seconds, looking around in all directions. All she could see was the endless lakes that spread ahead, along with stalactites and stalagmites all around, which had been growing slowly and steadily throughout the ages. There was this dreadful silence. She wanted to call Sweet Tooth's name, but a feeling of respect and sacredness at the same time prevented her from disturbing this beautiful place. She stood another minute in absolute silence, and then she decided to walk back. However, she missed realizing that the key her mother had given her had come loose from her neck and floated onto the ceiling. Its shape was formed within the mist, which had started spreading along the upper part of the cave. She walked beneath it, and a sudden feeling of fear urged her to get out as soon as possible.

- 'Well? What did he say?' Alexander asked her as soon as she came out of the waterflow.

- 'I am afraid we lost him. I looked everywhere, and yet he was nowhere! I really cannot understand how he managed to leave so quickly...and where to?' were Roserin's comments.

- 'The fog spreads very quickly,' Henrietta said before Rosie started pondering for too long. 'I want to go home,' she said, and so they did leave at once. Some beautiful patches of gold that were as thin as Henrietta's hair, along with traces of golden dust made their appearance in the air. While the children walked through it, the patches would stick onto their faces. There was a strong magnetism around their bodies, like big drops of mercury that attracted identical clones.

- 'It is very humid,' Alexander said and wiped his face with a clean cloth. The cloth took his face's shape instantly and even seemed to be moving. Various shades of gold moved slowly to the surface; the same way drops of oil would behave in water. They remained within the cloth's limits without spoiling the basic shape. It looked as if it had been something more than just a cloth. It seemed to be alive! Henrietta, on the other hand, was covered by golden prints of leaves' skeletons. The patches of gold behaved differently depending on the person they stuck to. Due to the sensitive and caring nature of the girl's character, the patches had formed a most sensitive part of nature: some very fragile leaves, which also described a part of her very beautiful character. Roserin, on the other hand, was covered by thousands of particles that formed several keys. If she would have seen them herself, she might have remembered to check her neck for the key. Unfortunately, they were formed on parts of her body that were NOT noticed by her, like the back of her head. Her brother's print was particularly interesting. He carried one image only, which was the shape of a chameleon. But why did his forehead carry that particular shape? This is something that we will probably find out in the future...

Now, younger Bernard was a very different case. He was always happy and could very easily transfer his cheerfulness to any person who had the good fortune to meet him. He did not bear any image on his body whatsoever. The dust behaved in a very peculiar way. The positive energy he had in his body repelled it, but still kept it around him like a golden cocoon. And that was not all. The patches transformed into small happy faces! Faces of children and clowns and faces of ancient Greek masks- theatrical masks. At the same time, they would emit a dim white light around his face that made him look like another sun. Or perhaps like a firefly that had forgotten to switch off its light!

Astrapi was surrounded by a whole cloud of three-dimensional bones with some meat attached to them, and a few pieces of salami and ham here and there. Every time she tried to grab one, the particles would float away instantly, and then reconnect again the way they were before, only to make the poor African cat suffer...

Robert, as the last and cutest of the friends, was surrounded by smaller clouds, which had taken the shapes of miniature Angels, flapping their wings. They flew around a penguin-shaped cloud which bore a close resemblance to Robbie.

- 'We are very lucky to have Bernard with us right now!' Roserin said. 'How would we find our way back without his help?' she thought while they descended the stairs that lead to the bridge. Bernard's glow was so strong that the children couldn't lose him from their sights. They continued this way until, at some point, the boy stopped in front of them, as if roots had grown out of his feet, and looked puzzled.

- 'I cannot see any further than this. The fog is too dense now,' he told his friends with a tone of disappointment. 'All we can do now is wait until the second sun comes out.'

- 'But we cannot stay on the stairs!' Henrietta said. 'Who knows what could happen here in the meanwhile.'

- 'Well, do you have a better idea?' Roserin said to her friend. 'We cannot see further than our noses. Remember what happened to poor Timothy? He tried to guess his way back home, and as a result, he had this terrible accident...'

- 'Yes, I remember the day you told us the story,' Henrietta agreed. 'I do feel sorry for him.' She sighed, trying to bring the image back into her mind's eye, the image of poor Timothy descending the wrong stairs, the ones that had appeared suddenly out of nowhere. Some very strange things would occur every time the mist became as thick as a properly made candy floss. In the case of poor Timothy, who had chosen not to be patient enough, the tricky path had led him straight to the entrance of his aunt's house!

- 'Ouch!' a voice of complaint was suddenly heard. 'Stop kicking me all the time Henrietta!' It belonged to Bernard, who was sitting on a step on a lower level than everybody else.

- 'It was not I!' Henrietta complained to her cousin. 'Why do you always assume that it was me?'

- 'Alexander? Are you here?' Bernard asked his cousin, not only to find out whether it had been him who had kicked him, but also to make sure that he was still there, feeling slightly worried for not having heard him talk for some time.

- 'Where do you think I have gone?' Alexander replied.

- 'Is Astrapi with us?' Stamatis asked, all of a sudden greatly worried.

- 'He is right here with me,' Roserin answered her brother. She then tried to feel Astrapi's head with her hand, when she realized that what she felt was thin air where the African cat was standing only ten seconds ago. She moved her hand around in a panic, only to find out that her beloved cat was gone.

- 'He is not here!' she gasped, still trying to feel for him at a close distance with a trembling hand. 'He is NOT here!'

- 'What do you mean he's not here?' Stamatis asked. 'He was with you all the time!'

- 'And now he is gone!' Roserin almost cried. 'Alexander, Henrietta...is Astrapi with you?' she asked in great worry. After three seconds that felt to her like three whole hours, her friends replied that they could neither see nor feel her beloved cat around.

- 'I will go look for him,' she said to them and stood up.

- 'What are you talking about? Don't be crazy and sit on your...step!' her brother said, managing to control his tongue just in time before expressing carelessly a rather less kind word. 'I am in no mood to look for you too in the end!'

- 'Don't worry Rosie!' Henrietta tried to comfort her. 'I am sure he is somewhere close...He would never leave us alone.' As soon as she completed her sentence, she moved her hand around, looking for their beloved penguin.

- 'Astrapi!' Roserin started calling his name in the hope that he would instantly return to his friend. 'Astrapi!' she called again and waited for a few seconds; in case her ears grasped the sound of his steps. But unfortunately, there was no acoustic sign of his nails anywhere. 'Astrapi!' she tried again for the third time and feeling downhearted, she did not find the strength to call him for a fourth time. After seven seconds of absolute silence, Rosie looked behind her, from right where they had walked down from. A pair of deep red glowing lights that were coming down the stairs made her eyes pop out as wide as an owl's. This time, the children seemed to be right in the middle of the stairs of this huge temple, and it looked as if this pair of lights floated up, and up again, disappearing for a fraction of a second and then reappearing, but this time in a much bigger form. Roserin was too astonished to alert her friends. After a few disappearances and reappearances, the lights had reached an extremely worrying distance in no time. Rosie let a sound of surprise out of her mouth as the only way she could use to communicate. What on earth was that thing? A special kind of dragonfly? Or was it that tarantula creature that had somehow found a way to appear in their world? Henrietta told her about it once and it was horrific! Roserin hoped secretly that they would not have to encounter any unidentified jumping object, like the one that her friend had described her. Alexander turned around as soon as he heard Rosie's gasp.

- 'Hey! Look who is here!' he said full of enthusiasm. 'Our little red-eyed Bigeyes!'

- 'Bigeyes?' Henrietta asked in disbelief. Her face looked like a mask with an expression of the utmost astonishment that any artist would ever be able to depict. Rosie noticed at that moment that the cloud that was covering her friend moved further away.

- 'But if Bigeyes is here then so is Sweet Tooth,' Alexander said. 'Look at these eyes!' the boy thought. As soon as he had made his assumption, Bigeyes jumped a few stairs down and right above Robert's head, which he used as a base to step onto! Robbie made a loud noise out of fear and jumped high, flapping his flippers up and down. He caused Bigeyes to jump away and disappear within the fog.

- 'Where is he going?' Henrietta asked in fear that something bad might happen to the monkey animal, just in case he lost his way too. But Bigeyes sat a few steps away and stood as still as a monkey sculpture. He looked back at the children and released a shriek.

- 'Does he want us to follow him?' Bernard asked.

- 'I don't know what he wants, but I am not leaving this place without Astrapi,' Roserin answered back firmly.

- 'Rosie is right,' Henrietta told her cousin. 'We need to find Astrapi first.'

- 'There is no need for that!' Bernard said. 'He is down there!' he shouted excitedly and pointed his finger in the direction that they were supposed to follow. 'See? Right next to Bigeyes, waiting for us!' All five of them turned their heads and could, at last, see their cat friend with the long ears. Now his body had a slightly silver-bluish glow, caused by a certain flower's pollen that got stuck onto his hair. That was some very special pollen, as well as very rare. He had a beautiful shimmer that made him look like a moon cat!

- 'If somebody came to me one day and told me that this cat came from the moon, I would believe them!' Alexander said with a smile. Rosie had already rushed toward her beloved friend and gave him a big hug. It was she this time that shimmered, releasing a big cloud of moon pollen around them both as she patted Astrapi's body with love.

-'He discovered the shimmery flowers!' Stamatis answered his friend. 'They are the most beautiful flowers I have ever seen!' They both stood up, getting ready to follow Bigeyes. 'I cannot believe how my sister managed to run down these stairs! There is fog everywhere...'

Bernard, Robert, and Henrietta had already approached Roserin and Astrapi, trying to figure out where Astrapi had been, and where he had found such a special shimmery substance that looked like sticky drops of honey.

As soon as everyone stood again on the ground, the stairs behind them faded into the fog. Bigeyes moved further ahead and would look behind him occasionally so that the children could see his luminous eyes. After some time of tracing his steps within the clouds, they found themselves in a part of the woods that looked quite familiar to them.

- 'Please tell me this is not the place with that horrible freaky sound.' Alexander said to his friends and felt goose pimples on his arms. Everyone stood silently and looked at each other with expressions of curiosity and agony on their faces. They had no choice but to follow Bigeyes. They tiptoed so that they would not be heard by any monsters that might be hiding, and entered the darkest and most mysterious part of the woods. Bernard touched the medallion he was wearing on his neck that was given to the students at their school. It was a special kind of medallion with the embossed image of an owl's head, both on the front and the back. The boy pulled the front head downwards, which caused it to open into two halves. An inner embossed image of a sun, half embraced by the moon, appeared.

Right in the core of their union, there was a key- a key that represented the children's future and their destiny. This destiny was to discover and tame the greatest power that existed in the Universe...ever! The destiny to become lightworkers.

The moon had covered one half of the sun when the children entered into the woods. Bernard dared to follow Bigeyes first, even though he was the youngest and most vulnerable of all. He was still glowing inside the fog, with the only difference being that the hovering smoky smiling faces all around him were not smiling anymore. Their beautiful happy smiles had been replaced by horrified chattering teeth. Alexander, Robert, and Stamatis followed behind him, then Henrietta, with Rosie and Astrapi in the back. The fog had become less dense in front of them, but there were still areas where it looked as thick as cotton balls. The silver light that was emitted by the eclipse of the sun, made the clouds resemble luminous carriers of thousands of stars. It looked as if they were absorbing all the dispersed energy that existed in the air. The children arrived, at some point, to a place where the clouds had formed some familiar shapes. One cloud looked like a floating ship that was traveling quietly into another world. Its many oars transported it forward smoothly. The sparkling stars, concentrated in certain places, made the ship appear more lively and enchanting than any other ship that existed in this world. There were also shapes in the clouds of mirrors, rings, and doughnuts. Another cloud had formed the shape of a carriage that was being pulled by a dark horse, whose body looked like a puzzle of the Universe itself. In the position of its eye, there was a magnificent spiral of colorful stars. In other areas of its body, other interesting things were going on. A few stars would fall now and then, and a black hole was showing off its repelled positive atoms that were just about to form something interesting. Alexander admired some newly formed seashells and a blue lobster that had just floated past him. Then the children came across some sparkly light bulb-shaped clouds. The light had concentrated somehow on various points, which, when connected, shaped the outline of the source that produced the most beautiful golden color ever.

- 'Hey look!' Bernard shouted, excited. 'I am inside a light bulb!

Don't I look like an Angel?'

Before Robert had the chance to enter the bulb next to his friend, that horrible sound that froze their blood on their way to the caves sounded once again. This time, it made the light bulbs go dead and seemed to be spreading all around the children. Everyone froze like statues and Robert ran instantly toward Alexander in fear, and stood between the boy's legs. It sounded like the announcement of the coming of the most evil creature the world had ever seen...

- 'Run!' Alexander shouted to his friends, and they all started running as fast as they could inside the fog. Sometimes they had to pause to detect which way Bigeyes the monkey had gone. Roserin had stayed behind with Astrapi, as she did not have much energy left to run. She paused and took a few breaths when the scary sounds started enveloping her ears, and a bright white light was caught suddenly by the side of her eye. She looked to her left and was stunned to see a person sitting in the middle of the woods. He seemed to be the source of this light, as he was glowing even stronger than the light bulbs they had encountered before. He was sitting on some sort of chair- a chair that was impossible to see. He was using a feather pen to write in a book of many pages. It was placed on a table which was either see-through or had been constructed in such a way that would give anyone the illusion that it was simply not there! Roserin felt safe and walked toward the man. She could see his characteristics much clearer now. His long, light red hair fell down his back, and a rough beard gave him a unique, mysterious appearance. He was dressed in a long black velvet cloak, with sleeves that flared wide at the ends. Around his neck, a sudden sparkle made the girl notice a long purple Chevron Amethyst crystal wand that was fitted within a silver frame.

- 'Do not be afraid of the hallow creatures,' the man said, still writing his book.

Roserin was astonished she had been noticed already at that distance. The man had hardly turned his head! How did he know that she and Astrapi were there?

- 'They are your friends,' he continued seriously and looked at Roserin. The girl was amazed to see how much his eyes communicated when he turned his head toward her. They were a source of tremendous amounts of energy, and Rosie could feel the power and creativity that were bursting behind these talking 'mirrors'. She felt pleasant energy around her body, and a slight caressing sensation on her head, as if somebody had stroked her with a feather. After a few seconds of being hypnotized, she moved her head suddenly and looked onto the ground, for only just a second. A second, which was more than enough to make her gasp, since the man had disappeared! The book was still there, floating in the air. The girl ran toward it. Calligraphic letters sprang out of its pages then bounced gently before landing. It looked as if the book had been trying to catch her attention. The spreading of the letters resembled a fountain's falling water, to an extent. Roserin was enchanted by the mesmerizing image and moved carefully over to the 'letter fall'. She placed her hand into the core of the source and saw that they would still emerge through her hand. She smiled with pleasure and then looked at the text this man had written. His calligraphy was the most beautiful she had ever seen.

'I wish I could write in such a beautiful way!' she thought silently. She did not dare to speak out loud as she was afraid that she would ruin the beauty of these few moments of sacredness. Words would only shatter the bliss all around her. She read...

'I wish I could write in such a beautiful way!' she thought silently. She did not dare speak out loudly as she was afraid that she would ruin the peacefulness of these few moments of sacredness. Words would only shatter bliss all around her. 'I hope this man would not mind my reading of his story. It is so beautiful, I cannot resist! If only I could find that book again and see within its pages...'

Roserin walked two steps backward, overwhelmed and breathless by the discovery the book had offered her. These were her last thoughts and actions after the man had disappeared! 'Does this mean that he can write my future?' she thought. And what about the last sentence? She had not thought of any similar one so far, so what exactly did it mean? 'It seems these are my future thoughts. I will probably be looking for the book again,' she thought and leaned back over its pages.

'There must be something of great significance in here; I should look until I find it.' She looked at the end of the text, but all she could read was the same last sentence she had read before: 'If only I could find that book again and see within its pages...'

'I just do NOT understand!' the girl thought. 'I have made a few more thoughts so far, so why does the book not mention them? Maybe I should wait until the writer returns,' she pondered and tried to turn one page backward. The page melted down instantly, as soon as it had been touched, leaving behind a thin layer of gold on Roserin's delicate hands.

7. Confrontation with the True Self.

- '*Oh*, no! What have I done?' Roserin gasped, while the book started to disappear gradually, as if it had been a part of a vision. 'No! Don't go!' the girl pleaded.

- 'I am right here!' a voice sounded behind her, causing her to jump. Had the book transformed into a human being? Or was it the writer who had returned? Roserin turned around and came face to face to the person who had been standing behind her.

- 'Stamatis?' she said, as if she had experienced the most unexplained phenomenon ever, in front of her very own eyes. 'Henrietta!' she whispered, when her friends approached a few meters from the background.

- 'Who else do you think?' her brother replied. 'What exactly do you think you are doing here? Come on! Everybody is waiting for you!' he said impatiently and walked toward the main path. Henrietta, on the other hand, was slightly worried about her friend's unusual behavior. Roserin looked as if she were in a state of trance. Her eyes glowed more than ever before.

Rosie Protects the Coded Disc of Phaistos

- 'Is everything fine?' Henrietta asked her. 'You know, you really worried us. We thought we had lost you.'

- 'Yes, everything's fine,' Roserin replied while walking away, her glance fixed on a certain spot. She almost looked like those owls that could turn their heads a hundred and eighty degrees behind their bodies. Henrietta could feel that something was not quite right, but she could not stop and have a chat now that they needed to run. That terrifying noise was still all around them. A weird thing, however, had just occurred. Something that the children had still not realized: Roserin could not hear it anymore. She did hear something, which was very different from the goose pimpling sounds that made her friends run. She felt as if her ears had opened as wide as a dish, and she was able to sense the most beautiful sounds that a person ever had the luck to experience in their life. She thought she heard pleasant voices, singing and laughter of Guardians, or Guides talking to each other. And yet, they did not have any voices. Their sounds of communication more resembled the vibrations of Winter's crystals' dance, a river that was oozing of the world's sweetest chocolate, the pearl reflections of the shell's that mirrored the peak of Nature's beauty...as well as the book that had melted in Rosie's fingers. Henrietta kept dragging her friend until they reached the bridge. The bridge had somehow lost connection with the descending stairs, and had attracted, in a mysterious way, the woods behind it. Nature had a peculiar way of making herself noticed. Certain landmarks would appear in unexpected places. What nature wanted to achieve was to spice up life a little, by changing its form and appearance constantly. This time, the trees had placed themselves right between the stairs and the bridge, giving travelers the illusion that something was very wrong within their minds.

The children now walked onto the bridge. The scary sounds started to subside, and everyone but Roserin felt relieved to be back again on the misty bridge. Since the sounds had transformed into heavenly vibrations in her ears, she could not understand why there was such great hurry. She could not recall the fright that she had felt inside her heart. This calligraphic fountain book seemed to have absorbed all sense of fear and despair and had replaced them with joy and happiness instead. She was still wondering how the letters had formed her own thoughts and actions. She trembled at the idea of somebody having written down every single thought and feeling of hers. It did feel relieving, on the other hand.

'What about the moments I have been angry at others?' she whispered to Astrapi in worry. 'Oh, no! I will never dare think of anything ever again!'

- 'Did you say something Rosie?' Alexander asked her while crossing the bridge.

- 'No!' she replied abruptly to him, as she was not certain yet to whom to talk about her unexpected experience. She dreaded the thought that her friends might become curious on the spur of the moment, and insist on looking for that floating mystery book- the book that contained her very secret thoughts! Even thoughts that were not meant exactly to belong to an innocent girl, as she appeared to the others. Sometimes, she just could not help it! Was it that bad to be able to become invisible and scare away the people that she did not like? Or to be a little more mischievous and to add some fun to life every now and then? Like that time she had placed the clock's hands a few minutes forward in her class so that their teacher would think that the time was already up? She had only done this twice after all...Alright, three times to be honest. Maybe four? Alright! It was five! So what? All of her friends praised her in the end for having saved them from the possible humiliation of falling asleep in such a boring lesson on how to become a Lady and a Sir! Was it not a good deed that she had done? She had even protected the teacher from feeling bad, from the aftermath of such a possible scenario. The conclusion? He should be grateful to her! Suddenly, another thought crossed her mind like a thunderbolt. What if the book mentioned her teachers' own secret thoughts? It would have been absolutely wonderful if she could have a quick peek only! Just a tiny little paragraph?

- 'Be careful, Rosie!' her brother warned her teasingly. 'You have that dangerous, cheeky look on your face that usually gets you into trouble!' he said amusingly and brought his sister back to reality.

- 'What?' she said, as innocently as she could, but with apparent signs of potential trouble that was on its way.

- 'I am so glad we are out of the woods at last!' Henrietta said with a sigh. 'I wonder what kind of monsters were making that noise.' Roserin was the only person who would be able to give her an answer, but she was so deeply absorbed by her own thoughts once again that she had hardly noticed her friend's comment. Astrapi was the only one who could feel a great amount of positive energy around the girl, something he had experienced too at the same time, since they had been together. This great respectable man was the first stranger he had met whose limbs he did not wish to bite! This Calligrapher had transmitted to him instantly a great deal of warmth and trust somehow. His instincts had assured him that this was not a person with the slightest trace of hostility or malice whatsoever. On the contrary, this highly respectable man had made Astrapi's soul feel as if he was about to fly, becoming the first flying African cat in his world, ever! Astrapi was also the only one among them who was able to see the subtle waves of energy surrounding the girl. The waves twirled around and finally formed some interesting shapes of white bright books with calligraphic letters. The letters had butterfly wings, and their elegant bodies were being lifted away from the open pages. And then, having completed a journey of an approximate distance of ten inches, they paused for a while, then popped gracefully like fireworks in their entire splendor.

The children were now almost in the middle of the bridge, and tried to look toward their own statues. The fog, however, was so thick around them that it was impossible to make out what had happened to their stone shaped figures.

- 'What a shame! We cannot see if anyone else has passed by.' Bernard said. 'I wonder if there is a statue of Bigeyes down there! Showing us his true self.' Roserin rushed to see over the bridge, in the hope that she might be able to see anything more revealing that had to do with Henrietta's and her own possible futures. The clouds, however, were as persistent as her own head. After a few minutes of hanging over the bridge, Astrapi,

Robert, and their friends decided to move on.

At the same time and a long distance behind them, something unusual was going on. The floating book appeared once again, which was very normal you might say, but this time something very different had started to occur. The calligraphic letters that before sprang gracefully out of its pages, behaved in a much more bizarre way now. They looked like swarming bees that had been disturbed, and took a position that indicated aggressiveness. They flew around as a pointed arrow in sudden motions, and as soon as they had found themselves some distance away from their source, they formed a forked catapult branch that was just about to release its heavy load. A heavy "stone" of calligraphic letters was now being flung back toward the book itself. It landed violently onto its open pages, and the drop of ink that was spread around formed a drawing of a rather familiar picture. It was an unknown girl's statue, seen from the side. And then, something else occurred. The statue moved slightly toward the front and lifted her hands above her head as if she was hoping that somebody would pull her out of the page. A terrifying noise that sounded like a horn that was blown in a moment of the greatest danger ever came out of her open mouth. Three cracks appeared on the statue's distressed face.

All of a sudden, a hand appeared above the book, with a feather pen in its fingers and a pink fluorite stone embedded firmly on the top side of a ring, which was worn on the hand's middle finger. The calligrapher had reappeared, and he seemed to be ready to continue with his work. The page turned over by itself, while the statue's noise, which would freeze anyone to a statue themselves, was now starting to subside as if a door was closing right behind it. The man's sleeve covered the right page, and the way it hung made it look like a dark oozing substance that permeated throughout the page itself. The paper was not a flat surface, as it appeared at first glance. It was merely covering the hollow space of the book's unwritten story. Half of the sleeve that hung throughout and beneath the page looked as if it floated inside a strong current of invisible water. A few stars also appeared on the fabric, dancing on the floating sleeve. And then...he started writing. He placed his feather-pen on the page's central spot, vertically, and kept it still for a few seconds without removing its nib from the surface. A big drop of ink was released around it, which gradually caused the formation of the most elegant letters that nature would ever give birth to. The letters were formed one after the other, moving slowly and silently like butterflies on the top left of the page, positioning themselves in their chosen places. The first few sentences had now appeared:

"Three cracks started to appear on the statue's distressed face. My job has been accomplished. By having moved all the clouds in front of their stone reflections, their fears have been prevented. What still remains to be done depends on Rosie's actions."

As soon as he had completed his sentences, he placed his pen onto the page's surface that he had just created, and it was 'swallowed' gradually by the page itself, as if it were made of quicksand.

The children had now reached the last part of the bridge that was invisible to mortals' eyes. Bigeyes, as it was mentioned before, was a monkey that had come from the world of the living people. His perception was very different from his new friends', so he thought of course that the bridge was not complete, due to the lack of suspension cables. As a result, he jumped onto the branches of the closest trees. Using his tail as an aid for perfect balance, he landed onto the ground safely.

 - 'What on earth is he doing?' Stamatis asked with a smile. 'We have almost crossed the bridge, and he jumps onto the trees!' he continued. 'Let us hope that he will not be expecting us to follow him up there!'

Astrapi watched him climb from one branch to another, even higher, and he seemed to be thinking something similar to:

'Trying to be the center of attention, are we? If I had a tail like yours, I would be up there before you could even THINK to make your first jump! It is NOT the weight that prevents me. It is the shortage of a monkey's tail.'

His friends were now walking onto the invisible part of the bridge, and it was very interesting to see the way the mist behaved. On every single step they took, it looked as if they left trapped parts of mist hovering around their shoe prints. It happened in a similar way that cotton candy would behave, had somebody stepped right inside the middle. Since Astrapi's feet were a lot more puffy, they had trapped small masses of mist within their hollow parts, making them look more three dimensional than his friends' flatter footprints. A very thick cloud appeared in front of Bernard, who could hardly resist the temptation. Without thinking about it for too long, he waved his hand through it as if he were trying to catch a mosquito. Both the shape of his palm and its path were imprinted on the cloud. A thick mass which looked like a great amount of bubbles stuck together when examined closely, and like an irresistible mountain of cotton candy when seen from further away, was now sticking on his hand. It had the imprint of a face, the sleeping face of the Cretan Mountain 'Yuchtas', which was very close to the neighborhood where the children lived, and which imitated the profile of the Ancient Greek God 'Zeus'. Robert looked at the soft mass. Was that a piece of the Arctic seas' waves? Was it the waves' foam he had been enjoying in the North Pole?

- 'Yummy! It tastes even better than cotton candy!' the boy said cheerfully.

- 'Amazing! Look Henrietta!' Alexander shouted with excitement. 'There is some 'Fairy's Hair here! Do you want some?'

- 'Oh, yes! We are so lucky!' she said and grabbed a handful of clouds. 'These are so rare to find!' She expressed her thought while licking her fingers clean.

After each of them had their share, they wiped their mouths clean with their sleeves –apart from Henrietta who cleaned her lips gently with her finger which she wet with her tongue, and Roserin, who used the backside of her hand,- and walked toward the path that would lead them back home. As for their friend Robert, he was still staring at the separate piece of cotton candy cloud he had now stuck onto one of his flippers. He was so focused on the sugary piece that he bumped into an old olive tree's trunk as he walked, and fell onto the ground. They kept walking for some time under some very tall olive trees and passed above a big number of miniature stone-built arched bridges below them when the mist started clearing away gradually.

- 'Hey look! We can see a little better now,' Bernard said to his friends. He looked behind him when a strong gust of wind landed something that looked like a piece of paper onto his face. The boy gasped in surprise and grabbed it in his fingers.

- 'Pah! Where did THAT come from?' he asked and looked at the address that had been written on what seemed to be a posted old envelope. He read out in a loud voice to his companions:

- "Miss Rosa Stubborn

Recluse Road, Long Faced House

Lonely Island

P.C. Not known by any living or unliving human being."

- 'Did you write this Bernard?' Roserin asked her friend with suspicion, since she had not realized that this letter had landed from nowhere right onto the boy's astonished face. Poor Bernard had just become a suspect in Rosie's eyes, of trying to provoke the already agitated girl. 'If you think this is funny, your taste is really bad!'

- 'I haven't done anything!' the young boy complained. 'It has JUST landed onto my face! You SAW!' he said with an intense tone of surprise, feeling he was picked on unfairly by his friend.

- 'Oh, really? And who else was it then who wrote my name on the envelope? And why is it open?' she said even more angrily. 'I bet you took one of your father's stamped envelopes and you wrote my name on it! And why did you write this sort of comment as an address? You think I am that sort of person who...' but Roserin did not manage to complete her sentence before another envelope landed onto her face, with the following address:

"Mr. Alexander Pea Brain

Great Scientist's Road, Leavemealone Hill,

Lightbulbshire

P.C. Use your mind to find out!"

- 'Hey!' Alexander complained to Roserin instantly, since it was his turn now to be distracted. He had missed the envelope landing onto Rosie's face because he had covered his face with his hands in frustration about Rosie and Bernard's fight. 'What exactly is THAT supposed to mean? Did you write this?' he asked the upset girl who read out the address. 'You are calling me a pea brain? You think you are cleverer Miss Rose bead?'

- 'I did NOT write this!' Rosie shouted, shocked and annoyed at once, as it was HER this time who was experiencing Bernard's similar feelings of unfairness. She further defended herself: 'YOU two have planned this from the very beginning. Haven't you? You dropped the letters here for me to find them!'

- 'Now, wait a minute! You are calling me a 'plotter'? Is THAT what you are trying to say? Should this be the case, then I would do you the favor and write two other addresses for you so that at least you would be telling the truth. And...' The angry boy felt he was being accused unfairly and hardly completed his sentence before a third envelope landed onto his own face this time, with another fight- promising address on its back. Confused Alexander did not dare read it out loud since he already anticipated the consequences. Bernard grabbed it quickly out of his hands and read it out loud:

"Mr. Bernard Faceless

Buffoon Road,

Phlegmshire

P.C. Has run away from him."

As soon as his eyes saw what was written onto the envelope, he turned all red and shouted:

- 'I am NOT faceless! I bet it is you both who have prepared this and you think that I do not communicate with my brain to realize that...' he was about to carry on, when all of a sudden a big cloud of winged scrolls being pushed by a strong wind landed on them violently while the wind became even stronger. Henrietta felt goose pimples. All the scrolls had ONE thing in common: Their seals were all BROKEN.

- 'WHAT IS THAT?' Stamatis shouted to his friends in order to be heard. The wind whistled even louder than their own fights. Thousands of scrolls had filled the air and expressions of worry were formed on the children's faces. Astrapi sniffed in the air, with his instincts telling him that something was very wrong indeed. Robert, who was standing right next to his friend, jumped in the air and grabbed a scroll that resembled a fish tight within his beak. The scroll tried to fly away, but the penguin would not let go of it.

- 'This is the creepiest thing I have ever seen! WHERE HAVE THE MESSAGES GONE?' Roserin shouted to her friends. 'And where are the scrolls coming from?' Her heartbeat got very fast, and an expression of great worry affected her baby looking face.

- 'We'd better get back RIGHT NOW...something is very wrong here!' Henrietta shouted while having a few last looks at the laying scrolls all around her. She then saw, or at least thought that she saw, Stamatis' name in glowing letters on at least six scrolls that were carried past her, as close as they could fly and float next to her.

- 'Pah! I am not going to pick you up! You do NOT exist so you will not be able to hurt me!' she kept saying decisively as she walked through all these scrolls, which were attracted to her as if she was the most powerful magnet on the whole dimension, ever! 'You do NOT exist! You do NOT exist!' The more she resisted, the more letters and scrolls hovered around her in a hypnotizing, never-ending dance. She kept running away from them while Alexander, Rosie, and Bernard carried on arguing. Stamatis was trying hopelessly to put an end to the fight and Astrapi kept trying to calm down his friends, shouting to them:

'Come on! Stop it! You are acting up like baby kitties!'

During this chaos of intense argument and Astrapi's nonstop growling, the whistle of a strong hot Southern wind came from nowhere. Clouds of thousands of empty broken-sealed scrolls flew all around them, preventing the limited light that was still in the atmosphere from spreading around. The children hardly noticed one of their friend's sudden disappearance. Roserin was led by an envelope's dance into a silent hidden spring within the woods. A spring that contained a really big shell. A shell that reflected the image of a floating mermaid who smiled back to Rosie. Her hair hovered around her, and out of nowhere, a fish appeared suddenly and swam along the shell's ripples, right in front of Rosie's own reflection. The fish was within the shell's very own surface. It looked as if this shell contained a small piece of the vast enchanting world of the Sea. Any person who had the luck to find themselves in that place was able to see a piece of their own soul, translated into a few seconds of projection according to the secrets of their no-longer-locked heart.

Within the hollow part of the shell, a stone-carved mermaid was sitting right in the core, holding a big pearl in her hands. Some crystal-clear water flew from the top of her head, down her very long hair, and finally landed inside the shell itself. Rosie could hardly take her eyes off her. The rock on which the shell was firmly fastened was placed on the top of a small hill that was covered by soft green moss. A few more stones that had been placed around the spring in small concentric circles caught the girl's attention. The luminous blue color inside them made them look as if they had enclosed the strongest feelings of euphoria. But what had really drawn Roserin's attention was what was emerging right in between the stone circles themselves: A transparent kind of chocolate-consistency balloon which emitted the most beautiful lights of white chocolate and cherry syrup that a living entity ever had the chance to see.

- 'Chocolate balloons!' she sighed and approached them closely.

They looked like miniature balloons that had the same appearance as the moon itself. Roserin placed her fingers on the top and pressed a semi-circled part of it, causing it to break into small pieces. She pinched and broke the remaining pieces with her fingers, giving her the chance to take a peek within. A luminous star appeared in its core, which was surrounded by a few rings of precious, colorful stones. Rosie placed her hand inside the chocolate balloon; She grabbed the five angled star and without any hesitation, she moved it right inside her mouth. The balloon lost its light instantly, and the few colored minerals that were disturbed by Rosie's intrusion fell onto the ground and started already the formation of their descendants.

- 'Yummy!' the girl said with delight and wiped her mouth clean. 'Tastes like lemon chocolate!' She then decided to press another chocolate balloon and have one more little star. It was too delicious to stay there for all eternity! One more would certainly not hurt. She approached the second balloon that was available, and with trembling fingers of craving, she pinched it and instantly grabbed the luminous little core, only for it to end up on top of her tongue's taste buds. Some bright rays of light seemed to escape from inside her eyes and nostrils, for only a fraction of a second. Some more precious stones got disconnected from the main gas rings that surrounded the core and fell to the ground. More chocolate balloons were now in the process of being born. Roserin was covered by glowing dust this time, dust that floated among the colorful minerals. She decided to open a third balloon as soon as she had swallowed the second one, and after a few seconds, she proceeded to the fourth, and then to the fifth one. A whole bunch of newborn balloons had already started emitting their mesmerizing moonlight, and the place became even more luminous than it was before. Rosie was not able to stop eating their core stars. She was so enchanted by both taste and beauty that she failed to notice a pair of eyes that made their appearance through a pair of very thick bushes. Every time the eyes blinked, the pupils' long narrow slits became round for a quarter of a second and then stretched gradually back to their initial vertical shape. It was not certain whether these eyes belonged to a human, a reptile, or even a monster. One thing was clear enough: The entity that carried them had a dark soul, darker than the moon's eclipse itself. Roserin being unaware of its presence, and being in a position of longing for a few more 'delicacies,' was now getting closer and closer to the bush.

- 'Roserin!' A man's voice sounded all of a sudden and without any hesitation he opened the heavy oak wood carved door. Margaret showed up at the entrance within five or six seconds, still wiping one of her freshly washed clay pots dry.

- 'Sir Hipparchus! How nice of you to visit!' Margaret welcomed the well-respected man, whose air and appearance gave the impression of a very fair and well-educated person. 'I am afraid Mr. Marmeladas and his lovely wife are away, but...'

- 'Where is Rosie? Where are the children?' he interrupted her anxiously.

'I must see them at once!' he told the sympathetic woman and he looked around the living room in great worry.

- 'I am afraid they are not here!' Margaret answered the gentleman. 'They have gone out for a walk, but they should be here shortly. They were supposed to have returned quite some time ago actually,' she said, after having a look at the big cuckoo clock that was standing proudly in the living room. 'Would you like me to offer you something in the meantime? A cup of iced mixed juice perhaps? You could wait if you like; It should not take them long to arrive.'

Sir Hipparchus thanked her and made his way toward a big white comfy sofa built of bamboo. He sunk into it with great relief, at last being able to rest his painful body. It had been a long time since he had had the luxury to rest for a few minutes. He had been extremely busy completing and testing the latest invention of his. He could hold it in front of him finally and share its benefits with the rest of the world. But ONLY with the 'wise' brains of the world. He was happy now...it had been done at last. However, traces of worry were still apparent in his green, intelligent-looking eyes. He grabbed his long hair away from his face and caressed it backward using his fingers. His short chestnut trimmed beard was enough to make him sweat in this excessively hot, humid weather. He was feeling much better now as he used his handkerchief to sweep his face. He rested on the couch for a few seconds, his eyes gazing at but not really seeing a small wooden trunk that was placed right in front of him on the living room table. His thoughts had traveled far away from the mysterious rustic styled living room, which was decorated with the rarest and most precious antiques ever. Most of them were either covered or made from the finest pieces of oak wood. Like the elaborate mosaic pentagonal boxes that stood right beside the small trunk, hiding possibly some even more precious but also useful and practical treasures. Not one single object was placed in the house merely for decoration purposes. There was always a reason behind it to justify its existence.

8. Sir Hipparchus and the Star-Net Astrolabe.

- 'Rosie!' Henrietta's voice made her friend turn around after having swallowed the eighth star down her throat. At the very same second, the unidentified being that was lurking around the bushes beat a retreat, and the sounds of breaking branches made it obvious that it was a four-legged creature. 'What on earth are you doing here?' Henrietta asked her friend. Rosie turned her head, completely glowing this time due to the chocolate cores which had affected her protective aura. 'We need to get back before anything worse happens. I just have this feeling.'

However, Roserin's attention was distracted by something that beat every single chocolate balloon's presence in the area. Something divine...and there it was, standing right next to Henrietta, protruding among a few bushes that were loaded with marshmallows.

- 'Yummy!' she said with delight, and with a deep hypnotized look on her face, she approached the most beautiful sight that she had ever had the luck to experience. 'A GIANT glowing balloon, just for me!'

- 'Oh, no!' Henrietta sighed and looked at her friend. 'How many balloons have you eaten? You were not supposed to do this!' she scolded

Roserin. 'You will be having a toothache or something worse, and who knows for how long! Come on! We are going right now!' she said and grabbed the girl's hand.

- 'But it is just there! Have a look yourself!' Rosie complained and tried to pull Henrietta toward her big temptation. She wanted to open that huge chocolate balloon by any means. If she could at least admire the scenery inside and fulfill her eyes' longing to experience the most enchanting colors that the cores were ever likely to emit! Henrietta was compelled to drag her by force since the girl was not able to resist. On the other side, the boys still fought about the envelopes. And the longer they fought, the stronger the wind became, and the more envelopes appeared for them to read. Astrapi was still trying to separate them. The moment he saw Roserin and Henrietta, he ran toward them to draw their attention and said 'Where have you been? Quick!' then he ran back to the boys as fast as he could, trying to put an end to their fight. But there was nothing he could do. The anger inside their stomachs had charged their spirits to such an extent that one of the most terrifying phenomena that Astrapi's eyes could possibly experience occurred right in front of him, Robert and the girls. Waves of black matter emanated from around the boys' bodies and formed streams that moved toward the sky. Within a short time, the streams joined each other at some point and formed a thinner, long tornado that ultimately revealed a shape that very much resembled a giant spectral dinosaur of some sort- a dinosaur with the most terrifying head that Roserin had ever seen so far in her life. She noticed a slight resemblance to the Monster she had seen in her dream. Could it have been the very same Monster? she worried. A strange name came to her consciousness: 'Postosuchus.' The skin on the Monster's skull was almost see-through since it was as thin as a membrane. Its jaw was so strong that could smash the toughest tree like a toothpick, and its tail was so long that its end was hardly visible from where the girls were standing. It faded on the horizon. When it changed its direction, with a big whoosh, the powerful tail moved violently over the girls. Roserin almost fainted, but the worst was still to come. The girl ran suddenly toward the boys for some unexplained reason, while Robert ran the opposite direction, shouting and scared, and found refuge between Henrietta's legs, trembling in fear. Rosie stopped all of a sudden. At the same time, the sky started turning green.

- 'Look!' she shouted to her friend. 'It is one of those cute little creatures. They call it a meerkat! And it is carrying a chocolate balloon in its mouth!' she said, looking toward the huge Monster. 'And how cute it is!' She whispered to herself, hypnotized, as Henrietta ran in strides to save her from great danger. As she was about to grab Rosie's hand, the Monster turned its head, and with a swift motion that left Henrietta in a state of shock, it snapped its teeth right in front of them. They both fell on the ground and Roserin shouted intensely:

- 'Bad, bad meerkat!' and then she stood up and ran once again right into the source of trouble. Henrietta was too paralyzed by fear to even blink, let alone try for a second time to save her friend. Rosie's ongoing illusions were putting everyone in grave danger, especially her own self. When Henrietta saw the Monster turn its head toward her friend once again, she felt unable to make even the slightest sound. With her frustration levels having risen to the highest point, a powerful lightning bolt struck a number of trees that surrounded the boys. The deafening sound of a thunder clap's entrance interrupted the fight by force. All three of them fell to the ground instantly when the terrifying Postosuchus got swallowed up by its own tornado's eye. The tornado still hovered above the boys and shook its tail like a squirming fish that had just been taken out of its natural environment. And then, it became less and less visible, as it started losing its power. The wind was still strong though, the sky was still green, and the lightning-struck trees were now on fire. Robert ran toward Astrapi and remained as close to him as he could.

One of the strongest and most persistent thunderclaps was heard back at home. It almost seemed to originate from the window itself. A lightning bolt sent a beam of intense light to the very center of a chameleon's eye that belonged to a constellation. It drew Sir Hipparchus' attention in a very unique, effective way. The same beam that went throughout the eye's hyaloid canal and was then refracted from its cornea, fell onto a big piece of the mysteriously broken goblet that was found in the living room. Sir Hipparchus got up at once and walked toward the delicate piece. As a man who had a reputation of being constantly cautious and aware of any potential dangers, he pulled a glove from his vest's pocket. As soon as he put it on, he picked up the piece carefully and placed it gently onto the table. He sat back onto the sofa, and this time he pulled something equally delicate out of his pocket. It was a pair of glasses that looked rather unusual. Right above the main frame and further to the front, two miniature wooden triremes had been fixed firmly on the right and the left sides, above the two lenses. From within the trireme, a series of seven oars that seemed to play an important role protruded and covered a firm mast resembling arms that were placed underneath each side, forming the very base on which the miniature ships were resting. Roserin and Stamatis' friend put the glasses on and started lifting every oar one by one, from the lenses' side toward the background, from both sides simultaneously. With every lift, a new lens would make its presence noticeable under the triremes' keels, right in front of the main lenses. All of the newly revealed lenses looked exactly the same. Any skeptic might think that there was nothing special about them. The glass seemed to consist of the same thin surface that the basic lenses carried. However, as soon as the respectful scientist lifted the triremes' central masts that had been resting on the decks, something extraordinary happened. The rise of the two masts somehow worked as an automatic mechanism that pulled the trigger for a secondary function. The lenses were blurred instantly as if somebody had exhaled their warm breath against them, and traces of moving liquid were now apparent on the surface. The glasses looked as if they were not solid anymore. It was a unique phenomenon that gave anyone the impression that small drops of liquid had been trapped within the frames. Tiny bubbles started to emerge, and the live see-through surfaces even changed into colors of pink and turquoise green. And it was then when Sir Hipparchus could finally see what was lurking around the broken piece...

Three loud knocks sounded on the door, and the man fell back to the sofa, startled and with signs of great worry on his face. He placed both the glasses and the broken piece carefully onto the table and as far away from each other as possible. Margaret opened the door and after having placed her hands onto her hips she said with a sigh:

- 'What time do you call this my dear?' she asked Roserin with an intense tone of disapproval in her voice. She pulled the girl inside the house by her hand. 'First day on your own and you behave like a bunch of brainless bozos! Poor Sir Hipparchus has been waiting here for you all this time! Now go in there quickly and do apologize...and look at the state of your clothes!' She kept commenting like a restless locomotive. 'What have you been up to? Trying to return to the world of the living people by digging out your own graves?' Robert approached her and spread his flippers in an effort to hug her. What a relief it was for him to again see his most favorite lady, who always provided him with fresh fish!

As soon as everyone went inside, Margaret went back to the kitchen to bring Sir Hipparchus' iced mixed juice. The children stepped up the five wooden steps that led to the living room, whereas the Astronomer already walked toward them in haste.

- 'Uncle! How nice to see you again! Henrietta greeted her beloved Researcher, whom she admired so much, both for his pleasant attitude and his abilities as a scientist at the same time. He was not really her uncle, but children in Greece would ALWAYS call a grown-up 'uncle' when they are a relatively young age. That helped them feel more familiar with their father's colleague and closest friend. 'Have you invented anything new recently?' she asked, eager to see a new gadget that she could explore for the rest of the afternoon. She was hoping to see something similar to a very special mirror that would somehow do something very unusual, like show her the image of a friend and be able to contact them, or reveal invisible souls that were around them from other dimensions, or perhaps transfer her instantly into a place of her choice with the push of a single button. Or perhaps the creation of a chocolate soufflé that would instantly offer anyone who ate from it ALL the knowledge in the world so that they would not have to go to school anymore. The Researcher seemed to be worried about something though, so he interrupted her and brought his young friend back to reality. Robert was imagining the invention of a special copper pot that would contain part of a lake that ejected fish every time he looked at it.

- 'Henrietta! Tell me please, did something happen to you today?' he asked her with eyes full of worry. 'Anything that seemed unusual?'

- 'Well, lots of things happened,' Henrietta replied. 'Not to me, but there was this horrible noise in the woods and we all had to run, and after we passed over that bridge, Rosie found those delicious chocolate balloons, and...'

- 'I think we were in trouble Sir,' Stamatis interrupted his friend. 'We had this terrible anger inside us, and some very strange things happened around us. There was this very strong Southern wind, and the thunder, the fire, and it all started after we found those envelopes.'

- 'I know about the messages and the broken scrolls,' the man replied. 'Things are even worse than I thought. People's minds will be controlled soon and drawn into madness. Let me show you something,' he said with a sense of urgency and grabbed the glasses he had laid on the table. 'Put them on,' he asked Henrietta, 'and look at this broken glass. Be careful and stay at a distance,' he warned her. As soon as Henrietta did as he had advised her, once again he lifted the oars one by one. The solid lenses started transforming into moving liquid, and as soon as the two colors had appeared once again, Henrietta was finally able to see. After an unbearable six whole seconds of suspense, the girl released a frightening cry and moved backward as if she were struck by lightning.

- 'What's the matter? Let me see!' Alexander asked his sister, and within a fraction of a second he grabbed the glasses from his sister's face and put them onto his own. Henrietta felt too shocked to be able to comment. The boy looked toward the broken glass rapidly, but he was totally unprepared to face what his sister had just encountered. His eyes popped out, then they gradually closed, and soon, everybody around him became part of his feeling of a fading world.

-'Oh, my dear boy!' Margaret shouted as she came out of the kitchen with Sir Hipparchus's cup of iced mixed juice. She placed the mirrored tray with the cup onto the table, spilling almost half of the juice in her haste, and ran toward Alexander to help him recover. Robert followed her example and touched the boy's face with his beak softly. Bernard, on the other hand, was eager to see what was so scary that it made his cousin shout and his cousin's brother fall like a filled up sack of sand onto the floor. He ran and grabbed the glasses as soon as Margaret had taken them off Alexander's face and handed them over to overwhelmed Roserin. Bernard went a safe distance from the broken glass and put the spectacles onto his own nose. After one single second, he made the very same grimace of horror that was formed onto his cousin's face. He walked a few steps backward with his eyes popping out until he bumped against the fireplace that was right behind him.

- 'It's alive! The glass is alive!' he shouted as he kept staring in fear at what was happening between the broken glass that was resting on the table and Henrietta, who was now worried about Alexander's wellbeing.

- 'It is NOT alive!' the Inventor said firmly as he stepped toward him decisively and took the glasses off of his face. He then folded them and slipped them carefully back into his vest's pocket. He added firmly, 'NEVER allow yourself to give power to a negative thought! Now, tell me: How many pseudopodia did you see?'

- 'There are many!' the young boy replied, 'and they are dark and thick! They try to catch Henrietta! What is it, uncle?' Bernard asked in fear. 'I have never seen such a thing!'

- 'It is negative thoughts, directed against Henrietta,' The Scientist whispered so that he would not scare the girl off. 'Somebody tried to harm her but failed. And you need NOT let her know about this,' he warned the boy and touched him on the shoulders. 'We need to find out who is behind this, and we need to keep her away from danger. Never leave her alone...do you understand?'

- 'I understand,' Bernard promised his grown-up friend. He would always do his best to protect his beloved cousin.

Alexander was now lying on the sofa and starting to recover. Without a second thought, Margaret grabbed the iced juice she had brought and offered it to the boy. As soon as Henrietta approached the sofa to see how her brother was doing, Bernard felt in his consciousness a very intense image that appeared in front of him for only one second, despite the fact he was not wearing the glasses any longer. He saw in what manic way the negative energy's pseudopodia were trying to grab hold of his cousin. He also saw that they had no direct access to her. There was a golden egg-shaped kind of energy all around her that prevented the pseudopodia from reaching her. The boy's face became pale.

Bernard approached Alexander carefully by following the safest route as far away from the broken goblet's glass as possible. When Sir Hipparchus felt relieved about the boy's welfare, he said:

- 'What you have seen is not able to touch you. Not as long as you do not give it any additional strength,' he said and swept away the sweat on his forehead. 'You must NOT be afraid of it. Your fear is what it feeds on.' He looked toward Bernard and continued with a hypnotized stare. 'Something has occurred. It is a disrespect of the greatest kind. A number of evil souls have been freed into our land by the world of the living people. Some of these souls have found a way to transport themselves into our dimension. The Gate is no longer sealed.'

- 'Where did they come from?' Alexander asked, but Sir Hipparchus did not answer his question.

- 'And why did they set them free?' Stamatis wondered while Robert stood on Alexander's couch, still looking at him in a caring way.

- 'People have been incapable of controlling their egos,' the Researcher replied, 'their greediness to have everything,' -Roserin instantly took an expression of guilt,- 'and their illusion that they can control everything has caused us a problem of vast proportions. It is a problem that my colleagues have been trying to solve. Now you need to promise me that you will stay away from any situation that might put you into danger,' he said firmly, 'and NEVER give any information to anyone who may cross your path. Especially not of the situations that you have experienced here today,' he said with a raised tone in his voice. With his hands he lifted a well-hidden bag above his head that was hanging around his shoulder. It was a round leather bag with an extra front pocket in the shape of a hexagon. Right on it, there was a sewn figure of a hunter, holding the head of a lion in his one hand and some sort of weapon in the other one. Sir Hipparchus handed it over to Henrietta and spoke in a serious tone:

- 'Look at the surface, Henrietta. What do you see?' he asked her, taking a piece of rolled papyrus out of his vest's inner pocket at the same time.

- 'A hunter?' she wondered. 'He is holding something that resembles a lion's head.'

- 'That's right,' the Ancient Greek Scientist agreed. 'And here, what does this shape remind you of?' he asked the girl once again, once he had revealed a map of stars on his papyrus. Some stars were connected by a series of straight lines that formed various interesting shapes. The Astronomer pointed at one constellation figure with his finger, in which the brightest stars were identified with Greek letters.

- 'It looks like a coffee pot!' was Henrietta's reply.

- 'What else?' her adult friend urged her to think again.

- 'A coffee pot with a mirror?' she asked with uncertainty.

- 'Why would a coffee pot need a mirror, you silly goose?' Alexander teased his sister as he sat up straight on the sofa. Robert sighed in relief.

- 'I know what it is!' Stamatis shouted after having paid his full attention to a discussion that seemed to be most interesting to a person like himself. He liked exploring everything in his spirit life since he did not have much of a chance back in his living years.

'It's an hourglass!'

- 'Come on! It's not an hourglass!' Roserin replied to her brother. 'It is Orion's belt! Orion is supposed to be a hunter.'

- 'Well, it seems that Rosie has been paying full attention to her Astronomy classes!' Sir Hipparchus said with a smile. 'You are both right,' he continued and both Roserin and Alexander looked surprised. 'It is Orion's belt...but at the same time, our hunter transforms into an hourglass. And what does an hourglass do? It measures TIME. Now, Time is a very interesting concept here. If energy could be concentrated, a person could travel to any chronological period they were interested in,' he said and looked at Henrietta, deep inside her eyes. 'Orion's belt also works as a dimension 'vehicle' at the same time. The well-hidden hourglass, which is actually in front of everybody's eyes, rotates around its 'belt', and anything or ANYONE who enters inside it has the chance to travel into another Dimension.'

- 'But how can we control energy?' Stamatis asked, showing his interest in metaphysics, while Robert imagined himself controlling the speed of the fish in their efforts to get away from him as he swam behind them.

Sir Hipparchus smiled and looked toward Henrietta.

- 'Henrietta, would you please open the bag I gave you? Thank you!'

Henrietta obliged her older friend and took out a round object that looked like a flat disc. It was protected and surrounded by a bigger concentric golden frame. Right between them, the rest of the disc consisted of concentric plates with various markings of degrees. Ancient Greek numbers seemed to indicate Time. The main body of the disc was hollowed-out and contained a brass plate that resembled a 'star map'. It was dark, and various constellation figures like the Little Bear and the Great Bear glowed on the plate's surface. The brightest stars were represented by shiny diamonds, whereas the rest of the constellation's perimeter was formed by light blue glowing moonstones that looked as if they contained some blue frozen flames. All of the constellations protruded above a representation of the specific celestial sphere that was engraved on the surface. Right above the plate, a beautiful cut-out plate with a number of pointers and an ecliptic ring rotated around the astrolabe's center. The girls admired the unique refined cut-out design.

- 'These pointers look like a bear's claws!' was Roserin's comment. 'What are they for?' she asked the sympathetic scientist.

- 'They are 'star pointers',' he answered. 'Every time the plate is rotated according to the Time, the pointers show the new position of the stars. Now, about the three needles...' He drew everybody's attention to the marked up needles that were fixed firmly on top of both plates. 'The golden one points to the exact degrees that I would need to find the right constellation that would guide me by its turn to the dimension I needed to travel. The black needle shows me the month I would find myself in, and the frozen one...' he paused and smiled as if he had something precious to reveal. 'The frozen one is the needle that can freeze my own time,' Sir Hipparchus said proudly for having invented such a unique function. He carried on when he saw everybody's mouths wide open, Robert's beak included, an assurance that he had managed to catch their full attention.

'Now, about the fourth needle,' he said. 'I know. You do not see it. But it is there. As soon as Time freezes, there are more interesting things going on. Your chosen constellation becomes alive and shows you something very important, something that you always need to be aware of. It guides you to the right DIMENSION. It guides you to the way home...'

9. The Astrolabe.

*A*lexander wanted to have a closer look at this shiny enchanting device that was even more tempting than the cotton candy clouds that occasionally formed in their atmosphere. As he was getting up from the sofa, a few crystals of various colors and patterns fell out of his pocket. Robert grabbed one in his beak and ran outside to examine it in the garden, in peace.

- 'Here we go again!' Alexander gasped. 'I need to exercise my willpower a bit more and make the crystals stay IN my pocket,' he said. In the children's in-between dimension, everyone was trying to learn how to control their ego by emptying their minds and focusing their attention on what it was that they wanted. In this case, Alexander wanted to prevent the protective crystals from moving out of his pocket, but there was one tiny obstacle that prevented him from succeeding in his goal.

- 'Well, if you really focused and emptied your mind and BELIEVED that you could do this, it would happen!' Sir Hipparchus commented. 'Do not worry, it will happen in time. All you need to do is practice! Yes! 'Practice'. That would be the magic word!!'

Alexander frowned at the idea that he had to get rid of all the damaging noise that had accumulated inside his soul when he was still in the dimension of the living people, and which still buzzed within his consciousness. It was not an easy thing to accomplish. How much easier it would have been had he been a robot boy with a number of enhanced switches in his etheric body. 'It is not fair,' he thought, 'to discover all of a sudden that all the stress and anxiety were still attached to his consciousness. His passing had hardly prevented the attachment of unpleasant, negative feelings. And to discover that so many things he had been taught by some adults had not been valid either...

- 'They may not be valid to YOU. There are many realities,' Sir Hipparchus said to him as soon as he had read his mind. 'There is your own reality and there are other people's realities. The key is to discover what is most helpful in YOUR own Life, even if other people might disagree with you. But do let me know,' he said and looked toward the protective crystals that were now lying on the sofa, 'what sort of crystals have you got there?' He continued.

- 'And what does this hand do?' Bernard asked his educated friend before Alexander had the chance to reply, and pointed his finger toward another visible hand that was hidden right under the black one. It consisted of a reddish-brown material that seemed to shine intensely under the light.

- 'Ah! Now this one,' he said with a smile. He looked at it in a way that revealed his great admiration for this special looking hand, 'This one here is made of Alchemist's stone. See how beautifully it shimmers? This material is the result that the Alchemists produced in their efforts to transform metal into gold. It looks as if they have almost achieved this,' he said and stared enchanted at what looked almost like floating gold dust that had been trapped right inside this stone-made material.

A dark cloud of energy appeared all of a sudden out of one of the windows, taking the shape of a very repulsive collapsed face. Nobody seemed to notice.

- 'So what does it do?' Henrietta startled the Scientist from his hypnotic state.

- 'Forgive me…it shows TIME,' he explained, raising his eyebrows at the same time. The children saw the tip of the hand point to the Ancient Greek 'Acrophonic' numbers that protruded from the outer ring. The specific number that it was pointing at that exact moment was number 'seven' which consisted of the acrophonic symbol of five, and two vertical strokes on its right side. In this system of writing, the symbols originated from the first letter of the number's Greek name. Number 'ten' for example, resembled a triangle, and number 'one thousand' was represented by an 'X'.

'So if somebody wanted to travel to a specific dimension, they could set the hand to the dimension they wished.' He took a sip from the new freshly squeezed lemon juice that Margaret had brought for him. 'I could use the other needles in the same way. I could move the hands one by one to the month and week I want to find myself in, and the specific World I wish to explore,' he explained. 'Our own Dimension lies at sixty degrees,' he said with a certain emphasis on the words 'own dimension' and 'sixty.' 'This is the most important thing that I need to ALWAYS remember. There are many 'dimensions' out there, my children. Before setting out on an adventure, I am supposed to always know the way back home first and foremost.' He paused after the words 'way' and 'back' to show the importance of what he was saying.

- 'How many other dimensions are out there uncle? I mean besides ours, the dimension of passed souls and the dimension of Santa,' Bernard asked, eager to find out. Sir Hipparchus smiled and answered his young friend:

- 'There are some things that will be revealed when the time is right for you. For the present time, all you need to know is HOW to return home.'

Henrietta spread her hands in order to study the Astrolabe from a little closer up. Sir Hipparchus handed it over to her gently, and all the children moved next to her instantly, drawn by both its unique beauty and function.

'There is something I do not understand,' Roserin commented, 'Are there TWO hands that show the time?' she asked, while her friends and her brother touched the device softly. 'In what way is it different from the black needle?'

- 'The difference is that the black needle shows the Month that somebody may find themselves in, and it also changes color according to the season. So when it is autumn, it will turn yellow; When it is summer it will turn red. When it is spring, it will turn pink, and when it is winter, you will see it take on a dark blue color. Now, this hand here,' he said and pointed to the Alchemist's shimmery needle, 'does not really point to the exact day. The exact day WILL appear to you right on the hand's surface in a written form.'

Roserin looked amazed after the inventor's description of his unique Astrolabe, and she instantly felt a strong craving to become an inventor herself one day.

- 'Look, what beautiful stones! They make me feel so calm!' Stamatis commented on some tiny light blue stones that were placed one after the other onto the black background of the Astrolabe, in a way that formed some kind of perimeter.

- 'These are Aquamarine crystals,' Alexander explained, 'and the white ones are diamonds. Am I right uncle?' The boy looked at the Astronomer and received a positive nod. The diamonds that glowed like frozen drops of rain had been placed not at random places, but rather in very specific positions, as the shape itself implied. They seemed to be fixed firmly at every angle that the perimeter itself formed.

- 'Diamonds...' Sir Hipparchus said. 'They represent the brightest stars in these beautiful constellations you have in front of you. You see? Here is the Flying Fish that you will always find flying right under the Chameleon, and next to the Carina,' he explained. The eight friends noticed the enchanting shapes of the flying fish and the ship of the 'Argonauts' on the right side.

'I am so grateful to have received such valuable help from my new colleagues Pieter and Frederick,' he continued. 'How would I have known everything about such a unique constellation on the Southern hemisphere had they not introduced it? I am so fortunate for their input my dear children...yes! And so happy for their final transition into our own dimension. Happy for the sake of Science, of course, but rather sad for their own people and families who have lost them,' he added, feeling slightly guilty for his enthusiasm that the two Astronomers had finally passed away from planet Earth. But really, it felt to him like billions of light years had passed before he could finally welcome them into his world and work with them on the subject of his interest.

Henrietta touched the decorative cut out 'rete' that rotated around the main plate. It was now covering the northern part of what seemed to be the sky. She rotated it around the center and more constellations appeared, one after the other. The stars of Hercules' seemed to be especially brilliant, an element that indicated the calmness in his heart. The golden color of love and positive energy was apparent in Ophiuchus constellation, also known as Asclepius. He was a great healer who appeared busy at the moment in his great mission of reviving a passed soul. Serpent Caput, the snake found close to Asclepius, was now emitting a light green light from its own stars.

The girl rotated the 'rete' with the ecliptic ring back to its former position. Constellations like Hydra and Pavo the Peacock were the ones that were most prominent now. Hydra the multi-headed Monster seemed to be on high alert, and therefore on the run since her most dangerous enemy Hercules had been fit enough to continue with his mission. Her heads' yellow glowing stars reflected her fear, whereas the Peacock's white star lights had possibly been affected by Sir Hipparchus's current feelings of pleasure and pride in finally being able to present his most unique and refined invention to the world. Or at least to his own dimension. To him, this was not just a novelty that would serve its purpose and then be discarded and forgotten. It was a lot more than that. It was a device that contained a piece of his own soul deep inside its core. Not every scientist was in the position to create such a meticulous piece of artistic work that captured and depicted their soul's true essence.

Roserin rotated the cut-out surface with the pointers and to her great surprise, she saw that the constellations of Hercules and Draco glowed no more. It was an obvious sign that indicated Hercules was having a break. The shape of a little bear seemed to be glowing this time.

- 'Ursa Minor,' the girl read the constellation's scientific name. An expression of surprise and admiration appeared on the children's faces.

- 'What are these lines?' Roserin asked and looked toward Sir Hipparchus, pointing her finger at the ochre-colored engraved lines that were apparent on the main plate.

- 'This is a presentation of the celestial sphere,' the scientist replied. 'The lines change according to the plate that somebody decides to place,' he explained.

- 'So what does the Astrolabe do?' Stamatis asked.

- 'It can transfer somebody into another dimension. But I am not going to reveal this function to adults. It could be very dangerous. I have given it some serious thought and my decision is to make it known ONLY as a device that shows the positions of the constellations in the Universe, a device that shows Time. In the presence of another adult, I will call it 'The Clock'.

- 'And can we use it to travel to a certain place, at a certain time? There are these two needles that show the month and the time,' Roserin asked.

- 'No,' the Researcher replied, 'somebody could choose a certain dimension and place, but not the time. Such a function would complicate things. It is the Astrolabe itself that decides to transfer a 'Lightworker' at the 'right' time, a time that ensures that no living human being, animal, or creature is harmed by the fear or inability to comprehend something which is above their level of consciousness. Our Ego deciding what the 'right' time might be could cause the greatest damage.'

- 'So this device is truly alive!' Stamatis observed. 'After all, it is not just another object. It is made of Energy.'

- 'I have also given it a nickname,' the scientist added. 'I call it: 'The 'HIGHEST SELF'. What could possibly go wrong with the function of the Highest Self?'

- 'This is really amazing uncle!' Alexander almost shouted in excitement. 'But do tell us, what is it that you have inside your bag?' the boy asked with curiosity. 'I love its shape!' He stared at the open hexagonal leather bag that he had placed beforehand on the table, when Astrapi approached it and gave it a sniff.

- 'Oh yes, my bag! Of course' he answered in a tone of gratefulness toward the boy, who brought the bag to his attention, giving him the opportunity to present one more of his astronomical treasures.

- 'What you see here is an 'astronomical compendium.'' He started taking a hexagonal gilt brass box of some sort out of his bag. As he opened it, it revealed some more 'leaves' as they were called, which were bound together on one edge. Each 'leaf' was hollow, made by gilt brass in the same way the protective cover was made. It seemed to be functioning as a case that carried something precious.

'So this is how it is divided from within, and each 'leaf' can hold a few tools that might be needed for the Astrolabe.' The children saw a firmly attached round device with a needle in its center, something strange that looked like a ship with a long metallic piece that must have been its mast, an astronomical calendar, and a few tables of latitude that would always accompany the Astrolabe for its proper function.

'These rotating discs are 'solar volvelles' that show us the various phases of the Moon and the positions of the planets,' he explained. 'And this is a Sundial, which as you can see looks like a ship. We use it to tell the time by measuring the sun's angle above the horizon. We will not need it any longer now that the Highest Self exists in our dimension!' He said in all excitement.

- 'What are the tables of latitude for?' Roserin asked.

- 'According to the place where somebody might find themselves, the correct latitude table has to be placed inside the Astrolabe once the previous table has been removed. Each table depicts a part of the sky, the way it looks from a certain spot on planet Earth where the person happens to stand. The image would change if somebody moved to the celestial equator from the South Pole, or if they moved from the celestial equator to the North Pole. Now, do you know what this crystal is?' he asked as he took it out of a small pocket of his vest.

- 'It is Quartz Tourmaline!' Alexander instantly said, all excited for being able to identify the stone. 'It connects us to our Highest Self!! Oh my!' He gasped and looked toward the Astrolabe. 'Or should we say 'The Highest Self'?'

10. An Upside-Down Situation

- 'So does this crystal connect us to the Astrolabe? What does it mean?' Stamatis asked.

- 'It means that in case the Astrolabe and its owner get separated from one another, the crystal will bring it back to the person who has been using it. However, if the crystal gets lost, the connection will be very difficult to make. And I have not yet discovered another way to make it return all on its own. It is alive for sure, but it does need an agent to make the connection. The crystal is made of the purest energies that exist in the Universe, and this is the reason that it works.' There was a sense of magic in the atmosphere, especially because of the colorful way in which the well-respected scientist described everything to the children.

- 'I see there are a few dimensions here,' Bernard noticed. 'The dimension of Santa Claus' world- known as St. Vassilios to the children of Crete- the dimension of the Easter Bunny, and I also see the dimension of Alice. Oh! The dimension of the 'melomakarona' would be my most favorite one!' –melomakarona being the most traditional and delicious Cretan treat -

- 'There is also the Witch's dimension!' Alexander pointed with his finger. 'I hope they are 'good' witches. Oh! Look at that! There is Count Dracula's dimension, who would have thought!'

- 'Akashic Records,' Roserin read. 'What is that? I do not understand it.'

- 'This is one of the biggest and most reliable libraries that you could ever find in the whole Universe,' Sir Hipparchus answered. All pieces of information about both Life and Death are stored there, about ALL the living human beings and creatures that have existed in the whole Universe. And the information that we find there is always accurate my children. There is no 'lie,' there is no 'truth.' It merely presents what IS.'

- 'So, if I turned this hand to the living peoples' dimension…' Bernard said with curiosity, reaching his hand toward the Astrolabe. Within a fraction of a second he had turned the needle to the engraved calligraphic phrase: 'People.'

- 'NO!!!' Sir Hipparchus shouted, alarmed, but it was rather too late. The children, the scientist and the Penguin, who was outside in the garden, found themselves hovering upside-down in space in the living room. Alongside them were the Astrolabe, Astrapi, the Astronomical compendium, and the scientific bag.

- 'Bernard, what have you done?' his cousin Henrietta asked him.

- 'Hey! My crystals have remained in my pocket!' Alexander shouted, excited.

- 'What is going on?' Stamatis added his question.

- 'Why are we upside-down?' Roserin wondered.

- 'Hey, all! I see there are also the Fairies' dimension and the Aliens' dimension!' Bernard said as the Astrolabe hovered right in front of his face. 'The needles are all moving around like crazy! I see letters appearing and disappearing very quickly on the Time's needle. I don't suppose it has started…oh!' he gasped as soon as he realized what he had just done, with the feeling that he was currently in deep trouble.

Stamatis opened his mouth and drank droplets of the iced-juice that now hovered around him in bubbles.

- 'It seems the Astrolabe is working, but if it works, why are we floating in here?' Sir Hipparchus wondered, while at the same time trying to keep his shirt tucked into his knee length shorts. Astrapi hovered next to him upside-down and sneezed right in his face, causing him to cover it with his hands to wipe saliva off his face. Robert floated through an open window into the living room.

- 'Why is it dark?' Sir Hipparchus asked as soon as he took his hands away from his face. 'Are you all here with me, children?'

- 'I am here!' Roserin confirmed, and so did the others. She was worried about Astrapi because she could not hear or feel him near her. She was about to call the cat when Astrapi made his presence known with a strange sound as if he wanted to say: 'What sort of weird situation is this? Where is UP and where is DOWN?'

- 'Are these stars?' Alexander asked. 'You have not put any hovering glowing stars into your living room's ceiling, have you Roserin?'

- 'I have not!' the girl replied.

- 'Children, something is telling me that we are not in the living room,' Henrietta talked to her friends as if she were an adult, looking toward a big ring of what looked like a vast eye formed by thousands of golden grains of sand. There was light inside the ring's hollow space, and a formation of rays gave the illusion that this was the iris of an Eye. Right inside its dark vertical core, there was a bright star.

-Are we where I think we are?' Stamatis asked.

-'Oh, my True Source!' Sir Hipparchus said, excited. 'This is the 'Fomalhant' Star! I am giddy with excitement! Within this star, my children, it is very possible that new planets might be forming!'

- 'Planets? Are we in Space?' Roserin wondered. Robert floated in front of them along with an olive tree branch, rotating in 360 degree circles.

- 'Oh! The Astrolabe works!! It works! If only I had a tripod camera to take a picture!' The well-respected inventor expressed himself cheerfully as if he were a child, forgetting at the same time the fact that there was no solid ground in space to stabilize the tripod. 'We cannot take a good picture of our own dimension,' he added. 'It works! It works!'

- 'Did you hear that?' Bernard asked and stretched his ears. The sweet enchanting melody of some kind of instrument made its presence heard.

- 'Is that a harp?' Roserin asked. Nobody answered back. The musical piece lasted for a while, invoking feelings of calmness and happiness inside their hearts. Rosie felt waves of pleasant energy permeating her body from various sides and angles. She had never experienced anything like it before. As she enjoyed the gift, she felt that these feelings of utter joy in both her soul and her etheric body were probably a part of what people on planet Earth called: 'Heaven.' She did not want this to end. This was even better than enjoying her portion of apple pie dough when she was still on the dimension of the living people, and which she used to adore more than anything else in the world. What was happening right now was beyond description. But the music did stop at some point. Besides, they could not stay there listening forever. As people's invented 'Time' moved on, so did our friends need to move on.

There was total silence after that. They all felt such peace inside them that they hardly had the urge to ruin that with the harsh sound of their voices. They still floated within their own Heavens. After some time of total peace and silence, the noise of an animal's hooves was detected by their ears. They looked toward the noise's source. In a few seconds, they were able to see what it was that caused the noise.

- 'Is that a Giraffe?' Stamatis asked.

- 'It sure looks like one!' Henrietta answered her friend.

- 'That looks like the Camelopardalis constellation to me! Oh my True Source!!' The Researcher whispered, because he felt too touched by this moment of beauty to ruin it by speaking in a louder voice.

- 'Is she coming toward us?' Alexander wondered.

- 'I think she is,' Roserin said. 'What a beautiful Giraffe this is!' She admired the animal, especially because it seemed to contain a smaller Universe within it. Its body was formed by a milky way, many smaller planets, and some nebulas. A few falling stars formed its mane. Its outline was marked by a series of twinkling stars.

- 'Is it really moving? It seems to be running in the same spot!' Roserin wondered after a while.

- 'It is a good thing we do not need to go to the bathroom anymore!' Bernard said. 'It was really inconvenient when we were still alive. On the other hand,' he added, 'it was a good excuse to disappear every time we had visitors we did not like and stay in the bathroom until they were gone!' The children laughed.

- 'Imagine if we had to go to the bathroom right NOW!' Alexander said, amused. 'But what do we do now? Are we supposed to keep hovering?'

The Giraffe or 'Camelopardalis' was now standing right in front of them.

- 'I am glad I do not get scared as easily as I used to when I was still on Earth. I would have wet my pants!' Bernard said. Robert looked up along the Giraffe's neck. 'WHERE was the head?' he seemed to wonder.

-'Look how beautiful it is!' Roserin noticed and admired the breathtaking constellation in his long neck. She started floating upward, and now she could more clearly see the small planets that shaped the Giraffe's patches. As she hovered close to his neck, she felt the need to grab hold of it. Her friends floated up onto its back one by one, with the wise man following. The children felt the Giraffe's mane, consisting of hundreds of miniature stars, and they grabbed it. Sir Hipparchus grabbed the hovering Astrolabe, his bag, and his astronomical compendium, placed them inside his bag and hung it around his shoulder. Astrapi landed right behind Roserin and in front of Alexander. As soon as everyone was sitting on Camelopardalis' back, with Robert sitting in front, the giraffe walked three steps forward. After a few seconds, she started running. The children smiled as the stars went by at great speed. Some other stars fell, leaving a trace of dust behind them. The Giraffe started ascending at some point, and after a short time, she passed in front of the moon.

- 'I wonder how the man on the moon is doing. Is he feeling lonely, living there all by himself?' Roserin thought silently.

- 'He is fine,' Sir Hipparchus answered her by the use of his thoughts, preferring not to spoil the magic of the moment by opening his mouth. 'I can see him right now. He is still carrying all this wood on his back and he is waving to us!' he informed her using his telepathic skills.

The Giraffe continued to her destination, but none of them knew where they were heading. 'I assume we will find ourselves in the living peoples' dimension somewhere since Bernard pushed the needle to the word 'People,' the scientist thought. Before he could complete what he was thinking, the Camelopardalis constellation suddenly stopped. As a result, all of the children, Robert, Astrapi and the researcher were flung forward in space at great speed. They landed onto something that felt rather hard.

- 'Where did THAT come from?' Alexander wondered. 'I almost hit my head on this log. A whole open Universe all around me, and I had to land on this thing. What is this weird smell of fish?'

- 'Are we on a ship?' Henrietta asked and looked around. Robert jumped around happily; He was excited by the fish smell.

-'It is a Trireme!' Stamatis shouted from a distance after he looked down and saw the oars. Astrapi walked around, sniffing at every single corner and barrel that he discovered. He wanted to make sure that no hidden traps or negative entities were lurking there on this strange smelling deck.

The oars started moving forward and backward, and the ship was now floating with everyone running around on the deck. Bernard just managed to grab hold of the mast before he accidentally floated out of the trireme. Astrapi, on the other hand, moved his legs as quickly as possible, like the times he used to swim in the sea, holding his head as high as he could while stones and dust passed by him in waves. Due to the sudden departure of the ship, he floated slightly above the deck. As for Robert, he was ejected backward and crashed against the walls of a cargo hold then fell right into a barrel. To his great surprise, he fell onto something soft. Using his left flipper, he touched the surface nearby and lifted a…fish!

Roserin floated straight toward the Captain's wheel. It moved on its own. 'Had I still been alive, I would have totally freaked out!' she told herself. Then she looked above and ahead of the wheel. Her eyes opened wide and so did her mouth.

- 'This is even better than a dream!' she thought. 'I wonder what it is!' Light blue and magenta colors in the shape of a spiral were too powerful and beautiful to be ignored. Her encounter with this huge solid spiral object placed there in the middle of nowhere reminded her of the nice-shaped colorful candies that she used to enjoy when she was still among the living. The long light blue and magenta bands of dust twirled with one another; There was also the presence of an intense golden light within the spiral's center. There was a second golden light at the tail's end that faded into white mist far away from its center. The mist gave people the impression of a ghostly shaped astronaut.

- 'This is the 'Whirlpool Galaxy!' Sir Hipparchus answered Rosie's question from behind her back. 'Isn't it beautiful? It is one of the jewels in our Space!'

- 'Are we going through it?' Roserin asked.

- 'It seems the ship is heading that way. I know it feels too good to be true, but when you look for beauty and you believe in it, be certain that it WILL appear to you,' the man said with wisdom in his tongue.

- 'I have never seen anything like it before!' Rosie said, feeling touched in her soul. 'To think that I was not very interested in Astronomy classes when I was still on Earth...' Sir Hipparchus smiled, and the girl smiled back at him.

- 'I was one of the worst students in my class, you know. I was NOT born a scientist. But it is NEVER a child's fault when a teacher has not found a way to make their subject interesting,' he commented, thinking that Roserin could be feeling guilty, accusing herself unfairly. 'I was so bored in class that I used to make miniature shapes of animals out of paper. One day I made this shape that looked very much like the Astrolabe!'

Rosie smiled. The ship moved faster than they thought. They were now moving through the Whirlpool Galaxy and all the dust and rocks that floated above and under them glowed in light blue and magenta. Some golden dust that hovered in the center of the spiral Galaxy covered everyone's etheric bodies. The dust was so luminous that the children, Robert, Astrapi, and Sir Hipparchus glowed in golden light, in the same way that fireflies glowed on planet Earth. A few stones crashed against some of the masts, and the trireme wobbled a little dangerously. Bernard held tight to the mainmast. The ship was now covered in golden dust that made it look like a handmade jewel that had been constructed for somebody's beautiful neck. The Whirlpool Galaxy was soon left behind them. The children looked behind them and could hardly take their eyes off such a spectacular phenomenon that they had had the luck to experience. Now, they were passing through the white mist they had seen before from a distance. It almost seemed that they were now on planet Earth. Had they arrived already?

Rosie Protects the Coded Disc of Phaistos

- 'Ouch!' Alexander shouted suddenly in pain. 'What was that?' he wondered and turned his head to see what hit him so hard. He saw a painted bottle floating in space. He grabbed it to have a closer look.

- 'Look at that!' he said in great surprise. 'It is one of the bottles I used to paint and then throw into the sea with a message inside!' He looked at it carefully and he was instantly flooded with memories from his past life. He admired his painting of a white paper ship under a palm tree he had created at the beach, with his own depiction of 'Koule Castle' on the opposite side. He pulled out the cork and then the rolled scroll he had inserted.

- "When I grow up, I want to be strong, to help other people," he read his own message from the past and tears came to his eyes. 'I remember this,' he whispered. 'I remember the day I threw it in the sea.'

- 'Your wish might still be granted,' Rosie tried to comfort him.

A few seconds later, a shout of pain came from Sir Hipparchus' mouth. The children floated quickly toward him.

- 'What's the matter?' Stamatis asked, and he saw the scientist rubbing his head.

- 'Something just hit me on the head. What was it that probably caused a bump on my creative skull? A bottle?' he said in curiosity. 'Now let's see what this is…'The Alchemist's Muse'… Oh my True Source!!' he said as he liked to say every time he was astonished with the discovery of a strange phenomenon. 'Do you know what this is my children? This is the golden drink that we used to have in my youth, when I was still on Earth!' he said and admired the brown vintage still-sealed bottle and the dark yellow liquid within. On the bottom of the label, the following words were printed: 'Athens-Greece.'

- 'We are heading to the living people of Greece! We are on the right way! We are on the right way indeed…

Rosie Protects the Coded Disc of Phaistos

11. The Coffee Pot with the Mirror

- 'Ouch!' Roserin winced. Something had hit her arm. She rubbed it to ease the pain and looked to her right. A copper pot with a long arm was now hovering, spinning like a top from the strong impact.

'It's a 'briki'!' Stamatis told her, using its Greek name. 'It looks like the one that grandma used to make granddad's coffee!' He grabbed the tiny Turkish coffee maker to examine it up close. It was a funny looking pot that Cretan people used to make their Greek coffee, one that reminded Roserin of Pinnochio's long nose.

- 'It could belong to Pinnochio!' she thought and felt amused by the idea.

- 'It DOES belong to me!' The puppet's voice sounded suddenly within her consciousness. 'Help! I will not lie again!' was the second sentence that she heard right after. And then...silence.

- 'Why is the briki's main body so small? I always wondered why they made them so small,' Alexander said.

Before anyone had the chance to reply, Roserin was startled by something that pulled her backward violently. A dark arm was visible right in front of her stomach, as well as the same distorted face that had been seen out of Roserin's and Stamatis' house. Some parts of the face seemed to dissolve in dark energy, before it would connect its particles together again to form evil expressions. This face was one that was NOT afraid of crocodiles or any other threatening animals in its former life. Its eyes, with miniature crescent irises, were popping out all round, a hollow spot appeared in place of its nose, and it grimaced, showing a number of razor-sharp teeth. Its chin was doubled and had a few dark spots. But what kind of entity was this? The dark spots were spread on the rest of its face too, causing it to resemble a mountain of sand with pebbles in it. It was a Goliath's Tigerfish, the most terrifying fish of the Congo River in Africa.

On the ship's deck, everyone froze in their positions, apart from Robert, who ran away from the threat, terrified. Alexander ran after Roserin, while the dark entity used its fists to start hitting the girl on her sides continuously. Rosie cried in pain with every blow. She was now floating in space far away from the ship. Astrapi floated after Rosie and the entity, in his effort to save his friend. Everyone was now on the one side of the deck, not having the slightest idea how to help the girl.

   - 'He is taking her toward a black hole!' Stamatis shouted desperately. We MUST do something NOW!'

   - 'The Astrolabe!' Bernard shouted. 'We can turn back time! Then Rosie will be pulled back to the ship, and we will stop his attack!'

   - 'We cannot do that my boy!' Sir Hipparchus shouted to young Bernard. 'We cannot play with Time. It is the Astrolabe itself that will decide that. We can only freeze time…'

   - 'Let's do it then! Quickly Sir! My sister is disappearing!' Stamatis shouted in despair.

   - 'I would have already done it if I could, my boy. But you see…this device is more complicated than you think.'

Alexander suddenly took a crystal out of his pocket. It blazed in colors of turquoise and green on its surface. Henrietta turned to tell him that this was not the time to admire his pebbles, when the boy raised his palm and blew the crystal in the direction of Roserin. A rather long turquoise flame surrounded Rosie and formed a big round energy ball, from which emerged a face that blew the dark entity away. Alexander took another pebble, this time a blue one, out of his pocket and placed it onto his palm. Once again, he blew the crystal hard, in the girl's direction. The stone remained in his palm. Nothing seemed to be happening. Everyone stared in agony, unable to utter a word to ask whether something would happen. The words would not come out of the mouths of these souls, who felt their hands tighten in front of grave danger. After a few seconds of unbearable silence and no reaction, Henrietta's voice filled the huge void.

- 'Alexander?'

The sound of breaking branches made everyone turn their heads. And branches they were. They materialized from the trireme's mainmast. While everybody's attention was drawn to the newborn branches above, some thick roots appeared behind them and hugged the malus mast tightly. They seemed to be originating from Roserin's side.

- 'They are growing out of my feet!' the girl shouted from a distance. Everyone looked at these thick roots that resembled a Giant's long beard (if the beard's hair had been magnified a few thousand times). As the roots grew away from Rosie's body and wrapped around the mast, the branches grew toward the girl. They stopped growing right behind Astrapi, who was still hovering in the air. They were knitted to each other and formed a bridge. Roserin was suddenly pulled forward like a comet, almost past Astrapi. The African cat changed his direction and ran across the bridge, back to the ship. The girl was now standing on the deck, still glowing in turquoise-green light. Sir Hipparchus and the children all sighed with relief. The roots started to dissolve from her feet and the remains were now floating away from the mast.

- 'That was close!' Bernard sighed and relaxed. Henrietta's eyes popped out:

- 'Get away from there! Get away from there!' she shouted, panicked, at Roserin, while Bernard jumped as if he had just been electrocuted.

- 'How many are there?' Stamatis asked, terrified, and looked around in all directions.

- 'There seem to be more than there are stars...' Alexander commented, and in his panic, he grabbed something that looked like a mop, to defend both himself and his friends.

- 'Use the Mirror Rosie! Use the Mirror!' Sir Hipparchus urged the girl, in his despair to keep her, himself and the other children safe. Roserin stood still and focused with a decisive look in her eyes.

- 'What do we do now uncle? What do we do?' Henrietta asked in panic.

- 'Shhhhh! Let her focus,' the scientist replied. A big bubble of reflective material started forming around the girl.

- 'A Mirror!' Alexander shouted.

Human forms of what seemed to be shadows were attracted to the newly materialized ball, inside which Roserin had disappeared. Hundreds of evil-looking faces were now facing their own reflections. The image they encountered now was so dark and lifeless that they floated away in great terror.

- 'Had I still been alive, I would have passed out!' Bernard said.

- 'What kind of crystals did you use Alexander?' Henrietta asked her brother.

- 'The first one is 'labradorite' and the second one is 'lapis lazuli.' They are both very effective in dangerous situations.'

The mirror-ball that surrounded Roserin was now disappearing. No shadows were visible anymore on the ship or anywhere else. The black hole was now left behind. The almost-abducted girl looked at it and shivered at the thought of being dragged toward it. She looked at the long colored rings of gas that surrounded it, and at a luminous planet that was being sucked into it currently. The planet's light could not escape. Bernard sighed, relieved. And then it happened: The ship stopped moving.

- 'Why did we stop moving?' Stamatis asked. Everyone tried to keep their balance as the whole ship vibrated backward and forward.

- 'What is this noise?' Roserin was the next person to ask. 'Does the ship have an engine?' The noise came from the front half. They all ran toward the bow to check it out. In the meanwhile, Astrapi entered the poop deckhouse to look where Robert had been hiding.

- 'Is this what I think it is?' Henrietta asked, after her eyes had opened as wide as an adult Philippine Tarsier monkey's.

- 'It sure looks like it,' Alexander answered.

- 'It is huge!' Roserin added her own observation and leaned back onto a swan neck ornament.

- 'So this is where everything starts…' Sir Hipparchus almost whispered.

- 'Uncle, are we going to be safe?' Stamatis asked.

- 'We will be safe as long as we do not allow fear to control us,' the Astronomer replied. 'WE are the ones who have control, my boy. If we decide so, then it WILL be so.'

- 'Its shape is not very clear. It does look like a coffee pot, but it also looks like an hourglass,' Henrietta noticed, 'and it does move fast! We are not going to get in there, are we?' she asked as the big hourglass orbited around its center in quick circles. As soon as the top part completed a full circle, it delayed for a while until it fell downward again to complete another circle.

- 'Is that a real hourglass that exists in reality?' Stamatis expressed his question and admired what looked like, from where he was standing, flowing grains of stars.

- 'It is what YOU perceive it to be,' Sir Hipparchus gave an answer to the boy. 'To me, it is a beautiful lady that is floating in Space,' he said, his eyes fixed on yet another discovery that had touched him deep in his soul.

- 'So beautiful...' Roserin said. 'It reminds me of the day I was dressed as a teapot,' she said nostalgically. 'And what is that around the top of the hourglass? Is it surrounded by a... chameleon?'

- 'I think it really is a chameleon. And what a long tail it has!' Alexander admired the big round tail which looked like another spiral Galaxy in all its glory. The end of the animal's tail remained twirled in colors of green and yellow, draped right in front of the hourglass' base. The vessel started moving again at great speed. Everyone held tight to whatever they could, but the acceleration was so fast that Bernard and Stamatis floated away from the poop deck. Bernard tried to grab ahold of the mainsail, but it slipped past his hands. Stamatis fell onto the Jacob's ladder of the main mast and managed to entangle his foot around the rope. His little cousin was in danger of floating out of the ship. Bernard grabbed one of the buntlines of the fore sail but suddenly one end ripped apart.

The boy was barely holding onto the ship. As he struggled to keep holding the rope tight within his hands, the big eye that had been painted on the foresail looked back at him. Bernard thought it winked at him. As far as the huge hourglass with the chameleon wrapped around it was concerned, it changed its angle and continued orbiting, with the top heading toward the trireme this time. It was still moving at high speed.

- 'We are going to crash! We are going to crash!' Roserin shouted and lifted her trembling hand in front of her chest.

What was Astrapi doing inside the poop deckhouse in the meantime? While Roserin, Alexander and Henrietta were frozen by terror in the front part of the vessel, and while Stamatis started descending the Jacob's ladder to see what all the shouting was about, and while Bernard could do nothing but cling to his rope, hovering behind the trireme, Astrapi had found himself inside a really inviting space in which various glass bottles of all shapes and sizes had been stored. They all carried a label with the word: 'Pisti' written in the most beautiful calligraphic letters he had ever seen. He wondered which soul such creative fingers belonged to, which soul could create such enchanting script. 'What if I tried to grab a brush one day and make some calligraphic letters myself?' he thought. Although his paws were not very helpful due to his short toes, he told himself 'I think I would try it out with my mouth, or even with my eyes. Squirrels have the ability to do that. And elephants too. And human beings can. Why not an African cat? Where do these bottles come from I wonder? How did they get in here?' He looked at the letters once again. The word 'Pisti' was a Greek word; He knew because he had heard it a few times when he was still in the dimension of the Living People. But he could not remember what it meant. What was it? What was it?

- 'So here it is, 'Orion's belt'…and now is the moment of truth,' Sir Hipparchus said to the children. 'We cannot die again, so there is no reason to panic.'

The hourglass with the flowing stars inside it appeared bigger and bigger as the vessel came closer. It seemed to be even larger than the vessel itself, and the speed in which it rotated along with the deafening noise it created made it seem a lot scarier close up, despite the beauty of its glowing star sand.

The expected collision was about to occur any second now. But what could they possibly do? They could not go back anymore, it was the Astrolabe itself that had brought them here, so all they could do was do nothing, and see what would happen next.

The hourglass was now at its highest position and was about to descend. It would either smash the trireme this time or it would have to complete one more circle before the ship's fatal smash. Everyone was now petrified. Stamatis had just reached the others, Bernard was still hovering behind the vessel, Astrapi was trying to remember what the word 'Pisti' meant, Roserin had placed her right hand right onto her chest, Alexander was still holding the mop, Robert was inside the fish barrel having a nice meal, Henrietta took a few steps backward, and Sir Hipparchus opened his bag and took the Astrolabe out of it. The needles were all moving around at high speed. Now was apparently NOT the time to tamper with it. It was clearly doing something...

- 'Am I going to die for a second time?' Stamatis almost cried.

The upper part of the hourglass started its descent in slow motion this time. The chameleon was still holding tight, and as he descended he opened his mouth gradually. Everything was very dark now, when all of a sudden, the candle lamps that were attached to the ship's railings generated light that looked like sparklers imbedded into colored pieces of soap. The ship was now illuminated enough for the children to see where their friends were standing. The trireme entered right inside the chameleon's mouth very slowly, and kept moving for a few more seconds until it reached a big waterfall made of colorful glowing star sand.

- 'Hold tight wherever you can! Hold tight!' Roserin shouted to her friends. The vessel took a vertical position and started leaning downward. Before Sir Hipparchus could say 'Oh my True Source!' the ship was falling toward the direction of the star sand. Robert was now trapped in the fish barrel, since its opening had attached to the front wall of the cargo hold as the ship took the falling position. A few comets were traveling all around them in the same direction they were.

- 'Is that the Hale-Bopp comet? I do wonder...' Sir Hipparchus spoke mostly to himself when he saw a comet falling past them at a slightly greater speed, leaving a blue tail of gas and dust behind it.

- 'Oh look!' Henrietta shouted all of a sudden, while Bernard was trying hard to climb the rope back inside the ship. 'Isn't that the book that NOBODY read?' she asked. A book was falling ahead of them with the luminous signature of a person called Nikolaus Copernicus on the cover.

- 'Oh look at that! It really IS!' Sir Hipparchus replied. 'It seems the book is still yearning to be read!'

The loud sound of thunder made everyone jump, and a lightning bolt appeared among the stars.

- 'We are entering the dimension of the living people! This is so exciting! So exciting!' the Researcher expressed his happy feelings. Some heavy rain that appeared from nowhere made the vessel look as if it had just emerged out of one of planet Earth's wildest seas.

- 'I do hope Copernicus's book is waterproof!' Henrietta said.

After a few moments of traveling, the ship landed onto something that did not feel very stable.

- 'What is happening?' Roserin asked, trying to keep her balance while the vessel leaned in different directions. 'Are we there yet?'

- 'I do not think that our trip is over yet,' Alexander replied.

- 'Are we just about to fall through the hourglass' hole?' Stamatis asked. 'Where else could we be?'

- 'I think that is exactly what is occurring right now, my boy,' Sir Hipparchus confirmed. 'Let's ALL run toward the bow NOW! Bernard, where have you been?'

Bernard had finally managed to board the vessel and ran behind the others toward the Swan neck ornament that had been built on the bow. They all held tight onto the railings. The trireme leaned forward now for a second time. A heavy colorful star bumped on top of the Swan's head, and everyone felt that now was the time the ship would start its descent. But it did not. It seemed to be stuck.

- 'Why are we not falling?' Bernard asked, and looked downward, trying to detect the hole through which they were supposed to pass. 'Nothing is happening,' he said and took his hands off the bow's railing when Roserin noticed something sticking on his hair.

- 'What is that? Do you still have some cotton candy in your hair?' she asked him and batted a ball of cotton candy off his head. It hovered for a while in front of them and then landed onto the railing. The whole trireme leaned forward instantly, and the children along with the Astronomer managed to grab ahold of the railings in front of them at the very last second, except for Bernard who floated upward dangerously. And how was Astrapi coping or not coping during these moments?

Astrapi had been flung onto the entrance wall of the poop deck house from within, and was trying hard to remain inside. The bottles floated behind him, and once the vessel took its initial horizontal position, they landed back onto their shelves. Some of them were made of very thick strong material, and others looked more frail. Some of them were sealed with wax, others had corks, and others were even open and subject to losing the strength of their aroma. Some of the bottles had a special decorative appearance and style; They were so beautifully designed that anyone could hardly take their eyes off them. Others looked plain and not so attractive.

The ship was now traveling again at full speed. More comets fell along their route and a pendulum clock appeared above the trireme, traveling on its own. It hovered close to them, pendulum swinging and hands moving at high speed. From its side inspection door, a few wheels came out, small and big ones, along with a number of screws, two wooden pegs, the clock's case, a bottom door key, a winding key, and even an 'escape' wheel that seemed to be escaping! Something on the horizon seemed to be approaching the trireme. It seemed to be a solid object, and the only visible object to be ascending.

- 'Do you see that? Is that another book?' Stamatis asked his friends.

- 'Whatever that may be, it seems to be coming from the dimension of the living people,' Alexander answered.

- 'I think it is coming toward us,' Bernard said.

-'Look how much it glows!' Henrietta noticed the golden glow of the U.A.O. (Unidentified Ascending Object)

- 'We will soon know what it is; It seems it cannot float away from our same path. It looks like those chocolate pieces that are wrapped in golden paper!' Roserin expressed her own thought.

- 'Well, it glows a lot more than your chocolates, my girl. I wonder what earthly object would possibly glow so intensely,' the Researcher thought. 'What is that? What is that?' he kept wondering in his consciousness. 'Unless…' he thought, 'somebody is asking for help'

12. The Bottles of Life

Astrapi had not managed this time to remain physically inside the poop deck house. He fell right onto the main mast's velum, and the ship's opposite speed now pressed him to the sail like a stamp that had been glued firmly to envelope. A few of the bottles floated after him. Some of them fell right next to him, whereas others that were much lighter floated out of the ship like balloons. Some bottles opened and a colorful jello-like mass that glimmered got spilled onto the deck. It looked as light as the clouds, with the most harmonious combinations of colors. There were such beautiful combinations that would make anybody stare and feel unable to look again in a different direction. This substance looked as if it had been created for a very specific purpose.

The object that was permeated and surrounded by golden light had just approached the vessel. The children and the Astronomer could now see that it was a plaque of some kind, on which the figure of a man and a woman had been carved. Both of them had been depicted nude.

- 'It seems the destination of this plaque is the dimension of the Aliens,'' Sir Hipparchus said and admired the glowing etching as it flowed past them. 'I will not touch it, as its energy might be disturbed. It is not a parcel that belongs to us.'

- 'It is beautiful!' Henrietta admired it as it rotated around itself in slow motion. The two figures were upside down now. The man waved with his hand and the woman stood right next to him. Beside the man was the shape of a rectangle and another shape was carved behind him that looked like a half moon. On the plaque's left side were several carved lines that looked like rays emitted from a star, and on the bottom were a number of circles in various sizes which seemed to represent a series of planets.

- 'Look at the little ship above the circles!' Alexander observed.

- 'That's amazing!' Roserin replied. 'I do not suppose that could be us, could it?' the thought popped inside her consciousness.

- 'I do not know…' Alexander almost whispered and felt his hair stand up. There was a line right behind the small ship which seemed to mark the route it had followed among the planets. The plaque was now floating across the ship. More comets and star sand appeared to be traveling beneath, above, and past the two sides of the trireme toward an unknown place, if there was any specific destination. Everyone kept holding tight onto the stern balustrade. A sudden noise made Stamatis look over the stern's protective railings and he noticed the two front rudders moving forward and backward in repetitive motions. A few cracks sounded all around, which gave Roserin the feeling that the ship was alive at this moment and that it was trying to say something.

- 'Something is going on,' she said.

In front of them the peak of a stardust mountain shimmered at a distance. It seemed to be moving in all directions as if something was hiding right beneath it. It came closer, and closer, and closer. The trireme bumped onto it, and the bow landed in a horizontal position. Tons of stardust hovered now above the ship and covered it completely. The children, Astrapi, Robert, and Sir Hipparchus were not affected by it since their bodies consisted of etheric matter. Because of this fact, all the stardust and stars fell right through them. They were so light that they still stood above the mountains of sand. The vessel was not moving anymore. All they could still see around them was even lighter particles of stardust, which prevented a clear view.

- 'Is this the end of our journey?' Bernard asked.

- 'It might be, but it also might NOT be,' Stamatis answered. His young friend looked back at him with his head rotated a few degrees sideways and his eyes rolled upward, staring at him in a way as if to say:

'You have been so helpful!' sarcastically and funnily at the same time.

- 'It is very quiet don't you think?' Henrietta noticed. They all looked around, but the only thing they could see were particles of stardust, hovering and dancing in various directions, slowly and peacefully in a very tranquil atmosphere. They were now standing right in front of the poop deck house, along with Astrapi, who had landed onto the stardust covered deck.

- 'Stoop down!'

Alexander shouted to Roserin and pushed her head downward, when a pair of fiery eyes bore down on them. These two eyes glowed between two plaques that had been screwed together on one side. They released some heavy steam from within. The girl did stoop down, almost by instinct. Something was now pinned firmly against the poop deck house's door, right behind them. It kept swinging upward and downward.

- 'Is that a toaster?' Henrietta asked, startled.

- 'It looks like one,' Sir Hipparchus answered, unpinning the device off the door. 'It has teeth! I have never seen a toaster with teeth before! This is the first sign of the chaos that we see in this dimension. Did you see its eyes before?'

- 'I saw them,' Stamatis said. Everyone focused their attention on the scary-looking toaster and started examining it from all angles.

-'It was heading for me,' Roserin said. 'I know that. This is the second time it has happened. First, it was the shadows, and now it is the toaster. It is obvious.'

- 'We do not know that for sure,' The Astronomer replied. 'It could have been any of us standing where you were standing. Look at these sharp teeth! It looks like a Piranha toaster! And this brilliant white…Oh, my True Source! They are much whiter than mine!'

- 'Where are his eyes now?' Henrietta wondered.

- 'The energy was short but VERY aggressive,' Sir Hipparchus commented while he was exploring every single inch of the Piranha-toaster. 'We won't find anything else on here…'

-'Who would ever buy such a toaster with such teeth? How do the owners sleep at night? Are they not worried that their toaster might attack them while they slept?' Stamatis wondered, and lifted his shirt collar as he relaxed. Henrietta looked behind her and her face took on an expression of surprise.

- 'Look!' she shouted to her friends and with her finger pointed all around them. And they did look. They were gobsmacked to see that they were now standing inside a room. Robert, inside the barrel, was right next to them. He had passed out from the intense smell of fish.

- 'Is this a kitchen?' Stamatis asked.

- 'It looks more like a living room-kitchen to me,' Alexander said. 'It is beautiful! There are some traditional sweets on the table! Sugar doughnuts, goat cheese pies with sugar, weed pies…'

Bernard followed the nice sweet smell with his nose. 'We rarely had sugar doughnuts at our home,' he said and walked toward the big round wooden table. The sweets had been placed inside a basket and protected with a traditional red sewn towel on top. A plate with different kinds of sweets drew Roserin's attention.

- 'Look at the face,' she said. She could hardly take her eyes off the neatly placed cheese pies that formed a sad face. She pulled out a bamboo arm chair, one of the many that stood around the table, and sat down. She admired the round paper lamp that hung over the table. It reminded her of one of the planets. There was also a wooden couch with many comfortable cushions, on which Sir Hipparchus decided to sit and have a look at the Astrolabe. All the hands on the Astrolabe were now standing still. The golden needle pointed to thirty degrees, which was the Living Humans dimension. The Alchemist's needle pointed to the Ancient Greek Acrophonic number Eight, which was the Time. The black needle pointed to December I, and the 'I' that had been carved right under the Month stood for the First Week. The black colored needle had just started turning dark blue since they had found themselves in the middle of winter. Some faint calligraphic letters started to appear on the Alchemist needle's surface. The Astronomer waited until they were clear enough to read.

'It is Monday, ten minutes past eight. But where exactly are we?'

- 'I think we are home!' Henrietta said excitedly. 'If that bottle contains what I think it does, then we seem to be home!' She uncorked a cute looking small glass bottle which was resting on the table. She smelled it and moved backward very abruptly.

- 'I was right. It is the traditional drink of our area!'

- 'Are we back in Crete of the living people?' Stamatis asked. 'Where exactly are we?'

- 'I do not know that yet, Stamatis, but if we are in Crete then I had better change the latitude table,' the Researcher replied and took off the Astrolabe's rete. Then he took off the plate that had been in use and placed it firmly within one of the astronomical compendium's leaves.

- 'The Southern latitude of December would be the most suitable,' he said and picked up the plate that he was looking for from another leaf and placed it inside the Astrolabe. Then he covered it with the rete. Orion's belt constellation was currently glowing very intensely on this plate, along with the Horologium constellation, which was represented by the swinging pendulum clock they had encountered during their journey. The Camelopardalis constellation that gave them a ride to the ship now emitted a warm yellow glow. Alexander, who was now sitting next to the Researcher, touched the Giraffe's embossed shape with his finger. The figure of the Chameleon was glowing too, in colors of green and yellow, toward the Southern side of the plate.

- 'He travelled a long way to help us enter Orion's belt!' Alexander said, and the inventor smiled.

- 'What are these bottles here?' Stamatis asked. He had decided to explore the adjacent living room, which was one continuous space with the kitchen. Six nicely designed bottles that were shaped like various kinds of fish in the colors of red, blue, green, yellow, purple, and pink were standing on the living room's little table. They all had a label.

- 'It says 'Faith',' Roserin read, and held one bottle in her hand to observe it from closer. 'I have never seen such bottles before. These letters are beautiful! And the shapes... is that a salmon?'

-'I wonder what they contain...' Henrietta said. She was always eager to discover things before anybody else did. She got up from the chair she was sitting on and ran toward the little table.

- 'My intuition says these bottles are for you,' the girls heard Astrapi's voice inside their minds. 'I saw them on the ship too. I think you are supposed to drink them.'

Alexander, Bernard, and Stamatis approached them to see what they were talking about. Inside the barrel, Robert began waking up.

- 'Are these for us?' Bernard asked. 'Faith,' he read and grabbed one of the glass fishes. 'It smells like blackberry syrup!' he said after he uncorked it with an opener that rested on one of the shelves and smelled it. 'I love this sweet smell! What was that?' He paused for a few seconds and his face lit up. 'I felt some really pleasant energy all around my body. I felt a current that came from the bottle. It passed through my arm and ended in my heart! I am feeling wonderful! Yes, this is something that we need to drink!' he said with great enthusiasm and grabbed a glass that stood among others on a cupboard shelf. The drinking glass belonging to the family who were living in that house remained in its initial position looking dull. A clone of its body was now in Bernard's hands though, mysteriously materialized and looking vibrant and clean for the boy's immediate wish to use it. Bernard filled the glass with a light purple liquid and offered it to Roserin.

- 'Thank you!' she expressed her gratitude. She raised the glass to her lips and drank from it. 'That is delicious!' she said and her body glowed instantly in a light pink light. Her face looked happy and serene. She grabbed another glass; She filled it with some more Faith and offered it to Alexander.

- 'Thank you Rosie. That really made you glow! I do feel I need some of this too,' he said and took the second glass from Roserin's hand. He admired the glow inside the glass for a while and a drop of the liquid that fell onto his hand made his whole arm glow in pink light. He stood in a rather dark spot in the room, so his arm offered a few moments of intense Illumination. At the same time, some strange symbols appeared along the surface of his arm: a ghost, a man's head with his hair standing up on the top, a walking man, a flower, a disk with seven dots, a pigeon, some fish, two mountains, a snake, and something that looked like a branch that was used to detect water in the ground. Nobody seemed to have noticed. The boy brought the glass to his mouth and started drinking. The glass was soon empty, and his face glowed with a joyful smile before the remaining parts of his body felt the same rejuvenating energy. He took the third glass from the shelf and once again the original solid body of the glass remained in its initial position looking dull and lifeless. He opened another bottle, which seemed to be very well sealed. He poured liquid into the glass he had chosen and offered it to Stamatis. The boy thanked Alexander and smelled the drink in the glass. Then he started drinking it, but stopped.

- 'Why are we drinking something without knowing what it is?' he asked.

- 'You do not have to drink it. If it were harmful, our instinct would have warned us. But it didn't. How does it make you feel?'

- 'I am feeling lighter and more rejuvenated!' he said and without a second thought, he continued drinking until there was not a spare drop left in his glass. He smiled and a glow appeared on his face. Then his body became illuminated. Spirals of golden light twirled all around his body, arms, and legs. He looked at his hands where white light was being emitted from his palms.

- 'I am feeling wonderful! I also feel that somebody believes in me and is asking for my help for some reason…' Alexander said.

- 'Yes, I feel the same!' Roserin agreed.

- 'Me too!' Stamatis confirmed and filled another glass from a bottle that he had decided to open. He offered it to Henrietta.

-'That's funny…It smells to me like vanilla chocolate with a pinch of salt!' Henrietta enjoyed the smell and did the best she could to focus on the moment's pleasure. She relaxed and inhaled deeply. After three or four inhalations, she brought the glass to her mouth and started drinking from it. After she drank the whole Xiphias Gladius fish bottle, she rested her glass on the table. A sudden glow appeared around her like fireworks. She was hidden inside it and was hardly visible to her friends anymore. It lasted for a few seconds and then started fading gradually. Her friends were startled to see that she looked a little different now.

- 'Am I awake? Or is this a side effect of some sort?' Alexander asked. 'I KNEW I should not be tasting drinks I have never seen before,' he said as he moved his hands abruptly down to his waist with his palms open.

- 'You are made of chocolate!' Bernard was flabbergasted and he cut off two golden chocolate scraps from Henrietta's curly hair and placed them inside his mouth. 'And you smell like vanilla!'

- 'Leave my hair alone!' Henrietta said to her young cousin.

Everyone froze in front of the unusual sight, without the need to use the Astrolabe to achieve that. Eyes and mouths were all left wide open, staring at Henrietta's startling new appearance.

- 'If I was still alive, I would be laying on this couch right now,' Stamatis commented.

- 'What is so weird about it? We exist in the in-between dimension now,' Henrietta said. 'All of our thoughts, dreams, and desires can materialize at once! Our nightmares as well, I am afraid. We do not think with our minds anymore, just accept that we think now with our spirit! You left your mind back here somewhere in your graves.'

- 'As long as our desires do not harm anybody else, I concur that they will benefit us,' Sir Hipparchus added his thought to her consciousness. 'If a thought was meant to harm another person, it will come straight back to us and we will suffer instead.' His thought was complete. Henrietta looked thoughtful. Had she wished that somebody else be transformed into a chocolate person?

- 'You wished to be made of chocolate?' Stamatis asked her.

- 'I just wondered what it would be like to be made of chocolate. I thought: "What if the drink transformed everything it touched into chocolate?"' she sighed. 'I know. I allowed my mind to wander off once again...I mean my consciousness!'

- 'At least you do not look like a doughnut!' Stamatis giggled.

- 'Stop eating my hair and drink your own portion. Perhaps you will turn into a chocolate boy, and I can start eating YOUR hair for a change!' she told Bernard and offered him a glass that had materialized from the glasses on the shelf after she had poured some Faith inside it. Bernard rolled his eyes as he accepted the glass.

- 'It looks like pee!' he commented.

-'If you see it as pee, then it WILL be pee!' Roserin said to her young friend. 'Focus on its bright side!'

- 'Oh yes. I forgot all about that.' the boy giggled and, after a while, brought the glass to his mouth. He seemed to be very thirsty, as he gulped very quickly. As soon as he sucked the last few drops he licked his mouth. Everyone stared at him. He started glowing in a purple light.

- 'What were you thinking, that I was going to visualize something and transform into a sponge cake boy?'

The boy glowed, and when the intense light became gradually dimmer, an ecstatic smile appeared on his face. Something else was noticeable too.

- 'Bernard? You look a little more porous to me. A bit more…foamy?' Stamatis grimaced and approached him to see what exactly it was that he was looking at. Henrietta burst into intense laughter.

- 'I will never forget this moment for the rest of my in-between life!' She placed her palm on her chest while she kept laughing. 'I present to you, Bernard, the sponge cake boy!'

Her cousin looked at her, stunned, not yet having noticed what had just happened to him.

- 'What is going on with you? I did not wonder what it would be like to be made of sponge cake.'

- 'But you did mention it while the drink was still in effect,' Sir Hipparchus explained and observed the sponge cake boy's flexible pores. 'No worries though. The drink's effect does not last forever. Although you do look sweet!' he said. He poured some of the drink into another glass and offered it to Astrapi. The latter one smelled his hand and licked it, then he smelled the light pink drink and slurped. The African cat glowed with light blue light, and when the intensity subsided, he looked all white! The children were stunned.

- 'You do look beautiful, Astrapi!' Roserin admired him. Astrapi looked back at her and smiled.

- 'Well, our friend Astrapi, with some long white fur!' Alexander said cheerfully.

Sir Hipparchus unsealed another bottle, which was difficult to uncork. It looked like a tuna fish. When he did open it, some smoke of white light twirled and entered the astronomer's nostrils. He took a deep breath with his eyes closed. He held it for five seconds and then he exhaled.

Bernard took a glass and asked his friend to pour liquid in, to offer the drink to Robert. The Researcher obliged him. Robert was getting ready to put a big fat fish into his beak when Bernard pulled him out of the barrel, eager to see what effects the drink would have on the penguin. The boy poured it into his beak, almost by force. And then he waited. Robert glowed in turquoise green light for

a few seconds, and then the light disappeared.

- 'That is all?' Bernard felt disappointed.

- 'Penguins don't dream of sponge cakes, apparently!' Stamatis laughed.

- 'That's strange…I thought I had pushed all of the chairs under the table,' said a lady wearing a black dress who had just entered the kitchen. 'And what is this sweet smell?' she almost whispered as she looked around the kitchen. A cushion lying on the couch on which Sir Hipparchus sat returned to its original shape and no longer had the impression of his legs on it. The lady paused and stared in amazement. She had a cautious look and grabbed a thick walking stick that rested next to the couch. She walked carefully around the kitchen in a defensive pose. She looked quickly behind the old style shelves that were loaded with plates and copper pots, her fingers pressing her father's walking stick even firmer. The Scientist's eyes popped out as wide as a Goliath Tigerfish's when she jumped right in front of him, holding the stick above her head, ready to strike.

13. More Than Meets the Eye

The Astronomer's eyes opened as wide as a cat's when falling off a roof. Astounded, he let a girly sound out of his mouth when the lady jumped right in front of him, holding the stick above her head, ready to strike hard. Scientist Hipparchus started losing his height all of a sudden, until he reached both the height and the appearance of a ten-year-old boy. The adult Researcher was NOT an adult anymore. He froze in his position, and stared in terror at the stylish young lady dressed in black who looked like an agile, dynamic character. His fingers trembled in the defensive position that he had taken. He had raised his hands, by instinct, right in front of his chest. The lady, who seemed to be the current protector of the house, relaxed her body as soon as she saw that there was no human being who had trespassed her private space. The young scientist noticed how beautiful she looked with her long black fringed hair, and the sweet calm expression her face had taken when the tension evaporated into the white light of eternal protection.

- 'Now THAT is something we do not see every day!' Alexander commented and looked at the young-looking boy who now stood in Sir Hipparchus's position.

- 'Anemona! Are you done yet?' the young lady shouted to another person in the house. She placed the walking stick between the fridge and the sink, where it fit perfectly in the vacant space. Then she looked toward the kitchen table; She uncovered a basket which seemed to contain something edible since it was covered by a towel, and then she turned her back toward the invisible children and opened another cupboard which was filled with blue plates. She took out two of them, picked a few slices of bread from the basket, and placed them onto the plates. Finally, she opened the fridge and took out a covered glass container which contained half a block of margarine. With a knife that she took out of the drawer, she sat on a chair she pulled out and started spreading margarine onto the slices, after having placed the hemispherical glass cover onto the table.

- 'What has just happened? Why is everyone taller than me?' the young boy in the world of spirits asked the others. 'And why do my hands look young?'

- 'Uncle? Is that still YOU?' Bernard asked. He called all adults 'uncle' in the same way that other kids in Crete also used to.

- 'Of course, it is me, my boy. Who else could it be?' he replied.

- 'Uncle!' Roserin spoke to the young-looking Astronomer. 'You are a boy! Oh, boy!! You are much younger than I am!' she commented. 'What could that possibly mean?'

- 'Perhaps it is a late side-effect he is having from the drink,' Henrietta assumed.

- 'A late side-effect? I find it interesting that he transformed into a young boy as soon as he got scared,' Astrapi's voice sounded within everybody's consciousness.

- 'Hmmmmm…' Stamatis pondered, 'Are you saying that his fear caused this?'

- 'It looks like it to me,' Alexander added. 'I wonder if he will grow back,' he wondered.

-'I do not suppose he would keep getting younger if he got scared again, would he?' Rosie wondered aloud. 'This does not seem to have been caused by the drink itself, unless you imagined yourself as one of us uncle. You have not done so, have you?' Rosie asked. Robert approached the young Hipparchus and stared at him. What had happened to his older friend? He walked closer to him and touched his face with his beak.

-'Of course, he did not imagine himself as one of us. Sir Hipparchus is a Master of his Mind. I do wonder…Is it *us* perhaps who are having side-effects from this drink that suddenly appeared from nowhere? Oh no…' Stamatis said as he placed both his palms on the sides of his head. 'What is real and what is NOT?' he said in a state of confusion.

- 'Calm down my children,' the short boy said. 'There is no need to panic. I do have a confession to make. I cannot hide it I am afraid. I do transform into a little boy every time I am startled. There is nothing to worry about as long as I do not get scared multiple times, one after the other,' he expressed fear and looked pensive after his last sentence.

- 'We could not see you one day as a newborn baby, could we? Imagine that! Discovering uncle as a baby one day, now THAT would be hilarious!' Bernard giggled in amusement. The others rolled their eyes and looked at him using their etheric body language as if they wanted to say:

"Nice job Bernard. Uncle Hipparchus has not become a fetus yet."

Bernard stopped laughing at once and took on a serious expression as soon as he realized what he had just blurted out. Astrapi dropped one of the bottles and started licking the drink that spilled onto the living room table. The sudden noise caused the lady to look toward him. She stood up and walked to the little wooden table, right among the unseen children. She looked around in effort to detect the slightest motion. The children froze in their positions as she walked right through Henrietta. She stopped in front of the small table where Astrapi continued to lick the 'Faith' drink that had spilled onto the surface. The young lady sniffed a few times in the air.

- 'Chocolate…' she whispered, 'Where does it come from?'

- 'Where does it come from, indeed?' Stamatis chuckled, giving Henrietta an amused look.

The lady opened one of the little cupboards right at the bottom of the bookshelf. A few bottles of traditional alcohol and lemon liqueur appeared, which she had made herself. They all looked intact. So did everything else on the bookshelf, apart from the bottle opener that lay on the table. She closed the cupboard and kept looking around. She stood still for a few seconds intending to detect the slightest sound. Something glimmered on her neck.

-'What a beautiful pendant she has,' Roserin thought and admired the coffin shaped stone that was cut in such a way as to make the stone's rough internal glowing pieces visible. The surface glowed intensely in the colors of red, purple, and blue, mainly, although if looked at from another angle it glowed in the colors of yellow, ochre, and green.

- 'I must be losing my mind!' the young lady said.

A young girl about ten years old walked into the kitchen, opened the fridge, and took out two jars which seemed to contain some sort of jam. She placed them onto the table, glanced quickly toward the young lady and then to the table. She looked again at the lady dressed in black, stunned.

- 'Don't worry; I am not 'baboulas,' the young lady told her with a smile, referring to a Monster that some people in Crete used to scare disobedient children. 'I have already buttered a few slices; You can spread the jam on them if you like,' she said and walked into the kitchen. 'Would you like some warm goat milk?'

- 'Yes, thank you,' the blond girl replied, and started spreading jam onto the slices. The stylish lady took out a glass jar of milk from the fridge; She poured some of it inside a pot and placed it on the stove.

- 'Did she see us?' Alexander asked.

- 'Who, the lady? I doubt she did. But I bet she heard the bottle drop,' Stamatis said.

- 'Not the lady. The girl, I mean,' he replied to his friend. 'Didn't you see the way she was startled?'

- 'I think she DID see us,' Roserin said. 'I think she looked right at me.'

- 'Did she look right at *you* or right at her aunt?' Alexander asked her. 'I am asking because you were standing pretty close to her.'

- 'I think it is very possible that she DID see us,' Henrietta said. 'I thought she looked at me for a second or two.'

- 'But they CANNOT see us, can they? It must have been your imagination,' Stamatis doubted.

- 'Some people CAN,' The Astronomer said and looked toward the girl at the table. She had stopped spreading the jam and now stared at them. Henrietta released a shocked cry and moved a step backward, causing a few pieces of golden chocolatey curls to fall onto the floor.

- 'My hair just stood up. This is SCARY!' Stamatis said.

-'You can see us?' Bernard talked to her as she dipped the knife back into the jam and kept spreading it onto their breakfast. The lady who looked to be in mourning took the pot off the stove and poured the milk inside two mugs. Next, she placed the pot into the sink and took a jar out of a cupboard right above her.

- 'Some honey inside your milk?' she asked the young girl.

- 'Yes, thank you,' the girl replied. Then the lady pulled open a drawer right behind her and took out an old vintage teaspoon. She dipped it inside the honey and moved it above the girl's mug, watching the thin thread of sticky substance land inside the warm milk gradually as it broke into threads.

- 'This honey is of very poor quality. The threads break like cotton candy,' the little girl observed. 'It is not a good sign. You know what I mean…'

- 'I am afraid this is the only honey we have right now,' the lady replied.

- 'I was not talking to you…'

The lady froze. She looked at the girl and said:

-'What are you talking about? Anemona, you do worry me at times, you know that?'

- 'I was just talking to myself. What is so wrong with talking to myself?' she said and stirred the milk. The black-haired lady sighed in relief, 'It is allowed!' The girl calmed the young lady down.

- 'She DID see us!' Alexander said to the others, and stared at her in an effort to catch her eye again. Astrapi walked around the breakfast table and Robert approached the fridge, in the hope that somebody would open the freezer at some point. Anemona had managed to attract everybody's attention in her own way. She picked up a slice with jam and took a bite to eat.

- 'I am telling you, the girl is CREE-PY. She is NOT supposed to see us!' Stamatis told his friends.

-'Creepy! That is the word!' Anemona looked at the lady dressed in black. 'That is what this dress of yours looks like. Why did you design it that way?'

The children looked at each other, each of them stunned, while young Sir Hipparchus seemed to be making a few calculations.

- 'You don't like it? What's wrong with it?' the young lady asked the girl.

- 'You look like a black sarcophagus plant,' Anemona replied and looked at the encircling black stripes which were firmly fixed all around her companion. It looked, in a way, as if she had been caught by the vines of the most dangerous sarcophagus plant on the planet.

- 'What makes you see it that way?' the young designer asked her.

- 'Well…I don't know. Perhaps the red fabric you have added inside?' she said thoughtfully and took a sip from her milk.

-'Oh…' the dark-haired lady replied, and looked as though she had been caught in a major mistake. She looked like a rose that had been trapped by a deadly flower. 'I will make a better design next time. And everyone will be gobsmacked when they see it! I will return in two minutes dear, just carry on with your breakfast.' She got up from her chair and walked out of the kitchen.

Anemona took another sip from her warm milk and landed her mug back onto the table.

- 'Where do you come from?' she asked and took another bite of jam covered bread.

- 'Is she talking to us? She is talking to us!' Henrietta said all excited.

- 'She cannot be talking to us. And even if she was, HOW would she hear us?' Alexander said.

- 'The girl asked where we come from! Who else do you think she could be asking, her dead grandmother?' Alexander said in an intense tone. 'Oh my, oh my…a live girl talking to us passed souls,' he said and put his hands onto his head. 'I am getting goose pimples here. This is NOT normal. Uncle, I have seen enough. Let us go back home before it is too late for us. What if we got trapped in this world forever? Along with all the earthbound ghosts?'

- 'Are you afraid?' Anemona looked at Alexander. 'You do not need to be afraid in this house,' she said and got up from her seat. She took a few steps toward them. Robert was jumping, trying to reach the freezer's door. He jumped again. And again.

- 'Just stay where you are,' Alexander asked her. 'I am still not used to the idea that I have passed away, let alone the idea of being in the in-between world where all the suffering earthbound ghosts are floating around. And now a living girl from another dimension is talking to me? Now, this is too much. If I had a body, I would have collapsed onto your floor,' he said all flustered.

- 'We come from the dimension of the passed souls. We used to live in this city too, just at a different time and well...the surroundings were a little different too,' Sir Hipparchus explained to her. 'We have been exploring a new invention of mine, and we finally discovered that it worked! So, here we are!' he said proudly, while Robert kept jumping toward the freezer's door.

- 'You do not look like the others,' the blond girl replied.

- 'The others?' Bernard asked with curiosity.

- 'They have been attaching to people, making them do things.'

- 'Things?' Alexander asked. 'What things?'

- 'Like losing their minds and doing things they would not normally do. My cousin has been affected by IT too. She has not been herself lately,' she said and looked toward the kitchen entrance.

- 'Was that your cousin?' Roserin asked. 'She looked like a perfectly healthy person to me.'

- 'Areti looks healthy from the outside, but this thing is affecting her from INSIDE. I have seen it. It looks like a black tornado that is attracted to her as if she were a magnet. It twirls all around her and enters her head through her ears. It causes her fear and anger.'

Robert had just managed to open the freezer's door. A big block of ice fell onto the floor and smashed into pieces. The penguin stepped onto one of the pieces and started skating around the kitchen while the children talked.

- 'What do you think? Is this dress better?' Areti came back into the kitchen and Anemona turned around quickly to face her. Her cousin was now wearing another black dress. This one made her look as if she were right inside the mouth of a giant python. Areti turned around and presented the second dress she had designed to her young cousin. The python's glowing eyes, which were made of many stones similar to the one she was wearing around her neck, appeared on her back as she twirled around. The rest of the dress was narrow and had been gathered together in such a way that it resembled a snake's body.

- 'Well…' Anemona addressed her. 'If you like it, then I am glad you feel happy,' she replied tactfully, trying her best not to hurt her cousin's feelings.

- 'You have not eaten all of your breakfast I see,' Areti said and sat back at the table. She picked up her own slice of bread and started spreading it with jam.

- 'I am full,' The girl replied.

- 'At least take the rest with you,' Areti suggested. She got up, opened a cupboard above the sink, and took out a plastic container. She opened the lid, then picked up the two slices and stuck together the jam covered sides. She placed it inside the container, sealed it tightly, and gave it to her young cousin.

Robert now skated around the small living room. He used his left foot to push off the floor and slid on his right foot. He slid a long distance with great balance until he crashed against one of the kitchen chairs, where a heap of empty colorful plastic shampoo bottles in the shape of a fish collapsed on the floor, making a slight noise. Areti looked toward them, wondering how they fell on the floor. She didn't think she had touched that chair in any way.

- 'Thank you,' Anemona replied and walked out of the kitchen. Areti sat back down on her seat and kept spreading her slice with some yellow jam.

- 'There is nothing better than peach jam! It is a shame though that it almost finished. And I do need to earn some more money,' she whispered the last two thoughts. She stopped spreading the jam, and while she held the spreading knife in her right hand, she stared with a vacant expression, as if she were totally absent from her body.

- 'Let's go!' Alexander prompted the others. 'Anemona is leaving!'

- 'Is she going to be ok? She does not look very good,' Stamatis pointed toward Areti.

- 'I will stay with her,' young scientist Hipparchus replied. 'You can go and I will catch up with you later.'

- 'As you wish uncle,' Alexander answered.

The children floated through the walls along with Astrapi and Robert, and stopped at the outside yard, looking all around them.

- 'I have never seen such a thing...' Henrietta said, stunned. 'Look at this color!'

- 'It looks as if all earthbound ghosts have decided to have a conference here today,' Stamatis commented.

- 'This wind is terrible!' Bernard said.

- 'It is the typical southern wind that we have always had. But this time it looks a lot fiercer,' Roserin noticed. 'Look at this ochre light everywhere...'

- 'Good thing we have no solid bodies anymore! We would be

having trouble seeing with all the sand in the air,' Henrietta said.

- 'Good thing? It sure is! Imagine if we had to figure out a way to go to the bathroom up in space. We would have a few "meatballs" floating around!!' Bernard laughed. So did the others when they brought such an image into their minds and imagined the possibility of having to learn a new way of using the toilet.

- 'Where is Anemona?' Rosie asked.

- 'I do not feel her inside the garden,' Henrietta replied.

- 'Can she walk outside in such weather?' Stamatis wondered.

- 'If I had to stay inside every time we had such weather, I would have never left the house!' Roserin answered.

- 'I see a park in my mind's eye,' Astrapi's voice sounded in everybody's consciousness. 'Anemona walks through it. Somebody is right behind her...'

14. 'Georgiadi' Park.

All of the children turned their heads toward Astrapi, with worry depicted in their eyes. They started looking fainter until their etheric bodies disappeared completely. A crow with dishevelled feathers all over his body struggled to land in the stone-built yard, as the strong wind kept him floating in the air. A few lost feathers later, he finally landed in front of the door, with his black feathers pointing in all different directions, and pushed the half ajar door inward with his beak. He hopped inside, along with many leaves that were blown in by the wind. Sir Hipparchus had approached Areti while the children, Robert, and Astrapi were leaving. He sat on the same couch with the soft cushions he had sat on before.

- 'Money problems and anxiety. Now THAT is something I definitely do NOT miss from my life here on earth,' he said. 'It is true what they say, we only find peace once we have passed! We only have to keep working on our projects and kick a few ghosts' and monsters' butts every once in a while, but these are just some minor details. Earning money is sure not an easy thing, but don't worry lady, I see some great determination inside you. And an open mind. Yes...' he talked mostly to himself and put away in his bag the small telescope he had just looked through. 'All you need to do is see yourself already as a GREAT…whatever you want to be, and you WILL be! As long as you keep working on it and NEVER give up.

Just believe in yourself and your abilities. Nothing is impossible lady...' Sir Hipparchus tried to convey his message to Areti, from his spirit to hers. Then he looked quickly to his left side, then back to her, and right back toward his lower left side. His attention was clearly drawn by something.

'And who might you be?' he asked, and walked toward the crow. 'You do look somehow thunderstruck, don't you?' young Hipparchus said, and placed his pointer finger in front of the bird, prompting it to hop on. The bird did so instantly, then he flew and landed onto the boy's shoulder, prompting the boy to start growing back gradually to his former height. As soon as the black feathery bird landed onto his shoulder and grabbed hold of him firmly, Areti 's eyes popped out when she saw a crow floating in the air, holding onto something invisible, which was moving the bird upward as it became taller. The lady took a few quick short breaths and before anyone could say: 'Aspri petra kseksaspri ki ap ton Ilio kseksasproteri', she passed out onto her chair. This rhyme was one of the tongue twisters that Cretan people used to challenge their friends to say. It talked about a white stone that was whiter than the sun itself.

- 'Oh no! Oh, no!' Sir Hipparchus ran toward Areti as his height started changing once again, this time closer to the ceiling. He now looked like a young man around fourteen. The crow still perched on his shoulder. 'Wake up young lady!' he said and grabbed her hand. He patted it but nothing occurred. He let it fall onto the table. With both of his hands, he touched her face, 'Lady! Wake up! Wake up!'

A ten-year-old girl was chasing her woolly red hat in the wind when the children, Robert, and Astrapi appeared, half visible, in one of the city's parks. They hovered close to Anemona when a man approached her.

'-Wait girl!' he walked at a quicker pace. Astrapi was about to jump onto him from behind and wrestle him to the ground when Alexander hovered toward the man and looked over his shoulder. He was holding a book in his hand.

- 'You dropped this. Your bag has a big hole it seems.'

Anemona looked at her bag and discovered that it had been ripped open by force.

- 'Looks like somebody was looking for money in your bag,' the man commented. 'No wonder- the way things are right now,' he said and walked in the other direction after he had handed the book back to her. She looked at her bag, examining it with her fingers, and sighed when she came across the hole. She kept walking, holding her book in her one hand. Then she stopped for a while and seemed to be immersed in thought. She proceeded suddenly in a different direction, right into the heart of the park. She chose a quiet spot on the lawn, right under a touyia tree, and dropped her fabric bag.

- 'You can appear now. I am on my own!' she said.

A few faces started appearing more and more clearly in the air, floating around Anemona. The more visible they became, the more their hair gradually stopped floating and started being blown by the wind. They looked like ethereal apparitions who had come back to life. They took a few steps down as if they descended from a staircase, and came to stand on the same ground as the girl herself.

- 'So, how may I help you?' The girl asked. 'I am Anemona by the way.'

- 'Hi, Anemona! I am Alexander; This is Stamatis, Henrietta, Roserin, and Bernard. And of course, our African cat Astrapi, and Bernard's penguin Robert,' the boy said, and pointed in turn at Astrapi who was busy jumping in the air, chasing birds, and then Robert who ran toward the blond girl. As the African cat that Astrapi was, he loved chasing and catching his food on his own. He would rarely accept being fed by somebody else or being served a 'prepared' meal.

- 'Thank you for offering to help, but you see…we hardly know why we are here. Sir Hipparchus was showing us his invention when Bernard pushed this needle, and we found ourselves traveling in space. Then, we realized at some point that we were inside your house,' Alexander explained. 'I know that NOTHING happens by chance, so there must be a reason why we are here. I am just not sure what that reason is.' Everyone looked serious, apart from Bernard who opened his mouth every now and then, trying to catch all the broken chocolatey curls of Henrietta's hair as they were blown by the wind.

- 'You will start coughing hairballs soon, you sponge boy! Just wait and see when I look like the normal 'me' again,' Henrietta told him in an amused tone.

- 'Are you here on your own? Where are your parents?' Stamatis asked Anemona.

-'They are not here. They had to leave to America to work; I am at home with my cousin Areti. She designs clothes!' she said with a tone of enthusiasm at first, but after a short time her face turned gloomy. 'But she is not herself anymore. Nobody is,' she almost cried. Roserin disappeared all of a sudden. She was just not there anymore. Nobody seemed to have noticed, because their focus had been on their new friend.

From a short distance away, a man approached with a portable cotton candy machine. He seemed to be looking for a spot to park his trolley and create some cotton candy for the people and the few children who were at the park's market. Men were selling a variety of vegetables, whereas ladies had set up tables that carried various kinds of home-made sweets, jams, Cretan delicacies like 'kserotigano'-a sticky kind of hard-cooked dough leaf in a spiral shape, covered with honey and sesame-, various kinds of herbs planted in pots, jewellery, even miniature cars with chocolates inside them. Roserin appeared right next to the man with the cotton candy machine.

- 'Kalimera my ladies. It is rather windy today, isn't it?' he wished them a good morning.

- 'Kalimera Mr. Petro,' a lady replied. 'It will be quite a challenge for you to keep that 'old lady's hair' on the sticks today, won't it?' she asked the man, referring to his cotton candy the way it was called in Crete.

- 'Well, we can't have everything, can we? And you with your lovely pots, are you going to be alright? Hi Niko!' he greeted a friend who was passing by and started talking to him. Roserin noticed that the path toward Anemona lead downhill slightly. She also noticed that Mr. Petro had stabilized his cotton candy cart by placing a stone against the back wheel. She took the stone away and pushed the cart quickly toward the girl.

- 'Here is some cotton candy for you Anemona!' she shouted excitedly as she pushed the cart harder than the wind. People could see nothing but a cart running on its own!

-'Mr. Petro! Your cart is gone!' a lady shouted all of a sudden. The man ran behind his cotton candy machine without being aware that a mischievous spirit had been responsible for its departure. Rosie stopped pushing once she was only three meters away from her new friend. As soon as the man saw that his cart had slowed down, he slowed his own pace too, since he was quite overweight and could hardly run the long distance. He panted and stopped to catch his breath.

- 'Kalimera there!' he told Anemona as soon as he saw her. 'Are you alright? Sitting there totally on your own?' Everyone turned and looked at him as he approached. He could not see the children since they were visitors there from 'Iraklion,' a town from their faraway spiritual dimension.

- 'I have been better,' Anemona replied.

-'Are you not going to school? It is half-past already.' He peeked at the watch he had placed inside his shirt pocket. It was a vintage pocket watch with an embossed Santa and his elves on its cover. 'I think I know what you need to get you going,' he said. He put a spoon of sugar in the center of the cotton candy machine and turned it on. Then he picked up a stick and started rotating it in the bottom of the machine. The cotton candy started forming all around the stick after a small twister of sugar threads became visible in the center. At first, it looked like a small, inflated balloon as he moved it downward, then after a few seconds it started taking a very characteristic and well-known shape to the children.

- 'Look at that! Is he making a U.F.O.?' Henrietta asked, all excited.

- 'It could be a planet!' Alexander thought.

Then the man dipped a long spoon into some brown sugar crystals. He filled the spoon and placed it inside the central hole. Some brown cotton candy started materializing this time all around the stick. Mr. Petro took another stick and pushed the cotton candy slightly at some specific points by holding the stick vertically. With the help of other tools, he sculpted it in a very unique way. He now held something that resembled the basic shape of a ship in his hands. Next, with his long spoon, he added some white sugar into the central hole and kept rotating the upper part of the stick. Some more cotton candy started materializing above the ship, this time in white. Once again, he took the necessary tool in his right hand and sculpted three sails that were being blown by the wind.

- 'Here you go, my girl! Enjoy it!' he said and handed it to Anemona.

- 'A beautiful ship!' Roserin admired.

- 'Thank you!' The young student smiled as the man pushed his machine back to where it had been. She glowed as she examined the great edible artwork from all sides carefully. The wind had subsided, and Anemona could now taste her sugary ship easily, without her silky hair getting in front of her face.

-'Now THAT is a treat!' Stamatis said with excitement. 'What other ship on this island could be more delicious than this one?'

Anemona smiled happily and moved her fingers through the sticky mass.

- 'Would you like to taste some?' she offered some to her new companions.

- 'I would not mind tasting a ship and letting you know what I think!' Bernard instantly touched a piece and took it apart.

- 'Do help yourselves to as much as you like. I cannot eat it all by myself. Besides, I do need to go to school in a while,' Anemona said. The children took some cotton candy from the ship and tasted it.

- 'Ah, the same old candy taste!' Alexander said. 'And there is no danger of our teeth getting rotten anymore! I do not know about you, but I sure enjoy my spirit life! Although, I do miss the shiny enamel surface of my teeth...'

While everyone took a tuft of 'old lady's hair,' Roserin's attention was drawn by a round glowing object which looked like a disk, right under Anemona's turtle neck. As the spirit that she was, Rosie could easily see right under a person's clothes to what other object might be there. As she continued enjoying her own portion of candy floss, an etheric figure identical to herself squeezed out of her head and floated toward Anemona. She spread her right hand in front of the girl's throat, and a new materialized clone of what Anemona was wearing around her throat floated into the air, magnetized by Rosie's hand. It was a round wooden disk with various symbols carved on it along a spiral path. The surface was dark brown, with small traces of gold leaf pressed onto the symbols. There were symbols of what looked like flowers, people's heads, circles which contained other smaller circles in them, and a symbol which looked like either the Greek 'Ypsilon' letter or a forked branch used as a water detector. Other symbols looked like boomerangs, and there were even shapes that made her think of ghosts. Other shapes looked like a flowing river, a pair of mountain tops, something that resembled a kind of weed, a few leaves, the 'H' symbol, and perhaps a number of paddles. There was one carved shape that looked like a balloon. There were fish, -Robert approached to look at them and decide whether they were edible- and some human faces that were depicted with their hair pointing upwards. Roserin suddenly saw a few carved people walking on the disc. She wondered what some other raindrop-shaped symbols could mean, along with a triangle, a few hands, and a certain shape that resembled a hanging tissue.

- 'Are these two…huts? I wonder…and this one looks like an oyster. There is also a bird and a lady.'

- 'I see a dog's head and a boat,' Astrapi's voice sounded in her head. 'And THAT looks like a goat. I see no relative of mine on that disk,' he said. 'But I do find that sword interesting.'

- 'Is it really a sword?' Rosie communicated with Astrapi via her thoughts.

- 'So, what do your parents do for a living?' Henrietta asked Anemona when Rosie's spirit floated back inside her body. She had seen what she wanted to see. Her eyes' absent-minded appearance returned to normal.

- 'Mom and dad? They are Palaeontologists. They work at the Smithsonian Museum in Washington.'

- 'Palaeontologists?' Henrietta asked. 'So they dig up dinosaurs?'

- 'Sometimes. Most of the time they dig up ammonites, minerals, and fossils. They have sent me pictures of those by mail. Some of them are very colorful.'

- 'How come you did not join them?' Alexander asked her.

- 'I wanted to stay here. My friends are here; Areti is here,' Anemona replied. 'Besides, we would not have been able to take Fterouga with us.'

- 'Fterouga?' Stamatis asked.

- 'Our crow. His home is here. And he is here with his mate.'

- 'You saved one of his little ones when she fell into your fountain,' Roscrin described all of a sudden. 'She was drowning, and you took her out…'

- '…' Anemona's attention was drawn at once to her spirit friend.

'You saw me? You were there!!'

- 'No,' Rosie replied, 'I just seem to know somehow. Fterouga felt grateful to you and he has never left your side.'

The young girl smiled.

- 'Yes. I remember he flew onto my shoulder and I could not get him down! Then he made this really mesmerizing, soothing sound that brings the image of an exotic bird to my mind.'

A lady with long straight red hair, fringes on her forehead, and an olive green ancient Greek styled dress appeared in the distance. The southern wind blew her glowing hair and the silky shapes of gargoyles on her dress, which fell graciously from the waist down. Her right shoulder was bare, whereas her left shoulder was covered by a wide bell sleeve; Some more of this precious-looking fabric fell like a water fountain covering her arm in ripples up to her elbow. Despite sitting quite some distance from her, Bernard's vision was sharp enough to notice that there was a vague pattern of tornadoes that were ripping houses apart on her green silk dress, sewn by a light green thread. He noticed her shimmery copper boots and then he looked right inside her green eyes and beyond the pupils of her eyes. He saw something he had never seen before in his spirit life. He saw the figure of a gargoyle, chained at its wrists and ankles, struggling to be freed as it floated, trapped in controlling chains, somewhere in outer space.

The lady was stunned. She turned and walked away. Her very long copper-colored hair waved toward the children.

- 'Who is this lady?' Stamatis asked Anemona. 'A friend of yours?'

- 'I have never seen her before,' the girl replied.

- 'Pffff! What is this bad smell?' Alexander asked as he covered his mouth. 'It smells like a wet cat combined with rotten eggs and bone sauce for dogs…'

Everyone covered their noses

15. Where Did the Mysterious Lady Go?

Anemona got up from under the tuyia tree where she was sitting and moved toward one of the main paths which led out of the park.

- 'I'd better go. It is almost time we got inside for the first class,' she said to her new friends, right after she closed her hand watch. It was a heart-shaped watch with a delicately engraved design of almond tree branches in bloom, with a three-dimensional crow attached to the top of the watch. Anemona placed it back into her pants pocket. 'I know I will see you later!' she told the children. She grabbed her bunny shaped bag carefully so as not to lose anything else from the ripped side, while holding the stick with the remaining cotton candy ship in her other hand. She caressed Robert softly on his head using the tips of her fingers, and then she headed to the main exit path.

- 'The bad smell drove her away!' Bernard said.

- 'Come on!' Stamatis said. 'We should follow this lady.'

- 'Follow the lady?' Henrietta wondered whether this was a good idea.

- 'Yes! I have a feeling that this is what we should do right now. There is no other sign,' Stamatis confirmed.

- 'Let's do it then!' Roserin and Henrietta said in one voice, right after they had looked at each other. They got up and ran in the direction of the park's main road, where the mysterious lady had walked away. They ran hard, with Astrapi and Robert following right behind. Robert found it difficult to keep up as he ran. Besides, it was still early morning. What were his friends thinking running like this at this time in the early morning? They reached a point where they jumped into the air; They froze right at the highest point they had reached. Their etheric bodies started fading away until they could not be seen anymore.

At another place in town, their figures appeared in the air, still looking frozen as if unable to move. Once their opacity was closer to a hundred percent, they landed onto the ground.

- 'Where are we?' Bernard asked. He looked at the entrance of a long green building in front of him with several big posters with illustrations of dinosaurs hanging out of the windows.

- 'We are at the Museum of Natural History!' Alexander answered his cousin. 'She must be in there. Come on Robert!'

- 'Well, I do not have the slightest idea why we are following this woman, but this sure is a good chance for a tour! I never had the chance to visit the Museum before I...' Roserin said, and then she paused abruptly as if she had realized suddenly that she had better not continue her sentence. She proceeded toward the entrance with her friends. They walked through the glass doors and since spirits do not need to pay for tickets in the world of the living people, they went past the lady on their left side who was now selling tickets to a family from Germany. The children moved on straight ahead and walked under the skeleton of a big dinosaur, three vultures who were sitting right on the green metallic support beams of the Museum's

Rosie Protects the Coded Disc of Phaistos

main architectural skeleton, and an eagle. On their left side was a screen with a light green impression of a hand on it, and a second big flat screen that had been firmly secured onto the wall which presented a three-dimensional animation of a green feathered dino bird with a yellow beak, in flight.

- 'Where is she? Do you see her?' Henrietta asked Astrapi who had run ahead of them.

- 'I do not. But what I see here is a very interesting, fantastic wildcat! Is she single?' Astrapi's voice sounded in Henrietta's head, and the African cat walked toward the immobile Cretan wildcat. Henrietta rolled her eyes. Alexander walked further ahead and looked over the railing, but the only things he could see were huge skeletons of dinosaurs in the lower level, along with the imitation of a massive Deinotherium that resembled an elephant. The children passed by a model of a dinosaur with printed calligraphic letters and dates on his back. They looked toward the left and spotted the displays of a few stuffed animals positioned against big, illuminated photos in the background of their natural habitat. There was a wolf, a bear, a Eurasian Eagle Owl, a red fox, a little owl, a large rodent described as a 'Crested Porcupine', a wild boar, and a few more animals. Their backgrounds were lit up prints of either the desert or the woods and they emitted a natural light that made the animals look almost alive. Robert ran toward the exhibited animals, looking for penguins. Had there been any relatives of his around?

Henrietta decided to walk to the right on the ground floor, looking for the lady with the red hair. When she found herself at the parallel section, she came across a whole display of a dinosaur skeleton that was in the process of being unburied. A video of archaeologists explaining the whole process played near the exhibit. She also came across a few dino eggs with dinosaur embryos inside, a number of skeletons of 'dwarf dinosaurs', and a skull of 'Piatnitzkysaurus Floresi,' as the girl read on its label, but there was no lady with red hair in her sight. There was only a 'Buitreraptor Gonzalezorum', which was a bird-looking dinosaur with red feathers grown all over his body.

Roserin decided to walk down the stairs to the Minus One Level. As soon as she got there, she saw there was a main corridor. A parallel section to it was described as the 'Living Museum,' and a discovery center was on the opposite left side, which was called 'Erevnotopos' in Greek. Its meaning was the 'place of exploration.' She decided to move toward the latter. She walked straight into the main area, without wishing to waste any more time in front of a big poster that depicted a girl fishing, and where people had the choice to put their faces behind a big hole that would make them look as if they were the ones who were fishing inside a lake. She saw two big rocks resting on a table under two big magnifying glasses. Right next to this space, there was a low entrance leading into a cave. She read the sign above it which stated 'The Secret Cave.' People had to stoop down to get inside it. So did Roserin. Right to her left in the dark, a pair of earphones had been secured on the wall along with a small adjacent cupboard. There was also a sign with some written instructions:

1. 'Lift the headphones and listen to the sound of an animal that can be found in the cave.'
2. 'What animal can it be?'
3. 'The right answer is behind the little door.'

She took the earphones and placed them over her ears. She then heard a sound.

- 'That's easy! It is a bat!' she whispered to herself. Then she opened the cupboard right next to the earphones to see what it would reveal. A model of a lit-up baby bat was hanging from the upper part of the glass protected area. She closed the cupboard and opened the next adjacent one. The instructions were as follows:

1. 'Do approach and touch.'
2. 'What can it be?'
3. 'The right answer is behind the little door.'

Rosie Protects the Coded Disc of Phaistos

The girl put her hand through the hole and felt the mysterious object.

- 'Hmmmmm....it has a rough surface,' she thought. She opened the little cupboard, and a beautiful glowing stalagmite revealed itself under the light. She admired it for a few seconds, and then she noticed another display on the wall which had these directions: 'Press the button to listen to the story.' She decided to press the button which set in motion the recorded description of a story in English. The image of a boy appeared onto a mirror that was attached to the wall. He started talking about his dad, who had been working as a Speleologist. Some more images appeared one after the other. The boy mentioned how much he admired his dad, and that his dad used to take him and his sister to a cave at dawn for some exploration. He talked about a moth and a cricket that they had found in the cave. Right at her right side, Roserin admired the lower part of the cave which was full of stalactites and stalagmites in the dim light. In the meanwhile, in the 'Living Museum' section something else was going on...

A 'Horn-Nosed Viper' which was covered in sand jumped onto the glass which contained it in a transparent container. Somebody's hand, which was resting on the see-through surface, had provoked the attack. The hand belonged to a female human being with long straight red hair and a very childlike, innocent-looking face. The lady smiled and proceeded to the glass box that contained a number of cat snakes. She read the label and saw that this kind of snake was described as 'Saint Snakes,' in Greek. Right at her left side, a pair of very big iguanas was resting after their meal of salad. She did not show a particular interest in them; She moved on to see 'Milos Viper' instead, which had been resting inside another glass container with a nice 'fresco' painting on the walls as a background, depicting the particular animal's natural habitat. At Milos Viper's glass container was a fresco of a stone wall with part of the sea visible right behind it against a clear blue sky. A beautiful environment had been created with stones and holes inside which the snake could hide. The lady proceeded to the next glass container of her choice, one where the 'Blunt Nosed Viper' was resting right in front of the glass. A big thick trunk of a palm tree had been placed in the back left corner, along with a few ochre-colored rocks. Some more rocks and stones had been painted on the background against the blue sky, along with a few weeds which were painted right onto the tree's left side. A light in the cage's cover gave away the trunk's beautiful texture. The lady returned to the glass container where the Horn Nosed Viper had been resting. She spread her hand out and touched the glass. As soon as she touched it, the glass's hard surface turned to liquid, allowing her hand to pass through. The snake crawled onto her hand, up her arm, then onto her shoulder, and slithered into her dress on her back side.

Alexander and Stamatis had decided to look for the lady on Minus Two Level, where all the Dinosaurs were being displayed. They walked down the green stairs until they found themselves right in front of the 'Earthquake Simulator.' Alexander saw there was a Museum map resting on a bench that had been placed near them. He approached it and picked it up. There was a beautiful image on the cover of a 'Kingfisher' bird, intense colors of turquoise green and brown on its feathers. Right under the bird was the image of a rock that had a fossil of a leaf imprinted on it and there was also a cobalt blue butterfly on the right side. Some flowers could be seen toward the upper part of the cover. Alexander noticed that this map was in German.

    - 'Discover the Nature of Crete and the Middle sea,' he read. He unfolded it and felt attracted to a series of miniature pictures of various animals and flowers. Right under the pictures, he saw the Minus Two Level's drawing where they currently stood, along with the earthquake simulator, which was described on the map with the characteristic name of 'Egelados.'

    - 'I am not seeing the lady in the earthquake simulator unless she has transformed into a dinosaur,' Stamatis said to his friend as soon as he had looked carefully at all the people who had just entered the simulator.

    - 'I am going to the Dinosaurs,' he said and walked toward that section. Alexander watched the people who sat onto the wooden benches right inside the simulator, behind the protective bars. There were two walls: the one on their right side and the second one, which was right in front of them, on which a projector screen had been placed, along with a map on their right side. A lamp was hanging above the visitors' heads, and a few shelves had been attached to the front wall. An animation started playing on the screen with an audio description of how an earthquake occurred, and how people could protect themselves during an earthquake. Alexander's curiosity took over- he wanted to see the visitors being shaken by the first earthquake simulation. The time for this thrill arrived soon. A lady who arranged the fake earthquake by the use of a computer informed people that they were about to experience what an earthquake of 5.0 R magnitude felt like at the ground floor of a three-floor building. The simulator started shaking, along with everyone inside it. The map that was hanging on the wall moved intensely toward the right and left side, along with the lamp above their heads. A few minutes later, the lady told everyone that they would now experience what the same earthquake felt like to people who happened to be on the third floor of the same building. Once again, the visitors started shaking for a few seconds. When the earthquake simulation was over, the most destructive case of a 7.6 R magnitude earthquake in Chi-Chi, Taiwan was shown in the animation, along with photos of the disaster.

-'The earthquake that occurred in Taiwan was deep and long-lasting, whereas the earthquake in Kobe was strong but short,' the lady explained. 'You are about to experience the 6.9 Richter in Kobe, Japan, and the 7.6 Richter in Chi-Chi, Taiwan,' she said, and the violent shaking that had been felt in Chi-Chi, Taiwan began. A bag that was filled with food and which had been resting on one of the benches fell onto the floor instantly. A girl about six years of age was about to start crying when her dad, who was sitting at another bench opposite, calmed her down in the Japanese language. Everything shook intensely for about one minute. As soon as it stopped, another girl picked up the bag with the food that had landed onto the floor and placed it on her lap. Some more pictures of destroyed houses in Chi-Chi were shown this time on the screen. After a few minutes, the strong and short-lasting 6.9 Richter which had been felt in Kobe, Japan began, when Alexander decided to walk away to the dinosaur area.

A few excited children ran down the stairs, eager to see the section with the huge, bony animals. Two of them were attracted to a long glass container, which was filled with blue liquid and two miniature models of houses placed onto what looked like a yellow plastic base. A small tree also stood there, on the outer yard of one of the little houses. Two white fences had been placed in front of both houses. A sign on the top of the container read: 'Tsunami Simulator.' A few images showed the exact instructions of how visitors could create a tsunami by turning a handle counter-clockwise. The handle had been fixed to the bottom right side of the glass container. The children turned the handle without having read the instructions first.

The first model that Alexander saw in front of him was a huge elephant-like animal with two big tusks right under his jaw, turning inward. This was the 'Giant Deinotherium,' a land mammal five meters tall and seven meters long. Some more big dinosaurs appeared, like the 'Megaraptor Namunhuaiqui' and the 'Gigantosaurus Carolinii' who carried a very big head and weighed up to eight tons. Toward the end of the main corridor, Alexander saw a seventeen-meter dinosaur with a uniquely-shaped mouth because of its very wide lips and a large number of tiny sharp teeth.

    - 'Rebbachisaurus Tessonei.' And you weighed ten whole tons? Is that because of the rocks you used to gulp?' Alexander wondered when he noticed a few big stones laying in his stomach.

Stamatis had proceeded inside the 'Deinopedia' section, and when he saw that the lady with the red hair was not inside, his attention was drawn by the 'Patagonia Dinos' display- a machine that contained two screens and a little windmill with the instructions: 'Blow here.' He could not resist. The left screen changed the image that it presented at once and showed another illustration of a Dinosaur. On the smaller right screen, there was a description of the specific dinosaur. Stamatis blew the little windmill a second time when another image appeared on the screen and some music sounded simultaneously. This time, there was an illustration of a number of dino eggs on the ground. He could not resist blowing for a third time, and the third image of a red-feathered dino-bird almost made him jump.

'This must be a sign!' Stamatis whispered, excited. He proceeded a bit further and passed by a table where children seemed to be busy drawing the outlines of dinosaurs with oil pastels. Additionally, there was a second table for children where they were given the chance to do some painting and craftwork. The model of a dino head had been placed in the middle of the table. As soon as Stamatis walked by, the spirit of the dino head appeared and turned toward the boy. He did not realize what had just happened. He walked a bit further and stood right in front of a model of a little dinosaur that was dressed up as a gentleman. He looked at the egg-shaped chairs that people could hide inside and cover themselves by pulling down a white shell-like cover. One of them had its cover pulled down already.

- 'Could she be hiding in there?' he wondered. He waited with his heart pounding, feeling every second that passed as if it had been a whole hour. He did not know what to do. Keep standing there or run away? What if the lady really was hiding in there? He had had the impression of seeing a red reflection under the umbrella-like shape. Could it be her hair? Or was it just his imagination? And what if it really were her hiding underneath? What would he do when she revealed herself? What if she noticed that he was spying on her? What would he tell her in such a case? That he was just feeling that day like stalking a good-looking lady? That was out of the question! He decided to turn and walk toward the section's exit when the eggshell opened abruptly, and a child of approximately five years of age came out, running toward the table with the handcrafts and paints. He was wearing a red plaid check shirt. Stamatis jumped and sighed deeply. 'I must be losing my mind,' he thought and walked to the main department where dinosaurs' skeletons were being displayed.

Henrietta had decided to start her investigations on the first floor, where the 'High Mountains' and 'Conifers' sections were on display. She was in the 'High Mountains' section among a big group of foreign visitors. She kept looking for the lady with the red hair, but it did not seem to be an easy job. There were at least six women with red hair among the crowd. Henrietta did her best to observe all six faces as they moved around.

'If only they could all freeze for a minute! Where is Sir Hipparchus when we need him?' she thought. 'The Astrolabe would be really useful right now!' The Germans' guide walked toward the 'High Mountains' and started talking about the marmot, raven, and golden eagle that were on display right in front of a lit-up picture of their natural environment. Henrietta approached as close as possible to see whether the second lady she had spotted with red hair could be the lady they were looking for. As soon as she managed to reach the spot where the guide stood, everyone around her looked almost transparent, and time seemed to run much slower. The voices disappeared, a harmonious euphoric sound buzzed around her, and her gaze fell on some special 'feather grass' that had been planted at the scene, floating softly and gently as if it had been immersed in liquid. It looked like straw on which soft feathers had started blooming, dancing currently like the beautiful feathers of a white peacock's tail. Henrietta found it a lot easier this time to look around her and see who these ladies with the red hair were, by looking through all these people. They still moved, but at a much slower speed.

- 'I don't see her. Where could she possibly be?' she wondered.

A little girl about three years of age pointed at Henrietta and chuckled.

- 'Yes, I know you can see me!' Henrietta said and moved graciously like the spirit that she was. A stoat's spirit came out of its body where it was standing and approached the little girl, distracting her attention from Henrietta. The little girl chuckled once again and spread her hand toward the white-furred animal. Henrietta walked to the next section of conifers in a slow, gentle motion. More animals were standing there, an Ibex – which was a wild goat from the Alps- a lynx, a blunt-nosed viper, a short-toed eagle, a striped hyena, and a honey buzzard– which was a kind of an eagle. As Henrietta moved away from the High Mountains section, time returned to its initial rhythms, and the group's guide could now be heard talking once again in the usual way that live people talked. And as the girl approached the other animals, the blunt-nosed viper's spirit moved out of its body and went down the stairs.

But where were Bernard, Robert, and Astrapi in the meantime? Astrapi had been stuck in front of 'Shrublands' and 'Deciduous Forests' on the ground floor, where the Cretan wildcat had been standing proudly in her own natural environment. The Crested Porcupine's spirit was seen moving out of its large body by a little boy. The boy's mouth was now as open as Crete's 'Matala' caves' entrance, and the round red candy he had in his mouth dropped to the floor and rolled in a circle.

Bernard was watching a documentary about dinosaurs and excavators inside the Multimedia room, enjoying the impressive animation, when the blunt-nosed viper slithered right over his feet. The boy got a terrified expression, as if he had seen a live human staring at him, and climbed over the adjacent seats and straight out of the room. He chose to walk to the discovery center 'Erevnotopos.' He decided not to enter the 'Mysterious Cave;' He wanted to be as far away from the snake as possible. He instead chose to run up some stone-built stairs to another level. He found himself in a very welcoming space, where two stone walls had been constructed. A number of plants and bushes had been added to a limited area with some local nutritious red soil and small animals. A few miniature magnets with photos of these small animals had been placed onto a longboard, with the depiction of the stone wall that stood right in front of it.

- "What is hiding in the shrubland?" Bernard read on a sign from the wall that carried the illustrations of a bee, a flower, a mouse, and a snail. Another snake was hiding somewhere on the stone-built wall, which Bernard had not noticed. What he did notice was a series of little cupboards on which a sign could be read:

'Open. Smell. What herb is it?'

'Open for the answer.'

He proceeded instead to the restroom, and there he sat on a few big colorful pillows that were resting on the carpet surrounding two low oval-shaped wooden tables. He sat with his back facing the big window through which visitors could see the beach with its vast blue sea. He admired the bookshelves that stood right in front of him and contained various children's books for all ages. He got up and decided to pick a book at random by closing his eyes tight. He felt with his fingers and picked one up. He opened his eyes and saw that this was a book that was not exactly the subject of his choice.

    - 'Snakes! No more snakes for me, thank you!' His hair stood up as soon as he saw the photo of a Horn-Nosed viper on the cover, and he put it back on the shelf.

16. Now You Are Here, Now You Are Not.

Roserin decided to get out of the mysterious cave and went farther down, right under the level where Bernard was hiding. She came across a green tent and on the upper right side of the wall she saw a sign with glowing stars and an owl sitting in front of a big moon.

- 'A night at the campsite,' she read. 'Are we supposed to get in?' she wondered. She decided to do so, so she ducked and found herself inside a cave. It was rather dark inside. There was a glowing fire with a few logs that looked real, and a few tiny lights on the ceiling represented the night sky. A lady with a little child was already sitting inside, listening to the animals that were talking to each other. A beam of white light pointed every time at the specific animal that had something to say. There was a suspended owl on the ceiling with her wings wide open, holding a mouse in her beak. Some bats made their presence noticeable close to the top of the ceiling. Rosie also saw a badger, another badger at a safe distance from the fire, a ferret, and a few crickets. Roserin sat on a big stone and started experiencing the presentation. As soon as it was over, she got out of the tent, leaving the darkness and animals behind, and the lady with the little girl followed right behind her.

- 'This girl's name is Alice. How do I know this?' she wondered.

Rosie Protects the Coded Disc of Phaistos

When the lady and the girl decided to walk up the stone-built stairs where Bernard was, Rosie looked at the very big tree right outside the night camp. She walked around it and saw it was hollow from within. A sign outside stated: 'Plane Tree Cinema.' A big flat screen with a video had been fitted inside. The video was a documentary about turtles, frogs, and other animals. A wooden seat on which a visitor could sit and watch had been placed right in front of it. The lady with the red hair was not inside, but Roserin decided to enter anyhow. She felt attracted by the warm dim light fixed on the top right side of the internal part of the tree, which revealed some protruding parts of the trunk.

-'I wish we had such a tree in our garden!' she thought. She decided to get out a few seconds later and headed for what seemed to be a freshly painted boat, painted in colors of white, light red, and light blue. On the boat's 'keel', the name 'Tythis' was printed. The girl decided to get inside and inspect it. A big flat screen appeared in the center, showing a video of the town's castle 'Koule.' It looked as if the visitors were driving this boat in the port directly toward the exit that led to the sea. There was a wheel along with a GPS map 172C, a fish finder 160 C with arrows, an ENTER key, and a MENU. Rosie noticed there was also a sphere attached to the board containing a round compass with a metallic needle that pointed at the letters 'N,' 'S,' 'E,' 'W' as it moved around. The video started showing an underwater scene, and the camera travelled through a ship's sunken skeleton. One more main screen was attached to the main board, with four smaller images. One of them showed homocentric circles on a map. Another one showed a man working outside on the ship's deck. The third showed another map, and the fourth image showed the current speed of the ship at 78.8 ft. Roserin felt excited by the video showing the underwater sea world.

- 'A treasure could be buried down there!' she whispered when she heard a splashing nearby. She looked out of the ship and saw Robert enjoying the water canal that had been constructed in the same room. He let the water current drag him along to the canal's end. Then he climbed back to its start and slid again all the way down.

At the museum's ground floor, Stamatis was having a very close look at a red-feathered bird, with the name 'Buitreraptor Gonzalezorum.'

- 'So…here you are again birdie. But WHERE is the lady?' The boy's attention was drawn within a few seconds to a small case of a glass containing and lighting up 'Alvarezsaurus calvoi', and the skull of a meat eater 'Piatnitzkysaurus floresi.' Somebody seemed to have forgotten their museum map in front of a four-and-a-half-meter dinosaur's feet. Stamatis picked it up. It was a map written in English and had a chameleon climbing on a tree branch on its cover, along with the museum's logo of an ibex. 'I do need to focus. Let's see now…Where would the lady go?' he asked himself and looked at the map's various levels. As he looked at the sections, the lady with the red hair walked right past him and approached the red feathered dino-bird 'Buitreraptor gonzalezorum,' which Stamatis had just seen. She caressed the bird's head and smiled. The bird's spirit moved within its body, and when the lady stretched her finger right in front of the bird's chest, he grabbed hold of it with his beak and she pulled him out of his body. She walked toward the main 'Fossils' section and the bird followed. Stamatis was still studying the map when Alexander walked in from the upper entrance. He admired the wall painting on his right side that depicted two big dinosaurs against a dark background and a dinosaur's skeleton that was laid on the ground in its excavation process. The tools that were being used by the Paleontologists had been placed around the scene. Another screen on the left had been added to show a documentary describing the whole digging process. The boy walked past a few big dino eggs which were being displayed on the ground along with a few baby dinosaurs in them, and then he moved toward Stamatis.

- 'Have you seen her?' he asked his friend, while the lady walked right behind the section parallel to theirs, heading to the stairs with the dino bird following behind her like a slave.

- 'No. I wonder whether the girls have seen her, or Bernard perhaps,' Stamatis replied.

- 'I am pretty sure she is in here. I can feel it.' Alexander said. 'I feel as if I am just about to touch her.' He exhaled in a ponderous way and walked toward the exit. He looked outside to the 'Fossils' corridor right at the moment the lady was turning toward the stairs.

- 'No. She is not here. I am going downstairs,' he told his friend and walked through the corridor on his way to the stairs. As soon as the beautiful lady reached the stairs, she elevated herself slightly a few inches from the floor and floated up to the top level- the 'High Mountains' and 'Conifers' section, where Henrietta had been searching before.

So, was the girl still there? The lady looked carefully on the upper floor to see whether anybody was there. Nobody seemed to be present. She floated toward the 'Conifers' section and approached the animals on display. She spread her arm close to the 'striped hyena' and moved her fingers in such a way as if she wanted to say:

-'Come to me. Come to me my dear.' The striped hyena's spirit moved out of its body gradually and approached her. She caressed him on his head.

- 'That's my boy!' She smiled at him. When she looked at where his body stood, it did not seem to be there anymore.

Two boys approached the same section, holding sketchbooks.

- 'I will draw the Lynx here!' the one boy said, as soon as he read on the informative label what kind of animal this had been, and he sat down on the floor.

- 'I think I will draw the striped hyena!' The other boy sat down as well and started drawing the hyena's outline. They had not seen the lady with the red hair standing right next to them, smiling, caressing the hyena's spirit as if he had been her pet. She floated toward the stairs and the hyena followed.

- 'Hmmmmm…the hyena makes me feel sad,' one of the boys said. 'I think I will draw the honey buzzard,' he said and used a different piece of paper to start drawing the white-headed migratory eagle.

- 'I do love him! And look at his beautiful white throat with the brown lines!' he said to his friend while he admired the colors on the eagle's feathers.

As the lady floated down the stairs along with the hyena, Alexander moved toward 'Erevnotopos' discovery center. On the right side of the entrance, a board had been positioned where visitors were asked to express their opinions about the museum by using an attached marker. Many people had already written down how much they loved it.

The whole space where Alexander stood looked like a real cave. Right in front of him, another board had been placed with some colorful images of a fish, a lizard, a flower, a dinosaur, and a number of other pictures that Alexander could hardly make out from that distance. The main title that was printed was the following: 'Get to know the Scientists.' His eagerness to find the lady however, led him to the adjacent room, where a screen had been fixed firmly between the rocks onto the table's surface. A collection of minerals had been placed on the table for closer inspection under the magnifying glasses. The boy read the main sign: 'The Secrets of Earth.' A set of red and yellow protective helmets had been hung outside the mysterious cave, one above the other.

- 'If only I had any idea of where the lady went!' Alexander thought. He decided to enter the Mysterious Cave. At the same time, the ethereal looking lady floated downward to another level of her choice. Stamatis had walked into the 'Multimedia Room' and looked with intention at each of the visitors who were sitting comfortably on their seats watching the documentary on the big screen. The boy was astonished to notice a new characteristic of himself: Somehow, his vision became brighter and helped him distinguish every single person that was sitting in the dark. Not only that, but everything looked light pink!

- 'A few children with their parents and a few grandmothers and grandfathers are sitting in here. But WHERE is the lady?' the boy wondered. A big dinosaur appeared on the screen, the 'Noble One' as he was described by the narrator, when Stamatis felt a hand touching his left shoulder. He screamed loudly, right over the Noble One's loud scream on the screen. He turned around, startled.

- 'Henrietta! What are you trying to do, kill me twice?' he said to his friend.

- 'Sorry!' she replied. 'Where are the others?'

- 'There are four levels in this museum; they are all walking around. Have you seen her yet?'

- 'No! I have been on the first level upstairs. I keep looking. You have not been sitting here watching the movie have you?' she asked him, suspecting him of indifference.

Stamatis gasped, 'Just what exactly do you think I have been doing? Relaxing here on my butt, eating my popcorn? Let's get out of here and you will stick next to me now, so that you can see with your own pretty eyes what I have been doing so far,' he said and pushed her out of the Multimedia Room. It was at that time that the lady with the copper shiny hair had just descended the stairs of their own level, still heading for the dinosaur's section. Right at this point, her green-colored dress changed to yellow, and the pattern on it changed into another thin sewn design of high waves at the sea against tiny, fragile ships. As soon as she arrived on the Minus Two Level, she looked at the 'Egelados Earthquake Simulator' while people were getting inside to experience the next strong earthquakes. The lady guide who was helping people board the attraction saw her.

- 'The next earthquake is just about to start. Would you like to join us?' she asked her. The lady with the red hair smiled at first and then she burst into laughter, leaving the guide in front of her puzzled. She moved ahead to the dinosaurs.

- 'Where are we going now?' Henrietta asked Stamatis. 'What if we tried 'Erevnotopos'?'

Rosie Protects the Coded Disc of Phaistos

Bernard was enjoying the soft colorful cushions inside the children's room when the lady and the girl who had been inside the 'night camp' approached. Their first stop was right outside the children's room. They approached the little wooden cupboard, which had been placed on top of each other.

- "OPEN. Smell. What herb is it?" the lady read on the cupboard. "OPEN for the answer," she read on the adjacent cupboard. 'So what do you smell? Put your nose a bit closer,' she said to the girl. The girl did as she was told. 'What is it? Can you guess?' the lady asked her.

- 'It must be sage!' the girl said. The lady opened the other cupboard on the right side and read the answer.

- 'It is sage indeed!' she said as soon as she saw both the written answer and some sage herb being stored behind a glass container. 'Well done, Lily! Now, do smell in here,' she said and opened the cupboard underneath. The girl approached some small holes, through which the smell of a specific herb came out.

- 'I think this is oregano,' the girl said. The lady opened the other cupboard, and there was some oregano indeed, resting behind the glass.

- 'And how about the third one?' the lady said. 'Open it and sniff it!'

The girl opened up the third one and sniffed.

- 'Aaaaaaargh!' This one smells awful!!' she moved back abruptly and shut the cupboard.

- 'It smells awful?' Bernard thought as soon as he overheard. 'A bad smell is a bad sign,' he thought.

-'It smells awful? Now, what could that possibly be?' the lady wondered and opened the next little cupboard for the answer. Okay this is some 'malotira' herb, it is not supposed to smell bad,' she said and sniffed it herself. 'Pfffff! You are right!' she coughed. 'It smells horrible!' she said and covered her nose, right after she made sure the cupboard was closed tight again the way they found it. They decided to go inside the children's room under the impression that they were totally on their own. They could not see Bernard. 'What beautiful space it is to sit and relax in!' the lady said. 'And look over here Lily, so many nice books on the shelves! Most of them seem to be about animals: 'The Little Frog with the Golden Eyes,' she read and started browsing the pages of fairy-tale-like illustrations. But Lily's attention had been distracted by something toward the side of the window.

- 'Look mom! There is a ghost Pirate ship outside!' she shouted with excitement and stuck her little hands onto the window pane, watching the sea that was right outside.

- 'A WHAT?' both Bernard and the lady exclaimed at the same time and looked outside.

- 'I do not see anything dear,' the lady said to the child, 'but if you say there is a ghost Pirate ship, then I do believe there is one.'

Bernard stared at the sea.

- 'A ghost Pirate ship indeed,' he whispered. 'What exactly does that mean? I cannot be having any illusions since I am in the spiritual world, so that ghost ship must be REAL. And the girl can see it too. I wonder what they are up to,' he thought. The ship had a flag with a print of a head that was wearing the traditional red 'fez' cap that Turkish men used to wear on their heads. The sea had big waves; The ship, however, moved quickly toward the town's 'Koule' castle. 'Had I been still alive right now, I would never have believed it,' Bernard whispered to himself. 'A ship without a parrot? How is that even possible?' He looked astonished. 'Where is the parrot?' He stared more intensely when his vision changed all of a sudden, and he realized he was able to see right onto the ship's deck. For a few seconds only, he managed to distinguish an owl perched on one of the ship's railings- an owl who was wearing a red fez herself.

Roserin was inside the museum shop on the ground floor, admiring a three-dimensional pop-up book that enriched readers' imagination about the jungle. She enjoyed the sounds of the various animals that it made every time she turned a page. 'What wonderful colors these are!' she whispered to herself when she saw a variety of colorful bugs resting on some leaves. She browsed all of the pages, and then looked toward the shell craft construction kits that had been placed to the left on the shelf by the shop's employee. She picked up a three-dimensional owl which had been constructed out of a number of shiny shell pieces.

- 'How cute!' she said. A small piece that had been attached as part of one of the little owl's feathers fell onto the floor. Rosie picked it up and connected it back onto the body. She then placed the little owl back onto the shelf. Some fluffy dinosaurs nearby drew her attention, as well as an art kit for much younger children. She held the mini plastic see-through art kit bag in her hands and saw a set of oil pastels inside, along with a few dinosaurs outlines for them to fill in with paint. She looked again at the shell craft construction kits.

- 'There is also a penguin, a monkey, a goat, a koala I see, an elephant, a polar bear…There are so many! Even a flamingo, a chameleon, a panda, a puma, a raccoon, and all these dinosaurs too! How wonderful!' she said. Then she went back to the shelf that held all the children's books and re-opened the colorful book about the jungle. She opened to a random page which depicted some animals that were full of color. A few mixed sounds were released by three cute looking koalas. One of them sounded like a lion. A 'Saimiri' monkey protruded in the middle of the page; A few colorful frogs were close to him, some 'Alluette' monkeys, and a chameleon with intense colors were there too. Roserin enjoyed the sounds and the illustrations, especially on the left side where a monkey had climbed onto a tree branch holding a stolen camera. 'What a cute little face!' she thought. 'And what a beautiful background! It looks like a peaceful rainy day in the jungle…' She dreamed for a few seconds until the lady who was supposed to be at the shop's till returned from the ladies' room.

- 'I swear I heard some sounds in here,' she said to her colleague who stood at the ticket desk. 'Did you hear anything?' The other lady moved her shoulders upward, taking on a facial expression of ignorance. The till lady returned to her post just as Rosie managed to place the book back in its place. She did not want to shock the lady who would enter all of a sudden and see a book floating in the air. The lady in charge went behind the till and looked carefully at the bookshelf, all ears, ready to catch the slightest sound.

Henrietta and Stamatis were now standing right at the entrance of 'Erevnotopos' Discovery Center. On their right side was the board on which people could write their opinions about how they liked the museum. Stamatis looked at the board for a second, then back at the table with the minerals on it, then instantly right back at the board for a second time when his eyes landed on a child's drawing of a lady with straight, long, red hair…

17. A Very Powerful Stamp.

On the ground floor at the Fossils section where Astrapi was trying to get a response from the wildcat he had fallen in love with, the friendly-looking dinosaur with the printed letters on his back got a three-year-old's attention. The dinosaur's spirit appeared as it started moving within its body; He shook himself as if he were a wet dog and the letters were ejected into the air. They floated for a few seconds then landed softly back onto the little dinosaur's body.

Two children, a boy eight years of age and a girl of six years, were sitting on the floor of the Fossils section. The girl was making stamps of dinosaurs on a piece of paper, trying out an animal stamp set that her father had just bought her from the museum's shop.

- 'You are not pressing the stamp firmly enough. That is why it looks so faint,' the boy said to the girl. 'This is how you do it.' He grabbed a stamp; He pushed it onto the ink pad and pressed it firmly onto the paper. Everything shook around them all of a sudden. The walls moved like jelly, the floor moved, and the animals in the 'Shrublands' and 'Deciduous Forests' sections were ejected into the air. The red fox was ejected, a little owl flapped her wings while she found herself in the air, the Cretan wildcat, the Crested Porcupine, as well as the birds that perched on the branches all flew into the air.

- 'She jumps in the air because of happiness! She likes me!' Astrapi said ecstatically, as soon as he landed back on the floor along with the other animals, when he saw the Cretan Wildcat being ejected into the air.

The boy looked at the stamp, baffled. Was it him who had caused this intense shake? Or was something really strange going on inside the museum? The little girl chuckled. She grabbed one of the stamps and pressed it firmly onto the sheet of paper. One more earthquake-like shake occurred.

- 'What is going on here? I thought the Earthquake Simulator was downstairs,' Stamatis said to Henrietta, one floor below where the two little children sat. 'Is this another contraption of the museum?' he wondered.

Alexander had reached the upper level of Discovery Center 'Erevnotopos' right outside the children's relaxing area where Bernard was currently sitting. The strong earthquake had made the informative sign 'Exploration on the Mountain', fall off the wall and onto the rocky set that had been constructed right under it. The ibex, which stood further up, almost fell off when it landed back on the rocks, but he managed to climb back to his initial position. The magnets which had been placed on the long board that presented a printed depiction of the stone wall-which had been constructed on the front side- were ejected in the air and were pulled back to the magnetic board forming the outline of a dinosaur's foot.

- 'Now WHAT was that?' Alexander wondered. When the second big shake had been felt, a few of the cupboards on the 'smells and perfumes' board opened wide. Robert was still enjoying the internal water slide when he found himself in the air. He turned a somersault in mid-air and landed back on the slide.

- 'What is this? Are the Pirates on this ship attacking us with cannonballs?' Bernard asked himself. The lady who was inside the same room with him urged the girl to move under the door.

- 'Is this the earthquake machine from downstairs aunty?' the girl asked the lady, in the hope that she would receive a reassuring reply.

- 'I am sure it is another earthquake machine sweetie. Stay under the door,' she prompted her.

Alexander seated himself on the seats, feeling puzzled. Bernard came outside to see what had caused such great shaking, as his curiosity had affected him to a great degree. He walked past his friend without realizing that he was sitting there on his left side. Alexander was gazing outside the glass window when he saw the ship close to the shore.

- 'Is that a Pirate ship?' he asked, astounded. 'I must be dreaming! A ghost Pirate ship without an eye-patched Captain?' he said and looked at the mussel covered ship. 'How strange!'

Bernard ran to the museum's Gentlemen's room and turned on the tap water in the sink. He splashed his face with water.

- 'A ghost ship without a parrot! I hope I am not losing my mind!'

A man saw the water running and since he could not see Bernard, he walked toward the sink and turned it off. He shook his head and whispered: 'Here we are in a shortage of water, money, and food, and some unconscious 'malakes' leave it running,' he sighed after using the main national swear word. Bernard looked at him, stunned, as he left the bathroom.

Stamatis and Henrietta were on the stairs of the same level with the thought to walk downstairs to see whether these intense shakes had been caused by the earthquake simulator. The spirit of a 'Giganotosaurus Carolinii,' the big dinosaur fifty feet in length, was seen walking up the stairs. Stamatis' and Henrietta's eyes popped out, and they both ran up the stairs, as far away as they could get from the big-headed Dinosaur. Bernard came out of the men's room and walked toward the stairs. The dinosaur could not be detected by the boy anymore. The latter one was just about to descend the stairs when 'Rebbachisaurus Tessonei's' spirit, fifty-six feet in length and ten tons in weight, was caught by the boy's eye while the dinosaur was ascending the stairs. Bernard's eyes almost popped out, and he ran up the stairs, right behind Giganotosaurus Carolinii. The stones that were lodged within the dinosaur's stomach kept crashing against each other, leaving smashed pieces all over the stairs. The shakes kept occurring every time his feet stepped onto the stairs.

Alexander decided to walk down the stone-built stairs leading to the 'shrubland' section. He turned right under the big Plane tree cinema, then he walked past the 'Mysterious Cave' and the 'Secrets of the Earth' section where the various minerals were under inspection, and got himself out of 'Erevnotopos,' the area of exploration. He was heading toward the 'Multimedia Room' as the lady with the shiny, long, copper hair ran up the stairs.

- 'Ha-ha! Follow me, my babies, follow your mommy!' she shouted ecstatically as she ascended. Alexander was now right outside the Multimedia Room, which was on his left side. He looked toward the stairs, trying to decide where to go next. Then he looked to the left. As soon as he turned his head, the lady with the red hair turned to her right side and ran in front of the floor's elevators and kept running up the stairs. Alexander decided to walk toward the stairs on the right side. He stood in front of them for a few seconds, trying to decide which level to go to. The Giant Deinotherium with the two big tusks under his jaw was now walking up the stairs slowly. The museum's floor levels shook on every single step. Alexander decided to walk up to the next floor when the flying spirit of 'Taniwhasaurus Antarcticus,' a snake-like dinosaur fish with many small sharp teeth, floated above the boy. Alexander did not notice the presence of this threatening seventeen-foot-long fish.

In the meantime, as the red-feathered rooster-looking 'Buitreraptor Gonzalezorum' also ascended the stairs, the thirty feet long 'Megaraptor Namunhuaiquii' was now getting out of his body. The big head of an 'Abelisaurus Comahuensis' with really small eyes and sharp teeth chased around a teacher who happened to have the gift of inner vision. This helped her to be able to see it. The lady was panicked to such an extent that she

Rosie Protects the Coded Disc of Phaistos

ran toward the exit with her glasses barely hanging onto her nose. A few children who also happened to have the gift of spiritual vision hid themselves inside the cocoon chairs; Other children kept playing games they had started on the computers that were available on a table for them. One little girl ran and hid herself behind a big long dino bone which stood firmly on a black 'X' mark. A little boy was holding a stick with a dinosaur's head on top of it and moved it toward the huge dinosaur whose spirit was just exiting his body. The boy imitated a dinosaur's roars to scare away the big bony monster. His mother ran close to him and took him in her arms as she ran toward the stairs.

On the upper levels, more stuffed animals' spirits emerged from within their bodies. The scorpions that were confined within the glass container next to the stairs could easily walk through the glass and down to the floor. There was no solid obstacle on this planet that could keep their spirits trapped within a limited environment. The red fox stepped out of her "natural" environment, along with a flock of birds that had been resting on some branches. The Crested Porcupine moved the long quills on his back upward and walked backward to get out of his body. At 'Shrubland of Crete,' interesting things were happening to Astrapi, as the spirit of his beloved beautiful wild cat was returning to this dimension.

-'Oh...there IS a God! Baby, you are a LOT more beautiful in spirit! Not that you are not beautiful in body!' Astrapi's voice sounded. 'But you know what I used to say? It is the Spirit that makes the body!' he said, not able to take his eyes off her.

Next to come out were a goat, a crow, and an eagle at an adjacent display. The eagle flapped his wings and flew away, whereas the crow made a few nice pleasant sounds. A green woodpecker that had red feathers on his head flew to an opposite tree branch and got busy carving out some new holes. Life came back into these sections, with sounds that made visitors turn their heads at once, all ears. Two teenage girls were unlucky as a wild boar's spirit, weighing about 150 kg, ran full attack behind them. The girls screamed and dropped a bag of cupcakes they had just stolen from a younger girl. The wild aggressive boar would not let them out of his sight. There was obviously something about them that he did not seem to like. A bear had been trying to open a jar of thyme honey produced in Crete. It had been left behind on the corridor's seat inside a paper bag, as the owners had run away as soon as they had noticed a very hungry bear behind them sniffing out their honey. A lady ran at full speed as the Crested Porcupine, the rodent-like animal with the long quills on its back, ran backward in his effort to stab her with his thicker quills.

Rosie was having a closer look at some colorful crystal balls that hung on a rack on the table at the shop's entrance. From one moment to the next, the nets that were holding all the various kinds of glass balls became loose from underneath and all the pellets fell onto the floor. Roserin stood there with her mouth open. A man dressed in a business suit who carried a black case walked inside and stepped onto the 'Crested Porcupine's angry eye' glass balls, which had landed closer to the entrance. He slipped and fell onto his back on the floor. A lady who seemed to be a colleague of his ran inside and helped him back to his feet. During the time she had been busy doing this, the spirit of the dinosaur that was being displayed right outside the shop made his presence noticeable and moved his skull upward twice. Roserin fell onto the floor and started sweating. With her palm, she touched her chest.

    - 'Not again…' she said. She tried to inhale some air, counting five seconds. She kept it for another five seconds inside her, and breathed out at the same pace. She repeated this a few times, then the three-dimensional owl which had been puzzled together flapped her wings and flew toward her. She stood on Rosie's knees and released a few hoots. It was obvious that she was trying to tell her something.

    - 'This hand that touches me from within is so cold. So cold…' the girl said in agony, and lowered her head. The owl constructed from shells flew on Roserin's arm and glowed in golden light. A ray of the same light came out from where the bird's heart would normally be and permeated into the girl's chest. It emitted the light for a few seconds. Stamatis and Henrietta appeared, running through the exit doors. Giganotosaurus Carolinii scampered right behind them. The doors swung wide open when Bernard appeared, coming up the stairs and rushing toward the exit. Rebbachisaurus tessonei galloped behind the boy as if he had just discovered the most delicious prey. The lady with the copper hair and her current yellow silky dress headed to the main hall.

- 'Follow me my babies! Follow me!!' she called to the animals. The striped hyena followed behind her. The flying 'Taniwhasaurus antarcticus' snake-looking fish was next. It flew outside the museum's shop window at the moment Alexander arrived. He looked inside the shop and saw Roserin sitting on the floor with her head angled downwards.

- 'Rosie...' Alexander ran toward her and was just about to help her stand when the shell constructed owl flapped her wings and flew back to the shelf where she was positioned initially. She took her position and kept looking toward the girl.

- 'I can't. No...It is so cold inside me. So cold...'

- 'You are sweating.' Alexander observed. 'Some things are very wrong in here. I feel they have to do with this woman in some way. Would you be alright if I left you here for a while?'

- 'Yes. It will pass. It will pass...' she repeated with a trembling voice.

Alexander walked toward the shop's exit.

- 'I don't know what is going on here Rosa,' -he used her name in the Greek language- 'but we will set the balance back to where it was,' he said to his friend while he walked away. The little pearl-looking owl flew back and landed onto Rosie's shoulder, releasing hoots of comfort.

A little boy had his hands pressed against and was looking intensely into a glass container in his effort to detect the animal that was supposed to be kept within the container.

Rosie Protects the Coded Disc of Phaistos

- 'Where is the mouse dad? I don't see it.'

- 'It seems he is hiding somewhere. Look more carefully and you might see him having his coffee with his family! Oh! It really IS almost coffee time!' he said as soon as he had had a quick look at his watch. The boy looked more carefully this time at the upright straws on top of which the mice would usually climb. A background painting of wind-struck straws in a field made the image look more three dimensional. A clay dish with water had been placed among the red rocks but the mice were nowhere to be seen. What COULD be seen during that time, right behind the boy and his father, was the 'Viper of Milos,' which was crawling on the floor, along with the 'Blunt-Nosed Viper', the 'Four-Lined Snake', and the 'Horned Viper.' The 'Cretan Spiny Mice' ran away from their miniature caves and chose to climb up the walls as far away from the snakes as they could get. The big iguanas could walk through their big glass container in the corner as well. They walked slowly but steadily behind the snakes. One by one, the glass on each container transformed into a soft penetrable substance that looked like bubbly jello, forming a gate which enabled the animals to escape. The sparkly substance looked like a sheet of bubbly drink that had been frozen along one or two sides of the container. It was still sparkling vividly, as if it was making an effort to speak up and show that something of big significance was about to occur.

The Dab Lizard was now walking through the vivacious substance, which was changing its color currently into a deep cobalt blue. The fizzy bubbles had turned into turquoise green luminous bubbles. The 'Fat-Tailed Gerbils' were the ones who were now trying out their luck. The 'Freshwater Crab' and the 'Cretan Water Frog' passed through the live bubbly surface next. The glass container holding the little turtles disappeared suddenly and all the water it held fell onto the floor. The little turtles were now jumping and landing where the water was falling. The little fish that were inside the water with the turtles writhed at this moment on the floor, struggling to breathe. They did not have much time left, unless somebody ran to pick them up and put them inside another container that was filled with water with the right amount of oxygen for them to survive. A 'Yellow-Bellied Toad' jumped onto the glass within his own space when the glass vanished and became one and the same with the water, causing a big waterfall, which helped the toad land onto the back of a little turtle. The boy and his father stepped carefully over the little turtles and the fish and ran toward the stairs.

- 'Daddy! The fish will die!' the boy shouted in great worry.

- 'We will tell the people who look after them to come and tend them. There is obviously something wrong with that fish tank,' he replied. The man who had been looking after the animals appeared suddenly from the second entrance of the Living Museum's section. He ran toward the fish with a net and tried to save as many as possible.

- 'Stay in here for a while my sweeties, until I have found something better for you,' he said and put them inside the 'Common Tree Frog's' container. One strong shake in the museum's floors transformed the fish into flying fish inside the tank. The Giant Deinotherium was now standing at the museum's interior entrance which was also right in front of the shop's entrance where Rosie had fallen onto the floor. The girl was still there, and she had to quickly find a way to protect herself from this giant monster. She could be detected easily, since this was the SPIRIT of a Monster, and being a spirit herself, she had to find a way to hide from another spirit who had the ability to see her.

- 'THINK, Roserin, think!' she said to herself. The Giant Deinotherium was now turning its head toward the shop. 'Oh, I forgot! I have no brain anymore!' Rosie said to herself.

Astrapi followed the wild cat which had just run under the Deinotherium and out into the world. Roserin's friend hardly realized that the girl had been sitting on the floor, unable to move. He failed to notice that he had just walked under the body of a massive monster and that another one in the hall was just taking its turn to come to life. Astrapi and the wild cat ran through the doors as the Deinotherium moved its head through the shop's entrance…

18. Three Floating Octopuses.

𝒜 class of approximately fifteen young students - anyone would make a rough guess that these were children aged nine to eleven- was seen at the port where the 'Koule' castle was standing proudly. The fishing boats that had been tied up firmly at the quay floated more violently on the water when some incoming waves disturbed the calm surface. On the left side of the quay, people were jogging along the long trail that led to the castle, whereas persons of the older generation walked all the way toward the castle and beyond, in sheer determination to reduce their high blood pressure.

- 'Walk in pairs please, one pair behind the other!' a lady with long, brown curly hair caught in a ponytail said to the young students. She seemed to be one of their teachers. –'And I do NOT want to see any of you sneaking off to the Marina coffee shop. We are visiting the Museum of Natural History today,' she said sympathetically. She took off her brown trench coat when she felt she had started sweating and wiped her face with her fingers. The children stood in pairs, facing the way they were about to walk toward the museum. Anemona, along with another classmate of hers, stood right behind all of the other children.

The young teacher and her students started walking ahead when Anemona's attention was drawn by something on the horizon. She stood where she was and looked toward the ghostly Pirate ship which had just appeared in the sea. A slight mist made it difficult for her to see clearly. The ship seemed to not be moving anymore. Anemona slipped away from her class and entered the long pathway that led to 'Koule' castle. On the left side of the trail, a small number of merchants were selling a few canvases of paintings, which were resting against the wall. The little boats in the quay on her right side kept shaking vehemently as if disturbed by the arrival of the big ship.

The Southern wind became stronger and blew Anemona so hard that she almost lost her balance. Her Phaistos disc locket slipped out of her sweater as if an invisible hand had pulled it. It kept being pulled behind her neck by an unseen force.

- 'I have never seen such a thing in my seventy-two years of life, people starving to death and not doing anything about it,' an old man said to two of his friends as they walked past the girl.

- 'What we need is a leader,' one of his friends commented, 'a leader who will get us out of this mess…'

- 'Young Scientists decide to leave the country. They hardly care about what will happen next,' the third man said. 'It is the old ones who stay, the ones who have to deal with the problem.'

Anemona overheard them talk and recalled the day when her parents had to leave the country to be able to find a job in America. Despite her wish to remain home, all of her resistances vanished on the day of her parents' departure. All of a sudden, she had wanted to leave with them, whereas her mother had wanted to stay with her. But things were very unstable now as far as their finances were concerned, as her parents had expressed, so neither of them could do as they wished.

- 'Look at the state of my nets. Look at this,' a fisherman's loud voice interrupted the girl's thoughts. She looked at him. 'Who will pay for this damage? Who? Such great damage…I had to pay a fortune for these nets,' he shouted to three men who happened to be near him.

- 'What caused it?' one of the men asked him.

- 'The toxic lagokefalos caused it,' the fisherman replied. 'I am ruined. RUINED,' he said in despair. 'Something must be done about this.' Eyes filled with sorrow, he looked for more holes in his yellow nets.

- 'The WHAT?' the other man asked.

- 'The Lagocephalus sceleratus fish…' another man replied. 'They are toxic and a menace,' he added.

- 'A menace? A menace?' his tone changed when he expressed the word for a second time. 'They have destroyed me,' the fisherman cried.

A bit further, a man appeared with a big snake resting around his neck. He would let people pet it and have a picture taken with it around their neck, in exchange for five euros. On the right side, as Anemona walked closer to the Venetian built castle, another man who stood outside a blue kiosk was arranging boat tours to the opposite island of 'Dia.' Anemona read the yellow letters which stated 'boat trip' and a three-dimensional white shadowed word of 'Dia.' Two dolphins had been drawn in white, one on the left side of the word 'boat' and one on the right side of the main title, right above the word 'Insel,' which was also written in German and meant 'island.' A few colored photos of the island were shown on a map along with the depiction of a white compass and short pieces of informative text. The main name of 'Dia' was imprinted on the top part of the map in red letters. On the left side of the kiosk, the schedule for the trips had been written by hand on a long vertical piece of white paper in the Russian language as well for the Russian tourists.

'Giganotosaurus Carolinii' dinosaur was approaching the roundabout at this time, which had been built right opposite the long trail's entrance to the castle. He turned his head to his left side, where a traditional fish market was standing, and growled to the men who were selling the fish. One of them stopped at the spot where he was standing for a few seconds and lowered his head. He looked as if he had started losing all life force and energy from within at a very quick pace. He froze like the three dolphins that had been sculpted, one above the other, on top of some green stone sculpted waves. This sculpture was standing in the center of the roundabout that was opposite him, to the left side of the fish market. Before the three dolphins had the chance to get out of their own bodies, the man put his hands under a carton behind him which contained some salmon fish, and he threw it in the air with force. He then placed his hands under the next carton, which contained some prawns, and threw it in the air the same way he did with the first one. He grabbed the third adjacent box which contained some tiny smelt fish and did the same thing while releasing a loud shout. As he was about to throw the fourth box, filled with sea-bass fish, one of the other two men ran toward him as the third man stood there in great shock.

- 'There is no hope on this island for us; There is no hope. HOW am I going to feed my children? How am I going to pay the bills?' the man started shouting in despair and pushed the other colleague out of his way. With both of his hands, he grabbed another two cartons with mussels and calamari and threw them in the air. The third fisherman ran toward his colleague right away and seized him from behind, in an effort to restrain him. The man was so desperate that he moved backward with his colleague still on his back. With such a great amount of negative energy trapped inside him, they both fell backward onto the remaining fish-filled cartons. The dinosaur growled loudly one more time toward the fishermen. As a result, the main sign above their market which read: 'traditional fish market' in white with a blue background and a depiction of an Ancient Greek Fresco of a few Minoan dolphins on the right side and a boat with two fishermen on the other end and a painting of a Minoan human figure carrying fish in the center, fell onto the ground. The Giganotosaurus dinosaur kept walking toward the right side of the roundabout. Henrietta and Stamatis appeared on the same road as where the dinosaur had come from, where most of the fish taverns operated one next to the other.

- 'Where did all this fish and calamari come from?' Henrietta asked as soon as she saw the brick streets covered with seafood.

Rosie Protects the Coded Disc of Phaistos

- 'I think the fishermen might be on strike. What a waste for all these fish to be thrown like that on the street.'

When the children ran a bit further, they saw the two fishermen fighting with each other while a very thin cat with protruding bones approached and grabbed a fish in her mouth. She ran up the 25th August Street to enjoy her meal.

- 'You are malakas!' the one fisherman called his colleague the name many people used to call each other in Greece when they believed the other person had committed something unacceptable. 'Open your eyes and see what you have done! You have thrown the source of our income onto the road! Do you honestly believe your problems will be solved this way? You have a brain inside your head- Use it! Malaka!' he shouted while the third man was picking up the fish, the prawns, the calamari, the mussels, and the octopuses from the road and placing them back inside the cartons. As the dinosaur moved away toward a local tavern with a characteristic name: 'A Little Wine, A Little Sea,' the desperate man started to calm down. 'You are acting like a spoiled Princess! I will bring you a tutu dress to wear tomorrow morning,' his colleague shouted at him while raising his left arm in the air in despair. He walked among the fish toward the other man who had brought over a few boxes to pick everything up and put it back on the counter. –'A tutu dress!' the angry man repeated.

- 'I am sorry Vassili. I don't know what got into me,' the man apologized to his colleague. The dinosaur was now taking the right branch of the trail upward toward the town's center. This was the 25th August Street, where local people sold traditional souvenirs in their shops.

- 'Come on!' Henrietta urged her brother. They both ran behind the dinosaur, who was currently turning his head to the right side to look inside one of these small shops. A hat rack loaded with hats had been placed by the owner at the entrance. The dinosaur inserted his head deep inside the shop door and stared at the lady who was sitting at the counter. The lady was knitting something unique, as she was using some red wool with shimmery red sequins and had a comforted expression on her face. Some rays of white light emitted from around her head. The dinosaur backed up in a sudden movement, and as he moved his head out of the shop, a pile of hats got stuck on his head and carried outside.

- 'Oh, those earthbound spirits are taking my hats again!' the lady commented and ran outside her shop. 'Give me my hats back and go into the Light!' she shouted toward the visiting entity as she ran behind the flying hats. 'You pretend to be BIG, don't you? I may not be able to see you, but I know you are just as small as a lizard! Now, I want my hats back!' The dinosaur started moving quickly away from this lady. Something about her seemed to be alarming him. As he ran further up the street, he became smaller and smaller. By the time he had reached the fish foot spas on both the right and left side of the trail, he had shrunk half his size already. The lady ran, she jumped, and grabbed her cream-colored hats in the air.

- 'You are in BIG trouble if these ribbons have gotten filthy. You hear me lizard?' she shouted to the half-sized dinosaur, 'BIG trouble!' She started walking down the trail to her shop while Stamatis and Henrietta walked up the street. 'Oh! We have visitors in town!' the lady commented and looked right into Henrietta's eyes. 'My dear Margaret, I have not seen you for ages!' she said and hugged a lady who walked right through Henrietta. Henrietta stood still as if she had been struck by an earthquake.

'Rebbachisaurus Tessonei' dinosaur appeared at the starting point of 25th August Street, from the port's side. He lifted his head upward and growled. Right after, he lowered his head and looked to the front as his long, powerful tail whooshed at his left side and passed through a tavern right above the tables where people were sitting and through three octopuses that were hanging from the tavern's protective tent in the background. The octopuses moved slightly to the right side when some black misty energy left the tip of the dino's tail and permeated the octopuses. The dinosaur's tail moved backward, above the customers who were having their early lunch and who felt a strong breeze of air. The dinosaur proceeded up the street and three octopus-shaped shadows floated above the people who were eating. One of them landed onto a blond-haired lady's head and moved its black tentacles through her hair. The lady rested her head onto her fists with her elbows planted firmly on the table, when sudden spasms disturbed her body. A man and two ladies who were sitting next to her dropped their forks onto their dishes noisily and looked at her in a state of shock.

- 'What is wrong dear?' the man asked her, as a second black octopus figure floated out of the second hanging octopus and landed onto a child's head.

'Sweetie'? the man asked the lady and touched her on her right arm. The lady screamed instantly, and with a violent movement of her right hand, she threw the plates of food off the table. More prawns were now lying on the ground, along with 'tzatziki' yogurt- a traditional mixture of garlic and cucumber, a few fries, and fish, which attracted two starving cats under the table that looked like skeletons. A plate filled with red beetroot fell onto the white dress one of the lady's friends who had been wearing proudly, leaving stains that would be impossible to remove.

- 'I cannot take it anymore! I CANNOT do this anymore!' she shouted loudly in a state of total hysteria. People stared at her this time, when the boy on whom the second black ghostly octopus had attached started having intense spasms. While all the adults at his table were distracted by watching the lady react with total lack of control, they failed to notice what was happening to their little companion. The boy's face took on an expression of pain and agony, clearly a sign that he could not control what was happening to him. He grabbed the plastic-covered paper sheet under the dishes, which he had torn into various shapes with his nails some time earlier, and pulled it abruptly to the side. His parents, his uncle, his aunt, and three elder cousins of his all turned their heads, startled by the noise of the breaking dishes and the sensation of hot fries landing in their laps.

- 'Vassili! What have you done?' the uncle asked the boy. His aunt was preoccupied with scooping the grated tomato and sheep/goat cheese off her lap and then placing all of it back onto the oiled barley rusks, called 'dakos' in the Cretan dialect. Dakos was a traditional Cretan hard bread that had to be moistened first with water in order to be eaten without breaking people's teeth. As soon as everything was back on the soft surface of the bread, she placed it all onto an intact plate in front of her, which had escaped the great fall. The boy's parents were trying to figure out what had just happened when Vassili ran around the tables and shouted:

- 'Get out of me! Get OUT of my body!'

He started pulling his hair hard and staggered all around. 'No! No!' he shouted.

Henrietta rushed toward young Vassili; She looked at the tables nearby and pulled a plate of 'tzatziki' as close as possible to the boy.

- 'Eat the tzatziki! EAT the tzatziki!!' she prompted him.

Vassili looked at the second table in between him and the shocked customers and he spread his hands forward. He pushed the plates violently and threw them off the table. A young man who had just appeared with a number of new prepared meals, which he balanced along his right arm, froze as soon as he saw the two customers in hysteria and broken plates on the floor. He turned around and walked back into the kitchen where he came from. When the boy stopped to take a breath, a lady got up from her chair and walked with agitation toward the boy. Henrietta kneeled and as soon as Vassili looked straight ahead with eyes looking lost and vacant, she looked into his eyes and whispered.

- 'Vassili, listen to me. EAT the tzatziki!'

The boy's soul mirrors looked very sad. They moved a little, and Henrietta felt a connection.

'He feels trapped inside his own body,' she told Stamatis by the use of her thoughts, without being heard aloud. 'Go ahead, eat the tzatziki!'

The woman who had left her seat was now approaching. The tavern's owner had just appeared out of the kitchen, stomping heavily with his well-fed body toward the child. He inserted his hand into his pocket, which seemed to be loaded. His look was serious and austere. Vassili turned his head to his right and looked at the dishes that people had been enjoying before all the fuss had occurred. His lip lifted upward like a snarling dog's. A gentleman pulled two plates of fried zucchini and fries toward his side and placed them onto an adjacent chair on which a basket with bread and napkins had been resting. A lady of rather advanced age who was sitting at the one edge of the table close to the boy, raised her pointer finger toward Vassili and opened her mouth to tell him something, when, with a sudden motion, he dipped his fingers into the 'tzatziki' dish and then inserted them into his mouth.

-'Ah! Now, this is TOO much!' the lady with the pointing finger almost shouted. 'Somebody should teach this boy a lesson!' she said in great agitation.

Vassili stopped having spasms and his lip was not pulled upward like a snarling dog's anymore. One of the black octopus's tentacles was now visible as it flapped out of the boy's head. Then within a fraction of a second the whole negative entity was ejected out of the boy's body as if it had been placed inside a very powerful slingshot, a special slingshot which consisted of yogurt, onion, cucumber, a little olive oil, and the always very powerful and protective herb called 'garlic.'

-The number ONE herb against dark entities!' Henrietta said with pleasure and relief.

The owner of the tavern walked right in front of the angry lady who had gotten up and walked from the opposite table, and he stood behind the boy. He took his hand out of his pocket, holding a big calculator tight in his fist.

- 'Now let's see who is going to pay for all these broken plates?' he asked, and started pressing buttons. Henrietta and Stamatis were so concerned about the little boy's well-being that they had not noticed where the octopus' third black triplet had floated. It was not resting on any of the employees' heads. And the owner seemed to be clear too. So, where was it?

Stamatis took two steps backward and looked to his right where most of the tables had been.

- 'Where are you, you little piece of emptiness?' he thought and looked at every single person who was still sitting there. Everyone had turned their heads to their side, except for a little girl who was finally enjoying her meal without her grown-up cousin next to her stealing her fries all the time. Then, Stamatis turned his head to the left and studied the people sitting at those tables carefully. But no dark figure of a black octopus was there either, apart from a young man whose hair looked like tentacles.

- 'You are not hiding from us in there, are you?' he thought and walked toward the man. In the meanwhile, Vassili's father had gotten up from his chair as soon as he had recovered from the shock, and approached his son. The lady to whom the first dark octopus-resembling figure had attached started running toward the town's center, up the paved road, with her relatives following close behind her. She ran past a lizard which seemed to have a close resemblance to the first dinosaur that had escaped with the hats on his head.

- 'Come on; Let's go bring that lady back!' Henrietta urged Stamatis. But her friend's attention was drawn to the man with the tentacle-looking head. Henrietta ran outside the tavern's main space onto the trail when all of a sudden she fell onto the ground and looked at her palms. An expression of pain and despair appeared on her face. An electric purple liquid oozed through the lines of her palms.

- 'Stamatis…I am losing Life…' she whispered in agony. 'Help me…help!' A pair of black eyes appeared on her back and a number of thick tentacles firmly attached to her ethereal body. At this very minute, as the octopus was sucking out her soul, Henrietta regained her everyday physical appearance and did not look like a fresh chocolate girl anymore. Now, she looked like a pale sick girl whose golden light was now being taken away from within her solar plexus area, being sucked through the dark entity's plungers.

- 'Help!' she asked with the minimal strength that was still left within her, but her friend was still distracted by the man's strange-looking hair and could not take his eyes off him. And Henrietta was losing Life…

'Rebbachisaurus Tessonei' kept walking up the 25th August Street and growled loudly inside the fish foot spa. The little fish swam toward one side of the tank and remained there in one big swarm. The young lady who was inside started crying. She opened her purse, took out her wallet, unbuttoned the little sachet of coins, and put her fingers inside. She felt the coins' coldness on her fingers.

- 'Two euros and ninety cents,' she sighed. 'There goes the nice omelet once again,' she whispered and sighed again at the thought that she could not afford to buy an omelet for today's lunch.

As the dinosaur kept walking further up the street, a crack appeared on one of the four sculpted lions of the central 'Morozini' fountain. This was the town's central square, where people sat outside at various traditional coffee shops and restaurants and had the chance to admire the four lions that carried a big stone plate on their backs. The crack appeared on a lion's leg, right beneath his curly mane. A crow was unable to fly against the strong Southern wind and was therefore forced to land onto the lion's head. Henrietta was still struggling to survive on the street, not visible to anyone but her friend.

- 'I need Life uncle…I need Life…'

19. The Dragon's Eye.

The dinosaur that had been placed at the museum's entrance had an identical clone of himself by this time, standing in front of the shop. The Giant Deinotherium decided to walk outside, whereas the 'Carnotaurus Sastrei' carnivore theropoid was now looking in the shop's direction, magnetized by his discovery of a young girl sitting on the floor. The eight-meter yellow-eyed animal with the two short but robust horns above its eyes took the first step toward the shop's entrance when the form of an eagle that had been resting above the entrance doubled. His spirit exited from his body and flew through the main doors outside.

Roserin got up immediately and ran toward the till's desk. With trembling fingers, she grabbed one of the many net pouches which contained the small glass balls. These nets hung from some sickles. She pushed a ball through the black net's holes, and once she had it between her fingers, she threw it up in the air. The ball hovered for a while in front of her, while Rosie took a few steps backward. The crystal ball was now half-covered by a pair of eyelids. A pair of fluffy, deep yellow eyebrows appeared next; A pair of round, luminous, green-turquoise cheeks followed, looking in their initial non-solid state as if they had been shaped by immeasurable tiny particles of shimmery pearl ammonites which glowed in various shades between an intense cobalt blue and a turquoise green. A series of cream pearl teeth appeared next, and then a nose that looked as if it had been made of a blob of silver glitter jelly. Roserin's attention was then distracted by the appearance of a number of rice paper thin green-turquoise scales, which started forming a body that seemed to be the extension of the non-solid head. The half-materialized head moved backward, and some powerful yellow light flames were released against the carnivorous dinosaur. The wild animal backed off, winding through the information and ticket desk, then it kept walking right through the wall to the outside.

Rosie sighed with relief. She looked at her new friend that she had materialized with the power of her imagination. He had a long tail now that spread across the shop's adjacent room, which was covered by more rice paper thin metallic turquoise scales that moved softly and gracefully with every breath the friendly entity took. The scales looked as if they would melt onto somebody's finger as soon as they were touched. At the same time, inside the 'Multimedia Room' on Minus One Level of the museum, the 'Noble One' dinosaur that had been presented on the screen was an adult dinosaur currently, who now turned his head, staring at the visitors. He walked toward the camera and stepped out of the screen. None of the viewers had realized what had just happened. The Noble One, as the adult that he was by this time in the Spirit world, started looking for other existing entities of his own dimension, as a 'lunch' to be. A little baby that had been resting in his mother's arms noticed the diplodocus dinosaur's spirit coming out of his documentary and started crying. His mother looked at him at once.

- 'What is it my little truffle? This is not a real dinosaur!' she said and put the pacifier into his mouth. But the magical invention that seemed to work miracles at other times, did NOT work this time. Especially when the Noble One's tail whooshed out of the screen. It was an urgent matter that the pacifier would do its job.

- 'You are a Sea Dragon!' Roserin said as soon as the rest of his long, scale-covered tail appeared. Right after that, his main body and legs became visible to the girl. A set of six small delicate wings in the shape of drops appeared on his back. They stood gracefully, turquoise green at the center with a thin line of dark yellow glowing around the perimeter. There were three pairs of two thin oval neon glowing wings. One was on the lower side close to the main body and two more had grown on the upper side of the protruding supportive bones. A few yellow ochre stripes appeared on the turquoise-green surface around his neck while Roserin was admiring his seahorse-like wings. His snout and the rest of his head were now visible too. He turned his head and looked at Rosie.

- 'You have saved my Life!' Rosie said to the innocent-looking dragon.

- 'No. It was YOU who brought me here,' his voice sounded inside her head.

The Noble One was currently standing in front of the computer screen by the entrance, which depicted a green palm, on which visitors were supposed to place their own palms. The sea dragon lowered his body and Roserin felt the need to hop on immediately. And so she did. As she was stepping onto his leg, her new friend turned his head once more and blew a big soap-like bubble out of his nostrils toward her. The bubble surrounded her and filled her with golden light. The fragile-looking surface remained intact all around her while the dragon moved closer to the exit. The Noble One approached, and after releasing an equally strong growl in the air, he moved his head toward Rosie and opened his mouth. He snapped with force in an effort to grab the girl from her friend's back, but his teeth got electrocuted with the first contact. They could not get past the thin live surface of the bubble, no matter how strong and sharp his teeth had been.

He stepped back in pain. His retreat gave the sea dragon the chance to walk through the exit doors before the Noble One recovered. Roserin's new friend took four steps forward, flapped his seahorse-like wings, and found himself in the air. As he took off, the Noble One appeared outside, following them through the doors.

- 'Mommy! Look!! There's a dragon in the air!' a little girl four years of age said to her mother in sheer excitement. She was standing behind the windows of a Chinese restaurant on the first floor of a shopping mall on the same central street that led to the museum.

-'Yes, dear...' her mother replied while seated at a table with her back against the windows. She continued cutting the spring-rolls that had been resting on her plate.

- 'A dragon! Could it be somebody's kite?' a man who was one of the lady's companions wondered.

- 'No...she just has this habit of drawing dragons on the windows with her fingers right after she has exhaled her breath onto the glass,' she explained.

The dragon's scales glistened in the sun's rays before he reached an area further ahead where the sky looked red. The Noble One started walking toward the town's center slowly but steadily.

Anemona kept staring at the Pirate ship until it faded away into some fog that appeared from nowhere. She then turned around, ready to walk back to where she came from, when the lady with the red hair prevented her from doing so merely by imposing her own presence in the girl's way. Anemona gasped and froze right on the spot.

- 'So you can see me...' the lady said. 'I should not be surprised about this. You do seem to be a very special girl with gifts that not many people possess,' she commented. 'Now, that's a nice pendant you have there. Did your mommy and daddy give it to you?'

- 'No, actually it was my cousin who gave it to me,' Anemona said while touching her round Phaistos disk with her left hand.

- 'I see,' The lady said and smiled. 'Would you like to walk with me? Are you here on your own?'

- 'I have to go back now. I am here with my class and I have to catch up to them,' Anemona replied.

- 'As you wish,' the lady agreed. 'It has been nice talking to you,' she said to the girl, 'It is a shame you won't be joining me on this ride, but if you must go, then so be it.'

- 'A ride?' Anemona asked, harnessed by her own curiosity.

- 'You see that ship?' the sympathetic-looking lady pointed toward the Pirate ship. 'I will be embarking on it in a few moments. It is the town's new attraction you see. Have your teachers at school not informed you about this?'

- 'No...' Anemona shook her head right and left.

- 'Well...' the lady in the yellow silky dress said as the delicate orange sewn pattern of big waves and little ships being swallowed by the waves on her dress's surface started moving slowly. Two lighthouses emerged under the waves. 'The ship will be here soon to pick people up to transport us to 'Dia' and back. The whole process should take about thirty minutes, no more than an hour. And the ship has been decorated in a really fun way. Are you sure you do not want to come?'

Anemona felt an intense dilemma inside her. She felt she had to catch up with her classmates, but that ship inside the mist had hooked her. She had never embarked on a ship at sea before.

- 'Perhaps I could join you. The museum will still be there for me to visit,' she said and turned around once again.

- 'Terrific!' the lady said with pleasure, 'I will have nice company next to me.' They both headed toward the boulder-built Koule Castle. 'What if we went inside the castle until the ship has arrived?' the lady suggested.

- 'I would love to!' Anemona replied.

- 'Let's go then!' the lady prompted the girl and Anemona's face glowed in pleasure. The big sewn silky waves on her dress kept moving, swallowing ships and lighthouses.

They soon found themselves at the west-side entrance of the castle, beneath a plaque with a marble raised image of the winged lion of St. Mark. The pair proceeded inside to a dark, chilly, stone-built corridor. They left the heavy wooden door behind them and stopped in front of two paths. There was also a ramp, which led to the upper level of the castle.

- 'How about going upstairs?' the lady asked Anemona. 'We will be able to watch the ship from above while it's approaching the port.'

- 'Excuse me, young lady,' a man addressed Anemona all of a sudden. 'There is no such thing as a free entrance, especially these days.'

- 'Oh, I am sorry,' Anemona replied and unzipped her bag's front pocket. She took her bear-shaped wallet out and opened the pouch where she kept all of her coins.

- 'That will be three euros please,' the man said.

She gave him the coins and the man handed her the ticket. She turned toward the ramp. The lady was not standing next to her anymore. Anemona's eyes looked like a startled owl's. She ran up the ramp decisively, struggling to hold her balance on the slippery stones. She had to hold onto the wall on her left side to support her body while she climbed up. After some panting and sweating, the girl finally reached the roof.

- 'What took you so long?' The lady re-appeared behind her as soon as she stood on the roof. Her dress had turned deep red at the moment, with a pattern of light red sewn volcanoes and printed carnivorous red flowers with white spots sewn on their petals. 'It is so beautiful up here! There is also a tower on the Northern side,' the copper-haired lady said.

- 'Yes, I was just wondering…what your name is? I happen to be Anemona.'

- 'Let us go look for the ship!' the lady suggested and moved ahead to the battlements. 'Look! I see it!' she sounded as she stood between two merlons that were part of the crenellated wall.

Anemona sighed and decided to walk to the adjacent crenel. She looked at the sea and spotted the Pirate ship disappearing into the mist and reappearing after a short time.

- 'Now my dear...' the lady sounded behind her, 'you have something that I want and I am asking you kindly to give it to me.'

The young girl turned around with a sudden movement.

'I am talking about the locket. I need to borrow it for a while and I will return it to you as soon as my mission is complete.'

- 'My pendant? But this is a gift. What do you want it for?'

- 'Let's say that it works like a key to something that needs to be unlocked. I do realize it is a gift, but it will be treated with the outmost respect, I promise,' the lady replied. 'As soon as it has served its function, I will return it to you with my own hands.'

- 'No,' Anemona said firmly.

- 'My dear girl...It seems you have not understood me correctly. I have asked you to help me kindly, as a true lady would do. Perhaps a little girl like yourself cannot comprehend the vast importance of this. Yes, I am sure this is the reason of your refusal. But I need to insist before it is too late. A few lives are at stake here.'

Her little companion looked worried:

- 'What lives? Who are you?'

The lady approached her slowly. She looked at the embossed surface of the pendant and then back to Anemona's face with an air of confidence and control. She walked closer and closer until she stopped right in front of the girl. She grabbed the girl's wrist and pushed it up and backward abruptly.

Anemona hardly had the strength to resist. She fell backward through the crenel, and before she had the chance to realize what had just occurred, she felt herself falling into the void.

- 'Go and get me that disk,' the red-haired lady commanded somebody. A vulture appeared on her shoulder out of nowhere. It flew above the area where the unfortunate girl had fallen and then dove toward her while she was falling fast into the sea. Anemona's disk of Phaistos was being pulled upward currently as she fell, appearing as a desirable target to the vulture that made an effort to grab it and pull it away from her neck. He opened his beak in the air and the disk was almost inside it when his peripheral eyesight was distracted by a big moving surface underneath. It was a textured surface of glowing turquoise-green and cobalt blue scales that blinded his eyes and made it impossible for him to complete his mission.

- 'You can grab ahold of his neck. Just move forward through me,' Roserin told Anemona as soon as the latter one had landed onto the sea dragon's back. Anemona pushed herself forward, right through her friend's ethereal body, and grabbed hold of his neck as tightly as she could. She trembled intensely after her shocking experience, whereas the lady with the beautiful copper hair reacted in quite a different way.

- 'You STUPID bird! You would not be able to grab a little disk in the air even if it was hovering right in front of you,' she shouted outraged with her lip lifted upward due to her great anxiety. She clenched her fists while inhaling and exhaling intensely. Tornadoes of air showed up around her. Tornadoes with flames…

- 'The sky has turned orange. That is definitely NOT a good sign,' Roserin observed. 'What happened up there, Anemona? You sure scared me good when I saw you in the air.'

- 'That woman. She tried to make me hand over my pendant to her,' she said with a trembling voice. 'When I said no, she threw me off the battlements.'

- 'She wants your pendant? The one you are wearing now? Why would she want to have that?' Rosie wondered and pondered.

- 'I don't know,' the traumatized girl replied. 'It is the disc of Phaistos, given to me by my cousin as a present.' She forced herself to talk with a voice that did not come out of her throat easily.

- 'The disc of Phaistos? Well, it seems that your disc has something very special about it, and we need to find out what that is before she finds you for a second time. The shops on 25th Street are loaded with imitation medallions of the Phaistos disk. Why does she need yours so badly?'

Roserin was lost in her thoughts while the sea dragon flew right over the mysterious Pirate ship, the Dia island that had the shape of a laying dragon's body, and also the statues of the three dolphins that rested gracefully in the middle of the roundabout on the road that overlapped the starting point of 25th August street. Henrietta was still lying there on that specific street, but she was not seen by the two girls from above. The dragon kept flying, looking for a safe place to land. Anemona's strength was depleted by the strong shock and her eyes started closing as she leaned on the dragon's neck.

- 'You need some 'Life,' Anemona. Your experience has been traumatic...' Roserin said. 'Dragon! Would you please take us to Anemona's house?' Rosie's new friend changed direction and flew toward a lighter area of the sky that had not turned red yet. He flew straight into a crow-shaped cloud and disappeared.

Bernard and Robert showed up in front of the fish market as the 'Taniwhausaurus Antarcticus' snake-looking fish floated just above them and turned onto 25th August street. The striped hyena went past Bernard and the penguin to make her way toward the fish market. She approached the man who had thrown all of the fish onto the road and bit him fiercely on his leg. The man stopped sorting out the fish into their open wooden boxes; He supported his body with a box by placing his hand on the ridge and he leaned forward and started crying.

- 'I am feeling depressed,' he said and took off his white apron. 'I am going home...'

- 'What the...' his colleague remained speechless.

- 'Let him go, we hardly have any clients today anyhow,' the other partner suggested.

The hyena jumped with two legs into a box that was filled with fish and started eating as much as she could gulp into her stomach. The second fisherman approached the box where the hyena was eating.

- 'Why do I...Why do I feel so ill and heavy all of a sudden?' he panted.

Bernard could easily see why this man felt so ill and heavy all of a sudden. The man's aura was visible to the boy's eyes. It looked like a colorful shiny vapor with holes in it. Twirls of black energy that had generated from the hyena's aura invaded through these holes into the man's personal space. They united and formed a big strong energetic tube which connected with his stomach area and started sucking vital energy away from him.

- 'Oh no...' Bernard said to himself. 'If only I could help him, but he has to ask for help with his own free will,' he whispered and recalled Sir Hipparchus having mentioned to them once that living people were really complicated by nature some times. 'We cannot intervene and help them out unless they feel open enough to receive help,' the Researcher had told them. 'It might sound strange to you, but many of them love to suffer, to get other people's attention. Or they might be expecting to receive help in such a way that their ego would be fed. This is NOT true help, but they can hardly see it. And we could never help them unless they decided to be open to true help.' These were the wise words of the Scientist. 'If we did, the consequences would be disastrous.'

'So, all I can do right now is 'listen' carefully and see whether he asks for true help,' he thought silently and approached the fisherman. The hyena kept sucking vital energy from him. Bernard watched the man losing his strength. 'Just ASK for help! Ask me!!' he urged the fisherman. But the fisherman would not ask for help. Bernard could not bear witness to this man's suffering anymore. It was too horrible a scene for him to endure. He stood in front of a man who was collapsing because he was allowing his ego to prevail. 'I cannot just sit and watch this,' Bernard almost cried. He placed his hands in a certain position in the air and a long golden shiny surface appeared out of thin air. It had a pointy edge on the top, leaning upward. An identical sharp vertical surface pointing downward appeared, and it seemed to be connected in the center with its twin piece. The boy grabbed the tool from its two round handles at their opposite ends on his side and took a similar position that a gardener would have taken when ready to chop off a carnivorous flower's choking vines. As for Robert, the fish's smell had already been detected by his sensitive nostrils.

20. The Rescue…

$\mathcal{A}$ light blue aura appeared from within the middle dolphin of the three statues at the roundabout. An identical etheric body of the dolphin jumped into the air and headed toward 25th August Street. He floated at great speed and then slowed down as he approached Henrietta. The mammal turned its tail to the right side and gave a strong hit to the black octopus that was draining Henrietta like a psychic vampire. The octopus was ejected beyond the three hanging octopuses under the tavern's tent, and the dolphin took such a position in front of Henrietta so that the girl would be able to climb onto his back and grab ahold of him. And so she did. The dolphin took off and Henrietta was now in the air, half unconscious. The supportive compassionate mammal entered a huge cloud in the shape of a big wave. At the entrance, its walls looked as soft as cotton candy. The further they proceeded, the more solid it appeared, like a glacier of ice that was about to come to life any minute and gulp down anything or anybody who had invaded inside.

The dolphin jumped a few more times forward until he reached a deep slide of ice. After a high jump in the air, he let his body slide along the long slide until he reached the bottom; The high speed caused his body to slide ahead and he was then ejected upward along a second identical glacier that looked like a frozen waterfall. As soon as he found himself floating on the highest point, he moved forward and passed through an open entrance which had been built on the glacier's base. A big strong wooden-looking door had both of its shutters wide open. As the dolphin was entering and Henrietta was still lying unconscious on his back, her reflection appeared on one of the golden framed mirrors that had been attached to the shutters' back side. She appeared looking in the mirror's surface with a smile. As soon as they entered, the neoclassical white door closed behind them noisily. This door was made of coconut and its windows had been made of melted sugar. The windows contained stained panels, with a thin delicate black line that formed the shape of a white baby seal on one shutter and a penguin on the other. More delicate frames had been carved around the glass panels, giving the impression of being made of whipped cream the way they twirled around. The door's design was complete with another two carvings on the shutters' base, looking almost as if a child had carved the surface of plush-looking ice cream.

- 'No…I don't see the third octopus on this man's hair,' Stamatis murmured and looked around. 'Henrietta?' he called his friend, 'Where are you?' The boy walked out of the tavern's main space while the young man who served the dishes grabbed a broom and started picking up the thrown food and the broken plates from the floor.

'Now, where would she go?' Stamatis wondered. He decided to walk up the stone-built trail and looked at the big plush fish that had been dressed in a white gown that stood proudly outside one of the two fish foot spas. 'You glow like a star!' he whispered as he noticed the white light that surrounded it. 'You have not seen my friend Henrietta by the way, have you? The fish remained quiet in its position. 'If only you could talk! So, I will just walk further up the trail to the 'four lions' square. Goodbye Fish!' Stamatis walked away, and did not notice the camera that had been hidden within the fish's mouth.

The sky was dark green by now, and the people at a market taking place outside the 'Lotzia,' a central Venetian styled building, lit a few Christmas lights they had hung around their tents. Stamatis admired the variety of the products being displayed. A lady was selling traditional bagpipes, bouzouki musical instruments, mandolin instruments, and she was busy wiping a big lute. Another lady had displayed various kitchen aprons and fabric bags with patched shapes of foxes, owls, and other animals. At an adjacent tent, creations of ceramic nature decorated the table- oil-burners, pots for flowers, mugs, vases, and decorative embossed pieces destined to be hung on the wall.

- 'They are selling marinated anchovy fish here. Where is Roserin to see that? I am sure you would soon smell your favorite fish Rosie, and you would get over here before I said: 'Mia papia ma pia papia, mia papia me papia,'' he expressed one of the most difficult Greek tongue-twisters. Its meaning had to do with a duck that had little ducks. Stamatis looked at the small plastic containers with the fish that rested on a big box filled with ice, which had been placed onto a table that was decorated with a fishnet that held a few entangled seashells. He admired a blue fish-shaped plate that was resting on a shelf, and then he walked past the next partition where its owner was selling jars of honey that had been produced in Crete. The boy looked opposite him and saw a number of Aloe Vera plants and a row of small round jars filled with beeswax ointment, which seemed to contain Aloe Vera gel within it, along with Masticha, a substance that came from another Greek island. This kind of substance was made from some sap that was released by the trees.

- 'Some nice bottles covered with bamboo,' Stamatis said. 'I wonder if they have any submarine,' he thought of the popular vanilla sweet on a spoon that people would dip into a glass filled with water. 'How much I would love to have some right now. And some nice herbs I see.' He sniffed in the air, enjoying the smell of bunches of sage, chamomile, malotira, and other herbs that had been placed within baskets. A bunch of red peppers were hanging from a wooden table within that partition, whereas on the table's surface, a few green apples rested along with a gourd, a scale, a basket filled with sage, and a decorative piece of wood with a painted papyrus on its surface that described the herb's healing qualities. Two red fabric traditional bags were hanging at the sides, and a few red juicy pomegranates had been placed on a shelf in a red piece of cloth. Stamatis noticed there was one more gourd with a copper lid resting in front of a fresh-looking painting that depicted a traditional stone-made oven with two big amphores, an olive tree, and a wooden table in the foreground. The gourd that stood on the left side of the painting looked like a three-dimensional extension of the picture. A little white flower that resembled a jasmine blossom had been painted on the left side. Stamatis stood there for a few seconds and admired the painting.

- 'This smell…It makes me feel as if I were inside this painting,' he whispered. He kept looking for Henrietta. As soon as he walked past the partition with the herb display, a few faces that seemed to be invisible so far on the painting moved toward the direction that the boy had taken. People were not able to detect them in the picture so far unless they consciously started looking for them. These were small faces with light and dark areas that could hide themselves really well from the live people. They gave the impression that they were part of the brush strokes, and only young children that were open and observant were able to spot their facial characteristics. They moved intensely, eager to see where Stamatis was heading. A man who sold bottles of wine was displaying his merchandise on a wine rack and also on two little tables. They seemed to contain wine of the finest quality. These bottles were dark with fine printed labels and an additional label attached by a string around their neck, indicating the wine's quality and origin. Another young man had displayed bottles of liqueur made of roses, cherries, oranges, apricots, and lemons in long rectangle elegant bottles. These were colored orange, yellow, red, green, pink, and dark red. Stamatis' eyes focused on another seller's ceramic mushroom-shaped candle holders, when some loud shouts attracted his attention.

- 'I do NOT want you to even look at me again! Ever!' a woman shouted to a man. 'Go to Hell!' The man approached the partition where the woman was selling her merchandise, grabbed one of the supportive pillars and shook it with rage. All of the glass objects that were placed on her shelves made a warning noise that caused Stamatis to run to the scene. An older man abandoned his seat under the lady's partition and walked toward the younger man.

- 'Uncle, no!' the woman pleaded with him. A few men ran instantly to keep them apart from each other and prevent a fight with possible serious consequences. Stamatis realized there was a dark entity that kept changing shape attached to the attacker's back. It was not clear whether it was a bat, an octopus, or a spider. The boy grabbed one of the Aloe Vera leaves that was resting against its owner's table, and said:

- 'Leaf of the white Light and healing wonders, eject this entity to the True Source!' He hit strongly against the dark entity by using an identical clone of the leaf which permeated out of the live leaf as soon as Stamatis had grabbed it. The leaf went right through all the men's heads and ejected the negative entity far away.

- 'Not another one!' Stamatis gasped as soon as his eyes were drawn by the black vine of a carnivorous plant that had spread all around the woman's body. 'See what happens when you allow your anger control you people?' he expressed his thought mostly to himself while approaching the lady, still holding the Aloe Vera's leaf in his hands. He held it in a vertical position, and with a sewing motion using the leaf's spikes, he cut the vine. White light appeared around the Aloe Vera and with a sudden decisive motion, Stamatis hit the light green carnivorous blossom away from the agitated lady.

- 'Away to the healing light with your blood-sucking flower!' he said and watched the dark entity being ejected into the air, glowing its light green color of negativity, along with its squeezing vines. 'Now...finally some peace between you two people. And I will now look for Henrietta and enjoy your market at the same time.' He tried to encourage himself, but he was still shaking. His face was almost white, still with a very persistent worried expression that was even more persistent than the entity itself. He then turned his head around and saw a dark entity attached on most of the present peoples' shoulders. Some looked like other kinds of carnivorous flowers, others looked like huge light green glowing spiders, others looked like light green glowing witches, and others resembled scorpions, octopuses, snakes, bats, vultures, Pterosaurs, Ornithocheiruses with their colorful crests, and faceless beings that carried no consciousness inside them whatsoever.

- 'Oh my world...' Stamatis whispered. 'I think I have just understood why I was meant to find myself back here,' he murmured. 'Henrietta, WHERE are you? I cannot do this on my own!' A human skeleton that had been attached to an extremely thin girl's shoulder turned his head toward Stamatis and jumped in the air aggressively. His deep purple glow became a lot more intense as he landed right onto the boy's chest. In his bony fist, he held a scythe very tightly. He moved his right arm backward, just about to strike against the boy.

In the meantime, the dolphin that had been carrying Henrietta was now landing in front of Anemona's house. He hovered in front of the door and positioned the girl in such a way that she could lean into the door of the house, and called for help in the dolphin language. He jumped back in the air right after and floated away. The door opened by itself and Henrietta fell unconscious on the floor. Sir Hipparchus turned his head toward the door and an expression of worry appeared on his face. It was now the young face of an eight-year-old. The Scientist's physical appearance had changed once again.

- 'Henrietta dear, what has happened to you?' he asked and pulled the girl into the living room by her arm. As the eight-year-old that he currently was, he hardly had the strength to lift her on the sofa so he just decided to lay her on the carpet. Henrietta opened her eyes.

- 'Life. I need some Life. Please...help,' she whimpered with anxiety. Young Sir Hipparchus grabbed a bottle of 'Faith' drink that was still standing on the table and helped her take a few sips straight from the bottle. While the Researcher was still holding her head, a sudden spasm permeated throughout her body. She glowed in golden light and her eyes were now filled with sparkles and life.

-'Thank you, uncle. I was in such great pain. Such great pain. In a dream, I saw this giant octopus in front of me, hitting me with its tentacles on my sides. The pain in my nerves was unbearable. It was so intense. And I was feeling so helpless. So helpless…But you know, it is strange, in this dream, I was NOT me. It was Bernard in my place,' she revealed, and the Scientist took a facial expression that indicated compassion.

- 'You were Bernard,' he said. 'His spirit connected with yours…' He pondered. 'You felt Bernard's internal pain.'

- 'Pain?' Henrietta asked with worried eyes.

- 'He is aching about something and he may not know what it is that he aches about.'

- 'Aching about something and not knowing what it is that he aches about? How is that possible?' She looked at the Scientist and spread her palms open to her right and her left side simultaneously.

- 'Well, it is. What we feel inside us is more real than anything else we may be seeing around us. And it will keep bothering us until we become aware and do something about it. Otherwise, it will remain and haunt us forever. Sometimes we forget what it was that once caused us pain so that we could focus on the moment and do whatever we needed to survive with the tools we currently had until a more appropriate time came to deal with it. With time we can obtain other tools that will help us overcome this specific obstacle. It may feel cruel at times, but these obstacles give us the motivation to take action, to search, and therefore find. To experience, and therefore grow like the souls that we are. I prefer seeing them as tools that help us become the highest self that we can possibly be. Bernard cannot see them as tools yet. He feels them like torturing piranhas that bite away his soul. In this dream of yours, his soul is asking for help from YOUR soul. It has not come into his consciousness yet that the answer lies inside him.'

- 'Can we tell him that?' Henrietta asked him.

- 'We can tell him as many times as we wish; He will hear it multiple times but he will only absorb it if he decides to be open to the answer. The 'one' valid answer.'

- 'Which one is that?' The girl wanted to know more.

- 'The one that will free his soul,' he replied. 'And he is the only one who will recognize it.'

- 'So there is only ONE answer for every single one of us,' Henrietta concluded.

- 'There are 'many' answers for every single one of us, but the answers that may be freeing to my soul may not be freeing to your soul. We are each destined to experience our own adventure and search to discover our own personal unlocking keys.

- 'Unlocking keys…' Henrietta repeated in a pondering way. 'But why do we have to suffer in life like that? Why can we not have these keys from the beginning of our life, and enjoy a happy time with each other?'

- 'We do not have to suffer in life. Whatever we have experienced in our existence, it has been our 'choice,' even an incident we might think we would never choose consciously to happen. But think about this: Imagine your life without any negative situations occurring in it. The positive would eventually fill you up, and without the proper balance, it would start turning gradually into negative to fill the void inside you. Let's say you want to keep eating cotton candy and submarine vanilla all the time. After some time, you would not want to see them in front of you anymore, not to smell them, no less to taste them.

- 'I think that somehow it makes sense,' the girl agreed. 'When I looked like a birthday cake's garnish, I liked it in the beginning. My eyes saw something different in me. Something sweet. I loved the discovery of it and it was also something new. But as time went by, I got tired of smelling chocolate all the time. I felt I needed some smell-free time for myself.' The Scientist chuckled. 'So it seems that Bernard decided once to grow as a soul, in a specific way that we do not yet know,' she thought.

- 'And so have YOU. And I. And everybody else. But we do not consciously remember the date of the agreement that we made in our spirit life. If we did, things would have been a lot easier for us in the first place, and we would not have the chance to transform with our own free will. We would be tempted to burn that contract at any time so our self would not reach its full potential. We would remain slaves of our own ego instead of putting it aside by our own free will for Spirit to replace it and bring us everlasting peace. Never focus on the tree, my girl. Always look for the 'woods,' he concluded. Henrietta looked confused.

- 'Where are we? I have never been here before, but it sure looks beautiful!' Roserin wondered as soon as the sea dragon landed at a private-looking area, right behind a highly decorated main entrance where a well-dressed guard was checking out who was entering. 'I see,' she said after having taken a rather revealing expression that indicated she had felt something inside her. 'The answer I get inside my head is 'Royal Mare Hotel.' Anemona looked at her new friend, surprised. 'I know…This is a new characteristic to you. When I need an answer, it will eventually pop up inside my head! It may happen to you one day once you get connected to Spirit! Now, let's see why we are here. Look at those beautiful tuyia trees! I have never seen such tall and fluffy healthy trees!' They both started descending the long road with the breath-taking trees that were lined up one next to the other along the road.

- 'I am in Heaven!' Anemona whispered. The dragon waited for them where he had landed. That was right outside the hotel's spa in the parking space that had been designed especially for dragons. The sky was not dark red at this place; There was plenty of light and a beautiful orange sunset fell onto the bungalows' snow-white chimneys, making them glow in a unique way. This orange light behind the palm trees as the sun was hiding behind the mountains offered an atmosphere of total peace and harmony. The negativity that had started spreading in the town center had not poisoned this sacred looking place yet.

Roserin and Anemona walked past the white bungalows with the white wooden frames around the windows and the brown protective railings on the verandas. As they were reaching the end of the long welcoming road, the very impressive main entrance of the reception glowed in orange light from a distance, within an open space that contained neatly built stone walls and ancient Greek busts.

- 'What a beautiful place to be! And look at those busts! I have never seen such beauty before. Not even where we currently live!' Rosie stared as if she had been hypnotized. A black crow that flew in front of her face woke her up.

'Now let's go inside and see what surprises await us!' Rosie tried to help Anemona focus her attention on something pleasant in an effort to help her get over her shock.

The two girls were now inside at the reception area, with their mouths wide open. The area was much bigger than they had expected, with a big shimmery chandelier hanging from the ceiling. The main desk was just on the left side, where the receptionists were helping a group of British customers. Anemona's attention was drawn by the stone carved statue of a mermaid that decorated the reception's side desk. Roserin, on the other hand, was drawn by a small internal pond that had been built in a nearby hall outside the toilets. She noticed it right after she had admired from a distance a little bag in the shape of a wolf in one of the hotel's internal shops.

- 'Look at this! How cute!' Rosie instantly loved the neat little pond that included a fountain and two parallel rows of a few rectangular flower pots, with the fountain placed in between them. A design made up of small wooden circles, triangles, and other shapes on the background wall offered a variety of feelings to all the different visitors. A delicate geometrical design decorated the glass that separated the toilets on the right and left side of the pond, whereas a few tiny but strong lights up on the ceiling were currently on. Roserin grabbed a stone from within the pots that hosted some Aloe Vera plants. She dipped half of it in the water.

- 'It looks so pretty now that it's wet. I'd better put it back quickly before anyone thinks they have lost their mind!' She smiled at the thought of a stone appearing in the air, and nobody holding it as live people might think. 'It is not easy being a spirit without a physical body anymore. You need to keep 'sanity' in mind,' she expressed her thought to Anemona. 'Although some foreigners still see goats in the olive trees and think they need to be seen by a doctor!' she laughed. 'But enough with those funny goats. We have to see where we can find some Life bottles for you.' She got up from the pond's surrounding wall and walked past the mermaid statue that looked frozen in a certain position.

Anemona looked at her.

- 'She is ugly,' she thought and her face took an expression of shock and disgust.

- 'Well, you cannot expect every mermaid to look like The Little Mermaid, can you?' the mermaid moved her head and talked. Anemona gasped and moved three steps backward. She looked at the statue that had turned its head toward her, and which had released a few little stones and dust onto the main desk during her neck's rotation. 'So…you are looking for Life bottles. How tasty they are!' she said and turned her head back to its initial position. Anemona approached her when she saw she looked as frozen as a statue once again. She stood there, still, staring at the mermaid as if she had found herself under a spell. Had this mermaid just come to life and talked to her? Or was it a spiritual experience? Or did she just lose her mind because of the hot southern wind outside? She kept staring. She could not take her eyes off her. The magic she felt right now in her heart was beyond words. It kept her frozen in the same spot, unable to move, whereas Roserin had returned to the sea dragon by now. She approached him and climbed onto his back as he kneeled down.

- 'I am sure Anemona will do fine. She will find her Life bottles wherever they may be hidden, and at the same time she will be safe here, away from that woman. Now, we need to go to a very special place, dragon. It is absolutely imperative that we do so. Fly me to the 'Akashic Records' as fast as you can!' The dragon flew down the long road with the tuyia trees; He jumped into the air and flapped his little wings. The last warm rays of the sun gave a warm glow to his air-thin scales, which released a slight mesmerizing sound that would make any soul's hair stand up at once. It was the sound of a few pieces of rice paper, so thin, so delicate, so precious…

21. A Trapped Spirit...

With a decisive motion, Bernard snipped the black energetic cord between the fisherman and the striped hyena. This giant pair of scissors was so sharp that the cord was separated instantly into two hanging tubes. The hyena saw Bernard and ran away in fear. The fisherman looked toward Bernard too, and his eyes popped out.

- 'Do not be afraid. I will not harm you!' Bernard said to him. But the man started sweating. In his own eyes, it was not a young boy that reflected in front of him at the moment. Despite Bernard's words, the man looked terrified. He stepped back, turned around, and ran away in panic.

- 'Why is he so scared of me?' the boy wondered. His eyes fell onto a little round mirror which the fishermen had positioned against a crate filled with fish. He approached and looked inside it. He saw the reflection of a big-headed boy with a missing face. He gasped. He stepped backward. 'What happened to my face?' he thought in panic and ran toward 25th August Street. 'Nooooo!' he shouted, confused and terrified with his discovery. Where had his face gone? And why did his head look so big?

The striped hyena saw the boy running away, so she stopped her escape back to the museum. She smelled in the air.

- 'That is my most favorite smell: Fear!' she thought. She changed her direction and ran behind Bernard. Bernard ran past the fish foot spa, the cute small welcoming traditional shops, and then he disappeared within a cloud of fog. He did not seem to come out of it into the local market where Stamatis currently was, and where people walked around with negative entities attached on their shoulders. A skeleton sat firmly on a ten-year-old girl's shoulder. He had taken two bones out of his side ribs and banged the girl on her head. At first, the rhythm was slow, then it became slightly quicker, after a while it was even quicker, after a few seconds it was much quicker, and in the end, it became extremely quick.

- 'Come on Daphne, why are you being so slow? We will be late!' a lady who seemed to be her mother urged her.

- 'I have a headache mom,' the girl replied.

- 'A headache? No wonder with the southern wind and the sand from Africa we are getting today,' she made the assumption and put her hand behind the girl's back. 'I am not feeling very well either. I feel weak for some reason. It seems we both need a bite to eat,' she said and kept walking with the girl next to her when a bat appeared on her own back. The nocturnal bird's head leaned into the lady's neck with its teeth firmly attached to her skin. It seemed to be sucking her blood with obsession when a little boy in shabby clothes approached the lady and asked for money. The bat turned its head toward the boy and with its lips pulled upward revealing its sharp teeth, it hissed like a snake. This particular bat seemed to be blind. The lady turned around as soon as the boy pulled on her coat.

- 'Get away from me! I have no money to waste on parasites of your kind!' She grabbed a lute that she found in front of her at the instrument section of the market and waved it toward the boy, while the lady who had been trying to sell them came out of her post in astonishment and ran toward her to stop her.

At a part of the center of town near where the main fish market used to take place, clouds of mist started spreading near some narrow paths. The tiny carnelian painted church that had been built within a complex of buildings and an underground garage was surrounded by clouds. Only a few plants and Christmas trees that had been planted around it along with a big silver water samovar for the visitors were visible. Bernard and Robert stepped down from within a cloud that floated in front of the entrance and walked straight into the church, closing the wooden door behind them. On their left side, a few candles were burning in a box that was filled with tiny stones and water that had been placed into a metallic partition. A few icons had been hung on the walls with Mary and Jesus; A vase with a bunch of white lilies was also a part of the decoration on the right corner, right under a big icon that depicted Mary holding Jesus in her arms. On the icon's base, a number of thin silver miniature embossed images had been hung by the believers, depicting every single person's wish that they hoped would be granted by the holy mother. At the front, the installation of a rope suggested that people were not allowed to step beyond the slightly raised marble, where space was considered to be sacred. Bernard looked upward gradually and saw a glass tabletop covered with a shiny silky tablecloth of small sewn crosses in the colors of red and gold. Underneath where the tablecloth laid was a red velvet curtain with a big sewn golden-red cross.

On his left side, he noticed a wooden book rack on a tall wooden base which had been carved to depict a peacock standing on a vine, and a protruding cross as a separate image. Another beautifully carved base was supporting the box with the lit-up candles on the very left side. A vine had been carved on the front surface, with a protruding cross in the middle. Right between the candle box and the book rack, a window with three smaller round windows, one on top of the other, offered a sense of peace, protection, and balance inside the sacred space. One of the reasons that contributed to the feeling of these blessings could be that the glass pieces were dyed in colors of yellow, red, green, and blue. An arch had been built on the top of the long narrow window. Bernard looked at the church's upper part, which consisted of a dome with eight smaller windows all around in the same style. What he noticed next was the silver candle lantern that was hanging in front of the big icon of the Virgin Mary and Jesus. And finally, his eyes focused on the main icon that was surrounded by a carved frame with the delicate design of a vine.

- 'What happened to my face? Help me! What happened to my face?' he asked the Holy Mother while grabbing the icon's frame firmly with both of his hands. Mary seemed to be unresponsive. So did Jesus. Bernard kept staring at her face. 'Why do you never give us an answer? Why do you leave us on our own?' he asked as he let go of the frame.

- 'She has not abandoned you,' a voice sounded behind him. 'YOU are the ones who do not make the effort to listen. But it is not too late,' the voice continued. Bernard turned around and saw a familiar figure sitting behind the book rack. He had long hair and stubble on his chin; He was wearing a long black velvet cloak and an outfit with long wide sleeves. A long purple chevron amethyst crystal wand fit firmly within a silver frame around his neck. Four books had filled the four available casings of the book rack. And all four books displayed the same cover. When Bernard approached, he distinguished a three-dimensional image that depicted an antique lamp made of glass with a round base. As soon as he moved slightly to the right side, a face appeared on this image- a face that was trapped deep within the glass lamp. To his great astonishment, he recognized his own face inside. When he moved to the left, the cover seemed to be open from above, but this time without his face inside it. The colors were vivid and there was enough depth of field within the two images to make the boy feel that he was able to enter into the cover when he spread his hand onto the surface.

- 'Is this where my face has gone?' he asked the Calligrapher.

- 'For the present time...' the Calligrapher replied.

- 'What do I have to do to get it back? Bernard asked. The white mask of an ancient Greek God appeared hovering in front of the area where his face should have been. Its expression looked distressed.

-'The best person to give you the answer is NOT I.'

- 'Then WHO is?' the boy asked in anxiety.

- 'Your own self,' the man replied.

-'My own self?' Bernard was not expecting such an answer. And it was at this moment that he felt frustrated. 'If I knew how to get my face back, I would not be asking for help,' he commented.

- 'So you want to have an immediate answer.' The Calligrapher noticed that Bernard stood there confused. Why was this man not giving him an answer? All he was interested in was receiving a clear answer to see what needed to be done to get his face back.

'There is NOT just 'one' magical answer out there, my boy. There are 'many' magical answers that wait to be picked up by people who will appreciate and recognize their function and compatibility in their own lives.'

- 'But I just want to have my face back!' Bernard said anxiously.

- 'You WILL get your face back if you really want to,' the man with the cloak replied.

- 'HOW?' Bernard asked in despair.

- 'My boy, the question you should be asking is NOT 'how'. The question you should be asking is 'when.''

- 'When?' his new little friend asked with intense anticipation.

- 'Since you are asking me, and you seem eager to learn, we cannot yet tell when that moment will be. Time is an interesting concept you see. Time does not exist in the universe. It has been created by people. The best answer I can give you at this moment is to count by 'Spirit,' NOT by 'minute.''

- 'Count by Spirit?' Bernard looked at the Calligrapher, puzzled.

-'When your Spirit is ready to accept the valid answers is the time your face will return to its initial place.'

- 'When I am ready to accept the 'valid' answers...' Bernard repeated. He was not certain what to do with the nonspecific answer. It was an answer, but not exactly the sort of answer he was expecting to receive. He looked toward the floor and pondered on this answer. 'But which are the valid answers?' He spread his palms open. 'And where will I find them?' He looked back at where the man was standing, but to his great surprise, the Calligrapher had disappeared. The four books were still lying on the book rack. Bernard approached the book that was lying at the man's side and touched the cover with his fingers in an effort to lift it. He had opened it halfway the way he had grabbed it.

- 'You must have done something that was not exactly allowed,' The Calligrapher re-appeared at Bernard's front right corner, where Bernard himself was standing before. The boy let the cover fall back onto its initial resting position, startled. He was not expecting the Calligrapher to return and continue this confusing discussion. He froze like a child that had been caught red-handed while doing something naughty. He stood with his mask's brows raised and mouth open.

'Sometimes we may want the best for others and do things that are supposed to improve their situation, but at some point, we are surprised to discover that what we thought would have been the best for them was actually harmful to them,' the Calligrapher pointed out. 'Have you felt this way recently?' he asked Bernard.

- 'Yes,' Bernard nodded and his hovering mask looked embarrassed. In the meantime, Robert had wandered off to the local fish market that he felt was very near to them. His friend had pulled him away from the market right at the time he had opened his beak to insert a fresh-smelling sea bass inside it. He HAD to find another one.

-'I see,' the man said and remained silent. A few seconds passed in total silence. An Angel came out of an icon and his steps were light to such an extent that he almost floated above the ground. With every step he took, there was the mesmerizing sound of tissue paper beneath his feet. Bernard could see some distortion of the environment under the Angel's feet, appearing as if a number of invisible sheets of tissue paper had blended with the environment in the same way that chameleons blended with the environment they found themselves in. This Angel was wearing a white long cape with a hood. His long, curly, blond hair emitted golden light. He moved toward the arched door and disappeared right through it.

- 'There was this fisherman who needed help. This hyena was drawing energy from him through a black cord. He was losing all his life. So, I used the scissors and cut it off. He saw me and he got scared of me. He ran away. Then I saw on a mirror that my head was big and I had no face,' Bernard described his misfortune.

- 'You cut off the cord. From a man who had not asked for help.'

- 'But he needed help! The hyena was draining…'

- 'Did he say that he 'needed' help?' the Calligrapher interrupted him.

- 'No, but…'

- 'If he did not say he needed help, then you were not supposed to intervene. He had the 'free will' to ask for help, and he also had the 'free will' to NOT ask for help,' the Calligrapher brought this new information to the boy's attention.

- 'But why would somebody chose to suffer?' Bernard was stunned.

- 'People do. They use suffering as a tool to draw other people's attention. You have just ruined this man's pay off, and you have also scared him away. He saw you. He was not prepared in his psyche to see you just yet,' he paused, giving Bernard some time to realize what had occurred.

- 'I do not understand. He was suffering. And it was the hyena that made him suffer. He did not want this,' Bernard said.

- 'He did not want this in his 'conscious' mind. But you would be surprised to see one day how many negative situations people attract in their lives with their own free will. Their OWN free will. And they cannot see it unless they make the decision consciously to look very carefully.'

- 'So did this man 'want' this hyena to come and suck his energy?' Bernard asked in disbelief.

- 'He did not ask for help. Not even from our own world,' the Calligrapher stated. 'You ruined his ego's wish to be in the center of attention.'

- 'Is that good or bad?' Bernard worried.

- 'Good? Bad? These are just words. There is only 'one' energy and people decide in what way to use it. This energy cannot be defined by words.'

- 'But have I harmed him?' The boy was not content with the answer he had received. His ego was looking for a simple 'yes' or 'no.'

- 'You have scared him away. But he will recover. All he needs right now is 'Time.''

- 'Time'…Bernard repeated in a lower voice. He tried to understand. When he was still alive in this world, he always had the impression that spirits knew everything about life. But how wrong he was. Here he was in the world of spirits himself, and he had to keep learning. Apparently, he had not escaped school just yet. He looked at the book's cover and saw his face still trapped within the calligrapher's lamp. Or was it 'Bernard's lamp'?

- 'You are a boy with much goodness inside you. You may be in a bit of a hurry sometimes, but you will learn in time when the proper moment is to take action. Now…please go and look under the red curtain. Something is waiting for you,' he prompted him.

Bernard turned left around the book rack and walked toward the sacred area. He passed through the restraining rope and kneeled close to the velvet curtain. Using his right hand, he lifted it. A small oval-shaped mirror appeared. He lifted it and saw his reflection. His head seemed to be somehow smaller now, and half of one eye had returned to his missing face. It was blinking on a broken piece of face that looked like a piece of porcelain on a doll. The fragment of face was white with slight traces of cracks. His other eye, another half of his eye, his nose, and his mouth were still missing.

-'My eye has returned!' he said excitedly and turned around to share his feelings of enthusiasm. The Calligrapher, however, was not there. Once again, he had vanished. Bernard looked carefully, but he could not see him anywhere. With the mirror in his hand, he got up and walked through the rope for a second time. He noticed that three of the four books that had rested on the book rack had disappeared too. All except one. 'Oh, no…I am not going to open it this time,' he whispered to himself but his right arm was raised by an unseen force and his fingers moved on their own, rubbing each other at the same time. His arm pulled him toward the book, and despite his attempts to pull it back by the use of his left hand, his fingers managed to grab the cover and open it wide. Two sentences had been written on the right blank page:

"Your level of life has dropped.

Drink from the silver springs of the big round dome."

'The silver springs of the big round dome?' Bernard wondered. 'Now where could that be?' He looked around to see whether the Calligrapher had reappeared. But he saw he was still alone instead. 'He does not mean the waterflows at the cave that we visited, does he? I need to 'think.'' His hand moved instantly on its own for a second time and turned to the next page. Another sentence appeared.

"Stop thinking. Use your intuition."

Bernard sighed and walked toward the door with the white mask still hovering in front of his face. He opened it and walked outside. The mist still moved there, and the place was unusually quiet. He looked to his right side and decided to walk around the church. A number of plants appeared from within the fog, one by one. Some of the little tuyia trees had been decorated with big red delicate Christmas balls. When he arrived at the other side of the church, having walked the semi-circle behind it, he saw the big silver water samovar with a cross on top of it standing right in front of him.

- 'It does look like a dome. And it has four different taps. Is this where I need to drink from?' he wondered as the mist became thicker. A pair of footsteps sounded at a close distance. They belonged to a priest, who was heading to the church. He put his hand inside his pocket and took out a set of keys. He was getting closer and closer. Bernard felt that this person had the intention of grabbing the blessed water-filled samovar away from him and locking it eventually inside the church. The boy had to drink as quickly as possible. He turned one of the taps and grabbed one of the silver cups that had been placed on the table for the visitors. As he was placing the cup under the water of Life, the priest with the characteristic tall hat grabbed the silver dome in his arms and walked inside the church.

- 'No! I do need some of this water!' Bernard shouted. But the priest could not hear him. The boy was in the spirit world, and the priest was in the world of live people. The latter one locked the door after having placed the silver samovar inside, and put the keys back into his pocket. Then he walked away...

'What do I do now? I am not feeling very well. Is it because of the mist?' he wondered. 'How do I get inside?' The Angel who had exited the church was now approaching the door and Bernard watched him. The angel stopped, took one step forward, and was now inside it.

- 'But of course! I will knock on the door and the Angel will open it for me!' Bernard thought. He walked toward the door and raised his fist to knock. As he touched the wooden door, his fist went right through the wood. His eyes popped out by surprise.

- 'Stupid me! I am in the spirit world now, I totally forgot!!' He looked behind him and sighed with relief when he saw that his cousins and friends were not currently present to laugh at his behavior as a live human being. He entered through the closed door. As he entered, he saw the Angel's back disappearing into the blessed icon. A blond curl of his hair was severed as he stepped into the icon and it landed in the sacred area. Bernard did not notice. His main priority was to receive his holy drink, as he felt his strength depleting. His vision was impaired too. He put the silver decorative cup under one of the taps that had a cross on top and turned it until it started flowing. Some holy water came out surrounded by golden healing light. He closed the tap and started sipping the drink of Life eagerly.

- 'Ah!' he thought, 'That's exactly what I needed.' He looked for the can for dirty cups in which to throw his silver cup. But he could not see one. He looked behind the book rack; He looked next to the main icon to see whether there was a tiny bin that he might have missed, but he could not see any around. 'Could there be one under the red curtain?' he whispered. He walked toward the sacred area and stopped. He saw the Angel's blond curl on the shiny marble and lifted it. Some tiny pieces of gold leaf were released and stuck to his hand, even though they were not detectable on the curl itself. 'Is this the Angel's hair?' Bernard wondered, and admired the natural blond shade. 'It looks so light and warm. I take it it would be fine with you if I kept it, since it was on the floor?' he asked and then decided to put it inside his pants' pocket. 'Thank you. It will give me courage and remind me of your presence.' He closed his eyes for a few seconds and stood there feeling grateful. An image appeared in front of him. He saw the Angel coming out of an icon, holding a beautiful mirror in his hands. The mirror had a nice Baroque-style golden decorative frame with black cavities that indicated the passing of time. An intense golden light that emerged from the frame hid the black traces. There was only light. Bernard saw his reflection on the mirror. He saw his innocent, laughing, cheerful self, dressed in nice olive green corduroys and an attractive soft looking dark red sweater with wide knitted plaits on the surface. On his head, he was wearing a red woolly hat that ended in a tail, making him look like one of Santa's elves. He looked at his feet and his shoes looked unique too. They were shiny red shoes with a front that split and curled both to the right and to the left side, causing it to resemble a joker's shoe. There were two bells attached to each shoe, one on each side of both split tips. Bernard opened his eyes and the image disappeared. He smiled. His next thought was to grab the little oval mirror that was lying on the sacred marble level. He took it in his hands and looked inside. He still had that one chip containing half of one eye on his face, with the second eye, his nose, and his mouth missing. He formed a pondering expression that appeared in half of his eye.

The one book that belonged to the Calligrapher and still remained on the book rack suddenly opened wide. One of the pages was torn out of it and floated toward Bernard's head, sticking onto his face. Or rather his hovering ancient Greek mask.

"Stamatis needs your help.

Now go!"

This was the message that had been written on the surface, and a mesmerizing singing voice sounded, reading the message out loud to the boy. He grabbed the sheet and gasped in surprise. He turned around and wondered whether to place it back inside the book. A strong shove to his back caused him to almost lose his balance. Was it the Calligrapher? Was it the Angel? Apparently, somebody wanted him to rush and meet his cousin.

- 'Alright, I am leaving!' he assured the invisible entity. 'I am going!' And he let the sheet of paper land on the floor. He walked through the door and disappeared into the mist. The torn piece of paper that was now lying on the floor flowed upward. It moved toward the book and landed in its former position, connected again with its adjacent page. No trace indicated that it had been ripped apart. The book was then closed. The image with the glass lamp was still there on the cover. Bernard's trapped face and hands were still visible from within the lamp's glass.

And how was Robert doing during his quest to discover the fish he had smelled? The penguin had found the fish market by the use of his nostrils and had picked a bream fish with his right flipper. This was a type of fish that caused people to have the most intense, continuous, and noisy gas release ever! He had placed it above his open beak when the man who sold them grabbed the fish away from him.

- 'I see no air today, yet my fish are floating in the vacuum. Must be mini-tornadoes…' he talked to himself and placed the bream back into its crate. Once again, the hungry penguin lost the raw delicacy from almost within his beak.

22. The Grapple.

$\mathcal{A}$ big red blossom of a Rafflesia Arnoldii flower with white bumpy spots on its round petals grew at the Koule castle's entrance. It was so massive that it could easily hide a human being within its petals. Several host vines started to emerge from within the brick's slits and grew half a meter long as soon as a visitor turned their head in another direction. Two more blossoms of luminous red petals with yellow fades in between appeared on the castle's outside walls. The bumpy spots on these petals looked yellow this time. Within the central hollow part of this flower, a big round core that looked like a yellow planet was firmly connected with red spikes protruding from its surface. Its yellow center was luminous, making it look like a volcano in its active moments. The atmosphere now had an intense orange color from the sand that came from Africa, which made the city look as if it was part of planet Mars. The sand almost hid the flowers with their impressive fluorescent colors. Some more blossoms started to emerge.

Past the heavy wooden door at the entrance, a father turned his head and looked at his little girl.

- 'Which side do you prefer? Left or right?' he asked her as soon as they arrived in front of the two separate corridors. The right side consisted of the ramp that led upstairs to the roof, and on the left side were the stairs that also led upstairs.

- 'I want this way.' The girl showed another corridor that led to some sealed rooms, sealed by the strong wooden beams that had been placed in front of another set of heavy wooden doors. They walked in that direction when some dust along with a rain of little stones fell right behind them on the floor.

-'I think there is also a prison down here somewhere,' the father said. Suddenly, two thick green fluorescent vines moved around their waists and pulled them toward the wall. The girl screamed. A mother with her young boy ran toward the side where the scream came from when more host vines permeated through the wall and wrapped themselves around their bodies too. The vines pulled them next to some big pale boulders, along with a whole class of young children who had entered the main corridor with their teachers. A grandmother, a grandfather, and their little granddaughter did not escape the host vines' squeezing activities either.

- 'Let me off this wall at once, or I'll grab your little flower in there and turn it into a stuffed 'dolmadaki' meal!' an American man shouted as soon as another Rafflesia Arnoldii flower grew on the wall opposite him.

- 'What's a 'dolmadaki' meal?' a friend of his that had been trapped right beside him asked.

- 'The courgette flowers stuffed with rice that we had for lunch. I did tell you that while we were eating, but you never listen to what I say, do ya?' the young man replied.

- 'What is happening?' a girl asked in fear.

- 'Don't worry, it must be a new attraction in the castle!' a classmate of hers who was being pulled tighter and tighter to the wall said to her while he was losing his voice.

- 'A new attraction? Are you sure?' the girl asked him, when all of a sudden the few lights that were on inside turned off.

- 'See? They have turned off the lights so that we can admire these fluorescent flowers!' the boy tried his best to calm her down. 'See how impressive they look?' he said to her while he choked.

- 'But this is very tight.' the girl said. 'I hope you are right.'

- 'Sure I am right!' he coughed. 'You see those cowboys opposite us? They must be actors! They are funny too!'

- 'You think so?' the girl asked her classmate. He did not reply.

- 'What ith that horrible thmell?' another boy from the same class asked. 'Doeth it come from the medithine my dentitht put in my mouth? It ith tho dithguthting!' he struggled to speak.

-'I think it comes from the flowers,' a girl covered her nose with her hand, as best she could move her tied-up hand onto her face.

- 'It smells like goat's shit!' an overweight boy made a facial expression of disgust.

-'It smells like your fart!' a friend of his teased him and all of their classmates burst into laughter. Then they covered their noses quickly once again with the backs of their hands.

- 'Look at that! My fingerprints glow when I bring them close to the thicker vines!' a boy with glasses shouted in excitement.

- 'Yes, you are right!' a girl answered. 'Poooooh!' she whispered to herself, and kept observing her glowing fingertips excitedly, which reflected the same light green color of the vines.

- 'Mommy, daddy…What is going on?' another girl asked her parents who had also been trapped on the wall's cold surface.

- 'Don't worry dear,' her father replied, 'I am sure it is part of the program,' he said, but his eyes looked worried.

- 'Idane tuto na?' an old tied up man asked a friend of his what was going on in his Cretan dialect.

- 'Da kateho? E tuto ne to pragma den eksanaginike,' his friend replied to him in the local Cretan accent saying that he had no idea what was going on and that nothing similar had ever happened before.

- 'Mom?' a little boy asked his mother, both firmly captured against the wall.

-'Yes, dear…' his mother replied.

- 'What is going to happen now?'

-'Somebody will release us, sweetie, at some point eventually,' she answered and looked at the other people who had been grabbed by the strong vines opposite them. One of them happened to have a knife in their pocket.

- 'I have had ENOUGH with this joke!' An overweight lady bumped her head backward against the sensitive planet-shaped core of a Rafflesia flower that had grown right behind her, smashing it into tiny pieces. The flower's tentacle vines loosened up, and the lady could now move her hands out of the loops that had been keeping her a prisoner. She slipped smoothly onto the stone floor and continued her tour of the Koule castle. Unfortunately, other people did not see the way she had freed herself since they had focused their attention on the fluorescent vines themselves. Nobody had, apart from the American man.

- 'Now THAT is the lady I have been waiting for my whole life!' He admired her and bumped his own head against the central spiky core of the big orange Rafflesia blossom that had grown behind his own head. 'And I DID feel like having some jam this morning for breakfast!' he said as soon as he smashed the lava looking center, 'although, you do look a lot more like one of those smash surprise cakes to me!' he said after he had turned his head around to admire the damage he had caused to this restraining, torturing flower. 'But I have to say, my dear flower, that you smell a lot worse than my own ass after having wandered for a whole week in the desert and outrun the worst hurricanes of your wildest dreams. These hurricanes would have turned your little blossom into a colored cuscus with a hot stew inside, so be thankful I am in a good mood today! Pretty girl, I am on my way!' he said and walked behind the lady who had freed herself on her own.

- 'Hey! Where you going?' his friend asked as soon as he saw the man with the cowboy hat walk past him. 'What about 'me?' He moved violently, trying to cause his own release, but in vain. The Rafflesia blossom's core that had grown behind him was still intact.

A young student, thirty years old, was being held a prisoner too by the strong host vines. Her parents were being held right next to her.

- 'It is all YOUR fault,' her father said to her. 'YOU and your CHOICES to come over here to this place.'

- 'HOW was I supposed to know?' the young lady said.

- 'You could have chosen another place to visit,' her mother replied. 'You could have chosen for example the Christmas market where we could very well socialize and sell our own products at the same time,' she said in a disapproving tone, and her daughter rolled her eyes.

- 'Mother! THIS is the place I wanted to visit! If you prefer the Christmas market, then you are free to go to the Christmas market. I paid for the tickets with my own money and it has been your decision to join me,' the lady replied. Her mother made a grumpy face and turned her head toward her husband.

- 'What else do you want me to tell her?' she asked him.

In the meantime, the Rafflesia flowers had multiplied inside and outside the castle. Some of them were intense pink with bumpy lighter pink spots on their petals. Others were orange with light green spots on their velvet-like surface. They had spread on the stone-built wall that led toward the central roundabout of the city with the monument of the three dolphins. There were more blossoms along the 25th August Street that led to the Christmas market. Some of them were still big round bulbs, whereas others had bloomed already, and their host vines had captured some more people as they walked by, keeping them prisoners against the old Neoclassical houses' walls until they could find a way to free themselves. The blossoms were really big and beautiful. The more impressive they were, the greater their ability to hypnotize people with their unique, exotic beauty was. Until the moment people sensed their bad rotting smell. This was the moment when they realized they had fallen into a really big, well-planned trap. From that moment onward, it was in their hands to discover the means to free themselves from the smelly flowers and their unpleasant consequences.

- 'It smells like my Chinese flatmate's cooking!' a student commented while he was hanging from the round dome at the inner part of the Koule castle.

- 'Yes, we are now all roasted,' a friend of his replied as he was tied up right next to him.

- 'WHO is SHE?' his friend asked him all of a sudden.

- 'I have no idea dude, but she sure looks like a babe!'

- 'Has she come to free us?' the boy asked.

-'Look at that shiny long hair!' His friend admired her and was apparently unable to close his mouth again.

- 'I love the color too! It looks like those juicy beetroots,' he said, forgetting his current situation as a prisoner. 'It seems she really loves red, and it goes really well with her green dress!'

- 'What is she doing?' his friend asked when he saw the lady approaching a big red blossom that had turned its head toward her. She looked into its planet-like core and spoke some words to it. As soon as she did that, all of the flowers turned their heads to their captives' faces; They pulled back for a second and spit out some kind of liquid onto peoples' ears.

- 'What is happening to me?' the little boy's mother shouted as soon as she saw her fingers turning into stone. She moved her stone fingers with the hinges that had materialized, while the rest of her arm was now transforming into a puppet's arm. At the same time, a white mushroom started to grow between her and her son on the wall. The stone kept spreading onto her neck, her head, her other arm, her chest, her stomach area, and both of her legs. She also found she had some strings attached to her head and on the surface of her hands which led to a wooden cross above her head.

- 'Mpampa?' a girl addressed her dad in the Greek language as soon as she saw him in the form of a marionette. 'Would you give me some money to buy a nice woolly hat I have seen? It seems to be warm enough too!'

-'Sure, dear! Here you are!' he replied and handed her ten euros. A white mushroom started growing on the wall in between them.

- 'Here is some money for you to buy a book that teaches us how to get out of this mess. It has been all your fault. We could have been socializing at the Christmas market now while earning some more money at the same time,' the mother said to her adult daughter and handed fifteen euros to her.

- 'Excuse me, but HOW was I supposed to know?' the lady replied to her mother-puppet. 'I see that the flowers have spread toward the center. It is no different out there,' she said while she looked through a pair of binoculars that she held with her right hand as close to her eyes as possible. While she looked all around her through the binoculars, a white mushroom started growing on the wall in between them, and another one in between the mother and her husband.

- 'No. It is YOUR fault,' the mother insisted. 'You are useless,' she commented, and her daughter took on a sad expression.

- 'Granddad! Would you give me some money to buy some fresh chickpeas? They sell them right outside!'

- 'You want some chickpeas? Let me see what I have here.' The marionette grandpa inserted his hand into his pocket. 'Five euros. Go and get them dear!' As he tried to hand the euro note to his little granddaughter, a white mushroom grew onto the boulders in between them. The grandfather's friend had become a grand puppet too.

- 'Give the child some more money to buy some cotton candy too. Here. It is my treat,' the senior man said, and inserted another five euros into his friend's pocket. Another white mushroom grew between him and his friend on the wall. As the grandfather puppet of the little girl accepted the euro note with his right hand, an unseen force moved the wooden cross above his head and made his left hand take the note back from his granddaughter's hand, and place it in front of the Rafflesia flower instead. His right hand that held his friend's note was moved upward too. The Rafflesia sucked both euro notes and closed its petals into a bulb. Both of the elder puppets' arms were set free; They fell next to their bodies and the senior men's heads fell downward with a sad expression. The two white mushrooms that had grown in between the two older men and between the grandfather and his grandchild had released a number of deep red blobs. Some of them were big, others were small.

Another unseen force manipulated the wooden cross that had been floating above the other little girl's father-puppet. As she was about to put the money into her pocket to buy the woolly hat she loved, her father's hand was guided by the strings to take the euro note back from his daughter's hand and raise his own hand in front of the Rafflesia blossom that had grown behind his head. The flower sucked the money in. The father-puppet dropped his head looking depressed. Two white mushrooms that had grown on the wall between them started bleeding.

The puppet-mother's hand grabbed a twenty euro note she had just given her son. The boy looked puzzled as the note pulled his hand upward instead of downward into his pocket. She raised her hand holding the twenty euro note, and the Rafflesia flower behind her that had transformed her into a puppet moved forward. The blossom core's red sticky spikes spread outward and stuck behind the euro's surface. They pulled it inward and the flower closed its petals. Three white mushrooms that had grown between them on the wall looked pink now, with multiple red blobs on their surface.

- 'Give that back to me!' the other puppet-mother of the student who was getting ready to buy a book about 'how to get released from a trap' said to her stunned daughter and took back the money she had given her for the book's purchase.

- 'What the…' the lady expressed her surprise and did not complete her sentence. Her mother passed the money to her puppet-husband whose hand was raised. He waved the notes in front of the Rafflesia flower that bloomed behind him. The blossom closed its petals within a fraction of a second, entrapping the puppet-father's hand within its core.

-'It is YOUR fault!' the puppet-mother turned to her left and accused her daughter one more time. The white mushrooms that had grown onto the wall in between them oozed with a red sticky substance. So did the other white mushrooms that had grown next to all the young students while all of their money flew out of their pockets. Both coins and paper money flew in the air and entered the Rafflesia flower's core.

-The lady with the red shiny hair walked closer to the little girl whose dad had been transformed into one of the adult puppets and stood in front of the innocent-looking soul. The imposing woman looked at her. The girl looked back at her with a fresh, innocent-looking face. She looked inside the lady's eyes. She shivered. From a certain angle, they looked warm and welcoming, but when she looked straight inside them, she froze. The lady stretched her hand close to the girl's neck and her fingers felt the child's scarf. It consisted of a warm, shimmery, golden surface with slight traces of black, thin, delicate material that would give anyone the impression it would crease and rip like a sheet of gold leaf. The lady pulled it from the girl's neck and wrapped it around her own neck. Without saying anything, she walked toward the exit. As she walked through the door, the scarf turned deep red. The same occurred with the woman's green dress, which took an orange tone at first before a deep cherry red replaced it and revealed her current deepest mood. New patterns of light red silk sewn thread appeared on the dress's surface. These patterns showed the Koule castle being swallowed by a tornado, which was moving around the sea, being drowned by huge waves. On the crest of these waves and within, some tiny fishing boats struggled once again to remain on the water's surface. A few of them had been wrapped by the Rafflesia flowers' host vines. Right after her dress's transformation, her own face lost the beautiful complexion it had had, revealing her skull's bones to the highest degree.

The sky still had an intense red light around the castle and beyond. As the lady walked out of the castle's southern entrance, more puppets appeared on the main trail, wrapped by the Rafflesia Arnoldii's host vines. Even the man who had brought his big pet snake for people to take pictures with around their necks had been cast under the lady's spell, and he now looked like a puppet himself. The terrifying lady approached him. She spread her left arm toward the python that had been resting around the man's neck. The snake moved and stretched its body toward her hand.

    - 'No! the puppet man shouted.

The lady moved her head abruptly and looked at him intensely. Her eyes had a fluorescent yellow light in them. The puppet lowered his head in terror. He shivered. The snake's body was almost hovering in the air. It looked as if it would fall to the ground unless the lady took one step forward. She remained in her position. The snake struggled to reach her and had proceeded to such an extent that it was now impossible to back off onto his owner's shoulder. The lady still remained where she was. Right in front of her feet, there was an invisible circle of blue light around this puppet man. It seemed to be preventing her from coming any closer. The snake was almost hovering in the air now, with only a third of his body touching his owner's shoulder. The lady with the child-like face that now looked like a skull, shook her arm impatiently, opening her fingers some more. At the same time, her lip moved upward spasmodically, revealing her teeth. The python jumped onto her arm and curled itself around it. She turned around and spread both of her arms toward the sky. Some light green flames appeared around her dress. They grew and twirled around her as she walked closer to the trail's exit. With a smile of triumph on her face, she had almost reached the exit when suddenly she stopped. She turned toward a man who had not transformed into a puppet for some unexplained reason. This man was selling canvases with paintings of local places to the tourists. As she walked close to him, two hook shapes were formed out of energy in front of the seller's stomach. They seemed to be emerging from within his stomach area.

The lady stopped at a safe distance, and an energetic tube came out of her own stomach, emitting a light green light. The tube grew more until it was firmly caught and fixed by the man's protruding hooks that had been hovering in front of his stomach. Some silver energy was being sucked out of the man's emotional brain –another description for 'stomach'- into the red-haired woman's body. The man kneeled and started sweating.

    - 'I am not well. I am not well…' he whispered to himself. 'I feel sick.' He tried to walk away. He staggered. 'My eyes. What is happening? What?'

More energy was passing through the energetic tube to this mysterious red-dressed woman. The flames were now becoming red, and a tornado started forming around her body. A passerby saw the seller feeling unwell, so he ran up to the man at once. He gently touched him on his arms in his effort to support him.

    - 'Help me, HELP!' the seller of the paintings pleaded while he was collapsing.

    - 'If you want help, you must do as I say. Are you willing to do so?' The seller nodded his head in agreement.

    - 'There is an energetic cord that comes out of a negative entity's stomach, and it has connected with yours. IMAGINE you have a big pair of scissors in your right hand,' he paused.

- 'I have a big pair of scissors,' the seller said.

- 'Now you can use it and cut the cord in front of your stomach,' the man encouraged him.

- 'I am cutting the cord,' the Artist panted.

- 'And now say: 'And so it is.''

- 'And so it is…' he said, and a circle of purple light surrounded him instantly.

- 'How are you now? Are you feeling better?'

-'I do. I do!' the seller replied as the red-haired woman lost her balance backward.

- 'Good job you have done there dude!' the man patted the seller on his back.

- 'A negative entity you said?' the seller asked the passerby in his wish to learn more.

- 'It does happen occasionally. They walk among us and we may think at times that we have caught a virus!' he chuckled and turned around facing the trail's exit.

- 'Now WHO would ever imagine…but wait a minute! You have just saved me. Who are you? What is your name, my friend?'

- 'I am a colleague of yours. You appreciate paintings. I appreciate and write letters…'

- 'You are a Calligrapher! Now THAT is something that I have never encountered in this town. A man who is a Calligrapher!' He smiled and lowered his head. 'And where do you work? Perhaps I could visit you someday and we could sit together at one of the fish taverns opposite and have a drink with a delicacy and...' he looked back, but the Calligrapher was not there anymore. 'Talk?' he whispered to himself and looked around in his effort to detect him. But the only entity who was still there was the red tornado woman who had now proceeded to her next victims. Another five energetic cords came out of her stomach and drew energy from five captured puppets.

Each of them was now losing their own energy and started collapsing within their own Rafflesia flower's vine-tentacles. The red-haired woman, on the other hand, could barely be seen anymore. She was hiding within a huge tornado that consisted of green and yellow flames that now reached the sky. As it moved toward the exit, its flames spread onto the small fishing boats that had been tied to the pier. The seller's paintings remained intact. For some reason, the flames extinguished as soon as they touched the canvasses' surface. The tornado, however, was strong enough to keep heading closer to the roundabout where the monument of the three dolphins was standing. Some marionettes walked on the streets, guided by their strings, watching the other puppets that had been restrained by the white-spotted flowers.

- 'Get up and take charge of your own responsibilities!' one female bald puppet shouted to another captive puppet.

- 'But my dream is to become an illustrator and a writer!' the abused captive puppet said.

- 'Your feelings are irrelevant,' the attacking puppet said. 'You will do as I say. If you keep creating, I will tear up your work.'

Then, an unseen force turned the shouting puppet's wooden cross above her head and moved her strings. Her legs were pulled forward to walk away from the captive puppet and led her toward the town's center. A male puppet approached her, and they both laughed sarcastically at the Artist.

- 'Great job! Now she will become our personal servant! Keep messing with her perception of reality. And try to find ways to distract her from her work. We can't let her become independent; Do you understand? You have been really convincing so far! How I adored that look of despair in her eyes! I love it!' the male puppet stated with hatred. 'And always remember: Every time we talk with each other and our friends, we will exclude her from the discussions! Make her feel…invisible. We will keep talking and control everyone,' they giggled.

Unfortunately for them, they had not seen the huge, powerful, fiery tornado that moved toward them. While the artist puppet escaped the hot swirling walls by turning her flexible head in all directions (after having cut off the strings with a pair of scissors she used to carry within her pocket), the two unaware puppets that were pretending to be fair and responsible to their friends were caught by the tornado's disastrous walls. They were now in flames and it was too late for them to save themselves…

23. Skeletons, Pirates, and Earthbound Ghosts.

- 'Where am I?' Bernard wondered as he tried to see past the white light that surrounded him and Robert within a big bubble. The bubble had a slippery white surface from the outside, and additionally, behind the boy, the bubble held a sliding green, glowing skeleton with a crushed skull. The skeleton held a scythe in his hand that kept sliding downward.

- 'Now THAT was close!' Stamatis' voice sounded with a tone of relief.

Bernard turned around and saw his friend standing with his back to him. 'I am still too young for such adventures, no matter how great they appear in movies!' Stamatis said. 'But where did this protective bubble come from?' he wondered. 'It looks like Bernard's bubble gum!'

- 'This one here is a lot smaller,' Bernard's voice sounded behind him.

- 'Oh my! My, my, my…my heart!' Stamatis jumped while touching his chest with his right hand. 'Where did YOU two come from?'

Before Bernard had the chance to reply, the cobalt blue glowing earthbound ghost of a man with a pair of old-looking Cretan pants, a vest on his chest, and a shabby gents' hat, jumped onto their thin white slippery bubble and slipped down, falling onto his back. Robert shouted, terrified, and moved his flippers up and down.

- 'We cannot stay here!' Stamatis said and walked forward along with the bubble. Bernard and his penguin friend followed. Another earthbound ghost of a local man dressed in black clothes with a black tasselled scarf around his forehead moved toward the children. In his right hand he was holding a knife. He ran and raised the knife above his head, ready to stab at a figure in front of him just now. In his eyes, it was the threatening figure of the notorious Greek monster 'Baboulas' that had a little boy in his grasp. Baboulas had the special ability to transform into the most horrifying creatures on the planet in his effort to compel children to go to bed for their nap at noon time every day. This time, he transformed into the massive sea monster 'Charybdis' -a monster with the massive mouth of a leech that could swallow the whole Morozini fountain with all four lions and its pigeons and smash them with his multiple razor-sharp teeth that were similar to a deep sea dragonfish's. His head looked deformed, and he had a pair of huge black eyes and two black nostrils right beneath. He moved with a number of thick strong crab legs and a few squid-like tentacles that derived from his whale-looking body. Unfortunately for the local man, he could not see that this was a projection of his own fears. He approached closer and closer, and Bernard took the Angel's curl out of his pocket. The bubble's outer surface transformed into beautiful decorative mirrors that were connected to each other all around. As soon as the man was ready to strike, he shouted, horrified, and turned around and ran away from the protective ball. An image of a skeleton dressed up in black clothes and a black tasselled scarf around his forehead reflected back to him. He was holding a knife that he was about to stab at himself…

The spirit of a man with a big turban around his head, a red fez within a small round crown on the top of his turban, and a golden owl with an eye patch on her left eye that shimmered with golden dust, wings wide open standing proudly on the very top, walked decisively toward the white bubble. He wore a red silk coat with small golden compasses that pointed

Rosie Protects the Coded Disc of Phaistos

to the letter 'B' in every direction as its pattern. This was worn on top of a deep green velvet blouse, along with an attached golden sword that carried rubies on its surface and a decorative black pattern. The sword was fastened onto his shimmery copper leather belt that was added above one of the small golden buttons which had been sewn on his blouse. In addition to that, it was his method of distracting his enemy's attention to wear a pair of leather boots that shimmered with golden dust on which he had apparently kneeled. A white cross was now visible on the mirrors' surfaces, a cross that looked as if it was made of pearls. It was firmly fixed onto his turban, and it carried a jewel in its center.

- 'Sultan Barbarossa looks good today! Ho!' he said to himself as soon as he looked at his reflection in the mirrors. He pulled his red beard hair downward, while his straight red hair floated softly in the air as if he were underwater. He lifted his belt, as it had slipped down his belly, and then walked away. The boys looked at each other nonplussed.

- 'Was that Barbarossa? Captain Barbarossa?' Stamatis asked Bernard. 'Did you see his brows?'

- 'They looked bushy!' Bernard commented on the pirate's connected brows. Robert looked at the Captain-pirate with much interest.

- 'Turgut! Where are ye my lad?' Barbarossa called to a young man who seemed to be one of his crew members. The well-built corsair gave him instructions in Arabic.

- 'Does he have ONE arm only?' Bernard asked his friend, but Stamatis barely had the chance to observe before as an earthbound ghost of a man jumped onto a girl's shoulders in front of them. His green energetic cord vibrated toward the girl's stomach.

- 'He must have been a relative of hers in a past life,' Stamatis said. 'Let's go!' They both ran toward the girl who seemed to be feeling unwell. Her eyes were closing, and with her hand, she touched her forehead.

The white bubble moved along with the boys and the penguin. It emitted such intense light that when the ghost man turned his head toward the boys, he covered his eyes in pain and fell off the girl's back.

- 'Ask him to move into the Light, and tell him that you have another father in this life,' Stamatis whispered into her ear without being certain that the girl had received his message. 'Imagine this entity passing through you, walking away, and NOT remaining inside your body or around it,' he continued.

- 'Can she hear you?' Bernard asked him. Stamatis did not reply. He kept looking at the girl. The latter one opened her eyes normally this time. She walked a few steps forward, and then she stopped. She turned around and her blond curls fell onto her shoulders softly.

- 'I do have a dad in this life. DO walk into the Light!'

The boys looked at each other in amazement and smiled. The ghost-father got up. He looked at the street that led to 'St. Titos' church, and floated at high speed past the little shop that sold 'crepes.' Intense rays of white light glowed in the background. A skeleton with a tall white hat that was getting wider on its top and had been partly covered with long stripes of white fabric on its sides that led to a crimson fez, bore down onto the boys' mirrored ball, and with his right hand, he smashed the mirrors.

- 'What is going on? Don't the mirrors work?' Stamatis shouted in fear.

- 'Does he have any eyes at all?' Bernard asked him.

- 'No! He is a skeleton. Have you ever seen a skeleton with eyes?' Then a moment of enlightenment made him realize an important detail he had missed. 'Oh…'

- 'If he has no eyes, how will he see his 'true self?'' Bernard pointed out.

-'Right. What do we do now?' Stamatis asked in a panic.

- 'THIS is what we do!' Bernard replied and ran to the front side of the bubble. As he ran forward, the bubble moved forward too. The skeleton fell over onto the ground and was therefore run over by the hard slippery surface of the protective bubble wall. It cost him a few teeth that fell out of his jaw onto the ground. These happened to be all of his golden teeth.

A lady's loud scream sounded at the Archaeological Museum of Iraklion. This museum was built at a much further distance from the town's center. The lady ran on her high heels, as quickly as they allowed her, to the entrance's main desk. She picked up the phone receiver and dialled three numbers.

- 'Mr. Bone! Mr. Bone! This is an emergency! If you would please come downstairs right away!' she prompted somebody. 'I think it would be best if you saw it yourself,' she replied after a pause. She hung up and walked nervously into the main hall. Someone's footsteps sounded descending the stairs on the right side of the entrance. The young brunette lady turned her head instantly. The man who showed up was unknown to her, and a blond lady followed behind him. The lady, who seemed to be one of the museum's main employees and had talked on the phone, looked toward the stairs on the left side of the entrance. She took a few steps closer.

- 'It can't be happening...it can't be happening!' she whispered to herself.

Some loud hasty footsteps sounded on the left side stairs. She lifted her head and seemed eager to see the expected person's familiar face. All of a sudden, the steps could not be heard anymore. A loud landing on somebody's feet indicated to her that the individual who was currently descending the stairs had jumped.

-'What the...' she wondered when a boy eight or nine years old appeared. She then walked back to the stairs on the opposite side, releasing an anxious sigh at the same time. The boy walked up the stairs he had jumped from, when some similar footsteps sounded again, descending the same stairs. The lady did not turn around this time. She kept walking toward the other stairs that led up to the 'fresco' paintings level.

- 'Miss Ring, what is going on?' a man in his fifties addressed the anxious lady who happened to be wearing a number of rings on her fingers.

- 'Please follow me,' the lady ran toward him, and then led the way to the main exhibition of ancient Greek artifacts. They arrived at a separate section and walked past two ceramic bathtubs and two ceramic sarcophagi of the Greek ancient times. The lady walked to their left side and stopped in front of an amphora that had a big hole on its front.

- 'THIS is what is going on,' Miss Ring said to the man.

- 'The Skeleton! WHERE is the skeleton?' The gentleman looked shocked and puzzled at the same time and walked quickly in front of a sarcophagus that had been decorated on its surface with two different brown patterns. 'This skeleton is missing too!' he shouted and grabbed his chest as he passed out. 'We MUST find the child! Miss Ring! Go and call the police!! Go!' he urged the lady to leave and let him deal with his fainting on his own...

Back at the Lotzia building at the town's center, a second skeleton that was sitting on a lady's back with a wide white silk headscarf on his head that resembled a mound of whipped cream with a cherry on the top -due to its protruding fez- jumped onto the ground and ran toward Stamatis and Bernard. His tight shirt's long sleeves covered his long bony fingers. Some more of them were revealed each time the long hanging fluorescent light blue fabric dangled as he ran. A light red, long piece of cloth had been wrapped around his waist as a belt, separating his ribs from the wide light green pants, known as pantolon, that he was wearing. His bony feet were hidden under a pair of fluorescent light red sandals, which appeared bigger and bigger the closer he came. He jumped onto the mirrored bubble, and right at the same time, two more skeletons bore down onto the protective surface, which did not seem to be that protective anymore. The second skeleton was wearing a tall white hat that looked like jelly, and a long fluorescent purple jubbah with a delicate light blue design of decorative curvy smoke that curled within a crescent's hug. From beneath the jubbah, a fluorescent ochre blouse covered his chest, arms, and legs, whereas a light red cloth called kusak revealed his extremely thin and fragile waist. A pair of green turquoise sandals that he wore, with a pointy front that resembled a speck of pepper, glowed above Bernard's head.

The second skeleton that had jumped right above the one with the green sandals was wearing a fluorescent red hat on his skull, which people mistook easily for a cobra's neck unless they had a closer inspection of the tall, bumpy, wavy surface. The white fur of the glowing red jubbah he was wearing had taken a light green glow that was a reflection caused by the skeleton's negative aura. Stamatis noticed the intense vibration of the red color that the jubbah had been dyed with. Right at this time he found himself under a luminous red cloth that carried a rich turquoise-purple design of dry trees with multiple branches that twirled and led to miniature coffins instead of leaves. He was diverted from this observation when the first skeleton took out a knife and started stabbing the mirrors' surfaces with force. Both Stamatis and Bernard ran toward the materialized slippery surface and pushed forward for the protective ball to move. The ball would not move a single inch though. Stamatis pushed on his side which would lead them to the central Morozini fountain, and Bernard pushed on the opposite side of Stamatis', which would lead them toward the roundabout with the three dolphins monument that was standing on the green wave. The second skeleton was now pulling another knife from a silver scabbard with a crescent curve, which was pointing downward the way it had been fastened under his waist's fabric belt. He raised the knife and brought it down on the mirrors.

    - 'Over here!' Stamatis shouted when the knife's point protruded through the bubble's surface. The void that existed in between the mirrors' frames made it possible for the blade's sharp point to get the boys' attention from within the inner surface.

At one of the most central restaurants of 'Morozini' fountain square, a skeleton stopped right outside the relaxation place and looked inside. So did a child's skeleton, with his see-through spirit attached to his supportive structure. He decided to walk through the tables with the bamboo seats and the table mats that showed a drawn picture of the restaurant, with its name: 'The Pirate's Peg Leg,' when a huge foot that belonged to a 'Titanosaurus' stomped into the same position where the skeleton and the child were standing, leaving a big impression of his foot on the ground. A 'Rhinorex Condrupus,' which was a dinosaur with a large beak and yellow rings along his tail, ran past Titanosaurus. The skeletons took one step forward, escaping the possibility of transforming into two flat archaeological discoveries. When they entered the restaurant, they encountered a few other skeletons-Corsairs enjoying their rum punch, sea biscuits, and their most beloved salmagundi salad. There was also a family that was having their dinner around a big, oval, long wooden table. They were a family of two young boys around ten or eleven years old, a little girl around five years old, along with their parents and a senior lady. As this family was enjoying their meal of Greek moussaka, spaghetti with prawns in red sauce, cooked in a traditional well-known alcoholic drink that local men adored, and an impressive big hollow barley rusk -hard bread- that had been filled with a Greek salad and goat's cheese for the parents, and grated carrot and apple for the children, a pirate got up from his seat. He walked toward the family, staring at them all the time. The fat golden piranha-shaped earring that hung from his nose glowed under the adjacent tables' candle lights. He was also wearing a red scarf around his skull that had yellow and orange shapes of various pirates, mermaids, and sea monsters. His sharp cutlass sword hung behind his spine. He approached the little brown-haired girl and placed his long bony fingers around her throat.

- 'Shiver me timbers! So sweet… so innocent… squeezing a soft, pretty wench today wishes I! Yo-ho-ho!'

A strong hit from nowhere caused him to be ejected in the air and land among his lads. The skeleton who had escaped Titanosaurus' foot readjusted his rib cage's bone into its former position, right after he had used it as a weapon to hit the pirate. He then walked to the table where the pirate had been sitting, grabbed the plate with the spaghetti, the prawns in the red sauce, and goat's cheese and dropped the content onto the pirate's skull. Next, he grabbed his hand and dragged him outside, where he dropped him in the middle of the main trail. Some stray dogs' barking sounded in the distance. They sounded as if they were approaching the restaurant. The pirate stood up with his new spaghetti hair. An extremely thin dog hung from one arm by his teeth; Another dog hung decisively on his left leg, and the skeleton started running as far away as he could from a herd of approximately fifteen dogs. They seemed to be starving and felt like having ribs and femur bones with spaghetti, goat's cheese, the usual traditional alcoholic drink, and red sauce on today's rare menu...

Bernard ran next to Stamatis and pushed the ball's surface forward. The protective bubble moved and drug the two skeletons along with it. Robert did his best to follow his friends to avoid running on the ball's inner surface like a hamster. He could not avoid it, and at one point, he found himself running on the wall behind the boys, downward, facing the ground. As the skeletons landed onto the ground, a third skeleton who was wearing a glowing orange shalvar -a Turkish word for men's loose pants - as well as a kavuk turban with a pair of green feathers, was suddenly visible on the top part of the bubble. He was being dragged behind the two skeletons against his will. Within a fraction of a second after Stamatis' and Bernard's decisive push, he was laying under the bubble as well with his hands crossed above his chest, looking like a sleeping fluorescent skeleton who got lit up like a lamp in a light green light against a black scarf with tassels that happened to be laying under his head. The boys moved further ahead when Captain Barbarossa approached on their side. His attention did not miss the three skeletons lying on the ground unconscious and he stood right above the one who rested his bones on the black scarf. He stared at him in a pondering way. Then, a smile appeared on his face

24. 'Dancing with Jack Ketch'.

*A*strapi entered the 'Lotzia' Venetian building through its main entrance into the rectangular open space that was used most of the time for various activities, mostly exhibitions of various kinds. It was also the Mayor's main work space. The African cat encountered a few people who had gathered around a small, restricted area. Some of them were holding puppies in their arms- puppies that had been dressed in sweaters with great care. A sign had been hung on a wooden fence that kept them together. The sign read: "Puppies to be donated." Astrapi walked around and looked at a number of big round sculpted discs that carried depictions of important personalities. They had been fixed firmly on the walls.

- 'Dominikos Theotokopoulos,' he read the name on a green colored disc. 'You are the painter, aren't you?' Astrapi asked him in his thoughts. The figure remained still. 'Nikos Kazantzakis…' he whispered as soon as he saw the famous local Writer on another green sculptured disc. The children's friend and guide moved away through the first three arcs that were built within and saw two heavy wooden doors on both his right and his left sides. Right in front of him were three more arcs, one next to the other. He walked ahead to an inner semi-circular space, and the first thing that drew his attention was a smaller semi-circle that had been constructed on the opposite wall. One more wooden door stood on the left side- a door that had been built with poor quality wood.

- 'A lion with wings...' Astrapi whispered as soon as he saw the sculpted miniature image on the wall. 'Whoever has thought of such things? Why not an African cat with wings?' he thought. 'Here I am being affected again by my own ego! Get away from me ego!!' The African cat chuckled as he observed his feelings with honesty, and looked at the rest of the sculpted images. One consisted of a round spiral disc, another one depicted a book with a sword and a Greek crest helmet, and the rest of the images depicted arrows, shields in different shapes, another helmet, more swords, a shield with a ribbon, even drums. 'And who might you be?' Astrapi wondered when he saw a face that was sculpted on an oval shield, but his contemplation was interrupted by a gang of pirate-skeletons who burst noisily into the yard. Some of them pulled a cannon and placed it in front of the two doors within the narrow area of the six arcs. They aimed at the door and fired. A ball of signed paper agreements smashed the door into multiple pieces. A 'Piatnitzkysaurus Floresi' sarcophagus dinosaur inserted his head inside the main meeting room where the Mayor was speaking with his counselors and growled loudly. The skeletons ascended the stairs while Astrapi witnessed a rather different situation downstairs in the semi-circular yard: A man approached the hemisphere of the wall where a stray dog had lied down. The stranger looked behind him, and then he inserted his hand into the leather bag he carried over his shoulder. The African cat saw a silver metal foil in his fist that seemed to contain something as the unknown man unwrapped it. All of a sudden, a dark cloud of energy appeared around the man's body, shaping into a second identical self with one major difference: The form revealed a hysterical man who was struggling to free himself from a straightjacket. It was still attached firmly to the man's body as he approached the dog. Astrapi felt alarmed and took a meditative position by closing his eyes. He now looked like a white frozen statue.

The man unfolded a piece of meat and threw it to the dog. The smell reached Astrapi's nostrils, who remained focused on what he was trying to achieve. The dog gulped the piece despite its big size, as he seemed to be starving. He then lied down and closed his eyes. The man approached and pulled a hood from the inner part of his long coat. He covered his head and attempted to enter the hemispherical area toward the wall. He had spread his arms to grab the dog when a strong push along with a serious scratch on his neck from a white panther caused him to fall onto the floor. The second self that was attached to him screamed hysterically as soon as he saw that six white panthers had surrounded the dog, forming an impenetrable circle. The man could not see them though. He stood up and approached once again, taking a leash and a collar out of his pocket.

- 'What was that strong light that hit me?' he wondered. He reached right in front of the white panthers and as his leg was about to cross the boundary, the panthers transformed into Roserin, Henrietta, Robert, Stamatis, Alexander, and Bernard, who stood there as Guardians, holding tall canes in their hands- canes that carried an owl on their tops. The stranger made a move toward the dog, and as his leg was trespassing the boundary, the children blocked his entrance by moving their canes into an 'X' position. Simultaneously, an intense white light came out of the children's hearts and blinded the man, who fell backward. The attached negative entity that had infected him pulled him with more hysterical screams out of the 'Lotzia'. The children and Robert remained Guards in front of the drugged dog and Astrapi remained a statue while the skeletons that had ascended the building's inner side grabbed the Mayor and his counselors.

- 'Let's dance with Jack Ketch! Ho!' a skeleton shouted in excitement as he was pulling the Mayor toward the window. So did the other skeletons who had grabbed the Mayor's counselors. They pulled them off their feet and hung them upside down outside the windows. All the coins and paper money that was inside their pockets fell into the inner yard. The euros floated in slower motion and they landed on top of the heavier coins. Three Pterosaurs flew above the yard, having dived down from the upper open space, and one of them landed on Astrapi's frozen head. The skeletons that had appeared at the windows and that held these men firmly in the air transformed into giant mosquitos with skulls. More skeletons entered the inner arcs and went straight to the hill of coins that had just formed. They grabbed coins, put them inside their mouths, and the coins fell back into the heap through their non-existent stomachs. Another skeleton dragged a mother of three children who carried a number of golden forks and knives in her arms. He waited until she had released them onto the heap, then he grabbed a ten euro note and gave it to her. The lady walked out with her children, and a couple of parents walked in, with a few more golden objects in their arms. It was their turn this time to sell their gold for a very limited amount of money. More people were being forced by skeletons to hand in their possessions, while several vultures landed onto the internal columns. They did not dare approach the children-Guards as long as the latter ones were still standing in front of the dog.

At the front space of the Lotzia, the face of 'Dominikos Theotokopoulos' retreated within the wall when the fifteen foot 'Herrerasaurus Ischigualastensis' dinosaur inserted his head through the main entrance and looked around while hundreds of coins slipped from his mouth. The wall behind the famous painter became see-through as 'El Greco,' as he was also characteristically known, walked through his studio and was seen hastily covering his paintings with a number of throws. While he was busy, the Writer Nikos Kazantzakis walked through the painter's studio toward the wall's right side where the sculptured disc of the well-respected Poet George Seferis had been hung. He was not inside the painter's studio any longer. He now stood inside George Seferis' office, still within the wall. He looked at the Poet, and the latter one pointed at his flat disc, as it now appeared to be. However, the following sentences that had been carved into it were still visible:

"Call the children to gather the ashes

to plant them.

What has come to pass, has passed right."

The Ornithocheirus' spirits -the ones with the colorful crests- flew past George Seferis' round disc, holding two middle-aged women in their claws.

As they flew within the exhibition space, their thin membranous spread wings reached up to twelve meters wide from tip to tip. Their two captives screamed while they were being carried into the Lotzia wearing a few golden jewels around their necks.

- 'I can't pay the bills!' the one woman cried. 'I can't pay my rent…'

As the Ornithocheiruses transferred the two women to the inner yard to sell their gold for a few euros, a giant 'Liopleurodon' of the ancient seas, with the unbelievable body length of twenty-five meters and with four long flippers that helped him move, held a young student between his huge jaws and sharp teeth. She was a girl with a lost expression and extreme unhappiness within her exhausted looking eyes. She had no energy to pull herself out of his teeth and free herself from the vicious bully whose only purpose was to convince people of the illusion that it was only natural to impose control over weaker souls.

- 'They don't let me talk…They don't let me talk…' the girl whispered with the very last energy that remained inside her, and closed her eyes…

25. A Wish is Granted.

- '*Ye* shall be my Jolly Roger!' the corsair shouted, excited, and pointed to the skeleton with his finger. The unconscious bony servant of Captain Barbarossa was lifted in the air along with the stretched scarf behind his feet. Barbarossa looked at him as he hovered and caressed his red beard. Then he moved his palm upward. At the same time, the skeleton's body rotated a hundred and eighty degrees vertically and was pulled onto the waving black scarf's surface like a magnet.

- 'Fore the Sea Rover! Abaft!' Barbarossa commanded, and his flag floated down 25th August Street on the way to the port, along with the attached skeleton on it. A local man with a thick moustache under his nose saw the black scarf in the air. He saw it from the other side of its surface.

- 'There is my scarf!' He pointed at it and ran behind it to catch it. 'Damn southern wind today!' he cursed when a boy's earthbound ghost that was attached to a skeleton his own height jumped onto the man's shoulders and messed up his long grey hair with his hands. The man with the black shirt, black pants, and black traditional boots kept trying to keep his hair away from his face as he ran, but the ethereal boy kept messing it up. A little girl ran behind the man- a girl who seemed to be a close relative of his. The spirit of a monkey, who was wearing a luminous deep red shalvar and a blue blouse with a luminous dark green turban around its head that depicted multiple shapes of yellow crescent bananas which engulfed precious coconuts, jumped onto the girl's shoulders.

Bernard and Stamatis looked at each other. Then they looked back at the people who were present at the market. To their surprise, the people could not be seen anywhere. Instead, an army of skeletons ran toward the boys, holding cutlasses and other blades in their bony fingers. Some of them were wearing lose strips of fabric, indicating the days of their mummification, whereas others were wearing some really big turbans on their skulls. A number of them had wrapped black silk scarves around their foreheads, on which an image of a white human skull with a copper-red glowing beard materialized at the moment. Bernard noticed the existence of skeletons whose earthly body parts were still visible under their wraps. Bugs kept moving in between their mummy wraps and their bones, maintaining their adrenaline at the highest levels.

-'I will catch ye and crash ye like a bug ye cowardly swab!' a pirate skeleton hit his chest's bony cage decisively, under which an unfortunate bug happened to spend its last moments of life. Stamatis' and Bernard's hair stood up as soon as they heard the deep, threatening, rage-filled voice.

- 'Did he say that to ME?' Stamatis shivered. 'We need to get OUT of here! Which way is free?' he looked around, his eyes struggling to detect the safest way out.

- 'I see NO way out!' Bernard shouted. 'There are skeletons EVERYWHERE!'

- 'There HAS to be a way out!' Stamatis shouted back. He kept checking the area, but despair built up inside him as soon as his eyes connected with the hollow parts of a skeleton's skull, where their soul reading eyes were once fixed. 'They are coming closer!' he whimpered, while Robert approached him and hugged his leg. His friend was clearly upset about something, so the penguin felt like giving him some comfort.

- 'Then why don't we 'trilocate'?' Bernard asked his friend.

- 'I don't think we can do that. I feel as heavy as a rock,' Stamatis replied while the skeletons approached. One of them took out his whip from his yellow cloth that was wrapped around his pelvis- a whip that consisted of nine black leather lashes that were loaded with fastened nails. They hung from one end of the main 'cat o' nine tails,' as it was characteristically known in the Pirate language. This skeleton was wearing a red fez on his skull- a really long fez with a black tassel hanging off the top. His feet were hiding inside a pair of short red boots. A black raven that had left the museum of Natural History landed onto the fez's top surface. As a scavenger, he had the feeling that there would be carcasses sometime soon at the scene. The Egyptian vulture that had left his position in the museum's 'shrubland' section also appeared. He was standing on the shoulders of another crew member that belonged to Captain Barbarossa. He sure was NOT going to allow that little crow to steal his potential dinner away from him.

All the skeletons ran and jumped onto the boys' and Robert's protective bubble. They could not see their reflections as 'monsters' on the mirrors, since they did not have any eyes any longer. One skeleton had multiple bullet holes on the reflection of his bones, an indication that he was gradually disappearing. Another one looked like an 'Ornithocheirus' dinosaur, with a pair of big thin membranous wings. More bugs appeared on the reflection of another mirror as soon as the skeleton that had crashed the bug onto his chest had jumped onto the bubble. A fourth skeleton's reflection revealed his true self with the depiction of a huge skull and one eye, whereas the image of a skeleton that was dripping with light green acid appeared on a different mirror. A sixth skeleton made his presence known. This one had been rather different from all his other peers. This one's bones consisted of big hollow cannelloni noodles, since he used to eat only cannelloni, pastitsio (a traditional local meal of big noodles, cheese, and cream in layers), and spaghetti in his life. The boys would have frozen paralyzed in fear had they seen the true self of a psychic vampire's skeleton on a different mirror's surface. This vampire had a really long tongue that was sticky on the end like a frog's, and green fluorescent eyes that dripped liquid yellow orpiment, a strong poison that contained arsenic. These drops were easily noticeable on his pale lifeless complexion. His long dark hair was tied up in a ponytail with a red velvet ribbon. Right on the next mirror, the reflection of a skeleton with a pair of big bat's wings on his back appeared on the glass. When one more skeleton jumped onto the bubble's last mirror, another figure, Mr. Proper, made his appearance on the reflective glass. Mr. Proper was wearing a dark costume with white parallel lines, a tie, and a white shirt underneath. He also had some jello spread in his hair. Other characteristics of his were his well-shaven jaw and a red glowing flower that had been inserted into his costume's front pocket.

- 'He is made of treasure maps!' Bernard pointed at a skeleton whose bones were not exactly bones. They looked more like old rolled sepia maps.

-'I don't care! We need to get OUT of here!' Stamatis shouted when another skeleton pulled a telescope from his back and looked through it toward the mirrored bubble's content.

- 'How?' Bernard asked.

- 'We need to find a way out NOW!' Stamatis panicked. His eyesight fell onto a skeleton's eye socket which was sealed off with a round golden pocket watch. This was a watch of an unusual sort. Both of its hands were skeleton hands that pointed to number 'zero,' which was placed at the position where number twelve was usually placed. As soon as Stamatis' glimpse fell onto the time, its cover closed abruptly, revealing an embossed human skull of a pirate with two red rubies embedded within its eye sockets and two swords crossed and fastened right behind the skull. On the watch's back side, a beautiful delicate design of jasmine filled the rest of the round surface. The watch's numbers could be seen through the pattern's holes. Stamatis shivered.

The golden steering wheel of a ship in the form of an earring that hung from a pirate's ear helped Bernard recall something. He inserted his hand into his pocket and pulled out the Angel's missing blond ringlet. He looked at it. He held it in front of him, and in their great need to receive help, he imagined the Angel blowing his trumpet, giving the signal to other Angels and spirits that their help was needed on the scene. As the spirit that Bernard was, this was the most effective way they communicated. Not with words, but rather with images instead- images of the desired result.

A sudden earthquake shook the ground for only one second. Some of the pirates slipped off the bubble onto the ground. The boys felt the earth shaking beneath their feet. After a few seconds break, a second stronger earthquake occurred. A skeleton with a black eye-patch that carried a colored embossed image of Barbarossa and his red glowing beard slipped down onto a lower level of the protective bubble, whereas another pirate who happened to slip off with an iguana on his shoulder pulled a gun and shot at others among his wild peers. The bullet went right through their ribs, and further on its route, it shaped a hole on a child's slice of cheese that the child had been holding in the air. It had the shape of a little pug, and it was pierced right through its one eye. It continued its journey into a nearby 'souvlaki-gyros' meat —as it was known in Crete- shop, where meat was being turned around slowly in front of the wall's electric stove for the clients to enjoy. The bullet cut off a piece of hanging meat that had been divided hastily by the man who prepared it. The released piece fell right into the special yogurt that had been spread inside an open laid pie which was being prepared for the next client.

Some bat skeletons that were hanging on the shop's ceiling flew outside. One of them bore a close resemblance to the woman with the red hair. The face was similar to hers, and so was its hair. While the pirate-skeletons had started attacking each other due to the random bullet that went through their ribs, the skeleton of a monkey with a pair of really long arms kept jumping from skull to skull. It rotated three hundred and sixty degrees whenever a skeleton struck with a sword and also grabbed a camera any time an unaware tourist happened to carry one on their shoulders. A pirate skeleton was noticed by Bernard at a distance, carrying his own skull in his hands. Another one walked around using his hands, since he had been severed between his upper part and his lower part. He was walking within the chaotic Christmas market when he suddenly disappeared with the snap of a crocodile's skeleton that was lurking around. He was now captive in the crocodile's long snout- one with multiple sharp teeth. The skeletons of six piranha fish floated toward a beautiful lady who was standing in front of the fish section and bit her on her butt. She turned around with an expression of pain and punched the man who stood behind her and smiled at her.

Another short but strong earthquake made everyone shake and jump a few inches off the ground out of fear. Right after it seized, the pirates kept fighting against each other, affecting people in a seriously unhealthy way with the use of their weapons. As a lady opened her wallet to collect the money she needed to pay for her child's grilled chestnuts, a whooshing sword ejected the coins from inside her wallet away into a psychic vampire's mouth. A man at another side of the market took out of his pocket the very thin pack of money that he held in a clip, and as he was about to pay for his son's boiled corn, a whip caught the few paper notes and the father discovered that the paper clip had no notes clipped together anymore. With a sad expression, he grabbed the fresh boiled corn from his son's hands and gave it back to the seller. The skeletons were still fighting when St. Minas' church bell sounded loudly, transferring its acoustic waves around and through the buildings. Another earthquake occurred, and all the skeletons found themselves floating in the air this time at a safe distance from the ground. For some reason, they were unable to keep fighting where they were. They could only float like blown dandelion flowers in the wind. The boy's stare, however, was not drawn toward the pirates. It was drawn toward 25th August Street instead…

An army of glowing skeletons appeared. These skeletons were rather different from the pirates who had caused chaos around the town's center. These skeletons were wearing quite a lot of jewelry on their bony structures, from the top of their skulls to the bottom of their feet. They seemed to have eyes that were consisted of square blue stones within a thin golden frame, which was surrounded by a series of pearls that were fixed next to each other. They also had bandages for eyelids, which partly covered the blue stones that seemed to be resting on balls of cotton that filled the eye sockets.

Their jaws had been covered by golden jewelry which contained rubies and moonstones. Under their noses, there were a series of round hollow bases connected to each other, which carried a number of white pearls. On some of the skeletons' foreheads, an attached wreath added to the decoration. It consisted of delicate golden leaves and a number of white pearls which had been attached in such a way that made them look like little flowers. The rest of their bodies were covered in precious stones like emeralds, sapphires, rubies, and gold, whereas their arms were covered by red sleeves of a certain luxurious red fabric that had been sewn with golden thread, forming delicate designs of flowers and nets. Long strips of the same fabric flowed from the shoulder down, surrounded by lace along the perimeter. The hollow part of their noses contained a golden jewel, and their ears had been covered by more jewels attached onto a golden base, which resembled a certain flower. The crowns that some of the skeletons wore on their foreheads were gold that had been sculpted in a unique delicate way, thus giving Henrietta the impression that they consisted of fragile golden ribbons. In the center of the front part of the crown, a light pearl stone in the shape of a tear drop had been placed upside down, with its pointy part pointing toward the nose.

The boys kept looking at them, unable to utter a single word. A lady skeleton was wearing a dress of light green fabric with a refined golden sewn design of what looked like leaves. The dress still allowed her chest's bones to be visible along with the jewels that had been fixed firmly onto them. The sleeves led the eyes to a rich golden fabric. They displayed an additional golden sewn design on them, as well as around her neck. More precious stones decorated the light-green golden dress on the surface. Its quality was so high that anyone who looked at it felt hesitant to touch the folds, in fear that the thin golden fabric might suddenly melt on their very fingers. This lady's face was still partly there. She hid death's unavoidable touch behind a thin veil which still visibly revealed the protruding cheekbones and decaying teeth. A blond wig was covering her ears. It had been attached tightly beneath a well-sewn hat-like band of fabric that covered her forehead. Stamatis could make out some more delicate sewn designs in golden thread on top of another design that had also been sewn, with a white thread this time, in the shape of what looked like a swan with his spread wings wide open. The whole pattern had been stitched onto red velvet. Some emeralds had been added on both sides.

Bernard noticed that some of the skeletons were wearing red capes with variations of a golden, luminous sewn design. Their spine, ribs. and sternum were still visible and were decorated with beautiful bracelets that carried precious stones. Their sternum carried some diamonds in a silver sewn pattern that had been attached above the sternum. More precious stones formed an oval circle around the bone, and their face was covered with a thin veil on which the eye sockets had been covered by golden patterns in the shape of eyes. The nose was decorated similarly, and both the eyes and nose carried some miniature pearls- blue and white pearls. Some golden ribbons that carried the same kind of pearls had been wrapped around the fingers, and several rings decorated every single finger with stones in the colors of fuchsia, yellow, blue, and green.

Two rubies glowed intensely from another skeleton's eye sockets, and a drop of sapphire covered his nose, which was surrounded by golden lace along its perimeter. Stamatis was speechless at the big number of jewels and pearls the skeleton had been decorated with. His bones could hardly be seen.

There were also the ladies who wore the richest dresses the boys had ever seen female skeletons wearing in their afterlives. One of them stood proudly; Within her wide sleeves of many folds of silk were a number of symmetric twirls carrying a colorful precious stone in their center, along with a series of more of the same stone firmly attached within the twirls that had been shaped on the dress's surface. Some of them looked like a peacock's feathers above the golden fabric. A crown of smaller golden leaves with several brooches attached to it decorated the upper part of the skull.

Bernard and Stamatis were so affected by the beauty and sacredness of the moment that they were unable to use their vocal cords. They did not dare blink either. One blink could possibly cause the disappearance of the mysterious entities. Who were they? Had they been Kings? Had they been

Saints? Did they come from the nearby St. Titus Church? Did they come from the port? The boys felt too touched by the sight to be able to even express their wonder in words. Their eyes had been magnetized by the ethereal movements of these majestic entities. And then, something happened. The pirates who had been hovering above their heads, vanished from their sight. They disappeared along with their bony animals.

The skeleton with the light blue stones for eyes that had been fixed firmly behind his thin bandage made eyelids, and the golden crown with the white pearl drop, stepped forward and bowed to Stamatis, Robert, and Bernard. So did the other skeletons. When they stepped back to their initial position, some unexpected fog of red sand that arrived from Africa formed all around the 'Lotzia' Mayor's building. The boys could barely see them anymore. Stamatis walked slowly toward the elegant, aristocratic-looking skeletons, whereas Bernard and Robert followed within the white protective ball. They walked carefully within the blown red sand, without attempting to speak to each other. All of their senses were alert, to catch the slightest sense of their saviours' presence. So far, they were not in sight yet...

26. At the Akashic Records.

- 'The sea dragon flew over a wide, long, stairway that would give anyone the impression that it was never-ending, no matter which side of it they looked at. The steps' vertical sides glowed intensely in the sunset's pale orange light, and Roserin noticed various spirits' descending from the stairs. Other spirits walked patiently up the stairs that led somewhere.

- 'Is that Plato? That was Plato!' she shouted in excitement while the ancient Greek Philosopher was stepping down the stairs. 'And he is wearing a mask! How funny…it was a mask of his own face! Why was he wearing a mask of his own face?' she wondered when she then saw Socrates going down the stairs. 'It is amazing!' she gasped. 'He is wearing a mask of his own face too!' She could hardly close her mouth as she was taken by surprise when the next spirit she saw walking downward happened to be another familiar figure. 'That was Aristotle! He is wearing his own face too!'

The sea dragon kept flying higher and higher. A rumbling noise puzzled the girl. 'What is that?' she thought and looked around. 'It sounds like an avalanche.' Roserin looked toward the stairway where more spirits appeared, ascending the stairs. Two big rocks also rolled down the stairs. These rocks seemed to have been created for educational purposes, since they had colorful textured patterns on their surface. The patterns looked like three-dimensional maps. The first rock passed right through one of the souls who walked upward.

- 'I KNOW who this is! This is 'Sosos' the Mosaicist!' Rosie said to the sea dragon. 'And look at the way he looks!' she expressed her enthusiasm as soon as she saw that the ancient Greek mosaicist consisted of mosaic pebbles that made up his body. 'Oh...I need to bring the others here to see them!' she said while noticing the second big rock falling toward another soul who walked up the stairs. 'Is that 'Hageladas' the sculptor?' Roserin wondered, when his hands suddenly lifted up the rock in a way as if his fingers were a magnet. Roserin could now see clearly that these rocks were sculpted representations of Earth, with the various countries painted in intense colors. Hageladas used his index finger to shape the three-dimensional representation of Greece in a much more detailed way. The country's solid outline became fluid, and Hageladas could now sculpt the image with ease.

A reflective figure of a man who ran up the stairs drew Rosie's attention at once. This man consisted of mosaic pieces of mirror. He ran at high speed, almost looking invisible among the well-known ancient Greek creators.

- 'WHO is that?' Roserin gasped. 'Dragon! Behind him!' she asked her friend to rush while a third and fourth globe rumbled down the stairs. More souls were on their way up. The mysterious man, who reflected everything back off his long coat and hat that were also made from both small and big mosaics of mirror, disappeared within some clouds of mist. Roserin tried hard to detect him but more rumbling noises from falling planets distracted her full attention. The dragon flew through the mist, gaining on the distance. However, the 'invisible' man was rather quick himself. Visibility was now almost non-existent.

- 'Good thing we still have the sun's rays falling on the stairs!' Rosie thought. 'But WHERE is HE?'

The sea dragon flew closer to the stairs. He avoided another globe that fell downward by flying right below it as the globe jumped in the air; It was a planet that resembled red Mars to a great degree. More planets followed behind, causing the most terrible noise.

'I wonder whether these globes went through the invisible man or did he have to avoid them?' Roserin thought. 'I see no shattered pieces of mirror so far.' One of the planet-globes jumped right over another soul, who too was dressed as an ancient Greek. 'That is 'Gnosis', the other mosaicist!' she recognized his face's identical mask. Gnosis –his name meaning 'knowledge'- was walking down the stairs in the opposite direction of where Rosie was heading.

'There he is!' she shouted excited as soon as she saw the sun's rays reflect onto a human figure that kept running as if he was under pursuit. The Mirror man avoided a planet-rock as it was rumbling down the long stairway and another one which looked like the Moon. After a while, he reached the top of the stairs on which a Neoclassical white building was standing proudly, with fluted shaft columns of the Corinthian order in the front. There were eight fluted shaft columns along with four composite pilaster ones, which included a triangular pediment with a raking cornice right above the central four fluted columns. Three sculpted figures decorated the façade. One of them was a standing figure that looked like a deeply spiritual person who was wearing an ancient Greek cloak. The second figure had kneeled down on the left side holding a magnifying glass. The third figure on the right side was leaning toward the pediment's base with her arm spread behind an open book. She was holding a pen. Behind the pediment, an attic storey with two lanterns built on the top of two coved domes with a parapet as their base added to the building's magnificence. A balustrade with a number of 'urns' enhanced the attic storey.

As soon as the invisible man arrived at the top of the stairs and in front of the four central fluted columns, the three sculpted figures that were within the triangular pediment looked at him. He entered the main door, while more spirits that wore masks of their own true selves exited through the two blind doors that had been built on the main door's two sides. A number of children pushed the planet globes down the stairs while laughing and shouting in great excitement. The children looked at them until they disappeared from view.

Another Greek man appeared through the blind door, holding a heated airtight boiler in his one hand and a pigeon-shaped wooden automaton on his other. This man was not wearing a mask on his face. He rested the heated airtight boiler on the floor and connected the pigeon's back side to the boiler's opening. Within a short time, the pigeon was ejected into the air and opened its wooden wings.

-'...' Roserin was stunned. She was so impressed that she could hardly say a word. She then noticed a slight change in the pigeon's flight. It had now pulled its wings back to its sides and was rocketing toward them. 'It is not flying toward us, is it? No! We are much quicker than this little thing!' she said cheerfully. The pigeon seemed to be flying diagonally toward them with a straight route that would seemingly end somewhere behind them. The steam that was released from its internal technical bladder was at its zenith power. It pulled in its wings for a few seconds more, then after a while it spread them wide open once again. It turned around and rocketed in full power. Rosie screamed as she ducked to avoid being shaved on the top of her head by this unexpected menace. After a few meters, the steam was released from the pigeon's butt and the bird started its vertical fall. 'Oh, NOW you have to fall!' Rosie shouted intensely and sighed in relief for still feeling her hair intact. She saw the inventor running down the stairs, looking for his bird. The sea dragon was now landing in front of the entrance. Something really strange occurred on the Greek scientist's face. It looked frozen this time, like an ice-statue's. A mask of his own face had materialized in front of it. 'I have JUST recalled his name!' Roserin shouted in all her excitement. 'This is 'Archytas' the Mathematician!'

The dragon landed at the entrance, and the children-spirits who were getting ready to push another rock-globe between the two columns had to walk a little further and roll the planet to the starting point. Rosie got off the

Rosie Protects the Coded Disc of Phaistos

dragon's back when her long hair stood upward. The children's hair was standing up in the same way. As soon as the girl felt her hair moving upward, she got a puzzled expression and felt it with her hand to see what had just occurred on her head. She looked up and saw the end of her hair floating in the air, as if she had found herself on the top of mountain 'Olympos'. Then she looked back on her eye level, and on her left side, she noticed a gentleman with wild grey hair who was sitting behind a wooden desk looking through a big magnifying glass. He peered at a round disk that had a metallic needle. Roserin hardly paid any attention to him; Her curiosity had already been drawn by the invisible man. She rushed inside and found herself on the ground floor of what seemed to be a rather big library, a little different from the libraries she was accustomed to in her own town. Yes, there were shelves loaded with books, but there were other things inside too. One of the shelves was filled up with pigeons. Another one was filled up with magpies that each seemed to be carrying a shiny precious object of some sort. Each of the birds was standing inside its own private wooden partition. A huge pair of glasses was hanging above the main desk from a pair of strong silver cords.

- 'These are uncle's glasses!' Rosie approached as soon as she recognized the multiple oars at the sides. And beneath the glasses, the main desk had been placed for the receptionist to welcome people behind it. A big, long, neoclassical desk with a sculpture of a golden eagle on the front it was and a golden floral design beneath the marble's wooden perimeter had been sculpted. An automaton of a servant who held a jug of liquid in her right hand stood right behind the table. She was wearing a green cloak above her beige dress, which suited both her green head and green hands very well. Roserin looked around in an effort to detect the reflective man. All she could see were long marble tables with respectable researchers sitting on wooden chairs, studying under their individual lamp's warm light. The smell of orange was sensed by the girl's nostrils. When she looked at the wall behind them, she saw big, round windows that consisted of baked orange slices- dry orange slices that carried a little black color around half the perimeter, with deep red and deep warm yellow toward the slice's center. Above the researchers' heads, a big air-hot balloon gained height

Rosie Protects the Coded Disc of Phaistos

every time the flame was released and would later fall back to its former height as soon as the flame had stopped. A wax model of the well-known writer and 'Queen of the Crime,' as she had been characteristically described by critics, was holding a big magnifying glass in her one hand as she leaned down from the side of the basket. A massive book with calligraphic letters created by a nib pen had been opened and placed above the basket. A sharp knife leaned onto its pages, and some red ink had been spilled onto the knife's surface. A wax model of her main detective hero was standing next to her, with his attention drawn to a small part of the balloon. He was focusing on a small number of grey cells that were part of the balloon's unique design as a huge colorful brain.

Roserin headed toward the balloon on the left hastily. She approached some tables on which some parchments had been resting and turned to the right further down. A second hot-air balloon was ascending and descending in front of her and above the tables with another well-known wax figure fixed inside the basket. The most famous writer in Crete was holding a book in his left hand and a pen in his right hand, looking thoughtful. On Rosie's right side, three portraits of well-known scientists like Madame 'Curie,' 'Archimedes,' and 'Leonardo Da Vinci' had been hung on the wooden wall behind the main staircase that led onto the upper floor. They were presented within well-crafted, golden, vintage frames. The girl rushed past the marble tables and the second air-hot balloon of the famous Cretan writer that was shaped like an ink bottle, and she looked for the chameleon man. The library's back side looked neat and serene, despite a few people walking on the soft carpet between the loaded shelves. As Roserin moved ahead, the silk carpet's Persian design changed into a different design that depicted Rosie sitting on a marble table, reading a very big book. Behind her seat, the face of an ancient Greek man with red eyes was looking at her. She hardly noticed the new design, since her attention was drawn to anything that moved ahead of her, especially if it carried multiple reflective surfaces of mirrors. The girl crashed against a miniature airplane that flew from one of the shelves toward a table. The young girl who received the plane took out a rolled scroll with the information she was looking for, and a few lemon chocolates that had been placed under the scroll. Rosie kept walking past

Rosie Protects the Coded Disc of Phaistos

the marble tables with the busy students, when a magpie startled her as it flew in front of her and landed on one of the tables. The bird carried a shiny ring, and let it drop inside the hands of an old gentleman. He petted her, and then brought out a special magnifying glass to inspect it in more detail. Roserin's attention was drawn quickly by an intense flare. She looked at a hollow window opposite her on the right wall's surface. The girl ran to the protruding stone-built window, as she was magnetized by the crackle effect a mirror seemed to be displaying.

Rosie looked at the puzzle-mirror, and realized an image was appearing on its multiple surfaces. She saw a young wizard carrying a mirror in Iraklion's center, and her own self running toward him. She then kneeled and whispered something to a little girl right outside the main 'Lotzia' building. Roserin stared startled until the image disappeared. She could now see her own reflection of her surprised face and the tartan plaid of the yellow-green Victorian flounce-tailed bodice of her dress with puff sleeves. She saw the sleeves' olive green silky ribbons and the lined brown-ochre corset with a number of patched combinations of smooth antique gold and shiny metallic, uneven, fabric cut out owl automatons on the surface, until the image faded out. Another image of Rosie sitting on a marble table reading a big book faded in.

- 'Am I supposed to read this book?' she wondered. A strange pair of red eyes appeared on the top left side of her projection. The pair of eyes looked fake, but yet they were so real. Roserin gasped. Her hair stood up. When she felt she could not look any longer at those piercing eyes, she moved to the library's front and ran up the wide, winding, marble staircase. Back at the window where she had seen her image, the mirror retreated to the inside part of the wall, revealing the back side of the invisible man. He walked away to the adjacent room behind the wall. Rosie knew nothing of its existence. One of the busts that rested on every third stair moved and looked toward the girl as she walked upstairs. It was the bust of Cretan survivor 'Asproula,' a beautiful white stray dog of Iraklion city that had survived an attempted murder against her by a negative entity. Some more busts of heroes that had had their own fight for survival within their

Rosie Protects the Coded Disc of Phaistos

lifetimes had been placed onto the side of the staircase, like 'Henrietta,' 'Robert,' 'Astrapi,' 'Bernard,' 'Stamatis,' 'Roserin,' 'Anemona,' 'Fterougas the Crow,' 'Petra,' 'Sweet Tooth the gypsy boy,' and a few more heroes. However, Roserin, did not notice their presence, since some kind of strong force was pulling her onto the upper floor. At the moment she reached the second floor, the winding keys that were on the owls' backs on her dress's pattern moved twice…

Our explorer looked at the creative glass domes above her head, and more marble tables were revealed in front of her with people keeping busy on various inventions and other creations as well as discoveries in the area of science. On every table, a big globe of the various universes with a meridian circle had been placed for the creators and researchers to study. They were mounted on wooden oak stands that each carried an astrolabe with turned supports and four feet. A printed horizon ring and a big number of colorful bumpy planets and crystal stars on the globe's dark surface added to their magnificence. However, despite their beauty and the mysterious shelves that seemed to be hiding much more besides their books, pigeons, and magpies, Roserin had no time to lose. She was here for a purpose. And somehow, she had the intuition she had to look for a big book.

- 'A big book…' Rosie whispered. 'Where is the section of big books?' She looked around, and then closed her eyes. 'I need to trust my inner eye,' she thought. 'Calm down Roserin. Calm down…' She focused on her inner vision behind her closed eyelids in the hope of receiving some guidance. The winding keys on the owls' backs on her dress started winding up the automaton birds. For a few seconds, she stood still at the main corridor, and her eyes were still closed. When her panting stopped and her breathing reached a meditative state, various colors and shapes appeared behind her closed eyelids. These shapes resembled books, shelves, tables, and… miniature antique lamps that looked as soft as…mushrooms. Green antique mushroom lamps grew one by one at random positions on the floor, glowing ahead of her in the same way the shelves glowed in warm ochre light. Rosie followed the miniature antique lamps to see where they led. Fifteen steps later, they kept growing to the left side, between a few more shelves that were loaded with crows on the right side and with books on the left side. She turned to the left, still keeping her eyes closed so she would not miss the experience. A big old olive tree stood in the middle of the corridor where the fungi seemed to be growing further ahead, and it was very probable that they kept growing in front and further ahead of the tree. The girl followed the glowing mushrooms, and she could now hear the crows from within their separate section on the shelves on her right. Some of them slept, others cleaned their feathers, and others played with their neighbors and teased each other.

Roserin took twelve steps forward until she reached the big majestic olive tree. She tried to spot some more lamp-mushrooms, but she could not see any more growing. She stood quietly and looked at the old tree. It looked as if it was about to walk away on its strong roots that were exposed above the surface. It also looked as if it was twisted around its base by its own routes, like a marshmallow. Rosie noticed certain shapes on the surface of the very old twisted trunk with multiple holes. Some protrusions gave her the impression of carved out faces that belonged to spirits, another shape looked like a dragon, another part of a melted-looking root looked like an octopus, and another one looked like a gargoyle that had been trying to hide among the soft marshmallow-like twisted roots. Or was it the notorious Minotaur in the maze? Roserin opened her eyes and walked past the strong wide trunk.

- 'It is hollow!' she whispered as soon as she saw its other side. She then looked at the bleeding mushrooms that had grown around its entrance. 'There is not much time left,' she thought as soon as she saw them, and entered the hollow part of the tree decisively. A light blue area that revealed some stairs attracted her attention on the left side.

- 'Blue lamp-mushrooms...' she thought. She walked up the stairs that were lit by the glowing fungi; The winding stairs led much higher than the tree seemed to be in height from its outer appearance. She ascended up and up and up...until she reached a long corridor that led to the left side. The tree's branches made their presence noticeable through the wall's holes. The wall had also been decorated by a number of precious paintings. They were portraits of important people. Rosie gasped when she saw the first person who was depicted.

- 'It is Bernard!' She was so touched and happy by this discovery that she could only whisper at this sacred moment. 'You look really good Bernard!' she thought as she admired the little boy, depicted with his complete face this time, glowing with light. He was wearing a deep red velvet jacket that gave him the air of a person who belonged to a higher class. Underneath his jacket, he was wearing a vest with a series of buttons and patterns of old cars on the fabric's surface. A deep warm yellow ochre color surrounded the old cars on the vest as a background color. His pants were a green color and made of corduroy, covered by shimmery sugar crystals that had landed softly onto the fabric from the doughnut he was currently eating. A white shirt under his vest with small red buttons on his sleeves offered him a fresh, puffy appearance. A top hat which seemed to be rather different from all the usual hats, attracted Rosie's special attention. This one belonged to Bernard. And Bernard would only wear hats he was especially fond of. This specific one was purple and had a diagonal blue wire mesh on the top. The person who put it on had the choice to put any objects of their choice onto its front surface. On this hat, there was a model of a doughnut dipped in sugar with a hole in its center, three truffle balls, the traditional sweets of Crete called 'melomakarona,' three local cheese pies dipped in sugar, a chocolate 'mouse' sweet, a few cupcakes, and some gingerbread men cookies that had been decorated with white sugar icing. Right beneath, two small drawers had been added in the central area of the hat, with two red knobs to pull them out. A series of yellow nails had been embedded around the hat's perimeter. More delicacies seemed to be hiding within the drawers if judged from the pink strawberry syrup that oozed on the hat's surface.

Roserin noticed the three glass tubes on his hat that had been fastened by a piece of fabric. The first tube contained some kind of chemical bubbly liquid, the second one was protecting a golden lock of hair, and the third one contained a certain amount of white fog that moved at the top toward

Rosie Protects the Coded Disc of Phaistos

the soft cork. Rosie's eyes fell next to Bernard's red shoes with turquoise blue laces.

She walked past the portrait, eager to see the next one. She smiled as soon as she saw her brother, posing in a Victorian embossed waistcoat with an ochre brocade pattern, a series of golden buttons, and two inset waist pockets. Underneath the waistcoat, she saw a silk red-purple lined shirt trimmed with two rows of lace, a green silk puff tie that had a brocade pattern, as well as the waistcoat. It gave Stamatis an elegant appearance, with just a slight divergence from what was considered to be proper and just 'perfect' at the time. Was it the wine red lined pants? Was it the invisible panama hat he was wearing on his head?' 'The hat is slightly bigger than your head!' Roserin giggled as she had the ability to see invisible things that actually did exist. 'Nice shoes!' She admired the green-red shoes with the golden laces and front golden curve. She walked further ahead and saw Henrietta's portrait this time. Henrietta was sitting on an ochre velvet classic ornate chair in a very relaxed position, wearing a dark copper butterfly straight velvet bodice. The silk copper drop waist fell gracefully from her waist down. And right behind her, an owl was sitting on the chair.

Next to Henrietta's portrait, Alexander's picture had been hung on the wall of roots. Alexander was wearing a waistcoat with a gold-black swirling paisley pattern with metallic threads. It had a pointed hem and five buttons that looked more like healing pebbles. A light golden Byron shirt with two rows of trimmed lace gave him the air of a well-bred young boy who inspired admiration, confidence, and a sense of freshness and a good taste concerning style. His olive green corduroys made Rosie feel a certain way.

 - 'You sure do look like a healer!' she whispered. She looked at the big glowing stone that had been fastened on his top hat. 'I KNOW this stone. But I can't remember its name.' She admired the intense red light and tried to recall its name. 'It's a Carnelian stone!' she talked to herself. 'Your shoes...'-she whispered. 'They are surrounded by golden roots. And I love your puff tie! Light blue with gold...What a great combination of colors!'

The next and last portrait presented her own self, sitting on a red velvet ornate classic chair, having taken a pose that betrayed her mischievous intentions. She was wearing a yellow-green jacket with gypsy velvet corduroy. And her eyes...her eyes were the first part of her body that talked to the creator of this masterpiece:

"Get on with it! I have something sneaky and important to do!"

Roserin touched a piece of root that protruded under her portrait. It broke instantly. She put the pieces that stuck onto her fingers into her mouth.

'Hmmmmmm...I am in Heaven!' She approached with her ear cocked and heard some more delicate sounds of cracks that resembled the sound of raindrops on a window. 'This is meringue!' she said in an ecstatic state. 'The most delicious I have ever tasted!'

A crow flew past her and passed through a small glass door that had been constructed within a stained glass window which depicted the ancient Greek Diogenes holding a lantern in his left hand, looking for a true human being among the crowd. The thin black lines around the painted figures gave the glass a sense of an elegant and fragile appearance. Some warm yellow light seemed to be illuminating the room on the other side behind the glass. Diogenes' yellow ochre robe was looking more intense now, as well as another man's turquoise-green robe within the street's crowd, and the red clothes that a child who stood next to a lady wore. Diogenes' lantern looked very bright too.

Roserin pushed the window's eye-shaped handle downward and climbed through the window into the next room. Some more glowing antique lamps-mushrooms appeared, but this time they emitted a cozy ochre light. A big number of them had grown around an olive green velvet ornate chair, on which a big book was resting against its back. The crow that had entered the room was perched on the chair's arm with a key inside his beak. Rosie picked up a glowing miniature mushroom lamp from the rooted floor and held it in front of the book. It was locked with a padlock that had the shape of an eye. Its cover consisted of a well-framed black surface, similar to the surfaces of the holograms that were displayed at the museum of natural history. Its wide frame had vertical sections of metallic golden-brown color. As she carried the mushroom toward the surface of the book, a dark mesh appeared, moving on the cover. It looked like some kind of creature.

Roserin's attention was drawn to it directly. Its body looked strong, with big legs, and as soon as its head turned forward, the girl gasped.

'Oh my…it is a 'Postosuchus.' Roserin felt alarmed as soon as she recognized the dinosaur's distant cousin. 'And what is that on his back?' She stared at the forming shape that moved in front of her eyes. 'What are you? Are you a gargoyle?' the girl wondered. 'You have these huge wings. A bat perhaps?' The head formed last, with a colorful crest on the top of it. Then the new creature's legs were sucked into the Postosuchus' back and became one and the same with his body. 'An Ornithocheirus,' Rosie whispered and touched her chest with her right hand as she observed the giant dino-bird flapping its wings, as if he was trying to escape. Then another part of the Postosuchus' body kept growing, which was its tail. Its tail did not exactly resemble a usual tail. Two long and thin green-naples yellow patched necks appeared, their heads indicating they belonged to the dinosaurs 'Coelophysis.' They both seemed to have a red mark on their heads. They released a hissing roar, and the Postosuchus turned his head toward Rosie. He opened his mouth and released a bellowing roar. His teeth were almost touching her fingers. She turned the book around quickly and almost dropped it on the chair. She grabbed it in the air and allowed the glowing mushroom-lamp to bounce on the floor. She sat onto a bunch of roots cross legged and opened the book from its back cover. She chose a page at random, and the first thing that appeared showed a hologram of the woman in the red hair…

An unusual thud of something heavy that had been dropped onto a surface caused Roserin to turn her head. A pair of two red eyes that belonged to an ancient man's stone-carved imitation head were looking at her. It looked like a complicated invention, with a bunch of moving objects underneath. These objects were golden and served a specific function. The sculpture of the head itself was within an arc, the latter one being made of two columns, two rings, and two statuettes. Through the beak that belonged to a golden bird, which was one of the statuettes, some water fell into a small bowl. A big cylindrical container with a nozzle had been placed to the right of and slightly behind the bowl. The nozzle seemed to be allowing the water to fall into a small container. Right under the container, there was a third separate section that contained a little golden tree, and under the tree, a big spherical volumetric container that prevented the falling water from leaking. The water reversed, and a pair of golden snakes slithered toward a pair of birds that were resting on the tree. They cried out frightened.

- 'So, you are a clock!' Roserin gasped in great admiration. 'It is eleven twenty p.m. already!' She was astonished as soon as she saw the façade's columns that presented the past few hours by the function of one of the two little statuettes. She looked back at the book which rested this time on one of the marble tables in front of the stairs she had climbed. She climbed out of the little room through the window and walked a few meters further before sitting on a comfortable velvet chair in front of the table. She sat next to one of those big universal globes and another small surprise caught her eye. A little olive was sitting on the table's surface in front of the lamp. She grabbed it and put it inside her mouth.

- 'Hmmmmmm…chocolate! With almond inside. Now let's see…Let's find some more information about you…' she whispered and looked back inside the huge book while she chewed. 'So…this is what needs to be done with your behavior…' she said after a few seconds of reading and sighed. She looked thoughtful. 'You have been a victim of your own brain…How unfortunate for you and other people. So that explains everything. You CAN'T 'feel.''

The clock that had followed her struck 11.30 p.m. and Roserin turned her head to look behind her shoulder. The eye color on the clock's head had turned green. Its long stone-carved beard and moustache looked the same, whereas the curls that fell softly on the front side of his head moved a little in a slight breeze of air.

- 'I need to go!' She closed the book, then locked it again with its eye-shaped padlock and left the key onto the table for the crow to recollect. She ran down all the stairs and found herself at the entrance. She looked to her left where the automaton lady servant was standing and approached the reception. She grabbed the pewter cup that was resting on the table and placed it into the servant's left hand. The latter one's right hand that held the jug moved downward and poured some sort of drink.

- 'Hot chocolate! It is the thick rich kind! My favorite!' Rosie whispered. As soon as the jug was half-filled, the automaton's left hand lowered further, and the flow stopped. Then a separate flow of milk started pouring into the cup along with a mountain of soft whipped cream. When it was filled to the top, the flow stopped, and the hand lowered even further. Rosie grabbed the great temptation she had in front of her; She smelled it and started sipping. 'Oh, I am in Heaven!' she thought as she enjoyed the pure rich chocolate. She looked as if she had been bewitched by a magical spell when she turned her head to the right and saw Sir Hipparchus working on one of the marble tables. She placed the cup onto the table in front of her and ran toward the Astronomer. 'Uncle! You are working on the astrolabe!' She waited for a response, but Sir Hipparchus did not seem to be able to hear her. She bowed over the table toward him.

- 'Uncle?' she called.

The Scientist did not respond. He had a number of drawings in front of him that depicted parts of the astrolabe. He had also separated the astrolabe's various parts on the table in his efforts to put them together.

- 'I am coming uncle! I am on my way! Don't worry, I have finally figured out what needs to be done!' she said to him, and returned to the main reception to finish drinking her thick hot chocolate.

In the town, a team of eight corsairs ran out of the Archaeological Museum's main entrance with various ancient Greek golden treasures dangling from their protruding ribs. Miss Ring hardly noticed their presence as she was connected with the police on the phone. A few coins slipped out of a pirate's pouch as they were heading back to Barbarossa. Another pirate had put a gold mask of a man with a wide smile and a raised brow on the back side of his skull, whereas another skeleton was wearing golden rings all over his fingers.

- 'Use your deadlights ye son of a gun!' a corsair who had a wreath of golden leaves on his skull shouted to one of his crew members who had changed his mind and turned back, bumping into him. A few golden leaves were scattered on the trail, along with some more precious coins…

27. Searching for the Hidden Treasure.

*A*nd what was Anemona doing in the meantime? When Roserin left her, she was standing next to the mermaid with the red flower on her head- the mermaid that had no hands. Anemona stared toward the statue's face, but the woman-fish kept still this time, frozen as the statue that she was. The girl decided to move back to the little internal pond that had been built between the gents' and ladies' rooms. She looked at the circles that had been embedded on the background wall. There were also squares with an 'X' on their surfaces. She looked behind her to see whether anyone was watching her, and when she saw everything was clear, she raised her arm above the aloe vera plants' containers and touched the circles on the wall. One of them was protruding a little more than the rest. She pulled it. It looked like a cover to something. She pulled and pulled, but it was rather firm. And then she pulled it with both of her hands. She almost fell into the water as the round cover was released from the wall into her hands. A bottle's base was now visible within the wall. Anemona pulled it from the specific position, which was next to the bathroom's decorative glass on the right. She was now holding a narrow light purple bottle in her hands that emitted intense purple light: a bottle with a cork, on which a miniature handmade owl was standing. She leaned her head to one side. It was an owl with an eye patch on her one eye, and one who was holding a coconut under her wing. The young girl pulled the cork; She smelled the contents carefully, and then she drank it.

- 'It tastes like coconut milk…with chocolate syrup,' she thought. She enjoyed the taste with the help of her tongue's taste buds for a few minutes. 'I think my strength is returning. There is not much left inside …' She put the cork back in and placed the bottle back in its hidden position. 'How good that was!' she thought and walked out of the pond. She then proceeded toward the main hall. She passed by the entrance doors that carried a decoration of stained-glass black dolphins that swam within some blue waves, the design of a star in the color of orange, and another design that resembled an octopus. She turned to the left side past the main desk that had some white ancient Greek pillars and a deep brown ceiling, as well as a glowing stained glass that was fixed on the wall of a big shell within the water and several types of fish. Its intense blue gave people a sense of freshness and relaxation. She then walked above a big mosaic of the same design that resembled an octopus, with a few fish present among its tentacles. From within their eyes, some miniature lights offered their intense rays on the spot. The mosaic pieces glowed like colorful pearls in turquoise, green, light green, blue, and pink. Some more blue mosaic square stones represented water, whereas the pebbles of smaller waves had been dyed in gold. Anemona decided to descend the stairs that were on her left. She had reached the floor beneath when she noticed the door opposite her with the following inscription: 'Restaurant.' She went down the next staircase to her right until she found herself in the basement, where some shops of furs, jewelry, scarves, and hats served the clients' needs. She walked past them and found herself outside at a big swimming pool. Some of the hotel guests were already swimming inside, while Anemona seemed to have started sweating. Despite the wintery month of December, the climate had been rather warm due to the warm southern wind.

- 'I need some more Life bottles. I wonder where I can find the rest,' she thought and moved further ahead. She walked over a few arched bridges; She walked through trails that were decorated with exotic flowers and discovered even more swimming pools that had been constructed in various shapes. One of them had a whole 'kaiki' boat inside it, as it was called in the Greek language. At some point on one of the trails, she walked past a few chefs who had been roasting some meat and vegetables as well as fruits for the guests. She was impressed and enjoyed watching the food sizzling on the barbeque. A small wagon that carried all the laundry drove by.

- 'I feel like it is important to follow it...' Anemona whispered. She decided to listen to her instinct, so she followed it up a path past three shops that displayed a number of fresh-looking silk scarves in variations of blue, turquoise, ultramarine blue, and green. She followed it until the little wagon stopped and the driver got off. Anemona walked up the trail until she found herself at a crossroads. Her eyes popped out as soon as she saw something in front of her- something she was not expecting to see.

- 'A Pirate ship!' she said excitedly. She stood for a few seconds as if she had been bewitched and stared at the big ship with the thick ropes. After her mind had absorbed the new exciting image, she kept going, looking for the entrance. 'It is too warm. I better return to the sushi bar and see whether I can have something to drink,' she changed her mind and walked back to the Japanese restaurant that was a few feet down the same road, on her right side as she walked. A number of children were sitting at the tables, having their Japanese raw meal. Anemona headed to the bar, to see whether somebody was currently ducking behind the counter. She walked to the side and saw nobody behind it. She looked toward the children right after. 'Nobody seems to be serving them either. Perhaps I need to wait for a while? I hope somebody will show up soon. I am so thirsty! I am sure somebody will. I am already grateful for the moment this cold glass of water will be offered to me! Thank you so much to whoever would bring it to me! Thank you. I am truly grateful!'

An ethereal figure of a floating little man appeared right behind her, above the counter. This figure looked like a cartoon that had just come to life. It looked as if he was made of ice. The miniature man spread his hand in front of him with an open palm and he blew into existence a tall glass made of ice which contained various fruits inside its frozen walls. As he placed the glass on the counter, it started filling up with water. The floating man with the sympathetic friendly face, who was thin as a strand of cobweb hair, inserted his hand into his heart and pulled something out. When he opened his palm, there were some ice figures of a heart, a star, a monkey, and a koala. He inserted all four into the refreshing drink with a slice of lemon, while his frosty hair with drops attached to it floated in the air. And then…he disappeared. Anemona looked behind her back once again and discovered the cold drink.

- 'A glass of water! And there is ice inside also! Oh! Look at those shapes! How beautiful! Is it for me?' she wondered. Since she could not see anyone around, she dared lift it. Some traces of snow-crystals were melting on the counter. She took a few sips at once, as she could hardly endure any longer, and then she admired the frozen raspberries, strawberries, and blackberries that were being preserved within the icy glass.

'Thank you!' She placed the glass onto the counter and walked away from the sushi restaurant. 'Let's go to the ship now!' she thought and went up the trail. She started sweating heavily.

'It is much warmer than I thought,' she whispered and swept her forehead with her right hand. 'Why are the trees drying out at such great speed?' she wondered while she looked at the closest trees around her. A zombie walked behind the girl- a zombie that looked most horrifying to anyone who encountered it. Its spirit was absent from its body and walked in slow, steady steps. Right behind it, the woman with the red hair appeared. She had spread her hands toward the zombie and seemed to be manipulating it. It attempted to pull Anemona's necklace from her neck. Her Phaistos disc was pulled out from within her blouse. It reached the top of her head and was about to float past her ears. One more second was needed for the woman with the red hair to grab it. Just one more second. A crow dived against the woman's face and caused her to lose her focus. The zombie lowered its arms and froze. The woman fell onto the ground and disappeared. Anemona's coded disc fell back in front of her face onto her chest.

'Fterouga! What are you doing here?' the girl asked her beloved crow when she turned back and saw him looking for something on the ground. 'Go home please! Go home!' she urged him and turned the other way when the crow flew again right above her.

The ship looked as if it had been waiting patiently for Anemona to explore it. Its Jacob's Ladder looked fresh and puffy, white and strong.

- 'I want to explore every single inch of it!' She ran up the gangplank, holding herself with the supportive ropes. As soon as she found herself on the deck, she looked around cautiously. She was currently the only child on the ship as it seemed, so she had the wonderful opportunity to be aware and absorb in her consciousness every single noise and smell that caused her to feel that this ship was 'alive:' Every crack on the deck, every blow on the sails, every rub of the ropes. The ropes had been wrapped around a big thick rectangular handle, known as the 'belaying pin-' thick ropes, thin ropes, and even thinner ropes. Anemona grabbed one of the thick ropes in her arms.

-'It is pretty heavy!' she said to herself. She then looked around and saw some abrupt stairs leading to the lower deck. She decided to descend them carefully. She noticed a few lanterns that lit the space from the ceiling- traditional lanterns with white Corinthian fluted shaft columns all around the corners. The girl noticed another unique characteristic which was very familiar to her.

-'The shapes on the glass…these are the very same figures as the ones on the Phaistos disk!' She admired them on both the glass and around on the wooden walls as well, as their shadows looked magnified in the cozy soothing candlelight, creating a mysterious atmosphere with these encrypted, puzzling figures. And right opposite the stairs, under an intense display light, a collection of nautical knots had been framed for children's educational purposes. 'An eye, a 'reef knot,' a 'hunter's bend,' a 'goose neck,' a 'butterfly knot,' a 'double carrick bend,' a 'jury mast knot,' a 'thumb knot,' and a few others…! How interesting!' Anemona whispered. 'And the 'cheesing,'' she commented as soon as she saw the way a certain rope had been wrapped. 'It looks like those lunch mats!' she thought. After a few seconds of admiration, she decided to proceed to some cabins further ahead on her right side. 'This must be the kitchen,' Anemona thought as soon as she entered and saw a few resin model-imitations of food on the main desk. Two big, round cheese balls made of sheep's milk, some dakos hard bread which was similar to the pirates' sea biscuits, a rabbit, some other kind of goat's and sheep's cheeses, green beans and okra, as well as a few red onions were hanging on the wall within a protective net. Three models of weasels were also near the food. A bottle was standing on the main desk, as well as some red tomatoes, and a jug that seemed to be made of pewter.

- 'A bottle!' Anemona shouted, excited, and grabbed it from behind the round masses of cheese. This bottle had a cork with a pirate's skull, which had been pierced by a blade. 'Is that the Captain?' Anemona wondered, as this skull was wearing a big impressive hat that would seem to belong to a Captain only. She uncorked it and started drinking the glowing drink, when she sensed a good sweet smell coming out of it. The intense glowing of her body could not be restricted within the kitchen. It permeated through the brown glass bricks that offered the whole space a unique atmosphere and lit the remaining parts of the deck for a few seconds. The glass bricks looked like lollipops.

- 'They remind me of those rooster lollipops!' Anemona thought. 'And they also look like luxurious chocolates…chocolates with a thin golden wrapping,' she fantasized, and kept staring at them in a way as if she had discovered the greatest treasure of all. She spread her hand and touched the surface. 'You could be a bar of chocolate with coconut oil inside…' she whispered, when all of a sudden, a bar of chocolate with luxurious wrapping materialized to her left on the main desk. But the girl did not notice, for the reason that she had no expectations. She would discover part of the treasure only when it was the most appropriate moment for her to appreciate its value. Not earlier, not later. For the present, she felt the need to absorb the rich image inside her mind, and then she decided to walk out of the kitchen. She entered another cabin with many windows at the front and the sides.

- 'This must be the Captain's cabin if I judge from the beautiful table. And these parchments look like maps,' she said and sat on one of the dark oak sculpted chairs. She unrolled one of them carefully, to see what they were hiding. 'It is too big!' she said and decided to grab an old kind of astrolabe as well as a spyglass that rested on the table and move them to the window sill. She then grabbed another two or three parchments and placed them under the windows. She went back to her seat and unrolled the big parchment. 'Oh my gosh! It really IS a map!' she shouted excitedly.

'Map of the Invisible World,'

She read on its base and admired the multiple figures that had been drawn all around the world. Then her eyes fell on the inscription that had been added right beneath the main title:

"Including Portals of Outer Universe Civilizations, Cities Underwater, Pirates, Civilizations of the Inner Earth, Monsters, Mermaids, Skeletons, and Zombies."

'Pirates!' Anemona said. "Treasure of the pirate Captain Barbarossa, hidden in 1535," she read on the drawn island of Mallorca, which belonged to Spain. 'And here are more pirates!' she said after a quick browse on the map's left side. 'Malaysian Pirates' she read under a drawing of a ship with a peculiar kind of sails that resembled a flying lizard's wings. The depicted pirates seemed to be throwing fishing nets into the sea to catch the day's lunch. It seemed they had caught a merman. Anemona looked further to the left, toward the Atlantic Ocean. 'Pirate Henry Morgan (17th Century) marauds Spain's Carribean colonies,' she read under the next drawing of a pirate ship with a black flag and heaps of human bones on the deck. This ship had the pirate himself depicted on board along with his tied up prisoner, Puerto Principe. Another Pirate ship appeared further to the left. 'British Pirate Mary Read (17th-18th Century),' the girl read under the next ship with an image of a lady as its Captain. She stood among her crew of a few wild-

Rosie Protects the Coded Disc of Phaistos

looking mermen who held swordfish and big jellyfish in their hands. The upper part of their heads consisted of big shells. Anemona looked next further up in the Caribbean Sea, where one more pirate ship hardly escaped her attention. It belonged to British pirate Edward Teach, known as Blackbeard. So many pirates and so many hidden treasures!' the girl spoke to herself. 'This map is wonderful!' she thought. 'I wish I could have an adventure with pirates!' she wished, without being careful enough as to what exactly it was she was wishing for.

She then decided to walk out of the Captain's cabin and visit another cabin. She discovered a table with a few pewter plates, some cutlery, four wine jugs, two candlesticks, two bottles, and a few buns inside a basket. The table had been placed right next to a blue velvet curtain that displayed an image of the sea world deep inside the ocean, with a range of devilfish, black dragonfish, deep blue angler fish, spook fish, a giant vampire squid, sea serpents (all of them wearing pirate eye patches), shells, and corals.

One of the mysterious lanterns that hung from the ceiling offered its light and coded symbols to the crew. The spirits of the Captain and his crew appeared in front of Anemona's eyes while they helped themselves to their dinner.

- 'They are having 'kakavia!' Anemona whispered when she saw the traditional fish soup that fishermen used to have inside their bowls. It was a really unique meal, with a number of different fish, potatoes, tomatoes, carrots, onions, and celery. The girl sniffed at the scent of lemon in the air. It was usually used in the making of such soups to give them a special flavor. This soup also had the additional characteristic of being very thick, and to achieve this, chefs had added a lot of onions.

Anemona decided to leave the spirits in order to let them eat undisturbed, and she also decided to walk down some stairs that she had discovered on the deck. As soon as she found herself on the lower deck, she saw a few bunks where the sailors slept. She barely dared take a breath when she thought she heard somebody snore. After a few seconds of not hearing any more noise, she dared to walk on, and saw a bunch of clay pots, pewter pots, and pans. They were lying on top of a few boxes, waiting for their turn to be used. And then, the snoring sounded again. Anemona turned her head, and it stopped. For a second time, she could not see anybody sleeping on the bunks. She took a puzzled expression, but then noticed the cannons that came out of the gun ports. Right next to the cannons were a series of coconuts that were placed one behind the other to be used as cannonballs. All of a sudden, the snoring sounded for a third time. The girl turned behind her very quickly and she saw a sailor's spirit sleeping on one of the bunks. She stepped on tiptoes toward the stairs and walked upstairs as quietly as she could. Some of the stairs were slightly noisy, and one of the steps' creaks interrupted the snoring for a few seconds. Anemona did not dare take another step until the sailor sounded asleep once again.

Our friend was soon on the upper deck and decided to walk back to the kitchen.

- 'Oh! Is this a chocolate?' she asked herself as soon as her eyes were attracted by the thin golden wrapping on the main desk. 'It was not here before!' she thought. 'I wonder whether it belongs to another child who forgot it here?' She grabbed the temptation and looked around. She walked out of the kitchen and proceeded to the dining area. The spirits of the sailors and the Captain were not there anymore. The only signs left of them were a few fish bones on their plates and parts of the soft buns with their fingerprints in them.

- 'One of the bottles is still corked. It must be a Life bottle,' she thought, and walked toward the table. She left the chocolate on the table's surface and looked back at the bottle. As soon as she did that, she discovered that there was another cork in the bottle this time. This cork had an imitation of the chef's head with two blades permeating his skull. His tall white hat carried a logo of a swordfish with an eye patch on one of its eyes. Anemona uncorked it and drank some more Life juice. 'It tastes like banana!' she said as soon as she had wiped her mouth. 'How good that was!' she sighed with pleasure. She then took the chocolate with her and walked back to the Captain's cabin. Another bottle was standing on the table this time. It was a bottle with a different kind of cork. Anemona approached, and due to her surprise, she forgot what her initial mission was. She placed the chocolate on the Captain's lustered table and took the bottle in her hands. 'A beautiful parrot with blue and red feathers!' She touched the parrot-cork with her fingers; She pulled it out and laid it on the table. She smelled it and then brought the bottle to her lips. She took a few sips and found it difficult to stop. 'Vanilla milk smoothie with strawberry syrup!'

In her state of happiness, the girl could not control herself anymore. She ran out of the Captain's room to the stairs that led downstairs. She descended the staircase without caring whether she would wake up the sailor's spirit this time and looked for another bottle. She searched among the pots, plates, and pans, and then she walked through the bunks. There was a bottle next to the bunk where the snoring was detected by her ears. She lifted it from the floor without paying close attention to its cork. She uncorked it quickly and took a few sips. After a few gulps, she rested and lowered her hand with the bottle, waiting for the new taste to sink in. She waited some more. There was no expression on her face. She still waited. At some point, she let the cork fall from her hand onto one of the bunks, and then she grabbed her stomach and stooped down. She started sweating and looked paler than the spirits she had encountered in the dining room. She dropped the bottle on the floor and ran toward the stairs. She tried to hold herself up with the rail and almost crawled onto the steps. She struggled to pull herself onto the upper deck and ran toward the Captain's cabin without being able to see this time the new cork that was rolling on the bunk where she had dropped it- a cork which had a lady's head on it. She was a lady with red snakes for hair and a pair of big innocent-looking eyes…

A little mirror with a decorative silver frame was now standing vertically on the Captain's table when Anemona went in. She looked inside it and saw that she had black circles under her eyes as well as a white complexion that made her look like a ghost. She ran to the windows and unrolled the other maps, hoping to discover the description of a possible antidote. However, all she discovered was that these were parchments of different kinds of maps. A few children who were holding blades and wearing scarves around their heads entered the cabin.

- 'I need help! Please...I need help!' Anemona asked them at once.

The children did not seem to be able to hear her or see her. 'I am NOT well!' she said, but they did not seem to be aware of her presence at all.

- 'Oh look! Treasure maps!' a girl with a ponytail of curly chestnut hair shouted. Her friends kneeled around the maps and started to unroll them. Anemona clutched her stomach once more and tried to support herself on the chair, when all of a sudden, the big map that she had unrolled before and which was now rolled up again on the table, jumped into the air. It unrolled itself and took a spherical shape. It currently looked like a big live globe that was turning in slow circles. Anemona approached it and saw that the sea's water looked fresh and very real. It had some low waves on its surface. Our friend waited until Crete was visible in front of her, after the globe had completed a full circle. She touched 'Iraklion' city, and the surface revealed a whirlpool within the water of the Mediterranean Sea. The whirlpool pulled at her hand, and within seconds, Anemona had been sucked inside the living globe...

28. Equilibrium.

- '*W*hat do we do now?' Alexander asked in distress, and his pearl shiny aura started tearing in the areas of his stomach and his heart. He was now subject to danger. Any negative entity could approach him and suck out his vital energy at the lion square.

- 'Grab as many bottles as you can and empty them!' Roserin prompted them as soon as she saw the bottles still standing on their shelves. 'Quickly!' she shouted as everyone looked at her with puzzled faces. Despite their surprise at seeing her all of a sudden, they approached the partition with the dark bottles that were filled with alcohol. They grabbed materialized clones of the bottles and emptied the alcohol onto the street. Henrietta and Bernard moved over to the partition with the round bamboo-covered bottles and turned them upside down. Some more wine and traditional alcohol spilled out onto the ground.

'Now, come over here and let's get as close to each other as possible, with your backs against them, and keep the area of your stomach well protected,' Rosie suggested.

Stamatis, Henrietta (who had also returned to the battlefield), Bernard, Robert, Alexander, and Astrapi ran instantly and shaped a circle with their backs exposed outward. Roserin was standing in the middle, holding the bottles that she had emptied.

- 'Now lift the bottles above your head and wait until it is done!' she shouted while a strong gust of wind started twirling all around them.

- 'What is happening?' Stamatis asked. 'Has she arrived? Are we inside the eye of the tornado?' he shouted so that he would be heard.

- 'Rosie?' Alexander shouted to her next, expecting to receive an answer as to what exactly they were doing there with the open bottles above their heads. He could feel a strong active force behind his back.

- 'Just focus! It will be over soon!' Astrapi's voice sounded inside their minds.

- 'Is that hiccups that I hear?' Bernard asked, but he did not dare look behind his back. Losing his face once was too hard a lesson, so he was not in the mood to experience anything else unnatural. Hiccups had been heard indeed. But neither the children nor the penguin dared look at what was happening behind their backs. Right at these moments, all they felt they could do was to keep the bottles above their heads and wait. Besides, they had the feeling that they had found themselves within the eye of a dangerous tornado. And when something like this occurs, nobody wants to approach the tornado's walls. The children had focused their sight on the bottles they still held, with difficulty, in their right hand. And with their left arm, they supported their tired right arm. Various instruments were now flying around above them. The lutes that Stamatis had seen, the bagpipes, the bouzoukis, jewelry that ladies had been trying to sell and which now looked almost like pieces of coal, some cracked wooden handcrafts like round honey containers, the aloe vera plants that were now almost dry, the Cretan herbs in the baskets, and some beautiful ceramic work that had almost lost its vibrant color were all up in the air. Even the fresh painting that Stamatis had admired was twirling around, looking dark, pale, and grey, as all the other objects now looked old, pale and grey.

'We release the fears, prejudice, bitterness, traumas, and anger from the cells of this life and any possible previous lives, to the White Light!

And so it is!'

Roserin shouted. The strong winds were drawn inside the bottles.

-'Now seal the bottles!' Rosie said to her friends, who grabbed the corks they had protected within their pockets and pushed them into the bottle openings. A strong white light emerged from within every child's ethereal body.

- 'What did we just seal?' Alexander asked, baffled.

- 'We have people's fears and other negative feelings in here now,' Roserin replied.

- 'People's fears? And negative feelings? What are we going to do with them? he asked.

- 'You will see in time!' Rosie replied to her friend. Bernard recalled the Calligrapher's words as soon as he heard his friend:

'My boy, the question you should be asking is not 'how.' The question you should be asking is 'when.' Since you are asking and you seem to be eager to learn, we cannot yet tell when that moment will be. Time is an interesting concept you see. Time does NOT exist in the universe. It has been created by people. The best answer I can give you at this moment is to count by 'Spirit,' not by time.'

- 'Count by spirit'…the boy whispered to himself. 'So when the right spirit comes, we will find the answer,' he said, increasing his tone, finally addressing Alexander. His cousin looked at Bernard with a pondering expression.

- 'Wait up!' Stamatis shouted to his sister as she headed hastily toward the central Morozini fountain with the four lions standing proudly around it.

- 'Why are we here?' Henrietta asked her friend.

- 'My intuition has told me so,' Roserin replied.

- 'Your intuition? So what do we do now?' Henrietta asked again while her friend was looking at the fountain.

- 'I am not sure,' Roserin said.

-'Well, we have to do something because she is approaching,' Alexander said.

- 'I have never felt such immense pressure before in my afterlife!' Stamatis commented. 'You'd better think of something fast!'

- 'We have to wait here,' Rosie confirmed.

- 'And do what?' Stamatis asked.

-'I am not sure,' Roserin replied. Stamatis and Alexander sighed in great anxiety. Alexander approached his friend decisively.

- 'Rosie. We have to do something NOW. She is getting closer and closer. What was your intention with the bottles?' he asked her.

- 'Do NOT stress me out. You are blocking the connection,' she said firmly.

- 'The…the connection?' Alexander repeated.

- 'Yes. I feel I am receiving something,' Rosie said and looked in front of her in a way that indicated she was seeing something that the others could not see.

- 'What is it?' Bernard asked. Roserin focused, and total silence prevailed. It was the kind of silence that to the others felt unbearable. It was the kind of silence that made somebody feel that they were as powerless as an innocent rabbit, and that their own life depended on somebody else's actions. Bernard took out of his pocket the Angel's curl and looked at it. It glowed warmth and gave him an air of protection.

- 'This is just too much,' Alexander said. I am not going to wait here and...'

A loud noise from behind him interrupted his thought. He turned around and saw a lion looking at them. It was one of the four lions that were guarding the fountain. The children shivered. Not only was he a visitor that had not been expected, but he also looked really big.

- 'Let's go!' Roserin shouted and ran toward the lion, whereas her friends and her brother turned the opposite direction and ran away from the lion. 'No! THIS way!' she shouted again, this time from the lion's back where she had grabbed ahold of his mane. Everyone stopped and turned their heads. They were stunned to see Rosie and Robert sitting on this powerful furry cat, along with Astrapi. Was the lion behaving like a big tame lion because Astrapi was an African cat? Perhaps he was a distant relative of his? They walked toward the animal with caution. 'You have nothing to worry about! I feel he wants to take us somewhere,' Roserin said.

Her friends climbed onto the lion's back. The lion still looked white from the stone in which he was encapsulated before. A cloud materialized in front of Daidalou street (the main shopping area), and the lion jumped right inside it. People who were present at the central square around the fountain were left with the impression that the fourth lion had been broken by the 'Noble One' who had hit the statue hard with his tail. Those had been the people who could actually see him. Others, who were too preoccupied with their own matters in life while they were enjoying a bougatsa sweet at a near café, could not explain the sudden explosion of the statue into smaller stones. The lion had managed to free himself right before the dinosaur's tail made contact.

At the Museum of Natural History, at the lower level where the earthquake simulator was functioning, another shimmery cloud started forming between the stairs and the two big posters that carried the title: 'The Earthquakes.' From within this cloud, the lion, the children, the penguin, and Astrapi landed onto the floor. The lion proceeded up to the level where the earthquake simulator was.

- 'Why are we here?' Stamatis wondered.

-'I think I know why. Follow me, and take the bottles with you!' Rosie said and walked straight into the earthquake simulator. So did Stamatis, Alexander, Bernard, Robert, and Henrietta. Astrapi preferred to wait outside the simulator. Inside, people were sitting on the benches, experiencing the various degrees of the earthquakes. The most devastating earthquake that had occurred in Kobe, Japan was just about to begin.

- 'Open your bottles! Quickly!!' Roserin urged them. And so they did. The big earthquake began, and two little children started crying. The map on the wall moved toward the right and then toward the left; The hanging lamp above them shook violently, moving in a semi-circle almost. A strong wind formed within seconds, so the children realized instantly what they had to do next. They formed a circle with their backs against everyone else, and with Bernard and Robert standing in the middle. They raised their bottles above their heads with the corks inside their pockets. A tornado formed around them so big and strong that the visitors were not visible to them anymore. They were carried away in the tornado's walls.

- 'Stay close! Stay away from the walls!' Alexander shouted. While everyone looked upward, laughing skeletons were seen by the children. They were being carried by the tornado unwillingly. They saw psychic vampires who hardly stopped talking and were kissing portraits of themselves, monsters, hypocrites who carried broken mirrors, bats, snakes, even scary teachers with strict faces and that terrible look they gave above their glasses. Ghosts were seen by Stamatis too, and gargoyles, crocodiles, zombies, and witches. The children's screams sounded inside the tornado.

- 'It is almost done. Stay close! Almost done!' Henrietta shouted with her hair being blown in front of her mouth.

- 'Don't turn just yet! It is not over!' Roserin warned. The simulator kept shaking, a lot more violently this time. The tornado seemed to be a lot stronger than before. Alexander was pulled backward when Bernard grabbed his hand quickly and pulled him back into the circle. Some more arrogant teachers holding long sticks appeared, flying around the tornado's walls. Some creepy-looking clowns were next, along with women with long red nails. Henrietta thought she saw Death with his long sharp scythe in his hand. Rosie saw the notorious 'Baboulas' being swallowed by these powerful walls of wind. He was captured in a long chain of Christmas lights, which even played Christmas songs and twinkled in various colors.

- 'This must be the 7.6 Richter earthquake in Chi-Chi!' Alexander shouted loudly. The tornado's whoosh alone caused the children additional fears. These fears were sucked out by the tornado's walls too. Roserin's phobia of darkness was seen by the walls of the tornado, so for a few seconds, she could see nothing. Everything was pitch black. When the darkness was gone, giant olive trees and bushes surrounded and trapped by spider webs appeared, swirling in the threatening air walls. This was Rosie's second phobia: spiders. Then some luminous olive trees with outraged facial expressions appeared, dancing at high speeds, passing by very closely. This was Bernard's phobia of scary olive trees. When the luminous faces were gone, Alexander saw himself as a successful actor, with pages of scripts floating around him and being swallowed by the tornado. Being successful had always been a deep fear of his, since he did not want his parents to feel embarrassed about their own lack of chance to succeed in life. His replica smiled at him while he floated along with all the other fears. Henrietta was put to the test too. A grandiose bride, a creepy-looking doll, appeared hovering in the tornado's eye, right above her head. As the doll hovered above her, she laughed at the girl in a very sarcastic way. Henrietta released a cry of fear as soon as she noticed the doll's presence, and she kneeled toward the ground.

- 'Get up!' Stamatis lifted her from her arm and also raised her arm upward, so that she would keep gathering 'fear' inside her bottle. Henrietta had become doll-phobic, and could not keep a single doll inside her room. A few more dolls whooshed past and a number of scarecrows came next.

Scarecrows always terrified Stamatis. When he was little, a criminal had trespassed on their property, dressed as one. His transformation had been so realistic that when the boy saw him in their garden, he thought his father had planted a fake scarecrow there. He thought his heart would never stop pounding when the burglar turned his head and smiled at him. One of the scarecrows that whooshed by had this thief's smile. Stamatis released a girly cry and looked down at his shoes at once. The ground trembled. A big sea lion with a big moustache and big sharp teeth approached Robert. The shocked penguin avoided its mouth snapping toward him and hugged Bernard's legs tight. His terrifying predator was sucked in again, away from the children, Astrapi, and the poor innocent Robert. The ground trembled for about three more seconds, and then it stopped. Stamatis looked at the others, and he saw that they were lowering their arms with the bottles. He put his hand into his coat pocket and grabbed two corks. He sealed the two bottles he was holding.

- 'I thought it would never stop!' Henrietta said with relief.

- 'I had the same impression, believe me!' Stamatis answered back.

They looked behind them and could see the visitors who were leaving the earthquake simulator. A few of their children's bags had fallen off the benches onto the floor. Two parents were making efforts to calm down their terrified children, explaining to them that these earthquakes had only been a part of the museum's attraction. The tornado and the phobias were gone for the present for Roserin, Bernard, Robert, Henrietta, Alexander, Astrapi, and Stamatis, as well as for the younger children, in the same way that the earthquakes had stopped for the visitors. Alexander, Rosie, and Bernard sighed deeply after coming face to face with their deepest fears.

- 'Come on, let's go!' Stamatis urged them before they had a chance to take a breath. They passed through the simulator's safety door and walked to the main corridor. The white lion growled loudly and extended his leg toward them.

- 'He wants us to climb on his back,' Alexander said. Astrapi got off

Rosie Protects the Coded Disc of Phaistos

the square 'vibrate yourself' machine on which people could step and create their own vibration, and jumped onto the big lion's back. So did Robert and the children, making great effort to keep the bottles safe. Bernard had the unique idea of using Roserin's long hair to pass through the bamboo bottles' loops and bind them together. He sat right behind her. Henrietta had decided to stabilize her bottles within Alexander's sweater, on the back side of his waist. Alexander placed his own bamboo bottles within the very deep pointy hood of Bernard's coat, whereas Stamatis who sat behind Henrietta and in front of Astrapi, tried hard to materialize a basket filled with straw with the power of his imagination.

He tried to focus by clearing his mind, and he imagined the basket was already sitting in front of him. Until he achieved it, he had to hold the bottles in his hands. He did the best he could to feel the enthusiasm he would feel as soon as he had achieved his target. The lion ran forward and jumped through the wall. One bottle fell behind Stamatis and landed onto the floor. It spun in front of the wall a few times and stopped.

At the Koule Fortress, the stone-carved lion that was touching a book with his paw at the upper part of the back walls moved his head up and down first, then he moved to the right side. Right at this moment, the white lion jumped from within, with the children, Robert, and Astrapi as his riders. He had grown a pair of big wings on his back in the meantime and flew above the castle. They headed toward 25th August street, where the fiery tornado of the woman with the red hair could be seen ascending the main trail. It had become wider and bigger and had started burning the cute, small, traditional shops on both sides. The white lion landed in the middle of the trail, right between the big green flames. The children, Robert, and Astrapi got off his back.

- 'Open the bottles! Quickly!' Rosie shouted. They uncorked them instantly.

- 'They ARE open! What do we do now?' Alexander asked.

- 'We wait!' Roserin confirmed. 'No matter what happens from now on, remain in your positions with your feet firmly stuck on the ground!'

- 'Why do I get the feeling that I am not going to like this? 'Stamatis asked.

- 'I hope that what you have in mind will happen soon, Rosie, because it is getting toasty in here!' Alexander said.

- 'What is that?' Henrietta pointed toward the twirling, fiery tornado.

- 'Grab your bottles and spread your arms in front of you above your forehead!' Roserin asked them. Her friends and her brother did what she had suggested, apart from Robert, who ran toward the dolphin monument. It was too warm for him to endure. As soon as he arrived, showers of refreshing water fell on him and protected him from the deadly heat wave. In addition to that, something else occurred. With his left flipper, which he moved three hundred and sixty degrees around himself, he materialized a small igloo of ice, within which he disappeared.

The floating spirit of the striped hyena floated toward the children, closer and closer. She appeared from within the tornado's walls. She now hovered almost above the children when she was suddenly sucked into one of Bernard's bottles.

-'Put the cork in Bernard! Quick!' Roserin shouted. Her friend grabbed a cork with trembling fingers and sealed the bottle. He put it inside his pocket, and undid Rosie's hair to take another bottle. He made another knot using her hair to bind the remaining flasks. He uncorked the second bottle next, and held it up in the air. Something bigger appeared in the distance, floating away from the horrifying tornado. It seemed to be round.

- 'Is that the crested porcupine?' Henrietta asked.

- 'Keep your feet firmly on the ground, Bernard!' Roserin said. 'It looks like it is heading YOUR way.'

- 'MY way? Bernard gulped. He saw the crested porcupine's long sharp quills being whirred, in a very characteristic position to attack, as it floated backward. The boy sweated as the animal came closer and closer to his position. The shorter, thicker quills it used to attack other animals and people were at such a close distance now that this moment was the perfect moment for a nature photographer to take a breathtaking shot. Bernard held his feet firmly on the ground; He spread both of his arms forward and above his head, moved his head downward, and closed his eyes when he felt an intense bump. The threatening spirit had been sucked inside the bottle.

- 'Good job Bernard! Keep it up!' Henrietta encouraged him.

- 'What is that thing coming over here? No way!!' Stamatis shouted while Bernard was sealing his second bottle with a cork.

- 'Is that a dinosaur?' Alexander asked as soon as he saw the spirit of Giganotosaurus Carolinii being sucked toward them.

- 'I am not going to become as flat as a 'souvlaki' pie! I will leave the bottle on the ground and get out of here! Besides, it has gotten too hot. We better retreat!' Stamatis shouted in anxiety as soon as he saw the giant Carolinii being drawn in his direction. The flames around him made him feel as if he were a gyros pie (as the traditional meat pie was called in Crete) being stuck onto the main impaling iron that chefs used to turn the meat slowly and gradually over the flesh-burning fire.

- 'No! Don't leave it on the floor! All the fears would be released from that bottle if you did that!' Roserin shouted to him. 'Keep it in your hands and ground yourself firmly with your feet steady on the stones!'

- 'Oh really? YOU come and stand in my place then and put this monster into the bottle!' Stamatis shouted.

- 'The dinosaur has chosen YOU!' Henrietta shouted to Stamatis a few seconds before Giganotosaurus Carolinii arrived above his head. Stamatis was stunned and did not make any further effort to lower and abandon the bottle on the ground. He turned to the left and addressed

Henrietta:

- 'And HOW do you know that? THIS–' he spread his right arm with the bottle up in the air, 'is a BIG-headed lizard weighing eight tons!' he shouted. The Carolinii dinosaur touched his bottle and was sucked within it right before Stamatis had the chance to turn his head back to the right. The children's and Astrapi's eyes popped out as wide as the plush white-gowned fish's that stood out in front of the two fish foot spas ahead of them. Stamatis was astonished that he had made such a strong impact with what he had said to them. Then he turned back to the right.

- 'Where is he?' he asked them. His friends could not respond. They had frozen in their positions with astonishment. 'He is not…' –he looked inside his bottle- 'Is he?' he wondered. 'Nooooo…' he said with disbelief.

- 'Is that a snake?' Bernard asked all of a sudden. Another spirit was on its way while the shops around them kept burning fiercely and the woman with the red hair was approaching the Christmas market. Another lady came out of the burning shops crying. She was holding an unfolded letter in her hands. 'I can't pay all these taxes. I don't have the money. I just don't…'

Taniwhausaurus Antarcticus, the snake-like dino fish, was being sucked toward Henrietta's bottle. The predatory lizard came closer and closer. The Rebbachisaurus Tessonei dinosaur appeared right behind the sharp-toothed Taniwhasaurus. The dino fish thrashed its body in the air, as if it had been caught by fishnets. It came closer. It opened its mouth wide and his white sharp teeth were about to bite Henrietta. She turned her bottle toward him. Her arm entered his open mouth along with the rest of her body, but as soon as the bottle touched the upper part of his mouth, he was sucked deep inside its belly. The girl grabbed a cork from her pocket and sealed the bottle quickly.

Rebbachisaurus Tessonei was now on his way. The stones still crashed against each other inside his stomach. His long throat looked even scarier from where the children stood.

- 'A ten-ton dinosaur is heading toward me!' Alexander shouted.

- 'What were you thinking, that you would get away with it?' Stamatis shouted back. 'Don't lose your nerve! It's only the idea that is so scary!' his friend encouraged him.

The dinosaur looked like a big mountain that grew legs and a big throat. It whooshed past other spirits of the museum that were on their way toward the children. The red fox, a flock of birds, a wild boar, a bear, an eagle, a crow, and the woodpecker with the red feathers on his head were all in the air, floating away from the tornado's walls that had transformed into lava. Alexander prepared himself for a big impact. He leaned the upper part of his body forward, with both of his hands holding the bottle firmly. His right hand was on the bottle's neck, whereas his left hand was right below its base, as he was worried that the bottle might slip with all the sweat that he had on his hands. The moment of impact was near. He closed his eyes. The wide-mouthed dinosaur opened his mouth and his multiple tiny teeth made their presence noticeable. The bottle's lips touched his tongue, and the dinosaur was sucked inside it. The stones that hung within his stomach fell onto the ground with a smashing noise. Alexander jumped into the air to avoid one of them crashing against him, while Henrietta had just captured the wild boar as he was pulled toward her. She sealed the bottle with a cork while Alexander tried to calm himself down.

- 'I am the one who has control. I am the one who has control!' he kept repeating to himself.

The big bear was now being pulled toward Roserin. The bear's big sharp claws on her feet could not go unnoticed as she was being sucked by her own craving to enjoy the smell of fear, prejudice, bitterness, traumas, and anger. This brown fluffy-looking beauty that emitted the illusion that she was as harmless as a soft toy had the proper defensive tools to protect herself from anyone who attempted to run toward her and squeeze her like jelly in their enthusiasm. She did two somersaults in the air before her paw revealed its pointy sharp claws to Rosie. The latter one could not take her eyes off the cuddly-looking bear with the sympathetic face until her snout

Rosie Protects the Coded Disc of Phaistos

was attracted by the girl's bottle. The impressive animal looked as if she was trying to detect some honey within that dark bottle. Roserin corked it very quickly while simultaneously the woodpecker with the red feathers on his head was trapped inside Henrietta's bottle. A few of his beautiful red feathers did not make it inside the bottle with the rest of him. Some little birds were now approaching Stamatis' bottle. They looked like little fluffy tennis balls orbiting around themselves as they struggled to find their balance in the air.

- 'I think only little animals are approaching us from now on; Things are getting easier now!' Alexander shouted. Then the next animal appeared. The Giant Deinotherium made its presence noticeable from within the walls of lava and fire. It floated in the center and then moved to the right side where Stamatis was standing. It kept approaching. Stamatis froze. When it reached the foot spa on the children's right side, it changed its direction and was now being pulled toward the center. Everyone ran next to Bernard to support him, as it seemed that the two-tusked giant was heading toward the boy. It did a somersault and fell onto Rosie, who had been unprepared. The two tusks under his jaw were just about to make an impact on the girl. She lifted the bottle in the air by instinct, as if it had been a toast that had just sprung out of the toaster. She targeted the Deinotherium's tusk from its inner surface, right from where it grew out. She was now standing between the two tusks under his jaw. Had Henrietta and Alexander not moved toward Bernard, the Deinotherium's massive body would have crushed them. Roserin seemed to have disappeared between the two tusks. The inner surface of his tusks barely touched the surface of her bottle and the beast was sucked inside effectively.

- 'The big ones are not yet all in the bottles! Get ready for the next ones!' Alexander shouted, when the next animal appeared at a closer distance this time. However, it gave the children the illusion that it was a lot further than it really was.

- 'What is it?' Bernard asked.

-'Is that a dino-bird?' Alexander wondered.

- 'It looks like a chicken!' Henrietta commented.

- 'It looks like a plucked chicken to me!' Roserin said.

- 'Is it a turkey perhaps?' Bernard asked his friends. 'Besides, it IS Christmas.'

- 'There was no turkey at the museum,' Stamatis said.

The unidentified floating bird (U.F.B.) was now heading toward Stamatis' bottle. It did seem to have the appearance of a plucked turkey with a very long tail. Stamatis placed his bottle in front of him and sucked in the bird with ease.

- 'That bird reminds me of somebody,' Stamatis thought when he looked at his bottle. Alexander had also not recognized the 'Buitreraptor Gonzalezorum' that they had seen at the museum. It was the proud dino-bird with the red feathers, who looked rather roasted now and more like the soy cooked birds that were seen hanging in the windows of the Chinese restaurants in China Town. This was also the first animal whose spirit had exited its body. Stamatis took another cork out of his pocket and sealed his bottle.

- 'She is heading toward us!' Rosie shouted all of a sudden when she spotted an owl with an eye patch being pulled toward Alexander.

- 'I got her!' Alexander shouted.

- 'Not her! I mean HER!' Henrietta pointed with her finger toward the woman with the red hair and her tornado. She had changed her direction toward the children. Now she was twirling with the same intensity of rage, wind, sand, and lava against our friends. The width of her tornado walls had not decreased either.

- 'What do we do now? The bottles will have melted as soon as she has reached half of the distance!' Roserin shouted.

- 'We cannot stay here!' Henrietta shouted back when a balcony fell and crashed at a close distance.

- 'What is that horrible smell?' Alexander asked and placed his hand in front of his nose. His friends sniffed in the air.

-'It smells like sulfur,' Henrietta replied. 'It is the characteristic smell of a negative entity. It is time we left. She is too close to us,' she warned.

-'But what about the people in the market?' Bernard asked.

-'It is us who are in danger now!' Henrietta shouted. 'She wants to get her puppets back…'

29. Projection.

- 'And what happens to the people here? They need help,' Roserin asked.

-'They will have to help themselves. There is nothing we can do,' Henrietta said and placed her bottles inside a basket that had JUST materialized on the white lion's back. It was the basket Stamatis had been trying to create. 'We now have the bottles in our hands with all the souls safe. We need to get them back into their bodies!' Henrietta shouted. 'Let's go!'

The children jumped onto the lion's back. Bernard sat almost above the head, holding his sealed bottles tight. Right behind him, Stamatis placed his own bottles within Bernard's deep hood, making sure to keep them safe. Henrietta sat behind Stamatis with the materialized basket in front of her, along with the bottles. Stamatis turned around and saw the basket.

- 'What the…This is my basket, is it not?' he realized, with feelings of both astonishment and enthusiasm that he finally made it possible to materialize what he wanted.

- 'Turn around! We are leaving now!' Henrietta urged him.

Roserin sat behind Henrietta with Astrapi in between them, whereas Alexander sat behind Roserin and bound his own bottles together using Rosie's hair. The lion and the children transformed gradually into a long line of smoke that danced gracefully in the air in a hypnotizing way. It was like the dance of smoke that could be seen every time a candle was being extinguished.

At the other side of the lady with the red hair's fiery tornado, the merchants grabbed as much of their merchandise as possible in their desperate efforts to save it from the fire. A man was carrying a number of Persian silky carpets away from his shop. He turned and looked, magnetized by the tornado. He wanted to get away safely, but he was also drawn toward the moving walls, like a spaghetti addict who really had to twirl those delicious-looking noodles with the traditional local kefalotyri cheese around their fork. Another man grabbed two of his ceramic candle holders in order to carry them as far away as possible, when his hands let them fall to the ground and they broke into pieces. The excruciating temperatures of the tornado had already affected the ceramics' temperature. With a cry of pain, the man flapped his hands in the air quickly to cool them down. A young lady was making great efforts to save her precious and sensitive herbs which had been placed in big bamboo baskets. Then she went back to save the beautiful painting with the depiction of the local traditional oven, the olive tree, the amphoras, and the table.

A long, thin line of candle smoke appeared at the market. The smoke became thicker and wider, then gradually showed some motion within it. The motion revealed an image of the white lion and the children on his back.

- 'What is going on here? I thought we were on our way to the museum's upper levels,' Alexander said.

-'And we returned on the other side instead!' Bernard laughed.

- 'It seems that our job is not done here,' Henrietta said.

- 'But WHAT is it that we need to do?' Stamatis asked.

- 'What we need to do right now is wait and see. And the solution will present itself. That is what I say when I have no answers,' Astrapi's voice sounded inside them. 'All we need is peace...' he concluded.

- 'Peace?' Roserin asked and observed the chaos and panic in which people all around them had found themselves. Astrapi remained silent. One merchant was carrying vases filled with honey, another merchant was carrying her Aloe Vera and Aloe Arborescence plants as far away as possible, and still another lady was trying to save her mandolins, lutes, and bagpipes from the twirling flames.

- 'I have never seen anything like that in my whole life!' a seven-year-old boy said to a friend of his. The bells of St. Titus church in the closest square started banging loudly, in the priests' efforts to let people know there was some sort of emergency. A puppet of a cow with strings was flying in the air with flames all around her.

- 'Angelina is in the air...' Rosie felt sorry to see such a scene of the cow puppet that used to walk in the central streets. The two Charlie Chaplins, a man and a young boy who were dressed like the well-known actor, were running away from the market too. The young people who were selling healing stones, jewelry, and macrame pushed their carts away to safety. The African American acrobats who danced and impressed people with their somersaults were now running away too.

-'I don't understand why we have to stay here and do nothing!' Alexander shouted. 'We are wasting precious time!'

- 'Sometimes to retreat one step backward is equal to taking one step forward,' Sir Hipparchus' voice sounded in their minds.

The partitions that were at the other end of the market caught fire as the tornado was approaching. People who had been trying to save their merchandise abandoned the rest of it and ran away before they were dragged into the lava walls of the lady with the red hair. Members of the rescue teams of Greece who were giving out first aid lessons at the St.

Mark's Basilica main exhibition space of the town urged everyone to leave. Men dressed in red clothes with white crosses on them, members of the Red Cross team that they were, walked away first of all.

- 'Where are they going? Are they not supposed to stay and save lives?' Alexander shouted in astonishment.

-'Apparently, you have never had first aid lessons. The first and most important rule in saving a life is to keep yourself safe first and foremost,' Henrietta answered his question. 'If they got roasted like turkeys, they would not be able to make themselves useful to other people.'

The fire started spreading from one partition to the next. A young dressed up wizard ran away from the market with rolled-up posters under his arms. A few of the posters of his upcoming show of magic tricks that he had stuck onto 'Lotzia's' central Venetian building had already caught on fire.

- 'Our town is being destroyed and all we do is sit and watch,' Alexander shouted.

- 'I think we are supposed to stay here and see something.' Henrietta thought silently. Her voice echoed within her brother's consciousness. She could not help but see a young girl of around eight years old pull a good quality silky carpet behind her. The difference between her and the other people was that she was running straight into the tornado.

- 'Look!' Stamatis shouted and pointed toward her.

- 'Is she trying to kill herself?' Roserin wondered silently.

The young wizard with the black eye shadow around his eyes was now exiting a nearby café with a big mirror in his hands. He put the mirror on his head to carry it and ran toward the fiery tornado. He ran past the lion and the children, and followed the girl.

- 'Where is HE going? Is he trying to save the girl?' Bernard asked.

- 'I have no idea,' Alexander said.

- 'I think I have seen him somewhere before,' Stamatis said.

- 'What exactly do they think they are doing?' Roserin wondered. 'The tornado will kill them!'

- 'We cannot interfere here. They are heading that way with their own free will. I am sure it has to do with their own life plan,' Henrietta said to her friends.

- 'Will we just watch them die?' Alexander said in distress.

- 'We do not know the future yet,' Henrietta replied. 'Always think of the best results as long as there is still hope!' she made her thought clear.

The little girl stopped at some point. She placed the Persian silky carpet right in front of her. Something unexpected occurred. A person who looked like a carbon copy of Rosie appeared next to the little girl and whispered something in her ear. The little girl unrolled the carpet wide open, facing the tornado. Roserin's lookalike walked next to the young wizard and whispered something in his ear. As soon as she did that, the wizard went to stand right next to the little girl and held up the mirror against the tornado.

- 'What exactly does he think he is doing? This is no time for a magic trick!' Stamatis said, and kept watching, unable to take his eyes off of the three souls.

The black-dressed magician with the golden moons and stars hid himself behind the mirror. The girl imitated what her hero was doing. She protected her head behind the big carpet, with her fingers still exposed. The tornado approached. The temperature got higher and higher.

- 'I feel like a chocolate soufflé that is being heated up inside the oven,' Bernard thought.

A few flames were falling onto the mirror's surface when a woman's silhouette appeared in the eye of the lava walls. She was wearing a red dress with sewn silky patterns of tornados, destroyed houses, and people being swallowed in the air. The images moved on the dress's surface. The lady's face appeared next, right behind the flaming walls. Her usual frozen expression –which was her only characteristic that was the opposite of the flesh burning flames- was replaced by an expression of both astonishment and terror combined. Something had drawn her attention to the mirror that the wizard was holding. She started screaming like a ghost that had just discovered her own dead body.

- 'What is happening?' Henrietta wondered.

- 'I don't have the slightest idea, but it seems that Roserin's body double has guided the magician to find out a way to stop our trouble maker,' Alexander said from behind the mirror. On the front side of the mirror, some unseen things started to occur…

A gargoyle with wings was what was reflected on the mirror's surface, moving in the same way that the lady with the red hair moved. It also carried a sign in front of its chest, holding it with its dangerous-looking hands. The word written on the rotting sign was 'Nephthys.' When her face took an expression of astonishment and terror, its face simultaneously took an expression of astonishment and terror. When she started screaming, the gargoyle started screaming too. The next thing that happened was that some red hair started growing on its head. It grew longer and longer, until it reached the same length as Nephthys' hair.

'Look! Did you see that?' Bernard shouted all of a sudden. 'There is a gargoyle in her place!'

Nephthys appeared behind the mirror's surface, and she felt the surface with her hands. She still had a terrified expression on her face upon the realization that she had just been trapped. The tornado's flames fell onto the carpet the girl was holding and burnt it in various spots. The burnt spots shaped an image of terrified Nephthys with her hands feeling the surface in an effort to free herself. The burnt areas were restored to colors of intense red depicting her dress, and pale brown depicting her new body that had been replaced by a gargoyle's. From within the mirror, Nephthys punched the surface and smashed it into multiple tiny pieces. She jumped outside of the mirror and as soon as her foot touched the ground she transformed into a little mouse. The tornado started decreasing in size. It also started losing its strength.

- 'Now look at that! Who would ever expect that this wizard had real talent!' Stamatis commented. His friends were speechless.

- 'Give me that carpet, my girl,' the young magician asked the girl after he leaned the mirror against a pillar. He rolled the rug and held it under his arms.

'This is too vibrant a design for people to display in their homes. Its place is in a more private collection. Thank you dear. Are you alright?' he asked her. His new young friend nodded positively. 'Your presence has been most helpful. You do realize I would have never made it without you,' the girl smiled at him. 'You are the bravest girl I have ever met!' he said. 'Now, do NOT touch that mirror. Let others deal with it. I am so very proud of you!' The girl glowed and ran away quickly to let her mother know that the town's well-known wizard had been proud of her work.

The tornado looked different now. It looked more translucent, like the glass-made bricks that displayed their frozen beauty. It also emitted something Christmassy into the atmosphere around it.

- 'I feel warmth and harmony inside me,' Roserin noticed.

- 'Me too!' Henrietta agreed.

From within the enchanting-looking tornado that started giving the impression of the softest jelly ever with traces of sparkling raindrop-like beads, the disc of Phaistos hovered inside the weightless eye. A young girl stepped out from the soft attractive mass and caught everybody's attention. The children looked astonished.

- 'It's Anemona!' Bernard said.

- 'How did she get here?' Roserin was stunned. 'Anemona is still alive. How did she get transported here?' she wondered.

The girl's necklace of the Phaistos disc kept hovering within the tornado's eye. Rays of golden light emerged from around its main symbols on both sides. A dove flew out of the tornado and landed onto Anemona's hand. The spirits of a number of men, women, and girls appeared around the half-destroyed market. Some of them were bald, others' hair was standing upward and looked like plants that had just popped out of the soil. They walked toward the burnt partitions with pieces of lumber, took the burnt parts down, and replaced them with the new pieces they carried in their hands. A woman was holding a big round ceramic disk with seven miniature planets positioned on its surface. As she walked toward the children, all seven planets started slowly lifting into the air, getting bigger in size, and the area around them became dark purple. A few distant stars appeared while the planets rotated around themselves and around other planets at the same time. A cluster of silverfish swam in the miniature universe in marinated oil and lemon that shimmered like the traces a snail would leave behind it on its passage. The fish landed into boxes that had just materialized at the fish department along with their marinating sauce. A number of these people carried a few ceramics to replace the ones that had been smashed into tiny pieces by the tornado's powerful hot winds. They placed them neatly onto new tables that some of their people had brought in. A lady carried in a bunch of flowers and started planting them in ceramic pots. She seemed to be expecting a baby, judging by her big tummy.

- 'Look! The flowers are turning into Aloe Arborescence leaves!' Henrietta noticed.

The children looked stunned.

A lady dressed in a long white ancient Greek dress and a long white cloak with white trimmed fur along its perimeter appeared in the place of the aftermath. She was a lady who was not like the other ladies that had appeared from within the see-through substance. This one seemed to share one common characteristic with the previous woman. She was carrying a baby under her white, elegant, and precious looking gown.

A golden light appeared on her forehead in the shape of an elegant line that ended in a spiral shape right in the center of her forehead. At the same time, green healing light glowed around her body. Her long, straight, black hair shone under the golden glowing jewel that had just materialized. Her face, young and wise, was like a child's soul- totally open to the creative powers of the universe.

Alexander noticed a golden brooch she was wearing- a round brooch that resembled the disc of Phaistos. It kept her cape tight on her shoulders. She moved. She walked. She walked with motions that were slow and calm. She turned toward the market's sections, and the children had the chance to see an embossed, sewn, delicate design of the Cretan mountain 'Yiouchtas' on the cloak's back surface. It was easy for them to recognize the mountain's sleeping head as it appeared to people when they looked at it from a distance. There were more shapes of white spirals all around the sewn mountain. Some of them were round, some others were oval, and a few others were a little more creative, with different distances between the lines. She also had a long plait, resting above the rest of her hair.

- 'Is this a Goddess?' Alexander wondered. As he stared at her, the front side of her body appeared at the back side of her back, as she was still standing still. She looked toward Alexander and smiled.

-'Was this temple standing here before?' Alexander asked as soon as he saw a two-level structure with a dome on the top and a pillar on its right side. The two floors were separated by a long floor.

- 'I have not seen this before,' Stamatis confirmed. 'I love the little river that flows out of it. I wonder whether it starts from the entrance or whether it flows inside it as well,' he thought and looked at it meandering with intense interest. Meanwhile, a bear had been making serious efforts to open one of those tempting thyme honey jars. A bald man moved a scythe against the bear a few times to make him leave. Then Roserin looked at a woman who had been trying to comb her hair with a device that looked like a comb which she held from the middle part that connected the two other parts that carried the forks.

- 'Do I see what I think I see?' Bernard asked his friends.

- 'I think we ALL do,' Stamatis replied.

- 'If I were still alive, I would really love to describe to everyone what I have just seen with my own eyes!' Henrietta wished.

- 'If you were still alive, you would NOT have seen it!' Alexander said.

- 'Don't be so certain about that,' Henrietta imagined.

- 'So, this is the mysterious disk of Phaistos which nobody has ever managed to interpret…'Roserin said, whereas Bernard felt too moved by the magical scene to be able to comment. Then Rosie remained silent.

- 'It does make sense,' Henrietta whispered. 'The symbols had been carved along a spiral. The spiral is the symbol of Creation…' she completed her sentence, unable to continue. She placed her hand on her other palm and focused her attention on the moment. They could hardly take their eyes off what was happening in front of them.

- 'The disc IS alive…' Astrapi's thought sounded in their consciousness.

- 'It has been the key to Creation. And that mother…She seems to be their Goddess. This is why Nephthys wanted to have it so badly. She wanted to destroy it,' Roserin said when she saw that they had found themselves within a huge hologram of a golden, lighted spiral that spread within the foreground that lay ahead of them.

People who had run away from the disastrous tornado before, now returned. The merchants approached slowly and looked at their new replaced tables and the untouched merchandise.

- 'That's it. I am paying a visit to Dr. Fengarakis today. First I see goats in trees, then I see a freshly painted table with all of my products intact after all hell breaks loose,' a young man from France said.

Some twinkle lights turned on all of a sudden, and a group of children ran to see what goodies would be there, to eventually ask their parents to buy for them.

- 'There are more tables inside the Lotzia building!' Roserin said with excitement. 'I smell cinnamon cookies,' she sniffed.

- 'If they have cinnamon cookies, I am sure they will also have kurampie and kserotigana,' Alexander said, and tried to recall the taste of the two most traditional Christmas sweets they used to eat in Crete.

-'I loved the melomakarona!' Henrietta added and imagined the honey-made sweets. 'However, cinnamon roll with tahini is also delicious.'

- 'I prefer Mr. Trouffakis' lemon pralines! I could not stop eating them! Do you remember? The ones with the Easter bunny and the lemon fairy printed on those shiny colored papers? I also love the loukoumades with honey and the kalitsounia with the cheese and cinnamon on top! They are both so nice and sweet! And the bougatsa! Do you like the bougatsa?' Roserin asked. 'It is so perfect for Christmas time when it's warm, and with the sugar on top...'

Some snowflakes started falling from the sky. People felt the soft flakes on their hair; Some felt them on their nose, and others tried to capture them inside their palms where their body heat would sadly melt them. A girl took a pair of black gloves with black fur out of her pocket and put them on. More people approached and started exploring what things were waiting for them on the tables.

- 'Daddy! I want this snowpenguin!' a little girl at the approximate age of seven, pointed to a well-painted wooden carved snowpenguin, which was being built by a wooden carved girl. On the snowpenguin's body, a variety of fish decorated the surface, in colors of blue and purple.

- 'I am so sorry dear, but I am afraid we can't afford it this year. See?' he told his little girl and turned his pants' pockets inside out, when a pack of euros fell out of it and landed onto the ground. He gasped. He kneeled and grabbed the money. He looked at it in such a way as if the notes were about to melt in his fingers any moment now, along with the snowflakes. They were yellow, well printed, fresh looking, and without the slightest crease on them. He was too shocked to say a word. He grabbed one with both of his hands and put it up in the air against the light.

- 'This money is REAL!' he whispered.

- 'Dad! Close your mouth! The snow is falling right inside it!' the little one giggled.

The children looked at each other and smiled.

- 'Oh! I can smell some sweet bread!' Bernard sniffed in the air. 'With raisins! I would love to have a bite to eat!'

- 'I would love to have some too!' Roserin said. 'But the only way we can have some is if somebody decided to leave a bun on a desk especially for us. I would not mind if they left us some of Mr. Trouffakis' chocolates to eat! Those in the shapes of Christmas trees and Santas were good too!!'

An older lady carried her portable table and chose a spot next to the other partitions to exhibit her own merchandise. On the table, she had a big linen sack which was filled with some things. It seemed to be light enough, soft and round. She looked at the white partitions' wooden walls to see where she could place her own merchandise. She opened her sack and took out some capes with fur, woolly hats, furry hats, and gloves. All in different colors and for any taste.

- 'It looks like a nice peaceful evening, does it not?' she looked at her adjacent colleague, trying to break the ice. 'And we do have some snow this Christmas! What else could we have asked for?' she smiled.

- 'Well, I sure hope we will have lots of people tonight; It has been too quiet recently. It kind of makes you feel like life does not want you anymore. Let us hope there will be some traffic,' the other lady who had also just moved into her own section replied.

-'There should be some. There is only one day left before Christmas!' she said. 'Never stop hoping my dear. Things will get better one day, and hopefully we will be here to see that. Imagine the parties we will be having!' she predicted and covered her mouth again with her white woolly scarf. The other lady nodded positively and then grabbed a pair of furry earmuffs from within her pile and covered her ears to keep them warm.

- 'Nutcrackers!' a little girl shouted in excitement as soon as she saw a table displaying a number of painted wooden carved soldiers. She approached the section with the bearded nutcrackers, and with excited eyes she inspected every single one of them. She was drawn by one in a red uniform with white buttons. He had a golden-red crown and a white, long, soft looking beard. She sighed. Nephthys had forced her father to take the pocket money he had given her out of her pocket to give it to the red-haired woman instead. The girl inserted her hand into her left pocket and felt it empty. Next, she inserted her right hand into the right pocket of her coat. Her fingers felt a piece of paper. She grabbed it and pulled it out.

- 'My money is back!' she looked at her twenty euro note with awe, and she was about to pick up the nutcracker she loved when her attention was drawn by a wooden carved Santa Claus. This Santa had three different sides, instead of one. On one side, he had vibrant colors on his robe: light red, purple, napier yellow, and orange cars on a deep red background. His woolly hat was deep red with an olive green fur, and on the surface of his right sleeve, the girl read the inscription 'Nice' that had been carved and painted in deep red calligraphic letters. He had a very festive-looking beard with plaits, and his face glowed with a smile. He carried on his right arm a baby goat with a red bow on around her neck, and a deep red sack that contained a penguin, traditional local homemade sweets, a doll that wore a sweater with a knitted African cat, a harp, a plush puppy, a colorful hot air-balloon, an airplane, and a little rabbit. He also held a list on which the names of the children who had been nice had been written with beautiful calligraphic letters in Greek.

On the second side of Santa, where his back was supposed to be, the girl read the inscription 'Naughty' along his sleeve. His colors seemed to be darker, and he carried a list on which the names of the naughty children were mentioned. He was holding a boot that contained a collection of underwear, and he was wearing a yellow bag that was loaded with fake money. His face looked serious on this side, with his brown eyes open and his beard wavy in this mood. His third personality showed him with deep brown colors on his robe, the pattern of cars appearing in deep ochre yellow. His face looked sad, and a few dry leaves seemed to be stuck onto his beard. In his right hand he was holding a scale, and under his left arm he was holding a big mirror. Along the surface of his sleeve, the little girl read the phrase: 'Very naughty.'

The girl grabbed the Santa instantly, who was known as 'Agios-Vasilios' in Greece. Right behind him, there was another wooden carved figure with two opposite sides. On one side, there was the figure of a tortured-looking gargoyle with its mouth open. Its hands were trying to grab a round disc that hovered right in front of its face. On the base of his feet, there was the inscription 'Naughty' in Greek letters. On the opposite side, a beautiful lady was there, with a red dress that depicted images of tornados that had ripped apart houses and swallowed boats within their walls. She had a young, innocent-looking face, with straight long red hair that made her look impressive. On the base of her dress, the inscription 'Extremely Naughty' had been carved.

The girl handed the paper money to the lady who sold them and took Agios Vasilios in her hands. She walked past the chestnut lady who also sold corn that had just been boiled. She sniffed in the air, sensing the warm chestnuts' smell. 'Thank you!' she said, looking in the sky.

-'Watch where you are going, kid!' a man who was carrying carpets that had been made out of sheep's wool said to her as she almost bumped into him.

A young man pulled his cotton candy cart to join the Christmas market, and the man with the sheep's wool carpets he had made after he had given his sheep their yearly shave, decided to carry his merchandise next to the lady who sold her furry coats, hats, and gloves, and opposite to the cotton candy man. As he was placing his carpets onto his own table at a separate partition, the cotton candy man placed a CD inside a CD player he had carried with him and turned it on. He then added some sugar with a long spoon into his machine. He grabbed two long sticks and turned the machine on. A spirit-lifting song started playing from his CD player, a Christmas song that caused Roserin and Henrietta to turn their heads.

- 'My most beloved song!' Rosie thought. 'Now what was its title? Something which has to do with fairies.'

- 'Cotton candy fairy?' Henrietta's reply sounded in Roserin's mind.

The cotton candy creator was now dancing, moving the sticks in the air according to the music's rhythm. The cotton candy was being created in floating threads, sticking around the sticks, offering a unique show to anyone who was around.

- 'He looks like a real wizard!' Bernard was impressed.

- 'You see the way sugar transforms into cotton candy? It looks as if he is working with spirits!' Stamatis said with enthusiasm.

- 'Apart from us?' Alexander asked amusingly.

People approached, drawn by the romantic classical music that seemed to be speaking to their hearts. Adults and children froze on the spot.

- 'Mommy! I found some money in my pocket!' a little boy said with enthusiasm. His mother responded in an unexpected way.

- 'Shhhhh!' She longed to attend every single second of the show, with her focus uninterrupted by all means. Her boy turned his head toward the cotton candy man and gasped. His own attention was successfully magnetized too. The only thing this man needed to have was their first glance.

Some drums sounded in the distance. The children turned their heads and saw a big team of musicians dressed up in red. It was the town's Philharmonic Orchestra that had just started parading around the center, playing the Christmas songs they had been practicing for never-ending hours.

At another part of the market, a mother with a little boy around five had just discovered a fifty euro note inside her own purse. She smiled happily and looked at her son, whose eyesight had been magnetized by a few gingerbread houses with a layer of bougatsa sweet on the roofs, craved by all children that happened to walk past them. The boy looked at a little house that was made with dark cookies on its roof and colourful sweets on its walls, and had a miniature model of a witch with a white cat along with three children out in the powder sugar-sprinkled garden. The lady offered the fifty euro note to the seller and grabbed the gingerbread house softly. In the meantime, the white lion started disappearing.

- 'What is happening?' Alexander asked. 'We are not leaving, are we? No! Not now that everything is getting so nice!' he pleaded. He saw that their feet had started vanishing too. Within a few seconds, they were surrounded by some thick fog. The music's nice sounds and people's cheerful laughs were muffled. The last object that remained visible in the children's optical field was a really big lit-up paper boat shape…

Inside a shop that seemed to sell various kinds of fabrics for all kind of uses, Areti (Anemona's cousin) was looking at some samples that were being displayed to her by the shop lady.

-'How about this one?' The lady unfolded a meter of a rather precious looking material on a long wooden table. 'It is polyester with viscose.' Areti's white sleeve fell onto the table from her elbow down, like medieval-styled sleeves behaved, as soon as she felt like touching the sparkly red material.

-'Yes! This is perfect for her,' she agreed. 'Five meters please…' she addressed the lady. The latter one took a meter and started unrolling the festive fabric from the big thick roll.

Anemona, on the other hand, was just stepping down the stairs out of a little shop with various toys and decorative gifts displayed in front of its window. Things like an animated carousel with horses, giraffes, elephants, and lots of tiny lights, a miniature oak theatre, a few healing pebbles in the shape of a star, a magic circus with acrobats, some lamps that were designed for children's bedrooms, and a traditional Cretan house which attracted the girl's attention somehow. Was it because of Santa's sleigh and the reindeer on its roof, or was it because there seemed to appear a fairy light with sparkles in every single room?

She stood in front of the window and watched. The windows were dark, covered by plexiglass, and therefore nothing was visible within. Not until the sparkly fairy light light turned on from inside. It revealed two parents sleeping in their beds. After a while, the light turned off and nothing was visible anymore. Another room was illuminated this time. Anemona saw a miniature model of Rudolph the reindeer sliding down the chimney. She looked intensely and admired the model's detail. Her eyes were fixed on Rudolph, while Santa was having a cup of hot cocoa with whipped cream in his sleigh. The light went off, and she could not see Rudolph anymore. She waited. The house looked cold and unwelcome now. The warm fairy light appeared behind the round stained glass of the front door. The door remained closed. After a few seconds, it turned off, and a different light in another room revealed a bedroom where children were sleeping in their beds. Anemona stared with full focus. Their room seemed to be poor, with hardly any toys. The walls had been decorated with a wallpaper that displayed various toys and little houses. The light turned off in that room, and the sparkly fairy light turned on inside the house's loft. A doghouse was visible this time, with a Pekinese sleeping in it. Rudolph was leaving a bone with meat on his plate, wrapped in a red bow. A few snores later, the light turned off, and it turned on in a different room on the house's ground floor.

- 'It must be the living room!' Anemona thought. She saw her beloved reindeer approach a Christmas tree with Santa's sack on his back. She smiled.

- 'If only I could…' she did not dare complete her thought. She turned to the right, still carrying on her shoulder the old bunny schoolbag with the hole in it. She left the shop's window with the amusing toys and festive lights. She walked toward the turn in the trail when her bag started changing its shape and appearance. It also revealed some intense colors. It now looked like a turquoise green dragon with a pair of delicate purple wings and some yellow ochre scales on its sides…

30. Centering the Souls.

-'Where are we?' Stamatis asked his friends and looked down at the surface on which they were currently resting.

- 'Is this a pipe?' Alexander asked. Roserin decided to get off the lion's back. She walked forward. She took a few steps, making sure she would not fall off the mysterious big pipe that spread into space. On her fourth step, she looked downward with a surprised look on her face. Her feet were not touching the hard surface anymore.

- 'Oh, I love it when this happens!' she smiled and hovered in the air. After a few seconds, she moved her hands and her body like a mermaid would have moved in the sea toward the pipe's end. She turned around and looked back at her friends. Her face glowed with happiness.

- 'So beautiful!' she thought, unable to express any other sound that would disturb this mesmerizing, heartwarming experience. Robert seemed to be a lot quicker than her as he ran and floated ahead of her, rotating around himself.

Henrietta felt attracted by this picture: two spirits that looked like floating happy spirits, so she took a few steps forward. On her fifth step, she was lifted into the air. She floated close to her friend, and then she turned around and looked.

- 'Hey! Where does all this spaghetti styrofoam come from?' Alexander touched with the fingers of his right hand a few long threads of foam that appeared resting on his left arm all of a sudden.

Bernard looked upward to see where they were headed to, when a big fat piece of chocolate cake fell onto his face. He wiped it away with his fingers.

Stamatis burst into laughter to such an extent that he bowed downward holding his tummy. His intense laughs caused him to close his eyes and stay in that position for a few seconds. He opened them after a while and straightened up to his initial position when he realized he was trapped within a big colorful soap bubble.

- 'What is going on here?' Alexander asked and decided to walk along the pipe. He reached one end and turned around. He gasped. 'Look at that!' he whispered and kept staring at the sight of a cheerful clown in a hologram who blew a party trumpet. His hands' palms were open and visible to the foreground and wore white gloves. He had a bowtie on his throat and a sparkly hat that was decorated with a big number of flat sequins the color of copper. A big yellow daisy had been added on the hat's left side, along with a sparkly miniature saxophone on the front. A few shiny copper sequins had been stuck onto the saxophone's surface, offering some additional beauty to the whole composition. The clown had blond curly hair and some basic black lines on his white face that shaped his smile around his mouth and his cheerful expression. Alexander was now hovering in the air and decided to "swim" toward the right side, to see the scene from a different perspective. When he reached a certain angle, the image changed. The clown now had a different expression on his face since he had thrown a plate of pie onto his own face!

- 'So that explains where this piece of pie has come from!' he thought of Bernard's sudden surprise to be covered with pie all over his face. He noticed some letters on the base of the paper plate, along with a child's drawing of a smiling girl. Alexander decided to float toward the hologram's left side this time, using his hands in the way a swimmer would. When he again reached the center, the original image of the clown blowing the party-trumpet re-appeared. The boy kept floating, "swimming," very slowly close to the penguin and Roserin, having a peek at the image every now and then until the image changed. From another angle, the clown was smelling a white daisy. There were also long strings of styrofoam hanging down from his hat. The boy floated a little to the left. The image remained the same. He moved further, and it was still the same. And then, at a specific second, it changed. This time, the clown was blowing a soap bubble through his miniature saxophone that he had taken off his hat. His face appeared more tranquil, with a slight yellow light falling right on it, and a green foreground on the clown's right side. The daisy was not on his hat anymore. Alexander looked mesmerized by the serene image in front of him.

- 'All that soap on my sweater! If mom were here to see that, I would need to learn how to become invisible!' Stamatis talked to himself right after the giant bubble burst all around him.

- 'Where are we? Do you see anything?' he asked his friends.

- 'Oh yes!' Sir Hipparchus' voice sounded. 'We are back at the museum! The new exhibition of the holograms has already started!'

- 'The museum?' Bernard was surprised and looked toward the Scientist who was now hovering behind Henrietta, Robert, and Roserin, and was closing the astrolabe's cover; He stashed it back in his bag. He still looked like a young boy.

- 'Uncle!' Henrietta shouted, excited.

- 'Yes, it does look like we are at the museum,' Rosie said and looked around. She saw a few more holograms with copper frames that revealed traces of black airbrushed color on them. Apart from them stood two big green round frames that looked like portholes. She thought she saw fish swimming against a reef-like backdrop. 'But why is everything so big?' she asked.

- 'Did the museum get bigger?' Bernard asked as soon as he managed to see again after cleaning up all that chocolate cake from his face.

- 'Perhaps it is 'us' who have become like the little sandman,' The Scientist, who was now back to his initial appearance as an adult (albeit a miniature adult), thought of the well-known character who distributed sand in children's eyes to help them have sweet dreams.

The white lion had shrunk too.

- 'So what do we do now?' Alexander asked.

- 'Well…All we need to do is release the souls and let them return,' Roserin said, still floating in the air.

- 'Release the…Are you out of your mind? What makes you think that they would return to…I don't know where, instead of returning to the center?' Stamatis asked her.

- 'THIS is their center. Without Nephthys controlling them, they have no reason to go where they don't belong,' Rosie replied. 'This is the only place for them to find peace.'

-'So let's open the bottles then!' Henrietta suggested and grabbed the first bottle to unbind it from Roserin's hair. She made big eyes and her jaw dropped when she saw that the bottle she had been holding in her hands was suspended within some kind of metallic device. The bottle's base was resting on a round hollow base, from where a robust golden spring started and led up to a thinner spring which looked as if it had been wrapped around the bottle's neck.

- 'What is this?' she asked.

- 'It worked!' Stamatis shouted, excited, from where he was standing. 'I decided to materialize a good bottle carrier to keep them safe. It worked!'

- 'YOU did this?' Henrietta asked with a subtle tone of doubt.

- 'Yes!' he confirmed.

- 'Is that a hole in the wall?' Bernard asked his friends.

- 'Where?' Alexander asked him.

- 'Right behind you!' he pointed with his finger and grabbed his penguin friend's flipper as he was drawn toward the hole.

His friends looked behind them and saw a big hologram of a hole in a wall, positioned inside of a rectangle that consisted of a few strong-looking bricks, in yellow and green.

- 'It looks beautiful!' Henrietta said. 'I love the lighting!'

- 'Look at THAT!' Alexander shouted all of a sudden, a bit further from the girls. 'Come over here! Quickly!'

The girls "swam" and floated toward him leaving Stamatis and Bernard behind.

- 'Is that a gun?' Roserin asked as soon as she saw a white-gloved hand with silver round covers on its knuckles pointing a long barrel toward anyone who stood or floated in front of it. It projected twenty-five centimeters in space.

- 'What else does it look like to you? A zucchini? But come over here and look down the barrel. It is just amazing!' Alexander shouted, excited.

Rosie looked through the projected barrel's hole.

- 'There's an eye! There's an eye!' she gasped. 'Is that the marksman's eye?'

- 'It looks like it!' Alexander replied.

- 'Show me!' Stamatis' voice sounded behind them, all of a sudden. 'Where? Here? Through the hole?' He closed his right eye and looked through the projected hole in space. 'Awesome!!' he shouted. 'It's an eye!' he said and looked through it once again. Bernard shoved him aside to see for himself.

- 'Hey!' Stamatis complained.

- 'Ha! An eye!' Bernard said excitedly. 'It's amazing!' He smiled at his friends. He moved toward the right side where Henrietta was. 'Look at that thing! It is so long!' he commented on the projected barrel that looked as if it came out of the main image.

- 'Will I finally be able to see too? Thank you!' Henrietta said and floated toward the position where her friends had looked through. She looked through the barrel's hole.

'Uncle? What are you doing in there?' she gasped, as soon as she saw Sir Hipparchus at the other end of the barrel. Her friends turned their heads as soon as they heard her.

- 'Sorry to block the eye, Henrietta dear, but this shape looks fascinating! I really had to inspect it from closer up. Those beautiful colors of yellow and green on the image where you are floating would hypnotize me and distract me from this well-drawn eye! It looks like my beloved astrolabe you see.'

- 'May I interrupt you from the tour and remind you that we still have the bottles unopened?' Astrapi's voice sounded in their consciousness, and everyone looked toward him on the party trumpet where he was still standing.

- 'Where is the white lion?' Alexander asked while Henrietta finally examined the drawn eye from within the barrel's hole.

- 'He flew back from where he came. He is busy with his own affairs!' Astrapi said.

The lion was returning to the place he had come from indeed. He flew up to the carved position where he had been created, at the back side of the 'Koule Castle at the main port. He placed his paw back onto the book he used to lean on, and turned back into stone. The sun that had been sculpted behind his head began shining a bright yellow light.

- 'I will open the bottles!' Bernard said and floated, along with the mask still floating in front of his face, toward Roserin's hair to unbind the first bottle from her hair. He took the first one, along with its stabilizing spring, and moved his hand toward the cork to uncork it.

- 'No, wait!' Astrapi shouted, but it seemed to be a tad too late. The bottle had such high pressure inside it that Bernard was pushed backward instantly. He fell onto Henrietta's back, and both of them were ejected along with the bottle through the gun's barrel, and got stuck on the laser-drawn black eye. A giant bear's spirit was released into space and moved toward the 'hole in the wall' hologram.

- 'I was afraid of that. Being shrunk like little sandman, and keeping tiny bottles with big entrapped spirits inside them does make you wonder how much pressure there is inside them. Good thing it was only a bear and not a dinosaur!' Astrapi said. 'Are you both well in there?' Henrietta could only release a sound, and Bernard had been too startled to make any sound at all. He was still holding the bottle in his hands and his eyes were fixed on one position. His mouth had dropped wide open.

The giant bear's spirit floated unwillingly toward the 'hole in the wall.' He then reached the area in front of the green-yellow heavy bricks and was sucked right inside the hole with the square light that showed in the background. The bear appeared behind the wall and walked toward the section where his embalmed body had been. He got inside the specific partition and vanished within his body. This time, his eyes looked more glowing.

On the other side of the ground floor's wall, the children, Astrapi, Robert, and Sir Hipparchus were still hovering in the air, looking slightly bigger.

- 'Did you see that? Did you see how the bear was sucked inside the wall?' Stamatis asked with a tone of enthusiasm. 'Had I not been a spirit, I would have never believed it in my live years!'

- 'We still have lots to see!' Rosie said, while Henrietta and Bernard were currently walking back to their friends through the gun's barrel. By the time they reached the other end of the round tunnel, their size had grown too.

- 'I will never forget such an experience. My whole afterlife flashed right in front of my eyes!' Henrietta said.

- 'I am opening the next bottle!' Alexander shouted from the surface of the clown's party trumpet and grabbed a bottle from the basket. He uncorked it, holding it as tight as possible in his effort to remain where he was instead of being catapulted into any distant unusual place. A little owl came outside and flew toward the hole. She hooted, and Robert stared at her as he floated in a circle around himself.

- 'I love so much the way she sounds!' Roserin said. 'Their sound is so comforting!'

- 'You do focus on beauty some more now, don't you? Such a good thing to see!' Henrietta said to her, and Rosie smiled.

As the owl sounded for a second time, it was sucked intensely into the hole in the wall. A few feathers floated in the air until they landed onto the floor.

- 'Let me open the next one,' Henrietta said, and untangled a third bottle from Roserin's floating hair. She placed its base on her chest, with its neck aiming toward the hole. She uncorked it quickly and a few long quills appeared at first; The crested porcupine appeared next. It floated forward until Bernard sneezed. The animal stopped and stomped its feet. It whirred the quills and charged Henrietta's back end in an effort to stab her. The girl's facial expression changed from serene to terrified and she lost her healthy color. Bernard pulled her toward him before she was fiercely pierced. The crested porcupine kept running backward, as Henrietta tried to realize what had just occurred, until it was suddenly sucked away by something else on the side of the wall.

- 'Are you well? Did he injure you? Let me see…' Rosie said.

- 'No, I am fine. Thanks to Bernard!' she panted.

- 'Henrietta dear, you were in serious danger. Good thing Bernard was close to you!' Sir Hipparchus said. 'I hardly had the chance to use the 'freezing time' needle.'

- 'Let me open the next bottle if everything is fine with you, Henrietta?' Roserin asked her friend, after a few seconds of allowing her to calm down. Henrietta nodded. Rosie untangled the next bottle from her hair; She aimed toward the hole and uncorked it. The wild boar came out, running forward in full attack. He could not resist the white hole's intense gravity, which sucked him right inside. At the same time, something else occurred.

- 'Did we get bigger?' Stamatis asked. 'We don't fit through the gun's barrel anymore!'

- 'We are WAY bigger than that!' Alexander replied and decided to swim toward the clown's party trumpet. He walked along it and approached the basket inside which the rest of the bottles rested. He pulled one out as carefully as he could and he aimed it at the hole in the yellow-green wall. He held the bottle firmly with his feet stable on the party trumpet so as not to lose his balance and uncorked it. The green woodpecker with the red feathers on his head flew outside.

- 'THAT is all?' Alexander asked and exhaled. Stamatis burst into laughter.

- 'Congratulations Alexander! That was really very heroic of you!' his sister giggled.

The bottle started shaking, and the spirit of 'Buitreraptor Gonzalezorum' came out in the form of foam. Alexander fell onto the trumpet's surface with a girly shout. The dino-bird with the red feathers assumed its everyday appearance and started chasing the green woodpecker. As she was about to snatch him, they were both sucked into the wall.

- 'I think you will be needing some help my friend! 'Stamatis landed close to him and walked toward the basket. Roserin and Robert were getting close, too. Robert felt too exposed, floating around like that.

- 'Astrapi? What are you doing in there?' Alexander turned his head instantly, for the second time in two seconds, back to Astrapi's position where he saw him surrounded by a really big soap bubble.

- 'Enjoying some centering!' Astrapi's voice sounded in his mind. Alexander's reflection appeared in various colors on the bubble's surface. He turned toward the basket and lifted a bottle. The one he chose seemed to have something really unique on it.

- 'A Christmas tree cork! Where did THAT come from?' Alexander wondered and took it out of the bottle's neck.

- 'I don't recall having seen it before,' Stamatis said.

- 'How cute!' Roserin admired it while Giganotosaurus Carolinii dinosaur squeezed out of the bottle. However, none of the three of them noticed the dinosaur, because they were completely distracted by the very creative Christmas tree cork. Henrietta, Sir Hipparchus, and Bernard froze in front of the handgun's barrel. The sharp-toothed carnivore with the pair of short arms, growled in the air. Rosie released a scream, Stamatis froze while his eyes almost came out of their sockets, and Alexander stepped onto the empty bottle that was lying on the flexible trumpet's surface. He slipped as it moved forward and crashed onto the party trumpet like the Giant Deinotherium would have if a harvest mouse had walked over the monster's feet. Giganotosaurus Carolinii's tail was caught all of a sudden by the white hole's gravity as he floated backward, and the huge dinosaur could not help himself from being sucked in.

- 'Just give me that!' Roserin grabbed the Christmas tree cork from

Alexander's hands, annoyed. 'You have distracted our attention! What would have become of us had his tail not been sucked in by the hole in the wall? I will open the next bottle this time.' she said and grabbed another bottle from the basket. She placed it carefully between her legs and uncorked it. The horned viper along with the blunt-nosed viper, the four lined snake, Milos viper, and nose-horned viper were ejected out of the bottle right in front of Roserin's own feet. Rosie screamed and fell backward.

- 'Get them away from me! Get them away!' she pleaded to her friends and moved backward with her arms and legs. But the snakes would NOT float away. On the contrary, they moved toward her. And the girl seemed to have a true phobia of snakes.

- 'They are attracted by your fear! You have to focus! Control your fear!' Henrietta shouted from where she was still floating.

- 'How?' Roserin asked.

- 'Make yourself believe that you are safe!' Henrietta shouted back.

- 'I am safe! I am safe! I am NOT safe!' she cried as soon as the horned viper touched her foot. Rosie moved toward another part of the room, away from them.

- 'Imagine they are spaghetti!' Bernard shouted to her as he was landing onto the party trumpet.

- 'I am never eating spaghetti again in my entire spirit life!' Rosie cried, and kept moving backward until she reached the clown's mouth. The snakes, however, kept crawling toward her.

Henrietta floated in front of a three-dimensional hologram that included a few colorful fish. She landed onto the soft sand of the aquarium and looked around. There was a big shell resting somewhere close to her. She "swam" close to it, grabbed it, and filled it with sand. She carried it in her hands and started "swimming" back to her friends like a mermaid. As soon as she arrived, she saw the horned viper standing in front of Roserin. She unloaded the sand into the air right in front of the hole in the wall by turning the shell upside down. The sand floated now in front of her. The snake turned around and floated quickly toward the sand. Within a few seconds, it disappeared right inside it.

- 'It loves to hide before ambushing its prey!' Henrietta said, but Roserin did not hear her.

- 'Ha! Finally, the snake has realized it would transform into my snack unless it got out of my sight!' Rosie shouted triumphantly. 'Get away from me you sneaky snail moving snarly noodles! Or I would snatch you and make you into a pastitsio meal!' Pastitsio was one of the most well-known thick noodle local dishes, with white cream sauce and cinnamon on the top, usually cooked with minced meat in the oven. The rest of the snakes moved backward now. Roserin's energy had changed, and the serpents could feel it. Was that a giant snake they had in front of them? It must have been a King snake! It would not have been so wise to challenge a King snake. If they did, they would lose their well spread reputation of being wise! They retreated and were lifted in the air. Then, Rosie imagined she was surrounded by a big, protective, white, slippery ball. She was right in the center of it. However, what the snakes and her friends saw was something different. They saw a giant eagle, whose attention had been drawn toward her food. The snakes moved instantly as far away as they could and floated to the pile of sand where the horned viper had been hiding. The whole heap of sand, along with the hidden snakes within it, moved toward the hole in the wall. As soon as it arrived, the snakes were sucked in first, leaving a few holes all around the ball of sand, which now more resembled a poked meatball. It was being sucked gradually inside the wall too. 'Ha-ha! Away with you!' Roserin shouted to the intended ingredients of her pastitsio dish.

-'Would you mind opening the next one?' Alexander offered her another bottle with a smile that revealed how amusing he had found his friend's behavior.

- 'I think I will let YOU do that one,' Rosie was slightly adamant this time.

- 'I must admit you did handle it very well with the rest of them though!' Alexander smiled and grabbed the next bottle firmly, while Roserin had a puzzled expression on her face.

- 'She managed to create the protective bubble which was most proper on this occasion. Well done Rosie!' Astrapi's voice sounded inside everybody's consciousness. 'The answer to YOUR problem came from within. Henrietta did make an effort to help you, but the real solution to your challenge lied within YOU,' He concluded, and Rosie smiled. She glowed while Alexander was making an effort to open the bottle. He pulled the cork out of the bottle finally, and the striped hyena appeared next. She struggled to float against the current that led her to the hole, but the gravity of the white hole had become even more intense. Her black stripes were sucked in before the rest of her ethereal body.

- 'Now THERE is something that I never expected I would see in the spirit world!' Alexander said, and Stamatis laughed.

- 'SHE was the one who made the fisherman sick!' Bernard shouted.

- 'The fisherman?' Henrietta asked him.

- 'At the fish market,' the boy explained but did not dare give any further details about his sudden decision to cut off the cord and not respect the man's free will to suffer. 'How confusing this world was at times!' he thought.

Henrietta grabbed another bottle from Bernard's deep hood. She aimed in space and released the cork. There was a noise of crashing stones and the bottle shook violently.

- 'Hold it steady. Something BIG is coming out!' Stamatis shouted from the opposite side, and Henrietta held it as tight as she could. A few stones were ejected out of the bottle, then 'Rebbachisaurus Tessonei's head squeezed out of the dark glass neck. It had not been an easy process for him to pop out with such a wide jaw. His especially long neck came out next with the red fox grabbing firmly onto it. His ten-ton round body followed, and along with the fox, he was swallowed by the white hole in the green-yellow lighted bricks.

- 'Good job!' Stamatis said to Henrietta. 'It was a tough one!'

- 'Thank you!' she replied with glowing eyes.

- 'I must say I am speechless!' Sir Hipparchus said while he floated back from the drawn eye. 'What have you been up to? I see you have been busy centering spirits!'

- 'Centering spirits?' Bernard whispered and a number of golden glowing question marks appeared in his aura.

- 'Yes. They return into their bodies and therefore they stop messing with peoples' energies,' Henrietta explained to her little cousin. 'Rosie! Catch this one!' Henrietta threw another bottle to her friend after having dove back into Bernard's deep hood. The bamboo bottle did a few somersaults in the air before Roserin grabbed it in her hands. She took the cork out with her right hand, and a big long elephant trunk started moving in every direction.

- 'The Giant Deinotherium!! Hold it steady Rosa!' Alexander called her using the local dialect, and watched in distress. Two giant tusks appeared, protruding under his jaw. Roserin aimed toward the hole in the wall. The rest of his body popped out like a thin stream of smoke which transformed into foam that filled its ethereal body. In the same way that the children had shrunk, the animals had changed size too, still in the same proportions according to the children's perspective. The Deinotherium was now floating toward the hole in the wall too. It was drawn in decisively by its long trunk. Once the giant was sucked inside, the children grabbed more bottles, with eagerness to release the remaining spirits. Stamatis opened one bottle and a big mass of foam fell onto the party-trumpet's surface.

- 'Get back! Another dinosaur is about to appear!' He stepped backward, and so did Alexander and Rosie. But nothing occurred. The foam remained on the paper surface. Roserin approached with caution, and she stared at it for a few seconds. She dipped her finger in to see what kind of mysterious foam it was. Where was the spirit which was supposed to have been released?

- 'Rosie? Be careful please!' Alexander prompted her.

- 'Get away from there! It can appear any second!' Stamatis said to her.

- 'It is champagne! Somebody filled the bottle with champagne!' Rosie said as soon as she smelled the foam.

- 'Champagne? These are wine bottles! 'Alexander wondered.

- 'It seems that somebody made a mistake during the filling of the bottles,' Stamatis said.

- 'It also means that one of us grabbed it without having released the drink out of the bottle!' Roserin said. Bernard gasped from the position where he floated in the air. He was about to say something, but he hesitated. He had just recalled that it was he who had taken the filled-up bottle with him in great haste, with the thought that he would empty it later at some point.

Stamatis took another bottle to open. He really HAD to release something BIG to feed his ego! Even just a bit. He released the cork, and the exciting moment came. Everyone seemed eager to see what would come out next. After a few seconds of silence, a stoat with its white fur appeared and floated in space.

- 'How cute!' Henrietta admired it, and Stamatis sighed as his ego had not been inflated. Instead of releasing a dinosaur, or a wild boar, or at least the Giant Deinotherium, he had released a cute harmless stoat. Henrietta turned toward Bernard's long hood. Robert tried to run toward the children as he floated, but the only result he achieved was to keep floating around himself in circles.

- 'I will open the next one!' Henrietta said and floated close to Bernard, while Sir Hipparchus was exploring a three-dimensional hologram of an American vintage car resting on a paved road with an open engine cover. The whole image was in shades of green and slight traces of yellow. Henrietta pulled the cork out by using all of her strength, and the 'Noble One' was released in space. The Noble One was now being carried away from the white hole's strong current, back on his way to the documentary that was being shown on the museum's Minus One level.

-'There go all the dinosaurs!' Stamatis thought and watched him float away. He released a sigh.

-'Give me the next one!' Bernard asked Henrietta, so she put her arm deep inside his hood. She chose a bottle at random and gave it to him. He pulled the cork, and everybody watched curiously. Robert's eyes were drawn to the bottle as well. The wild boar came out of it and did two somersaults in the air before it was carried away by the white hole's strong sucking current to the other side of the wall.

- 'There goes the wild boar too! Nice! Nice...' Stamatis whispered disappointedly.

- 'Did you say something?' Roserin asked him.

- 'No, no. I was just saying to myself what an amazing experience I have had with the spirits' centering here...' he replied.

- 'It has really been fascinating! Who would ever expect it that I would finally learn how to overcome my fear of snakes in my spirit life?!' she said in excitement.

- 'Who would ever?' Stamatis said with the least sign of interest. Roserin decided to open the next bottle and aimed it toward the hole in the wall. She uncorked it with her left hand. The wild cat came out next.

Astrapi's bubble burst instantly, and his eyes popped out. The wild cat was now being sucked back to her own body.

- 'Oh no! Don't go!' Astrapi said and ran toward the other end of the party trumpet that came out of the clown's mouth. However, the attraction that called the wild cat back into her body was a lot stronger than the attraction toward Astrapi. She was now being sucked through the hole to the wall's other side.

The children opened the remaining bottles, and more animals were released back to their centers. The Lynx was released, the honey buzzard eagle with the beautiful white-feathered head and white neck with the brown short lines, the ibex, the raven, a marmot, the golden eagle that was literally covered with gold, the scorpions, a wolf, the Eurasian eagle owl, and a number of little birds too. Then the children came across the last bottle. It was inside the basket that Stamatis had materialized.

-Why don't you open the last one? I feel somehow exhausted,' Alexander said.

- 'Yes, me too,' Roserin agreed.

Stamatis pulled it from the basket and the bottle started growling and shaking. It almost fell out of his hands. He uncorked it, but nothing happened. He started to look inside and see what was happening (or not happening).

- 'No! Keep your head AWAY from there!' Henrietta stopped him. Megaraptor Namunhuaiquii's big head appeared out of the bottle. Then his eight-ton, fifteen-meter body followed too. Bernard's attention was drawn to the sharp-looking claws that he hid in his arms. They were in the form of curved daggers. He made sure to stay away from him at a safe distance by holding tight to the gun barrel's surface. He was in no mood whatsoever to be pulled uncontrollably along with one of the biggest dinosaurs into his body and be trapped in there for quite a long time.

- 'It has been a wonderful experience indeed!' Stamatis addressed

Roserin with a smile. His wish had just been granted. He was given the responsibility and trust to release the forgotten Megaraptor Namunhuaiquii! Now THAT was a challenge that was not offered every day!

- 'Are we back to our normal size?' Sir Hipparchus asked as they were now standing on a different platform. The dinosaur had been sucked in by the hole, and the holograms that had been hung on the wall looked much smaller and flatter now. Bernard's sight caught a hologram of Gromit, knitting a pullover on a sofa. It was a nice comfortable looking sofa in the color of purple with yellow dots. The pullover he was knitting was orange and carried the letter 'I' in purple.

- 'I think we have grown a tad taller indeed,' Alexander answered, and walked toward the parallel corridor of the room they were in. So did Roserin. As they were exiting the museum's inner part, they saw the Eurasian eagle-owl entering into her own body. They smiled with pleasure.

- 'Look at her chest! I think I see a face on her feathers!' Rosie approached to see from a closer distance. 'It is amazing. There really is a human face on her throat! People will think it looks this way because of the different positions of the colors, but it is a face...' she whispered.

Alexander walked toward a glass display of the rarest meteor pieces which had been positioned in certain places. Bernard, Stamatis, Astrapi, Robert, and Sir Hipparchus came out from the upper entrance. Roserin walked further away from her friends and turned to the right side of the museum's main entrance. She stood in front of the big decorated Christmas tree.

- 'It is a REAL one! How pretty!' she whispered and put her nose close to its needles. 'It smells good too!' Then she looked at the red, white, and silver balls, as well as the big white and red snowflakes that were hanging in the branches. She admired a big number of miniature porcelain animals with intense colors and red bows around their neck that also hung on the big impressive Christmas tree. A sudden gust of wind that came from nowhere, blew some fake snow onto her hair and shoulders. All the porcelain animals' eyes suddenly moved toward the girl. Rosie smiled happily.

Sir Hipparchus was instantly interested in the mineral pigments, and Bernard looked beyond the ground floor level to the Minus One level and Minus Two level, trying to catch the slightest motion of the dinosaurs' bodies, or even something close to it. Uncle Hipparchus, as the children used to call him, looked spellbound by the colorful stones.

- 'Oh! Look at those beautiful mineral pigments!' Alexander approached him from his left side. 'If only I could add them to my collection! These colors, the contrast...'

- 'They are really worth living for and I love discovering such beauties in the world here and there. Look at this one. The 'Azurite,'' the Researcher pointed toward a deep blue stone with traces of green. '"It has been used since ancient times for the production of blue colored paint," it says here. "It is unstable in humidity and converts to green malachite,"' he read on the black informative poster that stood on the glass container's surface. 'Would you believe it? A stone that transforms itself into a different kind of stone!' he admired.

- 'Hey! Henrietta! You really have to see this!' Alexander called his sister.

- 'Look at that stone! It has gold in it!' Bernard admired a blue stone that shimmered with traces of gold.

- 'That's 'Lazurite'. It says here that during the Renaissance, lazurite had been named as the painters' diamond,' Alexander said and looked back at the stone and the little plate that held some ground light blue dust that had originated from the same stone.

- 'I like the Malachite too!' Bernard pointed at the green transformed stone. Henrietta was now approaching from a distance. From her point of view, a very clear image of a green foam-like stone with silver shimmery dust appeared on the informative black poster: 'Chryssocola,' She read easily, despite the distance. "Besides being used as a pigment, it has been used as glue for gold by jewelers," was the written explanation. When Henrietta reached her friends, she saw the intense turquoise powder that glowed on the small plate that had been placed right in front of the stone.

In the meanwhile, back in the town's center where people were now celebrating the coming of Christmas, something else was occurring. Right in front of St. Titus Church, the attention of the boy who had been exploring the museum's animals with his dad, had been drawn by a confused looking mouse that walked right over his feet.

- 'Look dad! It is the harvest mouse that I could not see in that glass container!' he told his dad with enthusiasm and grabbed it from its tail.

- 'What a funny little mouse!' his dad replied. 'Its fur is red! I have never seen a mouse with red fur before!' he said.

- 'We should bring it back to the museum!' the boy suggested.

- 'Perhaps we should. It must be missing its nice little glass house. I am sure it looks forward to climbing to the top of the hay grass too!' his father agreed while the mouse was shaking hard to escape.

"Cinnabar is a sulphide of mercury; It is toxic. Only the Emperor has the privilege to sign with it," Roserin read the information about the red stone she was looking at. The intense light red powder was being displayed on another small plate in front of it.

- 'Only the Emperor?' Henrietta pondered.

-I would not miss using it since it is toxic!' Rosie commented, but the flow of her thoughts was interrupted by an abrupt sigh that came from Bernard.

- 'This yellow stone is a poisonous one,' he touched the glass with his finger.

- 'Which one is that?' Alexander asked while Sir Hipparchus walked toward the 'Rare Historic Meteorites' glass container, which was positioned on their left side. "Orpiment is a mineral sulfide of arsenic. It has been used since antiquity as a pigment. Its name derives from the Latin aurigpentum (gold paint). It is a strong poison because of arsenic," Stamatis read from the guiding board.

- 'So this is where arsenic comes from!' Henrietta said.

- 'What is happening?' Alexander shouted all of a sudden.

-'The floor is shaking!' Roserin shouted back and her attention was drawn by a repetitive melody of some kind.

- 'Do you hear that?' Sir Hipparchus asked them. The children nodded emphatically.

- 'What a nice melody! Where does it come from?' Stamatis asked.

- 'It seems our Guides are here with us!' Henrietta said.

- 'Why is the floor moving?' Bernard asked and lost his balance.

- 'Hold on tight to whatever you can!' Alexander shouted when the museum's environment was not around them anymore.

-'Are we in space?' Rosie shouted, firmly attached to what looked like a meteorite.

- 'It seems to me we are on the way back home!' Astrapi's voice sounded inside her while he travelled on the same rock with her. As for Robert, he grabbed ahold of Astrapi's leg.

- 'Uncle? What did you do?' Henrietta asked. 'You were watching the meteorites, I saw you!'

- 'I did not cause this, if that is what you are asking!' Sir Hipparchus replied. 'It is funny though, we are standing on 'Red Meteorites'!' he shouted back and looked at the rock's green and red colors, which were being surrounded by a slight napier yellow aura. 'That was the meteorite I admired in the glass container. And for just a moment, I imagined how nice it would have been if we travelled on such rocks!' As soon as the well-known Scientist expressed what image he had visualized within his imagination, Alexander touched his forehead with an open palm while Roserin, Stamatis, Bernard, and Henrietta, froze instantly in their positions.

- 'If you can still travel with the power of your thought, then what did you make the Astrolabe for???' Alexander asked while the others remained speechless.

A mirror with a decorative frame floated past them, and Bernard happened to see his reflection on its shiny surface.

- 'My face! My face has returned!! My eyes, my nose, my mouth! It is all here!' he shouted and touched his face with his fingers, flooding with happiness.

The children, Sir Hipparchus, Robert, and Astrapi were now on their way back home; People in the town of Iraklion were enjoying their time at the Christmas market; Captain Barbarossa and his Pirates were currently floating in space; Areti was placing two big penguin mugs on the kitchen table along with red and yellow plates she had bought, a jar of local good quality thyme honey, and a chocolate calendar that depicted a number of jolly festive images; Nephthys was currently touching her paws behind a glass container as a harvest mouse in the 'Living Museum' section, and right inside the ground floor's parallel section where the new exhibition of the three-dimensional holograms was now being displayed, things were creepily quiet. For the present, there were no visitors inside just yet. The clown's hologram felt quiet, Grommit looked quiet, the fish in the porthole looked quiet, a hologram of Beano looked quiet, even a werewolf looked quiet. There was motion ONLY on the Star Wars Episode III hologram, where Luke Skywalker seemed to pass by. Until…a terrible scream came out of an orange-yellow hologram of a woman, and a few shards of glass were ejected from her mouth onto the floor…

Printed in Poland
by Amazon Fulfillment
Poland Sp. z o.o., Wrocław